Charles Parker Ilsley

The Wrecker's Daughter

And other tales of the forest, the shore, and the ocean

Charles Parker Ilsley

The Wrecker's Daughter
And other tales of the forest, the shore, and the ocean

ISBN/EAN: 9783337037031

Printed in Europe, USA, Canada, Australia, Japan

Cover: Foto ©Andreas Hilbeck / pixelio.de

More available books at **www.hansebooks.com**

THE

WRECKER'S DAUGHTER

AND OTHER TALES

OF

THE FOREST, THE SHORE, AND THE OCEAN.

BY CHARLES P. ILSLEY, ESQ.

————————

BOSTON:

ALBERT COLBY AND COMPANY,

20 WASHINGTON STREET.

1860.

PREFACE.

It certainly was not the intention of the author, when writing the stories contained in this volume, to give them to the public in the present shape. Written under the pressure of manifold duties, the most that he anticipated for them was a brief newspaper immortality — a passing notice and oblivion. Much to his surprise, however, many of them have continued to float on the current of popular favor; and by the advice, repeatedly received, not only from friends but strangers, he has been induced to make the present collection.

The tales, it will be perceived, are mostly of a traditionary character, although some of them must be received with liberal grains of allowance. We make this remark because a lady writer, now deceased, in encouraging the author to continue his legendary tales, wrote of them as follows: "They will be valuable to the future historian, perhaps, more than they deserve; for the sober, truth-telling air of your legends will expose them to being ranked side by side with

1*

veritable history. And," she added, with perhaps not a little truth, "they will doubtless have as good a claim to be so considered as much that has come down to us as history from remote antiquity."

The stories founded on the history of the early settlement of our State are entitled to more credence than those the scenes of which are laid on our seacoast. An exception should be made here in favor of "The Liberty Pole," a tale of Machias. All the incidents of that sketch are purely historical.

It has not been so much the aim of the writer to portray character as to describe scenes and detail incidents, in doing which he flatters himself that he has avoided exaggeration. He is not aware that his pages inculcate any particular lesson, but he feels perfectly assured that they contain not a word offensive to the purest morality. Such as they are, he submits them to the public.

C. P. I.

PORTLAND, APRIL, 1856.

CONTENTS.

THE WRECKER'S DAUGHTER.

CHAPTER I.

Along its solitary shore
Of craggy rock and sandy bay,
No sound but ocean's roar,
Save where the bold, wild sea-bird makes her home,
Her shrill cry coming through the sparkling foam.

DANA.

THE scene to which we would introduce the reader
is one in which nature exhibits herself in her wildest
aspect. Far along as the eye can discern, on either
hand, stretches a bleak, rocky shore, whitened by the
foam of the rough Atlantic, which chafes perpetually
against its jagged boundaries. Here and there a few
stunted pines, springing up on some headland, and
scattered patches of grass, dry and brown from the
poverty of the soil, serve rather to heighten than
relieve the dreariness of the scene. In clear weather,
under the most favorable circumstances, the view is
not one on which the eye, fond of the beautiful, would
delight to dwell; much less attractive is it in the
gloom of the storm, when nothing is heard but the
hoarse voice of the waves as they beat against the
cavernous shore, the strong rush of the gale, and the
shrill cry of the sea-bird mingling with the elemental

(9)

uproar, and nothing seen but the black, sunken ledges
that line at intervals the entire coast, hidden at times
by the sparkling foam, the stern, craggy cliffs, and the
gray, barren heath. And yet there is something in the
gloomy grandeur of the scene which often wins my
steps to its neighborhood.

Amid such an uninviting display one would scarcely
look for signs of human life, more especially at the
period of which we write. And yet they were to be
found. At one spot the shore abruptly recedes, in-
denting the coast for some distance, forming a deep
and rather broad cove, its sides lined with rugged and
precipitous rocks, but the bight terminating in a steep
shingly beach, the apex of which, owing to the wash
of the sea, is considerably higher than the adjoining
main-land. Close in shore the rocks on one side of
the cove jut out some distance; then, falling back at a
sharp angle, a snug little bay is formed, where, in the
roughest weather, a small craft might ride with safety.
Leaving the shingles you pass over a broad belt composed of fine white sand, intermixed with innumerable
tiny shells, and enter on a stony patch of some half
dozen acres, hemmed in with huge rocky fragments,
in the crevices and along the sides of which dwarf
trees may be seen, standing in every possible attitude
save a perpendicular. Here and there dark scraggy
bushes may be found, almost devoid of verdure,
although the greenness of summer be abroad.

On this desolate spot were erected three or four
huts, ill-looking shanties, built of various materials,
the foundations composed of boulders clumsily piled,
and the sides and roofs of plank and board, the dark
stains and paint on which showed them to be frag-

ments of wrecks. The aspect of these dwellings was
in perfect keeping with the place in which they were
located. From the fish which were spread out on
rude flakes near most of the huts, one would infer
that the occupants were fishermen. This was indeed
their calling in part, although a glance at the inside of
the habitations would lead one to the conclusion that
fishing was not their only pursuit. From the rough,
unpromising exterior, one would look for a correspond-
ing interior. But, instead of scant and rudely made furniture, a visitor would have been surprised to find the
apartments comfortably furnished, with quite a show
of gentility. More particularly would this have been
observed in one of the huts, which stood a little apart
from the rest, in a more choice situation, if there could
be a choice in such a place, and which appeared superior to the others in many respects.

The painted and panelled double door, evidently
taken from the state-room of some vessel, would first
attract the attention. Entering this, one would be
struck with the singular aspect of the rooms, all of
them being finished and furnished something after the
manner of a ship's cabin. In the centre of the largest
room, fastened to the floor, stood a heavy mahogany
table. Around the sides of the room ran a boxed
seat fixed similar to a transom. The walls consisted
of panelled boards, one perhaps painted green, its
mate white, and a third deeply stained to resemble
mahogany. Suspended around the walls were various
nautical instruments, sextants, spy-glasses, barometers,
and a number of rolls of charts, together with one or
two rusty muskets, grainse, &c. The bedrooms, four
in number, were finished in about the same manner.

Instead of bedsteads, bunks or berths were fixed up as on shipboard.

One of these apartments was quite tastefully arranged, the berth being neatly curtained, the sheets and pillow-cases of spotless linen, the window hung with a fringed drapery, and the walls ornamented with a mirror set in a handsomely-gilded frame, while the floor was covered with Venetian carpeting. There was adjoining this a small room, fitted up with a few shelves containing a small supply of books. The furnishing of this room evidently showed that it was intended for a sort of *boudoir*, — if such a fashionable term may be used in connection with so humble a dwelling.

This remote and obscure hamlet was the abode of a small gang of wreckers and fishermen combined, — the latter calling being followed when the former failed them. The company consisted of six or seven men, and it must be confessed, from their general appearance and bearing, one would be apt at first to cherish rather an unfavorable opinion of their characters. A more intimate acquaintance with them, however, would serve to do away with this impression.

The captain or chief of the band was a man whose gray locks and weather-beaten face told of years of toil and exposure, perhaps of suffering. He was a strong, hale man, nevertheless, and there was a light in his eye and a sprightliness in his movements that spoke of vigor unwasted and nerves well strung. The remainder of the crew were of various ages, all but one ranging past the meridian of life. This individual, known by the name of Antonio, was a young man of perhaps twenty-three, — a hardy-looking fellow, not wanting, despite his swarthy face and unshaven locks, in indications of manly beauty. There was in his countenance, withal, an expression that would lead one to prefer him rather as a friend than an enemy. He was of Spanish descent, as his name indicated, although from early life he had lived among Americans.

Save the females in the family of the leader, none of the gentler sex were to be found in this hamlet; and of these two we shall speak hereafter.

CHAPTER II.

Soft as the memory of a buried love,
Pure as the prayer that childhood wafts above,
Was she, the daughter of that rude old chief.
BYRON.

LATE one afternoon, in the fall of the year, at the time our story opens, two persons were standing by the open door of the dwelling whose interior we have described, which was occupied by the leader of the crew, gazing towards the sea, which was fast roughening under a smart north-easter. They were both females — one of them considerably past the prime of life. The somewhat masculine proportions of the eldest of the two, together with her wrinkled and sunburnt visage, set off by thin gray locks and an elfish-looking cap, gave her at first sight rather a repulsive appearance; but the gentle and affectionate glances that she directed toward her companion, and the mild tone with which she addressed her, were proofs that a warm heart was concealed beneath that rugged exterior.

2

Her companion was a maiden of about eighteen summers; her figure was very symmetrical, exhibiting a healthy, though by no means a coarse, physical development. Dark chestnut hair, arranged with a native grace, surmounted a countenance of more than common beauty, rendered more striking, perhaps, by the contrast exhibited in her companion. Exposure had thrown a slight shade of brown on her skin, but where her dress interposed as a veil, it was of a clear and almost snowy whiteness. Eyes large, full, and intelligent, shaded by long lashes, a slightly oval face, through the warm tinge of which the rich blood could be seen mantling, an exquisitely-formed mouth and clear red lips, around which, like sunshine on fruit, an arch smile loved to linger, a neck beautifully proportioned, and a full, swelling bust, — a model for a statue, — formed the maiden's charming contour.

Could it be that so lovely a bud was an off-shoot from so graceless a stalk? that so rare a flower had sprung up amid this wilderness of rocks — been nurtured among the rugged plants which surrounded it? Even so, in the by-places of this world, amid the sterile roughness of humanity, we sometimes find grace, beauty and intellect so predominant, as if nature sought a favored object on which to lavish her gifts, that she might not be without a witness of her lovely and beautiful creations.

"I am afraid we are going to have a severe gale," said the eldest of the females, as she cast an anxious glance seaward; "the wind increases in violence and the sea rises fast. I wish the schooner would return."

"Had I not better go on to the headland, mother?"

replied the younger female; "perhaps I may see her in the offing."

"Yes, go, my dear child, and take the glass with you. I, feel anxious about her, for it is growing dark fast, and it will be a bad night to be out in."

The young girl entered the door for the glass, and then, throwing her apron over her head, she started for the high bluff which springs up at the eastern entrance of the cove, skipping from rock to rock with the grace and lightness of the mountain chamois.

"If I see them, mother," she said, on leaving, "I will wave my handkerchief as a signal."

In a short time, although the path was difficult, she stood on the beetling cliff, gazing from its dizzy height with unshaken nerve. From that elevated point she had a full view of the ocean. The scene was not new to the maiden, yet she could not gaze upon the world of waters spread before her, rolling in from the outer deep with an unbroken swell, and dashing against the base of the headland with a noise like continuous thunder, without a thrilling sense of the grandeur and awful sublimity of the scene. She was not one of those, common as was the sight, who can gaze with an indifferent eye and unaffected heart on such an exhibition as was there presented; and, as the huge billows rushed madly in and beat upon the opposing barrier, and were thrown back in clouds of foam, a sense of His omnipotence who has said, "Thus far shalt thou go and no farther," touched the deepest chords of her soul, awakening emotions which she could not define or shape into expression.

For hours had she stood gazing, as at present, on a scene like this, silent and spell-bound, the working of her countenance betraying the agitation of her mind. Alas! the key to that inner sanctuary might never be applied, and its hoarded treasure never brought to the light. Her mind was like a hidden fountain, gushing with pure waters, but wasting its crystal currents in dark channels and murmuring unheard its subterranean music. Shall not the clods be removed, and the bright stream, sparkling in the sunbeams, flow gladly forth with its rippling melody?

Some time elapsed, so absorbed was the maiden in the contemplation of the scene, ere the nature of her errand occurred to her, when, raising the glass to her eye, and slowly sweeping the misty horizon, she hastily turned toward the house and suffered her handkerchief to flutter in the breeze. Afar off, heading for the cove, she caught sight of the object of her search. The vessel was a small fore-and-aft schooner, and was under a heavy press of sail, notwithstanding the gusts came stronger and stronger and the sea ran higher and higher every moment. She was evidently a fine sea boat, and bore herself bravely, riding lightly the heavy billows and nearing rapidly the shore.

"I must kindle a fire on the Head," said the maiden, as she gazed at the struggling vessel; "they will want a beacon-light to guide them before they reach the land."

The daylight was fast disappearing, and, feeling assured that it would be entirely dark before the vessel could make the harbor, the maiden, like one accustomed to the business, commenced collecting the brush which was scattered around the place and heaping it in a mass on the edge of the cliff. Having formed quite a pile, she started toward the house.

whence she shortly returned with a flaming pitch knot. By this time, night had shut in, hiding the little craft from sight, and leaving nothing to be seen but the sparkling of the spray as it was thrown up along the shore, and the occasional cap of a distant wave, the crest of foam flashing for a moment above the black billow like the lurid gleam we sometimes see playing on the edge of the thunder-cloud.

Carefully guarding her light, the wrecker's daughter bent down and kindled the pile of brush at its base. Immediately a bright flame shot crackling above the heap, followed by a dense volume of smoke, shrouding the light in its thick folds and threatening to choke the fire. The strong wind, however, soon fanned the whole mass into a brilliant blaze. At times, the tongues of flame would shoot high in the air, whirled about by the breeze, illuminating the surrounding scenery, and bringing out the neighboring cliffs in bold relief, while the crested waves would catch the lurid reflection afar off, seeming as if wreathed with fire. At other times they would bend low, as if licking the earth, darting serpent-like beneath and amidst the heavy black smoke that curled above them, while a tenfold gloom and darkness seemed to settle upon the troubled deep. The effect of this beacon-fire — light and shade thus alternating — was as singular as it was imposing, heightened as it was by .the deafening roar of the sea and the strong rush of the gale. Conspicuous on the headland, as the light flashed upon her form, stood the young girl, like some beautiful enchantress, gazing delighted upon the scene which her own magic had wrought.

2*

CHAPTER III.

Far o'er the watery waste a beacon-light
Beams its bright welcome to the seaman's sight ;
Exultant now he marks the whirling foam,
Nor heeds the growing storm — that light
　　　　　Guides to his home.

"A BLESSING on that girl!" said the old skipper, as he stood at the helm of his little craft, directing her through the wallowing sea; "a blessing on that girl!" he repeated more fervently, as his eye caught the first glare of the distant fire that served as a guide to his course.

"What light is that?" asked a young man in a feeble voice. The speaker was closely wrapped in a shaggy overcoat, lent him by the captain, and stood by the side, or rather reclined on the companion-way, near the binnacle.

"That light is kindled on Gull's Head, at the starboard entrance of the cove," answered the old man, "and by as fair a lass, young sir, though I say it, as e'er graced a prince's hall. A blessing on her, say I."

"Your daughter, I presume?" said his young companion.

"She calls me father, ay," replied the old man, with a little hesitation, "and never had parent more reason to pride himself on —— "

"Are you sure the light is kindled on the Gull's Head?" said one of the crew, interrupting the encomiums of the old man. "If it is on the Hawk's Nest we shall hardly weather Dead Man's ledge, if you steer your present course."

"Sure!" said the aged helmsman, "ay, my life on Nell's forethought. She has too much good sense to kindle a fire to leeward on such a night as this, knowing where-away we are. But keep a sharp look-out for'ard," he continued, as he bent a searching gaze on the distant beacon. "A bad ledge, sir, a bad ledge is that, with a bad name. It stretches here-away, about half a league from the Hawk's Nest,—the name given to a broad shelf that laps out from the larboard cliff, as we enter the cove."

The young man with whom this conversation was held was not, as the reader will infer, one of the crew. The wreckers had been on a cruise, during which they had providentially fallen in with a stranded ship, some leagues down the coast, from which, with much difficulty and risk, this young man was rescued. He was a passenger, and the only one saved, all the rest, passengers and crew, having been swept off ere the wreck was discovered. The survivor was not rescued a moment too soon, for he was nearly insensible and entirely helpless when fallen in with, and, had it not been for the old man, he would probably have been left to his fate. At the imminent risk of his life, he boarded the wreck and took the sufferer off. Owing to the heavy sea that was running, and the threatening appearance of the weather, they abandoned the vessel without attempting to save anything from her.

"Whence did the ledge you mentioned derive its name?" inquired the young man, after a brief pause.

"It has always borne that name since my knowledge," replied the old man. "There is a tradition among the few dwellers on this coast, that in the olden time a gallant ship, driven in by stress of weather, struck on this reef in the night and was shattered, so that when morning came not a speck was to be seen of her. One man alone, of all her crew, was found when the tide receded, cold and stiff, clinging with a death-grasp to the kelp and sea-weed growing on the ledge, and swinging about with the wash of the sea. Ever since, it is said, when the tempest is abroad, through the livelong night his lone wail can be heard mingling with the tumult of the gale. We are nearing the spot now, young man," added the old skipper, in a low tone of voice. "Look yonder — you can see it break under our lee-bow. Listen! there should be wailings from Dead Man's ledge to-night, if ever. I have often heard them in the pauses of the gale."

The old man bent his head, while his companion gave an involuntary shudder as he cast a glance on the long line of foam a short distance to the leeward, along the very edge of which the little craft was dashing with the speed of the wind; but it was not from a dread of hearing supernatural cries. He shuddered when he thought of the dangers he had passed through, and of the certain fate which must have awaited him had he been exposed to the fearful storm now gathering. He thought, too, of the companions of his voyage, now dashed about by the turbulent sea, or thrown, mangled corpses, on the rock-bound shore. Fortunately, among them he had to mourn no kindred lost, no friendly tie broken. As they approached nearer the shore, and the breakers sounded more loudly in his ears, still more vividly was he impressed with the horrors of the scenes through which he had passed, and a prayer of gratitude went up to Him who had vouchsafed his deliverance. He was aroused from this silent communion by a shout from the old man, and on looking up he found the vessel was in the close neighborhood of the cliff, on the summit of which blazed the bright beacon.

"Thanks, my brave girl! thanks for your light!" shouted the old man, gazing, as he spoke, towards the burning pile.

The young man turned his eyes in the same direction. At first the glare of the flames dazzled them so he could not discern any other object; but in a moment he discovered the person addressed. Standing, as it appeared to him, on the very edge of the cliff, which sunk sheer to the sea a hundred feet or more, he detected the graceful outlines of a female figure. In her hand she held a blazing brand, which she waved two or three times in the air, while " Welcome back! " came down from the dizzy height in sweetly musical tones. Once more swinging her torch in the air, she turned and darted from the spot, bearing with her the flaming brand. The young man followed with his eyes the light as it flashed along the maiden's path. One moment it seemed to run along the very brink of the tall cliffs — the next it would curve inward from the cove — now the light would pass quickly down some sharp descent — now seem to rise with less rapidity — one moment approaching, the next receding, until it at last faded and flickered to a dim twinkle, and then suddenly disappeared. Meanwhile, the sails having been lowered and furled, the schooner rounded the point we have described, where she was protected from the rough weather, and was shortly moored in safety.

We will not stop to portray the emotions of the

young man as he once more· placed his foot, on tho
land. Chastened joy mingled with sadness were his
first feelings, soon, however, succeeded by a deep, all-
pervading sense of thankfulness and praise.

As he stood apart, leaning against a huge rocky
fragment that had once formed a portion of the tall
cliff that frowned threateningly above him, scanning
with a bewildered gaze the blackened sky and the
stern scene faintly revealed around him, while the
crew arranged the boat for the night, the wrecker's
daughter, still bearing the burning brand, came tripping down to the shore, and, skipping on to a narrow
shelving rock that jutted over the tide, extended her
light so as to facilitate the work of the men, while
hearty greetings were interchanged, her sweet voice
and merry laugh calling forth lively echoes from the
gloomy caverns and dark clefts of the surrounding
rocks.

The young man, unobserved himself, had a full view
of her person. He gazed upon her wondrous beauty,
rapt in astonishment. The grace of her attitude, as
she bent forward with her torch, the animation of
her countenance, glowing with health and exercise,
the very disarrangement of her dress, which served
more fully to reveal her charms, rivetted the eyes of
the youth upon her. The encomiums of the old man
recurred to his mind, which he had imputed to a
parent's fondness, but his heart now confessed that
princely hall never was graced with a fairer being.
He thought of those flattering lines of the poet, and
here found their application :

> " Her eyes, her lips, her cheeks, her shapes, her features,
> Seem to be drawn by Love's own hand ; by Love,
> Himself in love."

Half doubting the evidence of his own senses, hardly knowing whether the lovely creature before him were an inhabitant of earth or a being of a brighter sphere, and completely fascinated with her surprising charms, an involuntary exclamation burst from the young man's lips.

The maiden started as the murmured exclamation met her ear, and, turning the light of her torch in his direction, made a movement of surprise, as she discovered him, a rich blush at the instant stealing over her neck and face. Her father noticed the action, and then bethought him he had not informed her of the stranger's presence.

"A young gentleman," said he, in a sort of introductory way, "whom we were so fortunate as to save from a wreck this morning; and you had better show him to the house, Nell, for a dry shelter and a warm bed would better befit his weak state than this damp night air, and these cold, wet stones. Never mind your light, — we can do well enough now without it."

"I was not aware of your presence, sir," said the maiden, stepping towards the young man in a free and unembarrassed manner. "You have been unfortunate," she continued, in a tone of unaffected kindness, while her features expressed the deepest sympathy as she gazed upon the pale countenance of the stranger; "you have been unfortunate, and perhaps need assistance. Permit me to show you to the house;" and with a tact and delicacy he little dreamed of meeting in this remote and wild spot, she carefully guided him over the broken and difficult way. There was that in her tone and manner, a warmth, tenderness and frankness, an absence of that awkward shyness, and of those coarse manifestations of kindness sometimes met with, and withal a propriety of language, that astonished the young stranger almost as much as did her unequalled and bewildering beauty.

CHAPTER IV.

Dreams in their development have breath,
And tears, and tortures, and the touch of joy.
BYRON.

There is a fair behavior in thee, captain,
And though that nature with a beauteous wall
Doth oft close in pollution, yet of thee
I will believe thou hast a mind that suits
With this thy fair and outward character.
SHAKSPEARE.

WARM and unbounded was the hospitality which awaited the stranger at the wrecker's dwelling. A glowing fire lent its cheering influence to bestow an air of comfort to the strange-looking apartment, which contrasted strongly with the forbidding aspect of the exterior of the hut. The constant yet unobtrusive attentions of the wrecker's family were as grateful to the heart of the new-comer as they were conducive to his bodily comfort. After a slight repast, worn and wearied with the scenes he had passed through, he gladly sought his couch. Fatigue soon induced sleep, but it was a restless one. There was no rest to his mind, though slumber pressed heavily on his eyelids. The poet Maturin describes his state, —

" He sleeps, if it be sleep — this starting trance,
Whose feverish tossings and deep muttered groans
Do prove the soul shares not the body's rest."

His excited fancy had placed him again on the stranded wreck, and the rocking and grinding of the vessel and the incessant beating of the spray were again felt. The waves again boiled in fury around him, and their deafening roar was in his ear. He felt the broad billows lifting the huge hulk upon their backs; then came the dreadful shock as it settled down on the sharp rocks, the dark wave bursting in a deluge of foam around him.

Yet ever amid the gloom and terror of that fearful scene there hovered about him one radiantly beautiful, whose countenance beamed angel-like upon him, and whose tones stole like soothing music to his ears. The last waking thought of the young man, as his cheek pressed the snow-white pillow, was of the fair hand that smoothed it; and the lovely spirit of his dreams and the wrecker's daughter were wonderfully like !

After the others had retired, the wrecker and his wife sat before the crackling fire engaged in conversation, the former indulging the luxury of a pipe, the blue smoke from which, after floating in aerial curls around his head, rushed in a broad ribbon up the rude-built chimney.

"So you saved nothing from the wreck?" said the wife.

"Not a single article," was the reply. "The surf ran so high it was dangerous boarding her, and it was at the risk of my life that I got the youngster off."

"We should be thankful for that, husband. One life is of more value than a thousand cargoes."

"Yes," replied the old man with great sincerity; "wealth may be replaced, but life once gone is gone

3

forever. The ship thrown on her beam-ends may be righted, but the craft that goes to the bottom, good bye to her; she will never rise again!"

The old man knocked the ashes from his pipe and continued: "The crew tried to persuade me from making the attempt, but I could not leave a human being to perish without one trial to save him, though, for the matter of that, his troubles were nearly over when I got to him. Precious little life was there left in him when I took him on board."

"It was a mercy you fell in with him, John," rejoined the woman, in a compassionate tone.

"You may well say that, wife,—it was a mercy, for by this time not two planks of that ship are left together. Two hours, with such a sea as there is now on, would grind the stoutest vessel that ever floated to splints, placed in the situation of the wreck."

"Pray God, no vessel be exposed to this frightful gale!" ejaculated the wife, with an inward shudder, as the strong blast swept over the house, causing the rafters to creak and tremble, while the deep, awful roar of the sea broke upon the ear in thunder-tones, and the rain and the driving spray plashed with a dull, dreary sound against the side of the building, and bubbled in the crevices of the small seaward window.

"Amen to that, Bess!" rejoined the old sailor, carefully laying aside his pipe. "God grant that no ship be abroad in this ugly night! Though wrecking is our business, and we are ready to take what the sea gives us, yet, *He* knows, I wish no harm to my fellow-creatures. They talk hard of us poor wreckers, wife; they give us a bad name; but, though other folks' mis-

fortune is our meat, sooner would John Brown pine
with hunger — ay, and often he has, too, as you well
know — than wrong his conscience by wishing ill to
others."

"What do they say of you, John? what can they
say of you?" asked the wife, in astonishment.

"They speak of false lights," said the indignant old
man, "set like bait in traps to lure the unwary to
destruction. And then they hint, if the sea spares the
poor sailor, the wrecker proves less merciful, — for
'dead men can tell no tales,' say they! No more
they can, wife, seeing as a cold tongue must needs be
silent."

"But have they any cause for giving you such a
name?"

"Why, the world is full of bad men, and there may
be some in our trade. I commenced the business on
Florida shore, — as good wrecking ground as you will
find on the coast, — and I have heard tell of men who
followed the trade in olden time on the Cape who
were little better than pirates. False lights were
kindled in dark, stormy nights, and when the devoted
vessel was lured on to the rocks, never one of the
crew escaped to tell the tale. If the surf threw them
ashore, there were always those ready to thrust them
back again, with a clip on the head, perhaps, to quiet
them."

"Cruel wretches! how could they?" murmured
the wife, in a low, half-whispered tone.

"A few years before I left the Cape," continued the
old man, "there was a report of a Spanish wrecker, on
one of the neighboring Keys, enticing a brig ashore
and murdering the crew. A number of bodies, it was

said, were found soon after washed ashore, all bearing gaping wounds, showing that the poor fellows had met other than a drowning death."

"I never liked the Spaniards," remarked the wife, with strong feeling; "they seem to be a cruel, blood-thirsty race."

"Not all of them, Bess. There is a set of despera-does among the islanders, but we must not judge of the national character by these men. There's Anto-nio, now, — he is a fine fellow, certainly."

"I don't know about that," said the old woman, with a shake of the head. "I can't say he altogether suits my fancy; nor more does he some one's else, though he tries hard to win it."

"What, does Nell look coldly upon him? Why, I thought he was just the one to catch a maiden's heart."

"Love will go where it is sent, John, and only there. You cannot change or check the current of woman's affection any more than you can the ocean tides."

"True, Bess, true!" said the old man, playfully; "nor, for the matter of that, her hate either. Ye are headstrong, stubborn creatures, and will have your way, right or wrong. But I am not sorry that Nell does not affect the lad, for he has a good deal of the warmth of his clime in his blood; you may see that in his eyes. With Nell's gentle and yielding disposition, I fear me she would find more of the master than the kind husband in him."

"She will find neither, with my consent," replied the wife, in a tone which, had it reached Antonio's ears, would have closed the gate of hope against him forever. "Who is this young Spaniard, that he should seek to mate with one like her?"

"We all know who he is," replied the husband; "but who is Ellen?" he asked, rather significantly.

"She is an angel!" was the wife's reply, a shade of sadness stealing over her face as she rose from her seat.

"Ay, that is she, Heaven's blessing on her innocent head!" responded the husband. A brief conversation followed, when the wrecker and his wife retired for the night, the sough of the storm, like the moan of a troubled spirit, filling their ears, — a sound too often heard to banish sleep.

CHAPTER V.

O woman! in our hours of ease,
Uncertain, coy, and hard to please;
When pain and anguish wring the brow,
A ministering angel thou.

SCOTT.

WHEN the young man awoke the next morning, with the angry strife of the elements still in his ears, for a while his memory played him false, and he gazed confusedly about the strange-looking apartment, completely at a loss to account for his being in such an unfamiliar place. By degrees, however, he became aware of the true state of the case, and he lifted his head from the pillow to survey the singular appearance of the room. Barely had he time to notice the neatness and taste with which it was furnished, ere a feeling of extreme dizziness forced him back to his

3*

pillow. The exposure to which he had been subjected,
coupled with the excitement he had undergone, operat-
ing on a frame not yet recovered from a debilitating
sickness, had proved too much for him. A burning
fever preyed upon him, and through the day the symp-
toms grew more and more unfavorable, so that by the
second night the violence of the attack was manifested by the frequent wanderings of the patient.

Well has the poet characterized woman, "a ministering angel, when pain and anguish wring the brow."
Such an angel flitted around the couch of Edward
Irving, while the hand of disease was heavy upon him.
Day after day he continued to grow worse, and, for the
many weeks he was confined to a sick-bed, on Ellen
devolved the duties of nurse. It was her hand that
smoothed his pillow, and it was from her hand he
received the simple medicines prepared by the wrecker's wife. During all the wanderings of her patient
he bestowed upon her the tender epithet of "sister,"
and often would she resign her hand to his burning
clasp while he addressed her in all those endearing
terms prompted by a strong brotherly love. Often,
too, would he speak of his mother, wondering that she
was not present; and then, pressing the hand he held
to his lips, he would thank the blushing girl for her
kind attentions. So accustomed at last did she become to the familiar appellation, that she immediately
started to do his bidding whenever he mentioned that
sister's name. And when at last the veil was removed
from his mind, and he inquired, in a feeble whisper,
forgetful that he was amidst strangers, for "sister
Caroline," she stepped softly to his bedside and gently
answered, "I am here, Edward: can I do anything for

you?"—the sudden start and the inquiring look he gave were the first intimations to the delighted girl that his delusion had vanished.

"Surely sister Caroline has been with me!" said he, as he gazed with an earnest look into the face of his lovely attendant.

She shook her head, while, in a tone slightly embarrassed, she informed him of his deception, at the same time cautioning him not to exert himself by talking in his then critical state.

"Then it is to your kindness and care I am indebted for —— "

He would have said more, but she gently checked him, imposing upon him for the present strict silence. He obeyed her, but expressed what he would have said by raising her unresisting hand to his lips, and breathing the word "Thanks!"

Slowly did health and strength come back to young Irving, and for a long time he was compelled to endure the irksomeness of a sick-chamber. But did the young man find it irksome? If he did, he exhibited no signs of weariness, unless on those occasions during the absence of that lovely being whose delicate attentions and gentle sympathy operated as a spell upon him, banishing the gloom of confinement and the ennui of inaction. In ordinary cases, perhaps, the attentions of a young female towards a stranger, thrown, as Irving was, upon the hospitality of the family, would have ceased in a measure during the period of his convalescence. But the artless and sympathizing heart of the wrecker's daughter saw no impropriety in still continuing the offices of a nurse. Indeed, so occupied was the mother in her household duties, that Ellen was compelled — nothing loth, it must be confessed — to attend upon the sick stranger.

It was a pleasure to her, during his slow recovery, to take her needle-work and sit by his side, and, when his returning strength permitted, to enter into conversation with him, or to read to him from the few volumes that by chance had found their way to this remote place. If Ellen listened eagerly to the words of one whose mind was richly stored with intellectual treasure, not less eagerly did young Irving watch the manifestations of a spirit congenial with his own, — a spirit shackled, as it were, to earth, yet striving, in obedience to its native impulse, to plume itself for a flight into a higher and purer atmosphere. If he had been surprised to find so much beauty, and so much that is endearing in the feminine character, in this wild and out-of-the-way place, not less was he surprised to find, united to this loveliness, so much of the germ of that which, in its development, is so ennobling to the other sex. Before him he saw a fair and beautiful field, in whose rich soil the precious seed were waiting for the invigorating rays to quicken them. Could he hesitate? He would cultivate this inviting soil; he would strive to repay the obligation he felt resting upon him for the care and kindness he had received, by aiding the growth of those powers which promised such rich fruition. Ah! the beams that lent the quickening warmth, darted they not from the *heart* as well as the mind?

It was a delightful task on which he now entered, — delightful to pupil as teacher, — for Ellen, although Irving had not hinted his intentions, intuitively seemed to fathom his designs, and, by her eagerness to gather instruction, manifested her ready acquiescence. Fortunately for the young man's purpose, the wrecker, on revisiting the scene of the shipwreck, had found in a neighboring hamlet, among other things, the trunk of Irving, which he succeeded in securing for a slight compensation. The contents of this trunk were peculiarly valuable to Edward, for they consisted of a large set of books, which, in his new character of instructor, were almost indispensable.

CHAPTER VI.

They read together, reading the same book,
    Their heads bent forward with a half embrace,
So that each shade that either spirit took
    Was straight reflected in the other's face.
                                        ANON.

EDWARD IRVING — for it is time to give some account of our hero — was a young Virginian. He was about twenty-four years of age. His personal appearance was certainly prepossessing, without laying claim to any distinguishing marks of manly beauty. His countenance could not strictly be called handsome; but there was an intellectual cast to his features, — an expression which spoke of an open and a generous heart, — that at once won him the good will of those with whom he chanced to associate. His father had been some time deceased, leaving a handsome estate to his family, which consisted of the widow, and two children, Edward and Caroline.

Unlike too many of the "chivalrous" sons of the Old Dominion, left in a similar situation, who spend

their time and patrimony in horse-racing and like
"manly sports," to the neglect of the higher and
nobler employments and enjoyments of life, Irving
determined to strike out a path for himself, to pursue
a loftier career; for which purpose he sought to store
his mind with those intellectual treasures which bestow
such a lustre on the character. He heard his fellows
boast of their "nice sense of honor," of their high,
chivalric feeling, but he was grieved to see so little
evidence of that which gives to man his only true
worth and dignity. He was not satisfied with the
poor, beggarly chaff which fed the ambition of many
of his acquaintance. His aspirations were not bounded
by the foolish desire of astonishing the gaping multi-
tude by the brilliancy of his establishment, by a prod-
igal waste of money, or by a wild and reckless course
of life. He sought for no such distinction as this: he
felt, with the poet, that

> "The suffrage of the wise,
> The praise that's worth ambition, is attained
> By sense alone, and dignity of mind."

Not unfrequently had he heard his companions
boast of their being the "sons of Virginia," the descendants of heroes and patriots, — good men and
true; but he was not content to bask in the reflected
glory of other days. True, he felt proud of his
native State, of the illustrious names that shed such
a halo around her annals; and, conscious of lofty
capacities, he resolved not to waste them, but, by
cultivating his powers, to render himself a worthy
scion of the proud old commonwealth, and, it may be,
to rub off some of the rust which perchance had

gathered on her escutcheon. With these views and feelings he had visited the North, and entered "old Harvard," where he applied himself to a strict course of mental discipline. Actuated as he was, it may safely be presumed he did not slight the opportunities afforded him. He bent his whole energies to the task before him, and, when he took his degree, his name stood first on the list of aspirants. So eager, indeed, had been his pursuit, he overtasked his strength, and about the time of his leaving college his health had become very much reduced. In the hope of deriving benefit from a sea-voyage, he took passage for a southern port, and met with the disaster we have stated.

The fall months had passed away and the winter set in ere Irving's health would permit him to leave the house. Even then it was so precarious he dared not risk the fatigue and exposure of a journey home. To the joy of the wrecker's family, he at last concluded to remain with them until a milder season, or until his strength was sufficiently recruited to permit him to travel with safety. He had ingratiated himself wonderfully with the wrecker and his wife. Uncultivated themselves, though not wanting in a natural shrewdness which preserved them from boorishness, they were not the less sensible of the importance of education; and it was with no slight degree of joy that they noticed the interest that existed between Ellen and the young stranger in their studies. Whether, in their simplicity, they ever cast a thought on the possibility of the young couple conning a lesson not to be found in the books, we cannot take it upon ourself to say. At any rate, they never evinced the slightest suspicion. The modest and frank bearing of the young man entirely won their regards, and they reposed the fullest confidence in his integrity.

As for Ellen, she had scarcely analyzed her feelings from the day the young man became an inmate of her father's dwelling. She was sensible that a brighter light beamed upon her pathway, that a new fountain of joy had been opened in her heart, that the world wore a more beautiful aspect; but she attempted not to solve the mystery of the change. With a mind all athirst for knowledge, it seemed to spurn the slow, laborious process by which it is usually obtained, and to grasp at once the prize. Scale after scale fell rapidly from her eyes, until, like sudden sight to the blind, she became dazzled and bewildered in the light that beamed around her. Her young teacher, albeit he gazed delighted on the almost miraculous workings of her spirit, found as much difficulty in curbing her impatient zeal as many do in spurring on the dull laggard.

Day after day, as Irving sat by the side of that ardent-minded girl, and watched the changes of her beautiful countenance as new truths constantly burst upon her mind, and witnessed the rich glow which ever and anon irradiated her face as some newly-encountered difficulty gave way before her unconquerable perseverance, — day after day, as he marked the unfolding of her mind, the development of powers so much more brilliant than he dreamed of her possessing, — deeper and deeper grew his admiration. He saw her striving to win his approbation by moulding her intellect in accordance with his own by imbuing herself with his spirit, catching the tone and

hue of his intelligent nature, turning towards him
ever, as the flower to the sun, with a sweet confidence; and as he thus contemplated her, his heart
grew to her with an affection stronger, if possible,
than love. She leaned upon and looked up to him
with such a childlike earnestness, pursuing her inquiries with such an artless familiarity, and abandoning herself to his mental guidance so unreservedly,
and yet in her unrestrained freedom preserving always
such a modest propriety, that the young man felt flattered as well as charmed by her devotion. Mingled
with that deeper and more impassioned sentiment
which had sprung up in his heart, he cherished toward
her the pure affection of a brother. He felt proud of
the task he had undertaken as he beheld the rapid
growth of her mind, and reflected that, but for him,
perhaps, this lovely casket would never have been un-
sealed and its precious treasures never revealed.

There was one, however, who viewed these proceedings with far other than pleasurable feelings.
From the first hour that the young man had found
shelter beneath the wrecker's roof, there was one who
had fixed a jealous eye upon him. This was Antonio,
who, as has been hinted, looked upon the young
maiden as a prize destined for himself alone. With
all the vindictiveness of his race, coupled to a mind
trammeled by ignorance and low associations, the
reader may imagine the feelings with which he witnessed the growing intimacy of the young couple.
At the very first the devotion of Ellen to the stranger
during the severity of his sickness aroused his suspicious nature, and as the young man grew better
and a closer union seemed to subsist between the

4

two, while broader and broader grew the separation
between the maiden and himself, bitterer and more
vengeful grew his ire towards the cause of this
change; and when at last Ellen withdrew herself entirely from his companionship, insensibly indeed to
herself, he was goaded to an almost ungovernable
rage. He swore in his heart the deadliest vengeance
against young Irving, although, with all that cunning
so often engendered by malice, he smothered the pas-
sion-fires that raged fiercely in his bosom, so as to
conceal them from the notice of others. Impatiently
he waited for the coming spring, trusting that the
young man would take his departure, brooding over,
meanwhile, a plan by which he might rid himself of so
dangerous a rival, should he still linger in his way, or
return to snatch the treasure from his grasp.

Slowly and drearily to him, but marvellously rapid
and pleasant to the youthful couple, passed the winter
months. To them it was like the passage of a brilliant dream, and they could scarcely credit their own
senses when they observed that the huge snow-drifts
had disappeared and the budding spring was at hand.
They could not be convinced that it had been a rough
and rude season, and the old folks chuckled with
delight and rubbed their hands in great glee at their
mutual astonishment, when they told them that a
" harder winter had rarely been known." O, the sunshine of the heart! how it softens and mellows
where'er it falls and whate'er it touches!

CHAPTER VII.

They had not spoken ; but they felt allured
As if their souls and lips each other beckoned.

BYRON

Though absent, present in desires they be ;
Our souls much further than our eyes can see.

DRAYTON.

THE time at last arrived when young Irving felt
compelled to tear himself away from one who had
woven so powerful a spell around his heart. Strong
as were the ties that drew him to his home, ardently
as he desired once more to embrace a mother and sister whom he fondly loved, still he contemplated the
hour of his departure with emotions of the deepest
sadness. He had never made an avowal of his love,
he had never sought an expression of the sentiments
of her whose image was enshrined in his very heart
of hearts ; yet well he knew that maiden's heart was
all his own. Why then did he hesitate ? What should
prevent his securing the treasure which it would
seem Providence had placed in his reach ? Not on
his own account did he refrain from declaring his passion and seeking a return. Nay, feeling that life
without her companionship would be a poor boon, he
had determined at some future time on revealing his
affection, and, if possible, securing her hand.

But he had reasons for delaying this declaration.
He belonged to one of the old patrician families of
Virginia. He was well aware that his mother was of
that class which cherishes — for the class is not ex-
tinct—peculiar notions in regard to birth and fortune ;

a class which shrinks from, or scorns, an alliance with
those in a humbler rank; which arrogates a superiority
above the common herd, as though the purple currents that course their veins sprung from a purer
source than that of the rest of God's creatures. Such
were the ideas early instilled into young Irving. But
as he grew in years his good native sense taught him
better. He saw among the different grades of society
no radical distinction; he saw those in the lower walks
of life, borne down and fettered by circumstances,
fitted to adorn any station in life; and, on the other
hand, he beheld those who boasted of their blood,
who were not, so far as true merit is concerned, worthy
to undo the latchets of many whose companionship
they spurned. Seeing this, he felt, with the poet, that
there is

> "No distinction 'tween man and man,
> But as his virtues add to him a glory,
> Or vices cloud him."

Well knowing his mother's views on this point, he
thought, for the happiness of all, ere he committed
himself, it would be best for him to confer with her.
It required, however, all the force of restraint which
he could command when he announced his intention
of leaving for home. He first mentioned it to Ellen
alone, and the manner with which the information was
received, the tone with which she uttered the words,
involuntarily, as it were, "Home, Edward! O, why
should our homes be apart?"—the deep dejection
which accompanied this artless though meaning exclamation—almost threw him off his guard, and he was
on the point of clasping the lovely girl to his heart

and pouring into her ear the tender avowal which trembled on his lips. Fortunately for his purpose, the entrance of the wrecker and his wife checked the impulse.

Many and hearty were the regrets expressed by the parents when informed of his intentions. He had been domesticated with them so long that they looked upon him as one of the family, and quite as much interest was manifested as if he were indeed their son. His preparations for departing threw a shade of gloom over the household, and only the reiterated assurances of the young man that he would soon revisit them in the least reconciled them to his going away.

We will not stop to describe the leave-taking: it was a sad one to all concerned. Irving alone was cheered with the hope of soon returning to claim the hand of her whose depth of feeling prevented her presence when the final moment of parting came.

With feelings little to be envied, the young man traversed the barren region that separated the small hamlet from the great living world, and, as he slowly journeyed, his thoughts constantly reverted to her on whom rested all his earthly hopes. From the depth of his own feelings, well could he imagine the state of hers. A change had indeed come over the spirit of her dream, and bitter to her was that change. The light which had beamed so brightly in her pathway was suddenly withdrawn, and the gloom of night closed around her. Still, one little star looked kindly down upon her. Like the silver sheen on the edge of the black cloud which veils the moon, so Hope threw its light on the darkness which enveloped her. Dwelling on his promised return, her spirits soon

4*

regained their wonted elasticity, and a cheerful smile
again came back, like a bird to its nest, as if loth to
remain long from the spot around which it loved to
linger.

Irving had left behind him all his stock of books,
and the lonely girl derived a pleasure from going
over them, reviewing her course of study, and fondly
dwelling on the many pencilled passages, thus marked
in order the more forcibly to attract attention. Every
moment not devoted to other duties was spent in the
little apartment used as a study, and there she held
silent communion with the absent; and, while she
sought to hoard up new treasures to enrich the mind,
daily did her love strengthen toward him who first
revealed to her their existence, and taught her to
appreciate their worth.

With a very wildness of joy, which he found it difficult to conceal, Antonio beheld the departure of one
whom he looked upon as standing in his way. He
had long flattered himself with the assurance that his
success in winning the wrecker's daughter was certain,
until the arrival of the stranger dissipated some of
his confidence, at the same time arousing his jealousy.
Far different was the love—if it may be dignified by
the name—he entertained from that which had been
kindled in Irving's breast. Antonio's was a grosser
passion. He looked upon her as a beautiful woman,
an object of desire merely to minister to the coarser
appetites of his nature. He could not appreciate those
intrinsic qualities, those higher and purer manifestations of character, wanting which, the possessor
of the most captivating personal attractions is but a
mere painted toy, a thing of art and show.

But a short time elapsed after his rival's departure ere, flushed with new hope, he began to prosecute his suit. Urged on by his fiery temperament, and seemingly unaware of the very evident fact that Ellen studiously avoided him, he boldly threw himself in her way and perseveringly sought to win her favor. If before the maiden had a distaste for his companionship, more strongly than ever did she cherish it now.

In point of mere external appearance, perhaps, the Spaniard had the advantage of the stranger; but, in the address and conversation, in everything that related to character, the contrast between the two was so great that distaste grew almost into disgust, which she found it difficult to conceal when in his presence. Still, notwithstanding she plainly evinced her disrelish for his society, the young man ceased not his annoying advances; on the contrary, each repulse appeared to stimulate him to renewed perseverance.

So marked at last became his attentions, that, to bring matters to a crisis, and so rid herself of his unpleasant pertinacity, she relaxed a little from her accustomed reserve, nor sought to avoid him as before. Seizing immediately upon the apparently favorable omen, Antonio lost not a moment in formally preferring his suit. Ellen calmly listened to his protestations of love, and then, in a voice of great mildness, blended with a determination which shut out every hope, assured him that, with her present feelings, she could not entertain his proposal. The young man gave an involuntary start as he listened to his rejection, and then, as if doubting whether his ears had not deceived him, pressed his suit anew, and with a more passionate earnestness.

"It is in vain, Antonio," said the embarrassed girl, as she gazed with a feeling akin to pity on the glowing face of the excited youth, "it is altogether vain: our paths through life must be separate."

This time there was no mistaking her meaning, and for a moment Antonio stood silently gazing into the maiden's face, his compressed lips trembling in spite of his efforts, and a sickly pallor overspreading his swarthy countenance, giving it the ghastly hue of death. Thus he stood, statue-like, the only sign of vitality being the nervous twitching of his lip and the slightly convulsive heaving of his breast, until the maiden shrunk from the very intensity of his gaze; when suddenly a fierce gleam lighted up his fixed and stony glance, and a wildly vengeful expression swept across his features. The change was so quickly wrought, and so complete, that Ellen began to tremble with a sense of undefined apprehension. She dreaded the burst of passion which she doubted not would follow this forcible manifestation of the struggle within.

"Ah ha! I thought as much," said he, in a low, sardonic tone, "I thought as much, and I may thank the pale-faced stranger for this reception!"

"Antonio!" said the maiden, startled at his remark, and somewhat indignant, "I cannot listen to such language!" and she attempted to leave him.

"Nay, nay, Ellen Brown, you *must* hear me!" he exclaimed, as he stepped in her path. "I have long suspected this. The stranger is at the bottom of it all. He has tampered with you; he has won your affections with his smooth tongue, and fooled your ignorance with his bookish jargon. He has robbed me, curses on him! and little he cares for —— "

"Let me pass, sir!" interrupted the wrecker's daughter, now highly excited at the reproach thrown upon the absent. "Your language is as unmanly as it is unjust."

The enraged Spaniard for a moment fixed upon the maiden a lowering look, in which were concentrated every dark and malignant passion; then, making room for her to pass, he muttered: "Go, proud girl! go your way; but know that I can hate as strongly as I can love. Your path is clear, but I give you fair warning, maiden. Tell your sickly paramour to beware, for, if ever he crosses my path, a worse fate will await him than that from which your foolish father rescued him!"

It is doubtful if Ellen heard the threat conveyed in the last sentence, for she hastily seized the opportunity to leave the presence of her infuriated lover, who turned from the spot, invoking the most horrid imprecations on the head of his rival.

Time passed on, and the excitement in Ellen's mind, consequent upon the interview we have just described, had given place to other feelings. Sometimes a vague fear would flit across her heart that Irving's return might be attended with ·danger. But this apprehension was soon banished, for Antonio appeared to have mastered his passion. Everything in his manner evinced an entire change in his feelings. He had become cheerful as ever, and he greeted Ellen with the same cordiality he had always manifested, insomuch that she deceived herself with the belief that he had forgotten, or was indifferent to, the repulse given to him. Ah! little did she dream of the horde of evil passions which nestled, like so many venomous serpents, beneath that calm and smiling exterior, awaiting only the return of the young Virginian to arouse them to action.

But would he ever return? The spring passed away, the burning summer came, and the glowing autumn drew nigh, and still he came not, — still came there no tidings from him. Was he sick? Had he forgotten her? The wrecker's daughter could not repress a sigh as she pondered these questions. Yet hope and faith triumphed over fear and doubt. The distance was so great, the opportunity of sending to a place so remote occurred so seldom, she felt she had no reason to expect a letter from him, although he had promised to write. Banishing, therefore, her despondency, she bent herself with renewed zeal to the acquisition of knowledge.

Not for the sake of knowledge alone did she thus task her energies, although to one of her cast of mind no other stimulus were needed. In all her mental strivings one motive alone impelled her, one desire only did she cherish, — to win the approbation of the absent one, to raise herself to his mental standard. Her great ambition was to assimilate her character with his, and thus render herself more worthy of his friendship. If a warmer sentiment inspired her endeavors, its existence was not acknowledged, although the shrewd reader may decide that love alone was the prime mover of all her actions.

CHAPTER VIII.

Love gives esteem, and then he gives desert;
He either finds equality, or makes it.
Like death, he knows no difference in degrees,
But flames and levels all.   DRYDEN.

Absence, with all its pains,
Is by this charming moment wiped away.
                            THOMSON.

O NO! Edward Irving was not forgetful. Nay, absence served rather to strengthen his passion. Though he moved among beautiful forms, and caught the winning glances of brilliant eyes, and encountered wooing smiles, yet his heart went back to the lone flower, blooming amid the desolate rocks, true to its first impulses. Courted by the wealthy and high-born, — for the possessor of so many rich acres was a prize coveted by many,—feted and flattered by designing mothers and worldly-minded fathers, mingling in that circle whose members affect to look down upon those shut out from its charmed precincts, still, young Irving forgot not for a moment the wrecker's daughter, cast not a single regretful thought on her humble birth, but only sighed for the time when he should take her to his home and heart. During his residence at the North, he had imbibed more strongly those notions (peculiar, as we believe, to New England) which lead one to measure a man, not by the false and contracted views of a clique, but by the broad rule which the Creator himself has laid down, — by a mental and moral standard which alone is infallible.

It was no slight undertaking to enter into an expla- -

nation with his mother. He had deeply rooted prejudices to encounter, — prejudices imbibed in earliest
youth, and which had grown and strengthened with
years. He had still more to overcome. His mother
had already fixed upon a choice for her son, and since
his return she had lost no opportunity in bringing
about the end she had in view. She well knew that
Edward cherished rather " vulgar notions " of " equality," and fearing that he might carry them out in
forming a connection, she thought it would not be
amiss to avert the calamity by selecting a partner
every way desirable.

Poor woman! her air-built castle was destined to
tumble to the ground, and its ruins laid heavily on
her heart. She could hardly listen patiently to Edward's avowal that he had already settled the affair.
Her very worst fears were more than realized. What,
her son marry a low-bred wrecker's daughter! The
proud blood of the Irvings be contaminated by its
sole representative uniting with the daughter of a
fishmonger, a half pirate! Alas, it was a sore trial
to the aristocratic widow; and vainly might Edward
have essayed to reconcile her to what she deemed the
degradation, had he not had powerful advocates to
assist him.

One of these was his own sister, a fine, intelligent
girl, who partook much of the spirit of her brother.
From Edward's representations she had been completely won over to his interests, and already had she
begun to cherish a warm regard for the humble Ellen.
From the glowing accounts of her brother, the ardent-
minded girl was impatient to welcome the object of
his affection as a sister. The other advocate on this

occasion was a widow lady in the neighborhood, the early companion and always friend of Mrs. Irving. Her opinions had great weight with the latter lady, and, by her influence, Mrs. Irving in time became somewhat reconciled to what, in fact, from her knowledge of the determined spirit of her son, she knew could not be avoided.

Mrs. Randolph had drunk deeply of the bitter cup of life. Though of a wealthy family, the possessor of much wealth herself, and moving in the same circle with Mrs. Irving, yet sorrow had chastened her feelings, and taught her to view objects in a different light from that of her friend. Her own wedded happiness early crushed by a peculiarly painful blow, by which she was at once deprived of husband and child, she had retired in a measure from the world, her heart too much wedded to the lost to permit her to accept the many offers to again enter the married state. Edward was an especial favorite of Mrs. Randolph, and he looked upon her almost as a second mother. The most perfect confidence existed between them, and he had revealed to her everything relating to his heart-affairs, and all her sympathies were enlisted in his behalf. The good offices she rendered have already been noticed.

Elated with success, and impatient to rejoin her whose image was ever present with him, Irving hastened to despatch some affairs relating to his property, and then left home, determined not to return without bringing with him the wrecker's daughter, not as a visitor, but as the wife of his bosom, the mistress of his mansion.

Night had closed in, and the broad harvest moon,

5

rising from out the ocean, had thrown a pillar of light along its unruffled surface, as Irving arrived in the neighborhood of the little hamlet towards which his path tended. It was a dreary-looking spot, yet the rays of the moon, as they fell on the still waters of the cove and lent their chastening light to the dark dwellings, gave to the scene a very picturesque effect. It will not be wondered at that to the young traveller it appeared one of surpassing beauty, and that the humble hut, whose dingy roof was just tipped by the beams of the rising moon, was more attractive in his eyes than would have been the most finished specimen of architectural beauty.

He had arrived at a slight eminence in close proximity to the clustered hamlet, and for a moment paused to look around him. Everything seemed hushed in the deepest repose, not a sound breaking the impressive stillness, save the low wash of the sea as it broke in gentle ripples on the shore. Before him spread out the ocean like a vast mirror, reflecting in its clear depths the queen of night with all her lustrous train, while on either hand rose the beetling cliffs, like giants set to guard the land from the encroachments of its ancient enemy, the sea. Here a lofty promontory stood boldly out in the pale moonlight, and there a vast chasm seemed to yawn, black as night's mantle, the whole forming a checkered and singularly grotesque scene, affording striking effects of light and shade. We know not how long the young man might have been absorbed with the view, had not his eye caught sight of an object which induced him to hurry from the spot, the beating of his heart keeping time to the rapidity of his movements.

Standing on one of those promontories which spring from the sea, fully revealed in the broad moonbeams, the quick eye of the young man detected the outlines of a female form. It needed not a second glance to inform him who it was. Striking out from the path he was following, he hastened in the direction of the maiden.

So completely abstracted were the senses of the wrecker's daughter, as she stood gazing upon the scene before her, that she was not aware of the young man's approach until, standing nearly by her side, he whispered her name. The first impulse of the startled girl, as she turned and immediately beheld before her the very being who at that moment solely occupied her thoughts, was to throw herself into the arms that were extended to welcome her. It was an involuntary act, and when she hastily extricated herself from his passionate embrace, —

> " How beautiful she looked ! her conscious heart
> Glowed in her cheeks, and yet she felt no wrong."

We will not attempt to portray the feelings that agitated her bosom at this unexpected meeting. The poet we have just quoted best describes them, perhaps, in the following passage :

> " Joy trickled in her tears, joy filled the sob
> That rocked her heart till almost heard to throb ;
> And paradise was breathing in the sigh
> Of nature's child in nature's ecstasy."

The time, the place, the little circumstances attending the first moment of meeting, all were favorable to the object the young man had in view. Can there be a doubt that he improved the propitious opportunity, or a doubt of the result of that unpremeditated interview? "By the light of the moon," as the old ballad runs, they exchanged their vows; "by the light of the moon" the young man sealed his pledge on the rosy lips of his betrothed; and "by the light of the moon" at a late hour they walked home, two as happy hearts as that planet, or any other, ever smiled upon.

There was one being lurking in the neighborhood, who, from his hiding-place, had witnessed the rapturous meeting, and listened to the murmured interchange of feeling, and who went home that night, dogging their footsteps, with a heart overflowing with all the bitterness of malignant hatred, and racked with the most vengeful jealousy. The sleeping serpents were aroused, waiting to dart forth their poisonous fangs!

CHAPTER IX.

> Nothing shall assuage
> Your love but marriage.   LILLY.
>
> O serpent-heart, hid with a flow'ring face !
>   SHAKSPEARE.

THE delight of the wrecker and his wife at the return of Irving was unbounded, nor was it at all lessened when he informed them of the object of his visit, and that their consent only was wanted to crown it with success.

"Take her, young man," said the aged wrecker, with a slightly tremulous voice, as he placed the hand of the blushing girl in Irving's, "take her and cherish her. She has been a treasure to us, yet we cheerfully entrust her to one who, we believe, will not slight the gift. We are rude and unlearned ourselves, and Nell has ever lived among these wild rocks; yet," he continued, glancing affectionately, and it may be with a touch of pride, at the object of his remarks, "though I say it, the proudest lady in the land need not be ashamed of her companionship."

A slight pressure of the hand he held was the assent given by the young man to the old sailor's plain-spoken encomiums.

Having won the blushing consent of Ellen that the "happy day" should not be postponed any longer than was necessary, Edward, to while away the time that must necessarily elapse in preparation, — the ladies know how much is consumed on these all-important occasions, — roved about the rocks, sometimes with his gun and sometimes with his rod, deriving pleasure and health from the exercise. In most of his excursions he was accompanied by Antonio, who seemed particularly desirous of cultivating his friendly acquaintance. Finding him such excellent company, Edward rarely started on an expedition without extending him an invitation. It is true at first he was not very partial to his companionship. There was a certain something about the young Spaniard which impressed him unfavorably. What it was he could neither define nor explain. Sometimes it was the expression of his eye, when, turning suddenly, perhaps, he found it resting upon him; sometimes it was in his lips, where he thought he detected a slight curl of scorn, or defiance, which grated harshly on his feel-

ings; then again it was a peculiarity in his smile, or
in the tone of his voice. This, however, in time
wholly wore off, and his partiality at length grew
quite as strong as had been his former prejudice.

It may as well be mentioned here that Miss Irving
and Mrs. Randolph had sent on by Edward, whose
assurance of success must have been undoubted, ample tokens of their love and good-will, in the shape of
silks and satins, and all those little etceteras of dress
and ornament which are deemed so essential to the
bridal wardrobe, and which they rightly supposed
would not be unacceptable. The letters which accompanied these munificent gifts touched the heart of
Ellen more than the rich presents. That of Caroline's
breathed the very spirit of sisterly affection, while
Mrs. Randolph's was couched in the endearing language of motherly fondness. Mrs. Irving, also, con-
descended to write, assuring her that, as the wife of
her son, she would be warmly welcomed. It must be
confessed that the wrecker's daughter lingered with
greater delight over the warm expressions contained
in Caroline's and Mrs. Randolph's letters than she did
on the rather formal tone of Mrs. Irving's epistle.

Time passed on, and it had been settled that the
proposed ceremony should take place at the expiration of a week. An itinerant preacher, — one of those
self-denying characters who go about doing good,
leaving the crowded thoroughfares of life, and striking
off into lone by-places, searching out the remote and
unvisited places of the earth, taking neither purse nor
scrip, but sacrificing ease and comfort, content so that
they can bear to their fellow-mortals the word of ever-
lasting life, — an individual of this stamp very oppor-

tunely paid a visit to this distant spot, and was invited
to remain and perform the nuptial rites.

Meanwhile, one pleasant morning, it was proposed
by Antonio that the young men should take the small
boat, which was fitted with a sail, and go on a fishing
expedition. Irving readily acceded to the proposition,
and, taking in a supply of stores, as they intended to
be absent until nightfall, they started, with a light
wind, and with a fine prospect of a good day's sport.
Everything seemed propitious. At an early hour they
reached the fishing-ground. Excellent luck attended
them, and, in the edge of the evening, they were on
their return, in high glee at their success.

About a league or so from the entrance of the cove
in a westerly direction, there is a sunken rock, which
at low tide is left quite bare at its summit, but when
the tide is full it is covered to the depth of ten or
twelve feet. It was about sunset when they reached
this rock, which was fully exposed, the tide being in
its young flood. Owing to some remark thrown out
by Antonio, apparently in a careless manner, respecting a certain species of cockle to be found upon it,
Irving proposed landing.

Antonio spoke of the lateness of the hour and the
distance from the cove, as if hesitating. "There will
be time enough, however," said he, "for we have the
wind, what there is of it, and the tide, in our favor;"
and he ran the boat alongside the rock. A savage
gleam of satisfaction lit up the eyes of the young
Spaniard as he sprang upon it, followed by his companion.

For some time they remained gathering the cockles,
from some of which a rich dye, similar to carmine, may

be obtained,—a species very common on our coast. While Irving was thus busily employed, the young Spaniard covertly stepped into the boat, gave her a hasty shove off, and was quite a distance from the rock ere Irving noticed his absence. Presuming, of course, that it was done in joke, he made some slight remark, and continued gathering the cockles. Having obtained a sufficient quantity, he hailed Antonio, who was now at some distance, to take him off. A scornful laugh was the response. Still free from suspicion, and, finding the space on which he stood was rapidly encroached upon by the tide, he again hailed his companion, requesting him to return. This time no reply was made, but Irving noticed that the sail of the boat was trimmed that she might head to the westward.

Now, for the first time, suspicion flashed upon his mind. Ellen had told him of Antonio's offer and of her rejection of his suit, and of the exasperated feeling he manifested on the occasion; and this was the horrid revenge he had determined upon,—leaving him on that lone rock to perish by a slow and miserable death!

Hoping that, after all, his fears might be groundless, —though he now vividly recalled the unfavorable impressions he cherished on first meeting Antonio after his return, which served to increase his apprehension, —for a third time he hailed him, in a voice as unconcerned as if he regarded it all as a matter of sport.

"Come, Antonio," he said; "it will be late before we get home. The tide, too, is coming in fast, and will soon overflow the rock."

This time an answer came back, and Irving's blood

receded coldly to his heart as it fell upon his ears,
for he knew that he was a doomed man; that the
Spaniard had decoyed him on to the rock for the very
purpose of leaving him there to his fate.

"Ha! ha!" he shouted, as he sat down in the stern
of the boat. "A pleasant night may you have of it,
my young buck!" he continued, in a mocking tone, as
the boat slowly receded from the rock. "The priest
you have bidden to your bridal may be wanted for a
less joyful occasion, if the sea should throw your
battered carcass on shore. I gave the maiden fair
warning, yet I have trapped you at last. Kneel to
your God, for in an hour's time it will be all over with
you." And another savage laugh floated over the
calm waters.

In an agony of mind which for the moment benumbed
every faculty, the young man stood as if carved out
of the solid rock, motionless, almost pulseless, his
cheeks blanched as death, every muscle strained to its
utmost tension, with his glassy eyes fixed in a despairing gaze upon the distant boat, now fast disappearing
in the gloom of the fading twilight. Her course lay
to the westward, probably tending toward some by-
port, there being a number of fishing-stations scattered
at intervals along the coast, whence the young Spaniard would doubtless make his escape.

The last faint glimpse of the receding sail had flitted like a vague shadow on the young man's sight
ere he was aroused from his death-like stupor, when
the full sense of his fearful and hopeless doom burst
upon him. From the far-off horizon, into whose misty
obscurity the boat had vanished, the gaze of the unhappy victim of treachery was directed, with a shud

der, to the water at his feet. Inch by inch the tide
was gaining on his narrow foothold, every moment
creeping nearer and nearer to the slight elevation to
which he had retreated. In a momentary feeling of
despair, he threw himself upon the rock, giving himself
up to the fate which appeared inevitable, — waiting
for the rising tide to wash him off to his watery grave.

In that hopeless moment, what thoughts tumultu-
ously crowded his brain! His home, his mother and
sister, dearer than all, his almost-bride, the endearing
associations that clustered around each and all of these
objects of love, the glowing hopes he had cherished,
the long lifetime of happiness he had anticipated, —
must he resign them all? At the very moment when
all he coveted in life was just within his grasp, in the
freshness and vigor of youth, must he be taken away?
Must he die? He sprang to his feet as the bitter
thought shot like a pang through his heart.

"God of mercy, spare me!" he cried, with a choked
utterance, lifting his arms on high, as he felt the swelling water plashing around his feet as it broke with a
gentle motion over the rock. "Spare me, heavenly
Father!" he repeated; "but, if it be thy will that I
perish, in mercy let my sufferings be short."

The moon had now risen, and a long line of trembling light shot across the ocean's surface, apparently
terminating at the spot where the young man stood.
Its gentle beams, resting so like a smile on the face
of the deep, seemed, to his frenzied feelings, as sent in
mockery to his sufferings; and, as they broke in fitful
flashes among the ripples that played about the inun-
dated rock, they enabled the wretched young man to
observe the tide as it rose gradually, each little wavelet

washing in succession up, up, higher and higher, sending a clammy, deathlike chillness through his frame.
Slowly, as the waters rose,—now reaching the instep,
now the ankle, now creeping, creeping stealthily up
the limb, its cold embrace feeling like the clasp of
death,—in the very calmness of desperation, the
young man entered into a calculation as to the length
of time it would take before the tide would be breast-
high, before it would reach the lip, before it would
prevent the last bubbling breath! A strangling sensation, as thus in imagination he followed the rising
waters, aroused him from the reverie, and, giving a
convulsive gasp, with a sickness of heart not to be
described, he was about turning toward the far-distant
shore, barely discernible in the thick haze which had
settled down upon it, it may be with the faint hope
of observing some sign of relief, though in what shape
it would come he had not even a vague idea,—he was
in the act of turning, we say, when his eye detected a
slight ripple in the water, some distance seaward, and
presently he discovered a black object slowly crossing
the narrow line of light. He started, and bent his gaze
eagerly in the direction, while his heart throbbed with
a tumultuous violence. At first he thought it was some
inhabitant of the deep, a shark, perhaps, attracted to the
spot by the scent of human prey, and a thrill of terror
shot through his frame at the idea of falling into the
power of the voracious monster. Although but a
short time before he had prayed to be relieved from
the torments of a lingering death, yet he trembled as
the idea occurred that perhaps the object before him
was the terrible instrument of relief, sent in answer to
his petition. He held his breath while the dark object

was crossing the track of the moonbeam, when suddenly a bright ray of hope flashed, lightning-like, through the gloom of his despair.

O, what a wild cry of joy rang over the waters, more like a maniac-shriek of mirth than a glad outburst of sanity, as, tearing his garments from him in frenzy, the young man plunged into the sea. Dashing the water aside in his swift career, a few vigorous strokes carried him to that dark object. God be praised! it was a floating spar, the fragment of the mast of some large vessel, drifting with the current. One nervous grasp, one convulsive effort, and the panting swimmer threw himself at length along its slippery surface, while a fervent prayer of gratitude rose to his lips. He was safe, safe! He felt that his deliverance was sure, precarious as was his situation. No longer did the smile on the ocean appear to him like a mockery: he now saw that it was a beam of mercy, sent in the darkest hour of his peril, and to Him who ordered it was poured forth thanks as devout as ever fell from human lips.

CHAPTER X.

Such tricks hath strong imagination.

SHAKSPEARE.

The dread of evil is the worst of ill.

PROCTOR.

BUSILY occupied throughout the day, and knowing that the young men did not intend to return until evening, Ellen did not at first regard their prolonged

absence; although, as the afternoon wore away and
the shadows began to lengthen, she cast frequent
glances towards the entrance of the cove, momentarily
expecting the return of the boat. As the sun went
down and the shades of evening deepened into twilight, she began to experience an anxiety which grew
stronger and stronger as the hour grew later. To
relieve her mind, she visited the promontory known as
the Hawk's Nest, hoping to catch sight of the absen-
tees.

A strong feeling of apprehension filled her mind as
she cast a hasty glance in the offing without perceiving the object of her search. A slight smoky haze
hung round the shore and prevented her seeing far
in the distance, yet at one time she thought she caught
the glimpse of a sail in the direction whence she
expected the fishermen. It was but a transient
glance, and vainly did she strain her eyes to obtain
a second. Nothing met her sight but the dull waste
of waters.

The anxiety of the wrecker's daughter momentarily
increased. She could not account for the prolonged
absence of the young men. The weather had been
pleasant and moderate, the breeze, which had fresh-
ened considerably since nightfall, and the tide, were
directly in their favor: what could detain them?
Some accident must have befallen them, something or
other have transpired to keep them out so late. What
could it be?

A fearful thought now flashed upon her mind:
strange that it had slumbered so long! She remembered her interview with Antonio, she remembered his
threatening language, the terrible warning (for it

C

reached her ears) uttered in that moment of passion.
The whole scene, the fiery aspect of the Spaniard, the
sardonic tone, all, all came freshly to her mind. Merciful Heaven! what should prevent the execution of
his jealous vengeance, when such an opportunity
offered, — alone with his intended victim, away from
all human help, with no scrutinizing eye to mark the
deed, no babbling tongue to tell the tale? It was but
a blow unawares, and the deed was done. Her fears
thus aroused, the whole minutiæ of the dreadful scene
was pictured to her excited fancy. She saw the little
boat floating a lone thing on the wide ocean, she
caught the dark glance of the Spaniard watching for
the most favorable moment. Ah! the murderous blow
was given. She beheld her lover weltering in his gore,
his impotent struggles; nay, so much was her imagination wrought upon, she thought she heard the sullen
plash as the bleeding victim was thrust into the sea,
and the last bubbling cry as the waters closed over
him. Shrieking almost with the intensity of feeling
excited by the scene thus conjured up, she darted
from the spot and hastened home, determined to pre-
vail on her father to go out in search of the missing.

The old man laughed at the fears of Ellen when she
informed him of her suspicions of Antonio's treachery, and tried to ridicule her out of her "foolish
whim," as he termed it. "My word for it, Nell, the
lad's honest. I've known him from a boy, and
though he is quick tempered, and ready to take
offence," said the old man, "he'd never commit so
foul a crime. No, no, girl, you wrong him. Fear
has made you unjust."

"But, father, what should keep them so late?"

inquired Ellen, not at all relieved by her parent's assurance; "the sun went down an hour ago, and still they are not in sight."

"What of that, my child? Perhaps the fish did not take to the hook freely, and, not wishing to come home without bringing some tokens of their skill, they did not leave the ground quite so early as they otherwise would; or perhaps they found the sport so good the time slipped away unnoticed. Cheer up, Nell; your lover is safe enough, and will be here betimes."

Not yet satisfied, Ellen still urged her request. She had never mentioned to her parents her rejection of Antonio's suit. A natural feeling of delicacy had prevented her making it known; but her anxiety now grew so great she determined on revealing it. She told the old man the whole circumstances of the interview, of the rage of Antonio, and of his fearful denunciation.

"Ah, there is something in that; the girl has reason for *her* fears, though I have too good opinion of the lad to distrust him," muttered the wrecker to himself.

His wife, who did not coincide in her husband's favorable estimation of Antonio's character, on hearing Ellen's story caught some of her alarm, and joined in persuading him to go out.

Yielding at last to their united importunities and to the too evident distress of Ellen, he consented to go in search of the boat.

"The breeze is freshening fast," said he, "and blowing right into the cove, and by the time we have worked our way out, no doubt we shall fall in with them, and be laughed at for our pains. However, the young fellows shall not know our errand;" and the old man started to muster a crew and get under way. It was not long ere the impatient girl was in some slight measure relieved by the sight of the schooner stretching across the cove, making short tacks as she slowly worked her way into the open sea.

CHAPTER XI.

No hand did aid him ;
Alone he breasted the broad wave, alone
That man was saved.   MATURIN.

I cannot speak, tears so obstruct my words
And choke me with unutterable joy.
                          OTWAY.

IT had got to be pretty well along in the evening by the time the schooner had beat out of the cove. A thin, white, luminous mist hung like a silvery veil over the land, enveloping the whole coast in its delicate folds; but about a pistol-shot from the shore the atmosphere was perfectly clear, and the moon looked down in unclouded brightness.

It was but a short time before the little wrecking-schooner emerged from the land fog into the clear moonlight.

"Strange, strange where they can be!" muttered the old man to himself as he threw a hasty glance over the glistening ocean. "Do you see anything there for'ard?" he demanded, in a loud voice.

"Not a sign of a thing, sir."

"Keep a good look-out, — they must be somewhere near."

" Ay, ay, sir ! " was the prompt response from one
of the hands, who was stationed in the weather fore
rigging, gazing into the offing.

The breeze had now begun to freshen fast, causing
quite a smart chop of the sea; the sky looked watery,
and there appeared every sign of a coming storm.

" Greasy-looking weather," said one of the men, as
he cast a glance at the southern sky. " There is a
south-easter breeding, and we shall have an ugly night
of it."

Throwing hasty glances around him without seeing
the object of his search, the wrecker himself now began to grow a little anxious. The wind had been fair
all day for the return of the boat, if she had gone on
to the usual fishing ground; and what could prolong
her stay was a mystery to him. He began to think
some accident had occurred, for he could not bring
his mind to believe that Ellen's suspicions of Antonio
were true.

The schooner had just weathered Dead Man's
Ledge, and was standing to the southward, close-
hauled on the wind, when one of the men forward
sung out that he saw something floating in-shore. The
words had scarcely left his lips when a distant hail
came from the quarter designated. All eyes were
turned in that direction, but for some time nothing
could be seen, even the man himself who first discovered the object having lost sight of it. Shortly a
second " Holloa " came faintly over the water, and in
a patch of moonlight, that glimmered about an eighth
of a mile or more on their lee quarter, a small object
was just visible, floating on the surface; but what it
was they could not make out.

6*

"It is the boat! She is capsized, and they are on her bottom!" was the startling exclamation of the old man, as he jammed the helm hard a-port and bore away for the object.

"It must have been a white squall," he continued, as the schooner wore, and was running down before a smart breeze — "a catspaw — a sudden flaw from the land: for we have had no wind on shore to-day."

As the schooner drew near the supposed boat, so that objects could be more distinctly observed, some one remarked there was but one person to be seen.

"Only one? only one?" said the old man, quickly; "then the other is lost. Pray God it be not young Irving. Boat ahoy!" he shouted in the same breath, and in an excited voice.

"Holloa!" was the answer sent back.

"Who — who answers?" again shouted the wrecker, with a tremulous stammer.

"Mr. Irving, sir."

"Thank God for that!" exclaimed the old fellow, in a hearty tone. "Where is Antonio?"

"Gone off," was the reply.

"Gone off — gone off," repeated the skipper to himself, puzzled at the answer; "'I don't understand. He means fell off. Antonio has slipped his hold, poor fellow, and gone to the bottom. You mean Antonio is gone — drowned!" again shouted the wrecker.

"Yes, sir, gone,—not drowned, but gone off!" was Irving's reply, emphasizing the last two words.

The old man was nonplussed; but he had not time to ask for a more explicit answer, as he had to attend to the duty of relieving the sufferer from his uncomfortable situation.

Running a little to the leeward, the schooner was dexterously brought up in the wind, so that, as she ranged ahead, her sails shivering the while, the supposed boat was brought close under her lee. Four men were stationed, two in the fore and two in the main rigging, ready to seize upon the young man.

"Holloa! what's this, — a log?" exclaimed one of the men, as the mast grazed the side of the vessel. The next moment Irving was in the brawny grasp of two of the crew, and almost before he was aware of it he stood safe and sound on the schooner's deck, though coatless, hatless, and dripping with brine.

"God bless you, my dear fellow!" said the wrecker, seizing the hand of the bewildered youth; and "How is this? how came you on that log? where is the boat? where's Antonio?" were the questions showered upon him from all quarters.

A few words sufficed to explain the whole matter, and curses, loud and deep, were invoked on the head of the treacherous Spaniard by the indignant crew.

"He cannot have got far with this wind," said one; "let us go in pursuit of the black-hearted villain."

"Agreed, let 's have him back!" was the response of the others; and had not Irving interfered and persuaded them to leave him to his fate, the fugitive would no doubt have been followed and taken, and, perhaps, have tasted of the mercies of the ancient Lynch law, which, among those rude men, it is probable would not have been very tenderly administered.

"Ay, let us leave him to his fate," said the old man, "and a sad one it will be, too, if I am not deceived in the present signs. If the wind holds as it does now he cannot make a harbor, unless he runs for the cove, which it is not likely he will do; and if he attempts to stay out and weather the storm that is breeding, the Lord have mercy on his soul, — he will never see daylight again!"

The old man's advice was followed, and in a short time the schooner was on her way running for the cove.

With feelings little to be envied, Ellen awaited the return of the vessel, trembling with apprehension as first one and then another hour slowly passed away without her arrival. Again and again had she visited the different headlands in the hope of catching sight of the returning sail; but the mist was so dense she could not pierce its thick folds.

At last the schooner hove in sight and entered the cove. The wrecker's daughter hurried down to the shore, and, crouching under a cliff, waited with the most intense anxiety to learn the result of the search. Her fears were painfully heightened when she noticed that the small boat was not in tow. A faint, sickly feeling crept over her at the dread silence which reigned on board of the schooner, for not a word was spoken. They had been unsuccessful, or perhaps the body had been found. As this terrible thought occurred to her, a dizzy, swimming sensation in the head caused her to lean upon the rocks for support.

But the poor girl was not kept long in suspense. Edward was the first to step on shore, and, just as the senses of the despairing girl were failing her, he happened to make some casual remark. The first word had barely escaped his lips, when a quick, wild cry of joy met his ear. Turning on the instant, he felt himself clasped in the convulsive embrace of the half-distracted maiden, who leaned trembling and sobbing like a child upon his bosom. That moment repaid him for all his suffering.

It was a happy household gathered beneath the wrecker's roof that night. And as Edward related his story, and told of the peril he had passed through, and described the feelings he experienced on that lone rock, away from all human help, night coming on, and the greedy tide creeping every moment nearer and nearer, bringing with it death in its most fearful shape; as he spoke of clinging to the drifting mast, weak and exhausted, and every moment in danger of losing his hold as it rolled and was tossed about by the rising billows; of the agony he experienced as he found himself borne slowly towards the breakers on shore, now whitened by the angry foam, certain, as he was, if he should be dashed among them his doom would be sealed,—as he dwelt on these circumstances, a thrill of horror ran through the listeners. And when the man of God invoked a blessing ere they separated for the night, and in simple though forcible language alluded to the events of the day, and with fervid eloquence returned thanks to the Omniscient and Omnipresent Being for the wonderful preservation and deliverance he had vouchsafed, there was not a dry eye present, while the wrecker's daughter gave expression to her highly excited feelings by audible sobs, which she vainly strove to restrain.

Nor was he forgotten who, with the foul crime of murder on his soul, was that night a fugitive and wanderer. Pardon was implored for him, the wrath of an offended God deprecated, and fervent petitions put up to the throne of mercy that he might be pre-

served from the gathering storm, and be led to a
hearty and sincere repentance. Such was the influence of that simple invocation, every evil feeling
toward the intended murderer was banished from the
hearts of those who listened to it.   Could their voices
have reached him, they would unitedly have echoed
the merciful injunction, " Go, and sin no more ! "

But the prayer of the good man did not avail the
wretched offender.   The storm came upon him long
before he reached the place of his destination, which
lay a score of miles or more to the windward.   As
he beheld its approach his cowardly heart at first
prompted him to run back to the rock and take off
his intended victim; but a moment's reflection convinced him that long ere then he must have been
washed away by the rising waters.   Not daring to
return to the cove, for he well knew he could frame
no plausible excuse for Irving's absence, he strove
with the recklessness of despair to work his way
along, carrying sail for this purpose until his frail
masts bent like rods, and at the perilous risk, every
moment, of the struggling boat's capsizing.   The wind
still continuing to freshen and the sea to roughen, he
was obliged to reduce his sail.   Ere long the gale
raged with such violence that his little boat was
tossed like a plaything amid the angry surges.   At
last he lost all control of her, and, shaking with
guilt and fear, he found himself drifting rapidly
toward the precipitous rocks that lined the shore,
forming an unbroken and inaccessible wall, against
which the huge billows thundered and recoiled in a
seething mass of foam.

The horrors of his hopeless situation were now

fully realized, and, with an anguish of mind which the pen can but faintly describe, he saw that the miserable death to which he had doomed another, a Greater than he had decreed to himself. He would have prayed, but when he lifted his eyes towards the black and frowning heavens, conscience was busy at his heart with her worse than scorpion-stings, and the half-uttered words died upon his white and trembling lips. Even he felt that it would be blasphemous to appeal to Him, who has said, "Thou shalt not kill," while the blood of a fellow-mortal dyed his soul.

On and on drifted the frail bark, now whirled amid the foam that crested the black billows, and now rushing down the watery hollows, in whose awful depths the rack and tumult of the storm was unfelt. O, in those momentary pauses, in that brief, dread silence, hemmed in by liquid walls, and plunged into a gloom as fearful as that of the eternal abyss, not daring to call upon his God, and scourged by the unrelenting monitor within, who can portray the soul-rending agony endured by that poor wretch?

Racked quite to frenzy by the horrors that thickened around him, at last he fancied he could hear, amid the tumult of the elemental uproar, the gibbering of unearthly voices mocking his fears; and, as he drifted near the fatal rocks, and caught sight of the angry gleam of the spray as it was dashed high up the sides of the black cliff, his imagination converted the sheets of foam into spectral forms beckoning him on to destruction.

A loud, piercing *howl*, rather than shriek, of anguish rose high above the noise of the tempest, as, lifted upon a huge roller, the boat was borne with lightning-

like rapidity toward the jagged rocks. Twice arose
the fearful cry, once on the wave and once high in the
air, whither the miserable wretch was thrown like a
weed by the shock of the giant-wave as it burst on the
shore, — and all was over! A fearful retribution had
been exacted. Who will question the dealings of a
just and righteous God?

CHAPTER XII.

Her gentle spirit
Commits itself to yours to be directed,
As from her lord, her governor, her king.
SHAKSPEARE.

His house she enters, there to be a light
Shining within, when all without is night;
A guardian angel o'er his life presiding,
Doubling his pleasures, and his cares dividing!
ROGERS.

THE day at last arrived to which the young couple
had looked forward with so much interest. To
Irving it was one of unalloyed happiness; and, though
Ellen shared largely in the same feeling, yet other and
conflicting emotions agitated her breast. She was
about leaving the home of her youth, the arms of
those who had ever shielded her with the most affectionate tenderness, to reside amongst perfect strangers. From the very depths of humble retirement,
she was about emerging into the great world of which
she had heard so little, and concerning which her con-
ceptions were so very indistinct. More than all, she
was about stepping from lowly obscurity into the

highest walks of life, to take rank and associate with those born to wealth and all the consequence attached to it, with those intimately conversant with all the etiquette of fashionable society, accomplished in manners, and possessing cultivated minds. No wonder, as she thought of her humble condition, her ignorance of the routine of the world, that she should shrink as she contemplated the path before her.

Limited as had been her education, untutored as she was in the usages of society, wanting, as she deemed herself, in those elegant accomplishments which lend such a grace to the person, how should she conduct herself? What would be her reception among those to whom she was about to be introduced? These reflections, natural to one in her situation, crowded with much force on her mind. It was some relief to her, however, that she was not to be ushered at once into scenes so entirely strange; for it was Irving's intention not to proceed directly home with his bride, but to spend some time on a tour, visiting various places of fashionable resort, possibly for the very purpose of affording her an insight into the manners and customs of society, where she could observe, without being obliged to mingle with, the gay throng.

At an early hour in the day the ceremony took place. The rites were performed by the itinerant sojourner, who alluded in his prayer to the peculiar circumstances of the occasion, praying that the bride might be kept unspotted from that world which she was now for the first time entering, and that he who had won her from the retired and quiet scenes of her youth would guard and guide her in the strange and crooked paths that

7

were spread before her. With a plainness of speech which evinced that his words came from the heart, he charged the young man to cherish the treasure committed to his keeping, for to him alone could she look, and on him alone could she lean, in those untried scenes on which, for his sake alone, she was now about to enter. It was a simple though touching appeal, and was not without its effect on the young bridegroom.

The ceremony was over, and the moment of parting arrived. Every one of the inhabitants of the little hamlet clustered around the door of the wrecker's dwelling, to bid farewell to one beloved by them all; and, amid the homely though sincere expressions of regret of the neighbors, and the blessings of her own family, Ellen left the humble roof, now dearer to her than ever.

Many and many were the lingering looks she cast, as the carriage moved slowly over the rough and untrodden road, on the cherished scenes she was leaving. Headland after headland gradually was lost to sight, fainter and fainter grew the murmur of the sea, — sound familiar to her ears, — and at last the broad ocean, sparkling in the gay sunbeams as if rejoicing in the happiness of the young bride, faded from her view. A tear glistened in her eye, and a sigh was forced from her lips, as the last strip of blue, by a turn in the road, was shut from her lingering gaze.

But, as she journeyed on, leaving the barren scenes she had ever been accustomed to, and entering upon others where nature assumed a more inviting aspect, — as for the first time she beheld dense woodlands, clothed in their liveries of living green, broad fields spread out in the highest state of cultivation, verdant lawns and blooming gardens, decked with flowers of every hue, — as these constantly recurring objects were presented to her view, and the sweet melody of birds at times broke upon her ear, her thoughts were turned into a new channel; sadness forsook her countenance, her eye kindled, and a rich glow lighted up her face, while she gazed with unsatiated delight on what appeared to her scenes of perfect enchantment.

"Beautiful, beautiful world!" burst almost unconsciously from her lips, as, ascending a slight rising in the road, a wide and charming landscape was revealed to the travellers' sight. The scene was one on which Nature seemed to have lavished her gifts with an unstinted hand. "Well can I enter into the feelings of the poet," she continued, "when he exclaimed, —

> "'O, how canst thou renounce the boundless store
> Of charms which Nature to her votary yields!
> The warbling woodland, the resounding shore,
> The pomp of groves, and garniture of fields ;
> All that the genial ray of morning gilds,
> And all that echoes to the song of even,
> All that the mountain's sheltering bosom shields,
> And all the dread magnificence of heaven.'

You need not smile : it is one of your own marked passages in your favorite 'Minstrel,' Beattie," added Ellen, blushing at her own enthusiasm.

Edward gazed with a passionate fondness into the face of his lovely bride, as she thus gave expression to her enraptured feeling. Is it not Moore who has something to say about the charms of nature, how much they improve when reflected from looks that we love? Be that as it may, our young traveller thought the world never appeared so beautiful, the fields so green, the flowers so fair, the sky so blue, the warbling of birds so delicious, as on that self-same journey. The weather was delightful, and all nature seemed to sympathize and to be in harmony with his feelings.

It would be pleasant to linger with the "happy pair" on their bridal tour, and paint the emotions experienced by the young bride as she entered upon the new and untried scenes that daily opened before her. But we must hasten on with our story.

After visiting various cities and watering-places, after presenting Ellen to the too-much-dreaded world, Irving gladly turned his face homeward, impatient to introduce his beautiful bride to his own family. He felt not a little proud of her, for her unshadowed loveliness was the universal theme of praise wherever she went, and her unassuming bearing won her the regards of all. Though she shrank at first, with a natural timidity, as she encountered successively scenes she was entirely unaccustomed to, her embarrassment soon wore off. Intuitively she caught that air and tone, that easy and graceful address, which characterize those who mingle in refined circles; and, though she could not repress a slight fluttering at the heart as she entered a brilliant assembly, yet there was nothing in her outward deportment, save, perhaps, a total absence of affectation, of those starched, artificial manners, assumed by those to whom Nature has been chary of her gifts, to distinguish her from the rest of the throng.

With a deep feeling of joy — for he longed for the quiet of domestic repose, the substantial enjoyment of home comfort — Edward Irving entered upon the last stage of his journey. Soon the familiar scenes of his childhood came in view; and, when he entered on his own inheritance, he began to anticipate with much interest the meeting so near at hand.

As the carriage rolled up the broad, shaded avenue that led to the ancestral mansion, he felt no small degree of anxiety as to the reception his wife would meet with. Well he knew the cordial welcome awaiting her from his sister and Mrs. Randolph; but he feared that his mother's reserve might throw a chill over the meeting, and thus wound the feelings of the sensitive being beside him, who looked forward to the coming interview with emotions the nature of which the reader will easily imagine.

The carriage drove up to the door, stopped, the steps were let down, and scarcely had the foot of the new-comer touched the gravelled walk ere she was clasped in the warm embrace of Caroline Irving, and welcomed with the affectionate title of "sister." Mrs. Randolph stood by to receive the agitated bride with an embrace and a welcome not less warm.

Hardly stopping to welcome Edward, they immediately attended Ellen into the house, and sought the presence of Mrs. Irving. Never, perhaps, did she look more lovely than in that moment of meeting, the excitement of the occasion lending an additional charm to her features, while her neat riding-dress exhibited to the very best advantage the symmetrical proportions of her figure. Even the aristocratic widow was not proof against so much loveliness. She started on her introduction, and, as she glanced with a look of astonishment on the wondrous beauty of the bride, the frost-work of her pride melted at once, and she

7*

folded her to her bosom with an earnestness and welcomed her with a cordiality that could not be mistaken. It was a happy meeting to all; to Edward a triumphant one; and he gazed on Ellen with an overflowing affection, and a very pardonable degree of pride, as she sat between Mrs. Randolph and Caroline, with an unstudied elegance of manners, conversing with an ease and freedom as if she had been habitually accustomed to all the etiquette of fashionable society.

If the impression made by Ellen at the first interview was so favorable, subsequent acquaintance only served to endear her still more to her new relations. Mrs. Irving was completely won over, and bestowed the full measure of a mother's fondness upon her, forgetting entirely that the object on whom she lavished so much tenderness was the poor fishmonger's daughter, who, but a few months ago, had aroused all her jealous pride. As for Caroline, she was wholly taken up with her new relation, and a congeniality of disposition and mind cemented a love between the two as strong as ever existed in human breasts.

Mrs. Randolph felt a peculiar interest in the young bride. Edward was her especial favorite; she had espoused his cause, and it was natural that she should cherish the object of his affection. It was not a common interest she felt. Her heart warmed towards Ellen with all the yearnings of maternal love; nor was the young bride long in discovering and reciprocating this ardent feeling. There was a reason for this tender interest on the part of one, which may be explained hereafter. At present we will leave our heroine, the humble wrecker's daughter, in the full

enjoyment of every bliss vouchsafed to us mortals.
We part with her, happy in the endearments of kindred relations, happy — it is a poor word to use here
— in the love of him who realized all her fond hopes,
and happy in the esteem of her acquaintance. In
taking leave of her we will adopt the language of the
great dramatist, —

> " And whether we shall meet again, I know not.
>   Therefore our everlasting farewell take:
>   *   *   *   *   *
>   If we do meet again, why, we shall smile ;
>   If not, why, then this parting was well made."

PART II.

CHAPTER I.

Go on, sir, with your tale — we 've waited long
Your pleasure.   OLD PLAY.

Beshrew my heart, but it is wondering strange ;
Sure, there is something more than witchcraft in them,
That masters ev'n the wisest of us all.
                                              ROWE.

In the last chapter of the first part of this veritable
history (if the reader's memory serves) we hinted
that Mrs. Randolph took an especial liking to our
heroine, the humble wrecker's daughter, then the
happy bride of young Irving, the reason for which
we did not explain. Trusting that a sufficient interest
has been excited to learn what further fate had in
store for the young bride, — for we must confess that

her gentle disposition and the amiable and lovely
traits she exhibited, and which we so poorly portrayed, have won for her our warmest sympathies,—
we will crave the patience of our readers while we
introduce to their notice a few more passages relating
to her somewhat checkered life.

It was on a fine autumnal afternoon that Ellen and
her sister, Caroline Irving, tempted by the beauty of
the day, were sauntering through the noble park-like
grove which spread out on either side of the family
mansion. The house was a simple and chaste struc-
ture, with a very inviting aspect, surrounded by every
variety of inland scenery; the residence, the situation, the improvements, all possessing an air of wealth,
comfort, and refined taste. It was just far enough
removed from the bustle of the world to confer upon
it a pleasing retirement, and yet not so far isolated as
to give it a semblance of unsocial rusticity.

"Really, it is too bad!" said Caroline Irving, in a
mock-pettish tone, as she occupied a seat fixed beneath a wide-spread elm, through whose rustling foliage the parting sunbeams flickered with a pleasant
light; "it is too bad, Nell! I declare, I shall become
jealous of you soon. Before you came I was the
acknowledged pet,—particularly of dear aunt Randolph,—but now poor I am thrust into the shade
entirely. I won't put up with it, that's poz!"

"But how are you going to help yourself? Tell
me that, my sweet-tempered sis," rejoined Ellen, playfully, seating herself beside her, and twining a wild
rose in the dark locks of her companion.

"I was willing to yield Edward to your enchant
ment," continued the maiden, in the same tone; "but

no, you were not content with throwing a spell over him. There is mother,—every thought of hers is devoted to you; and when aunt pays us a visit, if you happen to be out, the first words that fall from her lips are, 'Where is Ellen?' and when you come in there are no more words or looks for me. I am so glad I have no gallant, for I should expect nothing more than that he would be drawn away by the same witching spell."

"You had better be careful what you say, Caro. dear, or I may be tempted to exercise the same power over you. But you alluded to aunt Randolph," —for by that appellation was the lady in question addressed by the Irving family, although no tie of consanguinity existed,—"and you have promised to detail to me the incidents of her life, which, I fear, have not been so happy as her goodness would seem to merit. Will you not gratify me with the relation now? for I confess I feel a strong interest to learn something of her past history, that I may yield to her that sympathy which is always due to those who have known sorrow."

"Her story is indeed a sad one," said Caroline, in an altered and melancholy tone, "and will awaken feelings hardly consonant with the charming scene around. I will, however, recount the event, as told me by mother, which darkened her early years and cast a shadow over her whole existence. Let us continue our walk, and I will speak of her history as we stroll along." And the sisters locked their arms, and proceeded with a slow pace in the shade of the overhanging trees.

"Aunt Randolph was married," said Miss Irving to

her sister-in-law, "quite young in life, and never, perhaps, did one enter into the wedded state with a brighter promise of happiness. In the first flush of womanhood, tenderly beloved, surrounded by every blessing that affluence and warm friends could bestow, joy strewed flowers in her pathway and hope wove garlands for her future. But, alas! as the old poet asks, —

> " ' What are our hopes?
> Like garlands on affliction's forehead worn,
> Kissed in the morning, and at evening torn.'

"Captain Randolph, her husband, owned and commanded a fine freighting ship. In the third year of their marriage, in accordance with their mutual wishes, it was decided that aunt should accompany him on a voyage to Europe, which he had determined should be his last, as he was possessed of a handsome property, and had grown tired of the sea. He was passionately devoted to his wife; besides, he had another tie, in the birth of a daughter, that led him to abandon a pursuit which necessarily demanded separation and long absence from a home now doubly endeared to him.

"At first they thought of leaving their infant daughter at home, but, as the time of sailing drew nigh, aunt could not bear the idea of parting from her child. She evinced so much reluctance, it was at last decided to take it with them, and a nurse was engaged to accompany it.

"They had a fine passage out to Liverpool, and, after remaining some time in England, Capt. Randolph and his wife proceeded to Paris, and thence to Havre, to which port the ship had been ordered. Here they embarked for home. Nothing unusual transpired on their homeward voyage until the fatal night in which the dreadful event occurred that in the same hour rendered our dear aunt a widow and childless.

"The day had been lowery, but the wind, though it blew rather fresh, was fair, and they were cheered with the hope of soon catching sight of their native land. As it grew near nightfall the weather thickened fast, and quite a gale set in. There was nothing, however, to excite alarm, and the ship, under easy sail, dashed over the billows as securely, apparently, as if beneath a smiling sky.

"It was about nine or ten o'clock in the evening, aunt says, she was sitting in her state-room, preparing to retire for the night, her husband being at the time on duty. All at once she heard an unusual noise on deck, a loud shouting, the rapid shuffling of feet, mingled with the creaking of yards and blocks, all denoting sudden alarm and confusion. Immediately, high above the uproar, she heard her husband's voice shouting through a speaking-trumpet, 'Port your helm! port your helm, or you will be into us!' The startling exclamation had hardly died away when she heard a rush down the companion-way, and the next moment her husband burst into her state-room, crying, with a hoarse voice, 'This way, wife, this way! Up, for your life!' at the same time seizing her about the waist and carrying her by main force to the deck.

"What followed in the confusion that prevailed she can but indistinctly remember. She recollects seeing the crew running wildly about the decks, uttering the most terrific cries; of hearing a strange rushing sound in the water; then followed a tremendous crash, which caused the ship to reel and quiver as if a thunderbolt had burst upon her. Bewildered and horror-struck at the scene about her, she was only sensible of being borne rapidly along, amid the crashing of spars, the outcries of men, and the dashing of billows, until she found herself in a strange cabin, surrounded by strange faces. Imagine, Ellen, the agony, the heart-rending anguish of that moment, when the appalling truth was revealed to her, that the ship in which she then found herself had run down that of her husband, and that, in all probability, both her husband and child were lost to her forever! I will not speak of the horrors of that night. Language would fail me were I to attempt to portray them. Aunt never alludes to the event, never ventures to describe her situation, and the further particulars which I shall relate of that dreadful disaster were derived from another source.

"It appears," continued Miss Irving, in a voice slightly tremulous with emotion, "that the ship on board of which aunt found herself received comparatively but trifling injury, while her husband's was completely cut down. It was ascertained that Captain Randolph, probably knowing the damaged condition of his ship, immediately exerted himself to place his wife on board the strange ship. Having succeeded in this, he returned to his own vessel to rescue his child, who, with the nurse, was in one of the state-rooms at the time of the accident. He had barely got on the deck of his own ship, when the two vessels, which had become locked together by the head, were thrown apart by a tremendous sea. A second wave, it is supposed, must have swept the decks of the disabled ship, as she lay in the trough, carrying away

with it her unfortunate captain, for his drowning cries
were heard immediately after at a distance. It was so
dark and tempestuous, and so much confusion prevailed, that nothing could be done for his relief, and
in a few minutes his voice was silent. In the mean
while the two vessels had widely separated, and by
the time that the crew of the strange ship had somewhat recovered from their consternation, and restored
things to order, the other vessel had disappeared in
the gloom of the storm.

"Having mustered the crew, it was found that, with
the exception of Captain Randolph, the child, and its
nurse, there was no person missing. In the hope of
rescuing the last two, the strange ship laid-to during
the night, trusting that the Roanoke, the name of the
ill-fated ship, would be in sight in the morning, if
afloat,—a circumstance hardly within the bounds of
probability.

"Slowly the hours passed away, and anxiously was
the dawning waited for. Daybreak came at last, and
its cold, gray light revealed to the weary watchers
nothing but an angry ocean and a frowning sky. Not
a sign nor a vestige of the disabled ship could be seen.
As the weather moderated and the daylight increased,
the master of the vessel commenced cruising about in
various directions, until a late hour in the afternoon,
without seeing the missing ship, when he was reluc-
tantly forced to the conclusion that she had gone
down. With a heavy heart, he conveyed the intelligence to Mrs. Randolph, who received the tidings with
a calmness wholly unexpected. Indeed, the suddenness of the blow which deprived her of her husband
had deadened her sensibility. The cup had been

8

drained to its very dregs, but its bitterness was reserved for the dreary future. All that had passed seemed more like a fearful dream than an actual occurrence. The terrible realization of her double loss, the heaviest weight of her affliction, was left for after days.

"Fortunately for the comfort of the bereaved one, the ship she was in was bound to a port not far distant from her own place of residence. She soon reached that port, whence aunt left for her home. It is needless to speak of her desolation of heart on arriving there. Everything spoke of her loss, everything served to remind her of the departed. She almost sank under the crushing burden, but she was sustained by One who always regardeth the widow in her affliction. With a spirit of holy resignation she submitted to the chastening rod, and as time rolled on the bitter became sweet. A repining murmur was never heard to escape her lips."

"Dear aunt Randolph! I shall love her more strongly than ever, now that I know her sad story," said Ellen, with a sigh, as Miss Irving finished her narration. And the young ladies turned and walked in silence and sadness towards the house.

CHAPTER II.

Ah! sweet it is, to gaze upon the face
Long seen but by the mind, to fondly trace
Each look and smile again. * * *
And O, how pines the soul, how doth it crave
Only a moment's look!   DANA.

How frequently in our walks through life do we
meet with persons, utter strangers, who remind us of
some friend or acquaintance long since gone to his
rest. There may be nothing in the general features
that awakens the association, nothing indeed which
we can account for or define, yet there is a certain
something which seems to recall as by magic the
departed. Perhaps, if we scan the countenance in
search of the likeness, we are unsuccessful; and yet
a hasty glance reveals it to us in all its truthfulness.
A peculiarity in a smile, it may be, a particular expression about the lips or the eyes, a slight inclination of
the head or movement of the body, some such trivial
cause touches the electric chain of memory, and the
image of the loved and mourned is brought for an
instant before us, as in the fleeting phantasms of a
dream.

This was the secret of the strong partiality that
Mrs. Randolph felt for the younger Mrs. Irving. On
first meeting with Ellen she detected an expression in
her features, something in her manner, which brought
instantly before her the husband of her youth. And
yet, when she cast a second glance on the lovely face
which had called up such a sad remembrance, for
the very purpose of ascertaining wherein consisted

the likeness, the resemblance had entirely vanished.
Time and again would this or some kindred expression flash upon her, awakening a secret thrill, and still,
as she endeavored to scan it more closely, like the
meteor-gleam it was gone. She scrutinized each look
of Ellen's with so much interest that it must have
been embarrassing to her, had she been aware that she
was the object of such rigid notice. As it was, the
mournful earnestness of Mrs. Randolph's gaze, which
did not wholly escape Ellen's observation, aroused
feelings in her bosom which were both strange and
inexplicable.

In vain, however, did Mrs. Randolph endeavor to
fix that look which so haunted her with memories of
the past. She could not discover the least resemblance between the features of Ellen, when they were
in a state of repose, and those of the image enshrined
in her widowed heart. Hers were not the broad,
expansive forehead, the black, deep-set eyes, the
slightly aquiline nose, and the full, rounded chin of
her lamented husband. There was no single feature,
nor combination of features, that looked *natural* to
her; yet, let but a smile play over Ellen's face, or let
her engage in an animated conversation, and there was
the look, distinct, but evanescent, indefinable, yet not
the less striking and apparent. Mrs. Randolph called
the attention of her friend, the elder Mrs. Irving, to
the circumstance; but the passage of years had
rendered too indistinct the image of the lost on her
mind to enable her to recognize anew, or even recall,
the minute lineaments of the deceased.

No wonder that the lone heart of the widow clung
with undisguised fondness to the object who pos-

sessed the power of awakening associations so dear
to it. For Ellen's own sake, her amiable disposition,
her kind and devoted attention to her, she loved her;
how much the tie that bound her to the young bride
was strengthened by the circumstance we have mentioned, the reader can readily imagine. Surely never
did a mother's heart glow with a deeper love toward
the child of her affection than did hers toward Ellen.
She experienced for her all the solicitude which is
deemed natural alone to the maternal bosom, manifest-
ing an interest in her happiness, and in everything
that related to her welfare, by a thousand little acts
of kindness and tenderness, which spring, as it were,
from the instincts of maternity. Need we say that
Ellen was sensibly affected by these demonstrations,
and appreciated them to their fullest extent. She
strove to repay them in kind, while she was inspired
with that ardent affection towards her second mother
which would naturally be engendered by such entire
devotedness.

But, amidst all the happiness which surrounded her,
the love and kindness of friends, the comforts and
elegant ease of wealth, amidst all these, did Ellen keep
in mind the circumstances of her humble birth? Did
her thoughts go back fondly to the lowly wrecker's
wife, and did her heart remain constant in its affection
to her rough and untutored parents? O yes, most
assuredly, yes! Ellen was not one of those who grow
giddy by the gifts of fortune. Dearly as ever did she
cherish the rugged scenes of her youth, warmly as ever
did her heart cling to those who watched over her
childhood and guided her later years; and it was with
feelings of unbounded delight she anticipated a visit

8*

to that endeared spot. She longed to stand once more on the threshold of the sea, to hear the booming shout of the vaulting waves, and to watch the snow-white foam breaking over the dark, weed-grown rocks.

With what pleasure she looked forward to the time when, in company with Caroline (for she was to be her companion), she could rove over the giant cliffs, and revisit her favorite resorts amid the cavernous rocks, where nature is exhibited in an aspect of stern, wild grandeur, and along the pebbly shore, up which the billows curl and break with a never-ceasing roar. Not once did the humbleness of the home to which she would introduce her high-born sister-in-law awaken an emotion of regret, nor for once was her pride startled at the thought of her parents' poverty and lack of refinement. Affection hallowed the home of her childhood, and softened the rough aspect of the whole; and the lively and amiable Caroline was quite as impatient for the journey as Ellen. She had never visited the ocean side, and her curiosity was stimulated to the highest pitch to behold its wonders and glories, of which she had heard and read so much.

CHAPTER III.

Down her cheeks flowed the round drops ;
And, as we see the sun shine through a shower,
So looked her beauteous eyes,
Casting forth light and tears together.
                                        LANSDOWN.

A hundred thousand welcomes ! I could weep,
And I could laugh ; I am light and heavy ; welcome !
A curse begin at very root of his heart
That is not glad to see thee !
                                        SHAKSPEARE.

AT a pleasant season of the year the journey was
accomplished, and Ellen stood once more beneath the
wrecker's roof. How dear to her every familiar
scene! How like a flower-gatherer did memory retrace the shining track of the past, lingering by each
bud that gave her young years such delight! Tears
of joy glistened in her eyes as she witnessed the emotion of her aged mother on her meeting. But a feeling of sadness stole over her as she beheld, mingling
with the affectionate cordiality expressed by her parent, a certain deference toward herself,—a show of
respect, as if she regarded the difference in their con-
ditions, and felt that humility would best become her.
The sensitive heart of Ellen was pained.

"Mother, dear mother!" said she, as she clasped
her in a warm embrace, "I am not changed, I am still
as ever your Nell, still as ever, I trust, dear to you!"
and the bright tears fell like diamonds adown the em-
browned neck of the wrecker's wife.

"Well, I know you are not changed, my child," replied the mother, with choked utterance ; "and dearer,

far dearer are you to my heart at this moment than
ever. The choicest blessings of heaven rest upon
you for not forgetting your poor old——" What she
would have added was lost in the half-sob which
escaped her lips as she strained the lovely being convulsively to her bosom.

It was a happy meeting, and yet, like all such meetings, a tinge of sadness just shadowed the bright current of feeling that swelled in the heart of mother
and child. More particularly was this to be observed
in the wrecker's wife, in whose breast the bright and
dark tide seemed equally mingled. We will not specu-
late on the cause of this strange circumstance. The
sequel of our story may reveal it.

The wrecker was absent on a cruise at the time, for
Ellen's visit was wholly unexpected, and intended as a
surprise; but he was hourly expected to return. You
may be sure that the Hawk's Nest and Gull's Head,
the bold headlands at the entrance of the cove, were
visited more than once during the day by the impatient girl. She was always accompanied by Caroline,
who felt no fatigue in climbing over the rough rocks,
so new and exciting were the scenes and her pursuits.

Towards night the little schooner was discovered
from one of the promontories, on which the new-
comers had taken their station to watch her approach.
We will not stop to portray the emotions of Miss
Irving, as she gazed upon the magnificence of old
Ocean, never, perhaps, more striking than at that
hour, when the hues of the declining day had tipped
it with a glory akin to that which flooded the western
sky. It was altogether a new revelation to her, and
she stood spell-bound, as it were, with the splendid

spectacle, watching the changing colors, as the light faded gradually from the sea. As for Ellen, her thoughts were too much occupied with the coming sail to take much notice of the scene that fascinated her companion.

It was dark, for there was no moon, although the stars lent their feeble light, ere the schooner of the wrecker entered the cove. As she shot into the deep shadow of the cliff, Ellen, in the humble garb of former days, might have been seen tripping over the rocks to the landing, bearing a lighted torch. While those in the vessel were securing her for the night, Ellen stood on a projecting ledge, and flared the light over the waters in such a manner as to assist the voyagers without revealing her own person.

"Thank'e, wife," said the old man, in a hearty tone, as, having performed the necessary duty, he pushed off from the side of the anchored vessel in a little yawl. "You need not have put yourself to the trouble of coming down, Bess, for we could have got along very well without a light."

"Welcome home, father!" exclaimed Ellen, as the boat's keel grated on the beach, at the same time waving the torch so that its light should flash over her person; "welcome back! What luck?"

"Nell, Nell! Am I dreaming? Is that you? As I live, it is the dear girl herself! Why, where did you come from? how came you here?" burst in rapid tones from the lips of the astonished old man, as he leaped to the shore, and rushed to the spot where she stood, half-doubting the evidence of his own senses.

Could there have been a more delightful surprise, a happier meeting than that between the wrecker and

his child? Again and again he folded her to his
heart, with all the warmth of paternal love, as he
questioned her of her unexpected presence, while the
dark cliffs resounded again and again with the loud
cheer of welcome which burst involuntarily, as it
were, from the lips of the hardy crew gathered on the
beach, who seemed as much astonished and overjoyed
as the old man himself at the return of their favorite.
It was the tribute of rough and honest hearts, standing on no idle and formal ceremony, and Ellen received
with deep emotions their boisterous demonstrations
of joy and good will.

Never was there a happier assemblage under one
roof than that which gathered beneath the wrecker's
that night. Until a late hour they all sat in conversation, the old man full of spirits, declaring time and
again that he felt as if a score of years had been
rubbed out of his life; while his wife gazed with an
earnestness of affection on the countenance of Ellen,
which fully evinced that, if her emotions were not so
buoyant and cheerful as her partner's, her happiness
was equally as great. Caroline and Edward partici-
pated as fully as any in the joyful greeting, while
their sympathies were tenderly excited as they witnessed the touching and unaffected manifestations of
love bestowed upon one so dear to their hearts.

"Observe her," said Edward in an under-tone to his
sister, his eyes beaming with affection: "'twas in that
plain attire I first knew her and loved her. Do you
wonder at it?"

"No, no; how could you do otherwise? Dear
Ellen, you are an angel!" and the warm-hearted girl
stepped forward and impressed an affectionate kiss on
the lips of her surprised sister.

CHAPTER IV.

I had so fixed my heart upon her,
That, wheresoe'er I formed a scheme of life
For time to come, she was my only joy,
With which I used to sweeten future cares.
OTWAY.

A FORTNIGHT, the period allotted for the stay of the
visitors, passed most happily. Every day they strolled
over the jagged rocks, exploring the deep chasms
hollowed out by the constant beating of the waves,
and gazing upon the frowning cliffs, some of them
toppling to their fall, the wash of the sea having worn
away their bases, opening here and there, to their very
hearts, deep recesses and dark caverns, into which the
surges rushed with a dismal booming sound, gurgling
along unseen passages, and returning in rills of sparkling, milk-white foam; or they would

"Stand on some high beetling rock,
Or dusky brow of savage promontory,
Watching the waves, with all their white crests dancing,
Come, like thick-plumed squadrons, to the shore,
Gallantly bounding," —

sights and sounds which never sated the eye or palled
on the ear, and which thrilled the enthusiastic heart
of Caroline with emotions to which, ere this, it had
ever been a stranger. Frequently they were accompanied by the wrecker, who detailed to them, as they
sat on some bold height which overlooked the ocean,
some old legend of the sea, some tale of shipwreck
and peril, or some stirring adventure in which he had
taken part during a long and eventful life.

Another week, and at last a month, had nearly ex-
pired, ere they took their leave, and then with feelings
of regret they tore themselves away from a spot
which, despite its barrenness, had charms for them all,
and which was endeared to Ellen by considerations
already sufficiently explained.

The evening of the day on which they left, the
wrecker and his wife sat alone by the door of their
hut, the former in the enjoyment of his time-colored
pipe; but an occasional sigh from the latter seemed
to indicate a heart ill at ease.

"Come, cheer up, Bess!" said the old man, placing
his hand affectionately on her shoulder. "Life is made
up of partings. The dear girl is happy: what more
can we ask? A noble fellow is that husband of hers,
a worthy fellow; and a fine girl, too, is that sister of
his. And then to see how Nell and she take to each
other!"

"It is not the parting, John, that saddens me," said
the wife, in a subdued tone; "my thoughts were on
something else. Do you remember that it is just
twenty-two years this day since the lost one was
restored to us?"

"Twenty-two years! No, no, Bess; you're mistaken," rejoined the wrecker, taking his pipe from his
mouth and gazing into his wife's face with an expression of doubt.

"Twenty-two years this blessed day, husband."

"It can't be," replied the old man. "Let me see,"
he added, "it was in the year 17—," and with the stem
of his pipe he touched the tips of the fingers of his
left hand to assist him in counting the years from that
date. "I wouldn't have believed it; twenty-two

years!" he exclaimed, in a low voice, as he concluded his reckoning. "How the time slips away!"

"Am I right, John?"

"It can't be otherwise; it must be so. But what of that, Bess? are you sad that we are growing old and gray?"

"O no, that is not it, husband. It would be a sin to repine when He has crowned all our days with goodness. No, John; but I was thinking, as we shall soon be called away, and as *she* has got to be a fine lady, it is our duty to tell the dear girl the truth concerning her parentage."

The wife paused and looked toward her husband as if waiting his reply. But he was silent. With an abstracted air he sat gazing on the ground, as if revolving some unpleasant thought in his mind. The proposition suggested by his wife had of late often occurred to him, and engaged much of his thoughts. From the manner of both it was evidently not one of a very pleasing nature, for its consideration threw a shade of gloom over them.

"I don't know but that you 're right, wife," at length the old man said. "I have thought over this matter much of late, and it has troubled me not a little. Thinks I, coming home on my very last cruise, I will talk the subject over with Bess, and get her opinion on it. I hate to do it,—not that I think it will alter Nell's feelings toward us, that is, in the way of loving us; but it will seem like breaking a natural tie."

"Yes, John, I feel it will be as you say. The little one that was so early taken from us appeared given back again when she came, and the love which would

9

have been buried in the grave with the lost, revived
anew in the poor foundling. I am sure I yearn over
that dear girl as much as if my own blood ran in her
veins."

A tear glistened in the eye of the speaker which she
did not attempt to conceal.

"And well may we love her," added the old man.
"Has she not been ever as a child to us? In sickness
and health, in infancy and youth, we watched over and
cared for her,—and what more could we do for our
own flesh and blood?"

"Yes, thank Heaven, we have not neglected our
duty to her; and there is comfort in that. And, though
Nell's feelings may be changed when we tell her she
is not our own child, I know her affectionate heart too
well to fear that her love will be weakened."

"I had some idea of making it known to young
Irving during his visit," said the old man, after a brief
silence; "but I concluded it was best to wait until
they left, and talk it over with you first."

"I am glad you did, John, for the parting would
have been doubly painful had she gone away knowing that we had no natural claims on her; and yet
I should like to be near her when she is told, and
hear from her own lips that she loves us none the
less. Would to God, if the desire be not sinful, that
she were our own!"

Until a late hour the wrecker and his wife sat by
the door, conversing on the subject. How to convey
the information to Ellen was a point long discussed.
A letter might serve the purpose, but the old man
was averse to this channel of communication, for he

felt that he could not enter so fully into the details in
writing as he wished.

"No, no, wife; she shall have it from my own lips,
and every circumstance connected with the event that
threw her upon our care. And moreover, Bess, as
you have always been confined to this barren spot, —
not but that the place is pleasant enough, as how can
it help being, with the great sea forever rolling before
us in all its majesty and vastness? — and have never
been where the earth is covered by the green grass
like a carpet, and the tall trees wave and rustle in
the breeze, and beautiful birds build their nests and
make music in the branches, and bright flowers spring
up everywhere and fill the air with a sweet perfume,
just as the easterly wind brings in the scent of the
sea; now, Bess, you shall go with me and visit Nell
and her husband, and behold some of these wonders
wherewith God has blessed this world of ours. We
will accept their invitation, and when we are with them
I will make known the story."

This point settled, the honest old couple retired
to rest, with minds somewhat relieved, now that they
had come to a determination on a subject which had
burdened their minds for a long time.

CHAPTER V.

With wild surprise,
As if to marble struck, devoid of sense,
A stupid moment motionless she stood.
MILTON.

A FEW months after Ellen's return she was surprised, and not less surprised than delighted, by the arrival of the wrecker and his wife at her new home. Their coming was altogether unexpected, for they had given no intimation of paying her a visit. It is unnecessary to say how joyfully they were welcomed, and by no one more warmly than by the widow Irving, whose opinion of the wrecker, the half-pirate as she once stigmatized him, had undergone a wonderful change since his daughter had become a member of her family. Rough and unrefined as he was, there was something in the blunt old sailor which won for him the good opinion of all, and more particularly of the aristocratic widow. She saw in him none of those vulgar traits which she had thought were inseparable from poverty and humble birth.

The meek and retiring character of the wrecker's wife was altogether different, too, from the picture she had formed of one bred in obscurity. She now saw that there was not such a vast difference in the moral and mental qualities of those born in the upper and lower classes of society as she had been taught to believe; that kind hearts and gentle affections, and sterling if not as polished minds, were to be found clothed in the humble garb of the poor as in the costly "purple and fine linen" of those born to wealth. In fact, the high notions of the lady were levelled to quite a reasonable and proper standard, and the sharp points of her character had become rounded and moulded astonishingly. After all, we are inclined to believe that the pride and hauteur exhibited by many should be ascribed more to an ignorance of human nature than to a want of sympathy, to a defect in the judgment rather than an obliquity of the heart.

Intent on making known the errand which induced his visit, the wrecker sought the first opportunity that offered to divulge it. He first made Ellen and her husband briefly acquainted with the facts. The delicate and to him painful task was not accomplished without exciting strong emotions both in the speaker and his astonished hearers. Ellen listened as one in a dream, scarcely crediting her own senses. Her bosom was agitated with feelings it would be difficult to portray. A bitter, dreary sense of loneliness, a sadness and sickness of heart, a dull, desponding weight, oppressed her spirits. She gazed into the face of her whom she knew only as a mother, as if seeking there for a denial of what she had heard. The earnest, affectionate, tearful look that met hers, though it confirmed the dark story, stirred the dead calm settling like a poisonous mist on her heart; the fountain of feeling gave way; and, rushing toward the wife of the wrecker, she fell into her waiting embrace, exclaiming, with a tear-choked voice, —

"Be still a mother to me! Do not cast me off! Let me be as ever your child, let me love you as ever, let me still share your love!"

The scene can be better imagined by the reader than described by the writer. It was one calculated to

9*

touch the heart's deepest fount, calling up its tender-est emotions. It served, too, to remove any half-formed doubts in the minds of the old man and his wife in regard to Ellen's unchanging affection towards them.

After the agitation growing out of the unexpected development was over, it was proposed that the wrecker should relate in detail the facts connected with Ellen's history to the family. Mrs. Randolph was invited to be present on the occasion, and after the evening lamps were lighted, the company assembled, eager to hear the full relation of that of which they had as yet received but a vague hint.

It would have formed an interesting and touching picture, that little circle, grouped around the old man, and listening eagerly to the words that fell from his lips. The most striking figure in the group was Ellen, who, with a tearful eye and a pale, sad counte-nance, sat by the side of her whom she had always looked upon as her mother, holding one of her hands within her own and half-leaning on her shoulder, as she listened with a throbbing heart to the story in which she was so much interested. The earnest in-tensity of the glance which Mrs. Randolph riveted on the speaker, as she sat motionless and statue-like nearly in front of him, would at once have attracted the notice of a casual observer. A hardly less strong expression of interest was observed on the counte-nances of the rest of the listeners. The details as given by the old man were as follows:

"It is more from a sense of duty to that dear girl," said the wrecker, glancing as he spoke affectionately at the object of his remark, "than any promptings of my own inclinations, that I am impelled to make the statement I am now about to offer. Were it not in the hope that she may under Providence be benefited by it, I know not but that I should have carried the secret relating to her parentage with me to the grave. We have always regarded her as our own from the moment we received her in charge from her dying mother; and sure I am, we could not have loved her more if she had our own blood in her veins. She came to us indeed like a messenger from heaven, at a time when we were bowed down with a sore disappointment, and it seems now like rending asunder a tie of nature to declare that she is not our own, that we have no parental claims on her. But it must be done.

"Some years ago I was returning in my smack from a cruise along the coast, and had arrived within a day's sail of the cove, when I was providentially placed in the way of rescuing two of my fellow-creatures from a drowning death, one of whom is now present. For two or three days previous to this event the weather had been rough, and the day before quite a strong gale had raged. The day had just broke on the morning in question, but the weather was so thick that the light came slowly, when I found myself running close aboard of a wreck. I knew not at first what kind of a craft it was, for I could perceive only the stump of one mast standing. As I bore up for the wreck, however, I soon discovered that it was a ship. How she came to be in such a disabled condition I could not imagine, for, though the storm had been pretty tough, yet it had not been so violent, at least where I was, but that a ship could make very good weather in it.

"The waves ran so high at the time it would have
been dangerous to attempt to board her; but, as the
wind had hauled off shore and the sea was fast going
down, I determined to lay by her. Anxious to learn
if any one was on board, I ran close under her lee and
hailed her. It was then I discovered that she had settled considerably by the head, and that she was liable
at any moment to go down. From the shattered state
of her bows I was at once convinced of the cause of
her disaster. She had evidently been run into, and
that, too, very recently. No notice being taken of my
first hail, I repeated it, when I saw a woman spring
up on the quarter-deck. At first she did not perceive
us, but gazed wildly around for a moment to the windward. She soon changed her position and caught
sight of us, and, as she did so, she stretched her arms
towards us in an appealing attitude, uttering at the
same time a gibberish sort of cry. A moment afterward she staggered to the side of the vessel and
stooped down. When she again raised herself, we
observed she had something in her arms that appeared
like a child closely wrapped up, which she held in a
beseeching manner towards us, all the time uttering
the same incoherent cry.

"It was a sad sight, ladies, in that uncertain light,
to behold the poor thing on that lone wreck, her
clothes, heavy with wet, clinging closely to her form,
and her loose hair streaming in tangled masses to the
wind. We immediately shouted to her to be of good
cheer, and that we would soon take her off. But the
poor creature appeared bewildered, and evidently did
not understand us, for, as our craft ranged ahead, she
ran shrieking with her burden to the fore part of the

ship, stumbling over the broken spars and rigging that lumbered the decks, holding out her arms to us all the while as if praying for succor. My heart ached as I gazed on the piteous object, and I resolved to attempt her rescue at once, although I knew it would be at the risk of life.

"We got our boat out, however, as soon as circumstances would permit, and with four oarsmen pulled away for the wreck. We reached her with great exertion, although we were once or twice in great danger of being swamped. Nothing would have saved us in that event, for we left the schooner short-handed, and could have received no assistance from the crew on board. But at last, through God's mercy, we reached the ship, and succeeded, after many efforts, in making fast to her. It then became necessary to use the utmost caution in taking off the woman and child, for, as the ship rolled and plunged in the surges, wo were every moment in imminent danger. The woman, fortunately, instead of being a hindrance, seemed endowed with an energy almost superhuman, and greatly assisted us in our hazardous task. After repeated failures in our attempts, we at last succeeded in getting the sufferers into the boat, and ere long in placing them safely on the deck of our own vessel. We took them off not a moment too soon, for we had barely got on board the schooner when the ship began to settle fast, and presently, giving a lee lurch, she went down bow first. Ah, ladies! it was a dismal sight, that sinking ship going down amid the raging billows, the heavens hanging in blackness like a pall above her, and the sea whirling and foaming around her as if rejoicing over its prey."

Here the old man paused awhile in his narration, as
if dwelling on the sad spectacle he had been describing, while the sighs and long-drawn breaths of
his audience testified the interest they felt in his
description.   .

CHAPTER VI.

She gazed on us with fixed and anxious air, —
That look consigned her infant to our care :
We read the sign and quick assent implied ;
She smiled, then turned her face away, and died.

'T is she ! 't is she ! the lost — the mourned — my daughter !
                              OLD PLAY.

"But I had no time," continued the old man, after a
brief silence, "to indulge in the feelings such a scene
would naturally call forth, for my attention was immediately diverted to the case of the survivors, who
demanded all my care. Soon after reaching my vessel, the strength and energy of the mother, which she
had displayed so conspicuously in the moment of
peril, forsook her entirely. Every nerve became
relaxed, her spirits seemed completely prostrated, and
she became as weak and helpless almost as the child
in her arms. On questioning her concerning the particulars of the disaster, we found that her mind was
all afloat, and we could get nothing from her but the
most incoherent answers. Poor crazed thing! All
her thoughts seemed to centre on her child, which she
had contrived to protect from the weather in a wonderful manner. We could hardly persuade her to
trust it for a moment in our care, and she was restless

and uneasy until it was restored to her. It was a touching sight, ladies, to witness the endearments heaped by the wretched sufferer on her child; her heart still strong and gushing with affection, though her mind was all wreck and disorder. But she soon sunk into a state of imbecility, uttering only an occasional wandering word. I saw that she was failing rapidly, and was fearful she would not hold out until we reached our station. Having a pretty fair wind, however, we arrived at the cove just before nightfall, and succeeded in getting the unfortunates safely and comfortably housed.

"Every exertion that our limited means permitted was put forth in behalf of the poor suffering woman; but all our care was unavailing. Fright and exposure had prostrated both mind and body. She lingered for a day or two in a sort of lethargy, then died. A short time before she drew her last breath, she appeared to revive a little, and made signs as if she had something to communicate; but when she attempted to speak her tongue refused its office, and she only uttered a feeble, moan-like whisper. Thinking she might wish to behold the child, wife took it from its little couch, where it was slumbering, and carried it to her bedside. Her eye lighted up at once on seeing it, an expression of satisfaction shot over her face, and she made an attempt as though she would embrace it. But her strength was not sufficient for the task, and she sank back on her pillow, gazing wistfully first into the infant's face and then casting a meaning glance on my wife, as if she by that look consigned the little one to her care. My wife answered the silent appeal by pressing the child to her bosom. The dying one seemed to understand her, for a faint smile played over her countenance. It was the last gleam of expiring nature, for immediately a slight tremor shook her frame, she turned her face a little from us, gave one gasp, and her troubled spirit was at rest."

The sobs of Ellen here interrupted the narrative of the old man. "My poor mother!" was all she could articulate, as she leaned her head on the shoulder of the wrecker's wife, and gave way to the feelings which agitated her breast. The sympathizing tear glistened in the eyes of each of the group as they witnessed the emotions of the sorrow-stricken girl. It is true, she had never known that mother whom she mourned; yet the relation of her foster-father, showing forth as it did the strong love of that mother, triumphing even over the wreck of mind, and sending the last glow of warmth through the death-chilled veins, breathing out, as it were, in the last gasping sigh, touched the deepest and tenderest chord in her heart; while a contemplation of the extreme suffering she must have endured on the wreck, — suffering so great as to induce frenzy, — and her affecting death, awoke the most poignant grief. After a brief silence, the wrecker proceeded with his narrative in an unsteady voice.

"Yes, Ellen, it was thus she died; happy, I believe, in the consciousness that her child had found a protector. And warmly did we welcome the little stranger thus providentially thrown on our care. But a short month before we had consigned to the grave the only child with which God had blessed us. We were childless and sorrowing, but when you came we felt that our lost one had again been restored to us. Your ages must have been nearly alike, and we bestowed on you the name borne by our own child. Your lively prattle soon chased the gloom from our dwelling, and we forgot our bereavement. We made many inquiries to find out something respecting the lost ship; but we lived in a remote place, and the means for the transmission of news were not so abundant as at the present day, and all our endeavors were fruitless. We were content with the result, for our hearts yearned towards you with all a parent's love; and, as years passed by, and you grew dearer to our hearts, we ceased to think of you as other than our own, and such we shall always consider you, in whatever circumstances you may be placed, so long as Heaven shall spare our lives."

"You did not ascertain the name of the ship?" said Edward, as the old man paused at the conclusion of his narrative.

"It would have been a difficult thing as we were then situated, although I might possibly have done so. But, in the hurry and excitement of getting off the woman and child, we had no thought for anything else ; and by the time we had rescued them the ship had settled so that any attempt to ascertain it would have been fruitless."

"Can you give no description of the ship?" asked Mrs. Randolph, who had listened to the recital of the wrecker with an intensity of feeling which could not have failed of exciting the notice of the company had not their attention been wholly absorbed in the story of the old man. The tremulous and earnest tone in which the question was put attracted immediately the

10

observation of the whole party, while the interest of those who were acquainted with her sad history was awakened at once to the highest pitch. Ellen raised her head involuntarily from the shoulder of her foster-mother, and gazed anxiously in the face of the wrecker, breathlessly awaiting his answer.

"Let me see," said the old man, rubbing his arm thoughtfully across his brow. "I think I can, ma'am, for I took particular notice of her before she went down. If my memory don't deceive me, she was painted black, with a white streak and white mould-ings; I believe she had a small round-house on deck, and — yes, I am sure — a large gilt figure-head."

"Tell me, sir," continued Mrs. R., still more agitated, "the date — the year."

"It was in the year 17—, early in the fall — the 18th of September, ma'am; I know that well, for we always dated Nell's birthday from that time."

"Pardon me," said Mrs. Randolph, rising from her seat and approaching the wrecker, her face betraying excessive emotion. "I have a reason, a most im-portant motive for the question. Did you preserve the articles of dress found on the child?"

"Certainly, certainly," answered the old man, won-dering at the question and the agitation of the speaker.

"Where, where are they now?"

"I brought them with me; they are in my trunk," was the reply.

"Bring them here — let me see them. O God, if it should be so!" and the widow sank on the sofa and buried her face in her hands, while the wrecker's wife left the room for the articles.

Each individual arose, as she re-entered the parlor

with a small bundle, except Mrs. Randolph, who continued her position unaltered. A silence as of death pervaded the room as the wife of the wrecker unrolled the small bundle and placed a little frock, cap, and other articles of an infant's dress, on the centre-table. Mrs. Randolph did not look up. She seemed to shrink from a sight of that which was to confirm her suddenly-raised hopes or dash them to the earth. The rest of the company gazed on the clothing in silence, each countenance expressing the most intense interest, excepting Ellen's, who leaned on her husband's arm, with a face pale as marble; and yet, could her heart have been laid bare at that moment, what a world of contending emotions would have been there discovered!

"They are here, Julia," said Mrs. Irving, in a low voice, as she stepped to the side of her friend and touched her arm.

Mrs. Randolph arose. Her face was blanched and colorless, and her trembling limbs barely supported her as she staggered rather than walked toward the table. One searching glance was cast on the dress: it sufficed. A glow of ecstatic feeling lit up her face, and, with a wild exclamation, — "O God! they are hers; they are hers! My child, my long-lost daughter!" — she rushed toward Ellen, and mother and child, the lost and the mourned, were clasped in a convulsive embrace. The sobs and tears of the surrounding group burst forth unrestrainedly and heightened the affecting scene, over a further exhibition of which we must be permitted to draw a veil.

The interest of our story is over. Why need we attempt to portray the unbounded happiness of mother and child so long separated, so deeply mourned, so strangely and unexpectedly united? Why describe the felicity of that little circle, now knit by ties if possible a thousand-fold more endearing than ever? Why speak of the delight of the humble wrecker and his wife, on whom were lavished every endearment which love and gratitude could prompt? It is only necessary to say that the Irvings and Mrs. Randolph would not listen to the return of the honest couple to their former home, but urged and finally prevailed on them to spend the remainder of their days on the estate of the now happy Mrs. Randolph, where, in a neat little cottage built expressly for them, they lived in the enjoyment of every comfort that life could afford. Hardly a day passed that their aged hearts were not made glad by the presence of Ellen and her husband; nor did many years elapse ere first a little boy and then a little girl might be seen playing around their door and hailing them by the grateful appellation of " grandfather " and " grandmother," in the countenance of each of whom might be seen a striking resemblancé to their loved and idolized " Nell,"—for only by that name did they call the happy wife and mother.

We will only add, in conclusion, that the memory of the faithful nurse, whose tender care of Ellen amidst the horrors that surrounded her, and whose love, so strongly manifested in her dying hour, we have portrayed, was duly cherished, as the marble shaft, on which are recorded her virtues and sufferings, plainly testifies.

THE SCOUT.

CHAPTER I.

A CENTURY has rolled away since the events we are about to record transpired. A century! Brief period in the annals of history, passed over, perhaps, with the dash of a pen; and yet in that time what wonderful revolutions have been wrought, revolutions in manners, customs, and every outward condition of life! One hundred years ago the red man bounded in pursuit of the deer, or crept stealthily on the war-path, where now the husbandman turns up the teeming soil and reaps the golden harvest, or the merchant threads the busy mart. One hundred years ago the forest waved in glory or in gloom over regions where now are smiling farms, thriving villages, and crowded cities. One hundred years ago,—but perhaps the contrast will be made more striking to the reader by the relation of our humble story, the incidents of which occurred in that remote period.

A little over a century ago there was but a solitary log hut on what was then styled the "Causeway," but which in modern times has borne the homely name of "Horse Tavern," the location of which is about two miles from Portland, on the Stroudwater road. A particular description of the spot will not be necessary to the development of our story. It may not be amiss to say, that its present name was derived from its being the general watering-place for travellers on their way to and from the city.

At that time the "Causeway" was covered with a dense growth of woods, which formed a portion of the primeval forest that once extended over our whole city; although the sturdy arms on Falmouth Neck, as Portland was then called, had laid many a leafy monarch low. A man by the name of Wier, or, according to our present orthography, Wyer, had selected this out-of-the-way spot, as it was deemed, for his residence. He had made a small opening, just sufficient to allow room for the erection of his rude hut, and to afford a limited space for a garden. Why he chose this place, so remote from the settlement, when men clustered together for mutual safety and protection, it would be difficult to say. Some of the good people of Falmouth, who, like many of their descendants, were fond of indulging in groundless surmises, ascribed it to a sinister motive, shaking their heads very gravely and suspiciously as they spoke of Joe Wier's temerity in thus exposing himself to the attacks of the prowling red man. A number of well-disposed persons cautioned him of the danger which surrounded him, and advised him to move into the settlement.

But Wier was a strong, bold-hearted fellow, and a very honest one to boot, for all that we can learn. He had peculiar social notions of his own. He did not like a crowd, he wanted plenty of elbow-room. A creature of the woods, he feared nothing in human shape. Paying but little attention to the cultivation of the soil, he delighted in following the chase; for which purpose he would absent himself for weeks at a time, roving amid the green forest, and conforming in his mode of life more to that of the savage than his civilized brethren. Joe was not always a follower of the deer and the bear, for, in the frequent disturbances of the whites by the red man, he was employed as a scout to the expeditions sent out to punish and drive off the wily foe. Well versed in the cunning so characteristic of the Indian, and capable of enduring equal exposure and fatigue, the savage found in him an inveterate enemy. His prowess was so well known that his name had become a terror to them.

"The varmints know me too well to molest me so long as I have this trusty friend by my side," said he, slapping the breech of his rusty rifle, which had sent death to the heart of many a wild denizen of the woods.

This was no vain boast, for he was famous far and wide for the accuracy of his aim. Nothing could escape his practical eye. The bird on the wing and the fleet deer alike fell beneath his fatal rifle. His skill was so great, and his fondness for sport so well known, that in time he was only known as Hunting Joe, a sobriquet with which he was evidently not a little pleased.

Joe was tall and straight as an arrow when he stood erect, and, though spare in flesh, his form exhibited a muscular development which betokened great physical power. His face was bronzed by the weather, and from under a singularly-looking cap, made fr⸀ the skin of some wild animal, a few gray hairs str⸀ gled, telling of length of years. The expression of his countenance was rather mild than otherwise, though the wrinkles and scars of time had made sad havoc with features apparently once more than ordinarily good-looking. His eye, however, still retained all the fire of youth, and in its quick, penetrating glances seemed to take an instantaneous, comprehensive view of all that was transpiring around him. Besides the odd-looking cap we have mentioned, the Scout wore a loose hunting-frock, girt about the waist with a deer-skin belt, suspended from which was a capacious pouch of the same material, and a sheath containing a formi-dable knife. His lower limbs were cased in leggins, and instead of shoes he wore moccasins similar to those used by the red man.

In the year 1745, the fifth French war, as it was styled, broke out, the longest and most ruthless of those desolating conflicts. Time and again the savage hordes swept through the infant settlements with blood and flame, sparing neither age nor sex. The tender infant and the gray-haired sire alike shared the same terrible fate. What the tomahawk and the scalping-knife left undone the brand consummated. No one felt safe for a moment. In the fields, in the house of God, and by their bedsides, the gun was always at hand, ready at a moment's warning. Men who lived apart forsook their dwellings and congregated in block-houses for mutual defence and security; and when they ventured abroad they stole out warily, dreading each thicket as an ambush, and fearful that each tree concealed a foe.

In some instances the fatal tomahawk was arrested and the victim spared, not from motives of humanity, but from the lust of gain; for, though the French awarded what may truly be called blood-money for each reeking scalp, yet they offered a higher price for captives, especially females, delivered in Canada: so that cupidity often stayed the murderous hand when mercy plead in vain.

CHAPTER II.

In the summer of 1746, news was brought to Falmouth that a band of savages had suddenly appeared at New Marblehead, as the town of Windham was then called, a pleasant village about ten miles from Portland. The report stated that they had attacked the dwelling of a Mr. Hanson, and butchered all of the family save one female. The survivor they had taken into captivity. Early in the morning the distressing intelligence reached Falmouth, and the Scout, who happened to be there, was one of the first to hear it. About one hour afterwards, he might have been seen leaving the Causeway and plunging into the woods, with his long rifle at a trail, proceeding with hasty strides towards the scene of murder. There was an unusual fire burning in his eye, a dark red spot glowed on each cheek, and his whole countenance bore the expression of a chafed and angry spirit.

He was evidently on no common errand, for he strode the thick forest, right on through thicket and brake, crushing the dead limbs beneath his heavy tread, and dashing aside the dense bushes that beset his way, with a recklessness and haste which betrayed the

agitated state of his mind. The startled deer broke
from its covert immediately within his range, but he
heeded it not; the shaggy bear muttered an angry
growl as he roused it from its lair, but it served not
to attract his attention; the stealthy catamount raised
its terrific, half-human cry, but his ear heard not the
warning. He still pressed on, thoughtless of danger,
heedless of the opportunities offered for the exercise
of his boasted skill, and regardless of fatigue. With
his head slightly bent and his body leaning forward, to
have seen him one would have thought he was wandering at random through the mazy woods. There was no
defined path for him to follow,— a wild, trackless region
of towering trees and heavy underbrush spread out on
either hand, presenting at every step the same unbroken, unvarying scene. Yet the Scout hesitated not
a moment on his way. Now and then, perhaps, he
would raise his head, and, after casting a hasty glance
around him, gazing for an instant through the opening
branches on the sky, he would resume his former position, continuing his route in the same rapid manner.

Mile after mile was traversed in this way, until at
length, in an incredibly brief period, he had reached
what was then known as Mallison's, but now enjoying
the unpoetical cognomen of "Horse-Beef Falls," in
Windham. The dwelling of the murdered family was in
this neighborhood, to which his steps were immediately
directed. The house was deserted. He entered the
battered door, and, following a crimson stain that ran
along the floor of the front room, he proceeded to the
fatal bedroom. The stillness of death brooded over
the place as he stood there alone gazing on the crimson floor, still wet with the blood of the victims. A

vengeful fire gleamed in his eyes as his glance rested on the dabbled walls and hearth-stone. For a while he remained silent, his breast heaving with emotion, overmastering his utterance. At length he found words.

"Accursed race!" he muttered between his clenched teeth; "a life for each drop will be too poor a revenge!" and he clutched his rifle with a convulsive grasp, while an expression almost demoniacal shot wildly over his face.

For the reader to understand the cause of the emotion exhibited by the Scout, we need only say that the murdered mother of the family was his only sister, and the young female carried into captivity was his sole remaining child, who had been on a visit to her aunt during the summer, her own mother being dead. Good reason had he for his emotion, with the blood of his kindred all about him, clinging in clots to his very feet, as if crying for vengeance, and a knowledge of his idolized child's captivity, perhaps more cruel suffering and death, racking his mind.

Not long did the unhappy man remain in the chamber of death. With a moan, rather than a sigh, he left the room, and, tightening the belt around his body, he prepared on the instant to strike on the trail of the foe. Just at that moment a footstep was heard, as of one cautiously approaching the house. The Scout raised his rifle in readiness for use. The dry branches crackled beneath the tread of the intruder, but still he entered not the door. Half-hoping that it might be a prowling savage, the Scout loosened his long hunting-knife, and then crept softly to the window, disposing himself so as to catch sight of the one outside without exposing his own person.

For a time nothing met his sight. Presently, from behind a clump of bushes, there emerged, not the expected red man, but a youth of some twenty-three or four years of age. The young man was armed with a rifle, and fully equipped, as for a long tramp. He was moving carefully around, as if in search of some object, first examining the bushes on either hand, and then bending down and intently gazing upon the grass. At length, as if satisfied with his scrutiny, he was about plunging into the woods, when the Scout addressed him.

"My young friend — Mayberry — where now? This way a moment."

The young man started, and, with a look of surprise, turned and hastened toward the house, at the door of which he met the Scout. A silent grasp of the hand ensued. There was no occasion for words to explain each other's object.

"I have discovered their trail, sir," said the new-comer, with a flushed though sad countenance. "We have no time to lose; come."

"But you were not going alone?" said the Scout, as he stepped in front of the dwelling, glancing gratefully at the young man as he spoke.

"Alone, and to the end of the world, sir, for rescue and revenge! The rest are wanted at home for defence, and they tried to persuade me to remain; but my mind was fixed."

"One word more, young man," said the Scout, in a faltering voice; "are all gone, — all?"

"Not one saved, sir, but Mabel. Every soul of

them shockingly butchered. They will be buried from the block-house this afternoon."

The Scout hastily dashed a tear from his eye, then, grasping his piece, he said, "Let us forward,—follow me!"

And the two started, like hounds on the scent, in pursuit of the foe, the Scout leading the way, his more practised eye at once striking the trail.

CHAPTER III.

For some time not a word was said as they made their way through the tangled forest; each seemed to be communing with his own thoughts. The younger, a manly, athletic youth, with a fine, fresh countenance, and a determined expression in his features, followed close in the footsteps of his companion, whose tall, sinewy form gave evidence of great physical strength. Although he had long passed the meridian of life, yet age had not dampened his vigor. His face was brown with exposure and well seamed with years, still his rough features wore a kindly expression, although an occasional sternness would steal over them, and an angry, fierce glance gleam from his eye, as a passing thought of the object he had in view flitted through his brain. The long silence was at last interrupted by the Scout's addressing his companion, without checking his pace, however.

"An! so you were going in pursuit alone, my young friend? I honor your courage, boy, but it would have been rash. Unacquainted as you are with the cunning habits of these wood-fiends, how could you expect to cope with them single-handed?"

"I could die, sir," said the young man, in a determined tone.

"And add one more to the number scored in blood," rejoined the Scout. "No, no, young man, life is too precious to be recklessly thrown away. Stout hearts and strong arms are too scarce in the settlements, and we shall need all we can muster before this bloody war is over."

"But you were going alone, were you not?"

"Ay, but my life is not so precious as yours. If Mabel is lost, I should have none to mourn me. Then, again, I know the nature of these devils, and my chance would be better. I am glad of your company, however, and from my heart I thank you for the interest you take in me and mine. I have heard there was a liking 'tween you and the gal, and I am rejoiced to know that you are worthy of her. With the blessing of Heaven we may circumvent them that have her yet, and, if so be she is alive, and we all get back to the settlements again, she is yours, youngster. But, if they have murdered her —— "

"You do not fear that event?" said the young man, hastily, the glow on his cheeks giving place to the pallor of alarm.

"I don't know, James," replied the Scout, shaking his head doubtfully. "I am loath to think on it; but when their blood is up there's no knowing to what lengths they will go. If they suspected now that any one was on their trail, and she should hinder their flight, her scalp would dangle at their belts in a moment."

The thought of the possibility of such an event produced a protracted silence, as they strode on their way, brooding over the situation of the captive. Hour after hour passed away, and still they slackened not their speed. But few words passed between them; for, besides the necessity of restraining every possible noise, through fear of a surprise, they were each too much occupied with their own thoughts to continue a conversation. Many a mile had been passed over, when at last the Scout hesitated in his rapid gait, and shortly came to a dead halt.

The sun was getting low, and the forest was so dense, the fading light scarcely penetrated the thick foliage of the overhanging branches. So shrouded in gloom, indeed, had their way become, that it required the closest scrutiny of the quick-sighted Scout to detect the trail, which at first was broad and distinct, as if the savages had roved carelessly along, thinking pursuit out of question; but for some distance it appeared that they had grown more careful, for it was evident that pains had been taken, if not to conceal, at least to render their route as little marked as possible.

"It is getting too dark to travel farther to-night," said the Scout, in a low tone, as he leaned his rifle against the trunk of a fallen pine and wiped the drops from his brow. "Something has occurred to make them more careful, for I have observed the last hour or two the trail has been growing more faint as we proceeded. You see by the prints on the leaves all around us that they made a halt here, probably for consultation. And here you see by the bent twigs that they have struck off in this direction. If they were alarmed they had got over it, from the broad trail they made again; or this, may be some trick of the desateful beasts. As there should be a spring near, from the trickling of yonder water," continued the Scout, "we had better make a stop here for the night;" and he proceeded to disencumber himself of his accoutrements.

"But there is still daylight enough to follow their track," said the young man, impatient of delay. "Every moment is important: we have a broad trail before us, why not follow it?"

"Patience, patience, my boy," said the old man, throwing down his hunting-pouch. "'T is a hard lesson, but you must l'arn it. 'Make haste, make waste,' are words full of sound wisdom, simple as they read, my young friend. I am as anxious to overtake the varmints as you are, but there is more in the signs about us than meets the eye, and I want broad daylight to pry into them. We have travelled a smart piece to-day, and a good night's rest will refresh us for an early start in the morning."

So saying, the Scout set about those preparations for camping out which a long acquaintance with a forest life had rendered familiar to him. In a short time his arrangements were completed; everything was disposed to guard against a sudden attack; and, after partaking of a hearty meal of the humble fare they had brought with them, they sought their leafy couches, the evening breeze gently waving the tree-tops and producing a lulling murmur among the leaves, occasionally swaying the branches aside, and letting in the rays of the rising moon on the silent and apparently deserted spot.

CHAPTER IV.

THE sun was glistening on the tops of the tallest trees ere the young man awoke from a deep slumber, into which he had only fallen at a late hour. The mission he was on, the anxiety he felt in the fate of one so dear to his heart, had kept him restless and uneasy. He hardly thought of his own situation, of the dangers that surrounded him, although the occasional cry of some wild animal, or the sudden cracking of the dry limbs around him, would for a moment recall him to a sense of his own peril. It was sometime past midnight ere his perturbed mind was sufficiently composed to induce sleep. Even when, from sheer weariness, his senses were locked in slumber, his teeming brain was busy with images connected with the maiden's captivity, plainly manifested by his murmured exclamations, frequent shiftings of position, and sudden starts.

When he awoke, he sprang upon his feet and turned to arouse his companion, but he found that he had got the start of him. Another glance discovered to him the Scout seated on the mossy roots of a tall oak, with the provisions for the morning meal in waiting before him.

"Young limbs require more rest than aged ones," said the old man, with a smile, after saluting his companion. "While you have been dreaming there, I have been taking a look about us. One cannot pass through the woods as he would on the beaten highway. I told you last night," he continued, as he applied himself to the coarse viands before him, "that

11*

we wanted daylight to read the signs hereabouts, and the event has proved that I was right. If we had followed on the route proposed by you last night, James, we should have had a pesky tramp of it, and that is all, for our pains. Cunning varmints are them red-skins, but they are not foxy enough to cheat the old Scout yet!"

"Surely, sir, that is their trail branching off to the right, over the hillock yonder?" asked the young man in a tone of surprise.

"Sartin true, there's no mistake about that, boy. One with half an eye could follow a path marked as that. But see here: just go beyond that clump of bushes there by that cedar to the left, and bring me what you find."

The young man obeyed him, and after a brief search he returned, with a strip of calico, a mere shred, which he found attached to a thorn-bush.

"There," continued the Scout, "the strip you hold came from the poor girl's dress, either left by design or accident. If the former, it proves that she is not frightened out of her wits, at any rate; if the latter, I hold it as a sign that Providence is with us, and will guide us aright, if we will only do our part by using a proper discretion. I calkerlate now, that the savages began to suspect that they might be followed, and a part of them were sent off this way, leaving a broad trail for fools to follow, if they will, but not one so well l'arned in their deviltries as the old hunter," added the Scout, with a low chuckle.

"By observing the place," he continued, "where you found that piece of cloth, you will find, if you look sharp, Mabel's foot-prints, on one spot in particular, where she ground her heel into the turf,—the brave girl,—as if on purpose. Shoulder your pack, my good fellow, and let us be off. I reckon as how we shall be close on their heels by nightfall."

It took but a short time to get ready, and they immediately started off on the new trail, the Scout leading the way with such a rapid pace that his companion, no inexperienced walker, found it difficult to keep up with him.

The trail on which they now struck was that of three persons only, as near as they could make out, the great body of the party having probably gone off in another direction to draw off the pursuit, should one be made, or perhaps on some other predatory expedition. Ere long the Scout found it necessary to slacken his speed, and to examine more carefully to ascertain the route of those they were pursuing. At times the trail would be lost altogether, but the quick eye of the old man, which seemed to take in every object, however minute, at a glance, would soon discover it again. Great precaution was observed as they proceeded, for they knew not how far distant they might be from the foe. At times the young man was directed to ascend some tall tree, which commanded a view of the surrounding country, in order to detect any sign of the fugitives; at other times the Scout would come to a stand, and place his ear to the ground, for the same purpose. But, except the trail, they had as yet discovered nothing.

It was now getting towards noon, and the two in pursuit were moving steadily though briskly forward, for of late the trail had grown at every step more and more fresh, giving assurance that the party they were seeking could not be a great distance in advance of them, when the Scout made a sudden halt.

"Hist!" said he in a low whisper to his companion, pointing at the same time to a clump of thick bushes that crowned a slight ascent a short distance in front of them. "I don't like the looks of things yonder. See to your arms, my lad; we may have a use for them presently."

The young man hastily reprimed his piece and held it ready for immediate action.

"Wait here," continued the Scout, "while I take a peep about us. There may be mischief in the neighborhood." So saying, he plunged into the underbrush at his right and disappeared.

For some time the young man stood his ground, waiting in anxious expectation, with his eyes fixed steadfastly on the thicket. He could see nothing to cause the alarm exhibited by the Scout. Everything at first appeared as usual, and he began to wonder at the movements of his companion. Presently, however, he discovered a slight movement among the branches in the centre of the clump, which under ordinary circumstances would not have attracted his notice. In a short time the bushes became more agitated, accompanied by a snapping of the dry twigs. A moment more, and the young man was startled by the sight of a large catamount, which emerged from the covert along the trunk of a mossy tree, which had fallen into it, and stood crouched on the projecting butt immediately before him, lashing its tail, and eyeing him with an angry, flashing glance, in the very attitude of pouncing upon him.

As quick as thought the young man brought his

rifle to his shoulder, and was just on the point of drawing the trigger, when a warning from the Scout restrained him.

"Don't fire, youngster, don't fire. Get a tree between you, if possible, and leave him to me."

The sound of the Scout's voice seemed to divert the attention of the animal, for he turned his head in the direction whence it came, gnashing his fangs and impatiently clawing the decayed trunk with his cat-like paws. The young man seized the opportunity, and made a movement with the intention of securing the cover of a large tree a few feet from him. He had scarcely taken the first step, when with the quickness of lightning the formidable beast turned and gathered himself for a spring, uttering at the same time the peculiar cry which always precedes, or rather accompanies, the fatal leap. The young man gave himself up for lost; but at that instant the sharp report of a rifle rang through the woods, and the panther, bounding high in the air, fell struggling within a few feet of where he stood, spell-bound with fear.

"There's an end of that varmint!" exclaimed the Scout, bursting from a thick copse near by. "But take care of yourself, my lad," he shouted, "for the crittur is terrible in his agonies, and hardly safe when the life is gone.

"I have made worse shots in my life than that," continued he, as he pointed to a dark spot in the forehead of the writhing animal, whence the warm blood was fast oozing. "He's a wicked thing when his rage is up, and bad as a red-skin, every inch of him. But we have no time to waste over him. I was loath to fire, for the report may reach the ears of those who need

but the falling of a leaf to arouse their suspicions."
So saying, the Scout carefully reloaded his piece, and
hastened again on the pursuit.

Casting a glance on the expiring panther, whose
dying eye still gleamed ferociously on him as he
passed, young Mayberry followed his companion,
grateful for his late escape, yet fearful that the report
of the gun might betray their approach to the savages,
and thus jeopardize the life of the captive, or at any
rate put them on their guard, and so prevent a
surprise.

CHAPTER V.

THE same anxiety on account of the report of the
gun that troubled the young man's mind seemed also
to burden the thoughts of the Scout, for, after travelling along some time in silence, he remarked, in a low
tone, —

"These woods are master places for carrying sound.
I've hearn, 'fore now, when I've been out hunting, a
report go echoing through the forest, just as though
each tree had a tongue of its own, and so caught up
and repeated the sound to its neighbor, until it went
clean through the whole tract. But I hope there are
no such tell-tale trees in these parts, for if they should
bear that pesky shot to the red-skins we are in s'arch
of, it would be an evil report for us, I consate, though
we raised it ourself.

"Tread softly, my boy," continued the old man,
"and don't disturb the bushes more than you can

help. We must be careful of our trail, for there's no telling how many of the varmin there may be prowling around us."

Every step was now taken with the greatest caution. Particular care was observed to prevent the least noise, even the snapping of a twig, and our two friends pressed forward so softly and stealthily that they scarcely disturbed the dry leaves in their path. From the signs around them the hunter knew that the Indians could not be far off. At one spot, which they reached about two hours after their affair with the panther, the marks were so fresh, the Scout assured his companion that they could not have left it but a short time before. The savages had evidently set about preparing a hasty meal, and it was possible the report of the gun here reached them, for there were obvious marks of a hurried departure.

As the new-comers cast searching glances around them, the Scout prying into the neighboring bushes as if fearful of an ambuscade, the quick eye of the young man caught sight of an object which sent the blood with a warmer flow through his veins. The place in which they found themselves was a small area, nearly surrounded with lofty trees, whose overhanging branches cast a deep shade over it. On one side a massive tree lay stretched along the ground, its extremities concealed by the underbrush into which it had fallen. In a slight crevice of this tree, which had doubtless been occupied as the maiden's seat, as if placed there to attract attention, the young man detected a bead bracelet, which he at once recognized as a gift of his own to Mabel. It was a token to him that she anticipated a pursuit, and his heart was thrilled with a secret pleasure, for it assured him that she had confidence in him, and relied on his exertions to rescue her from captivity. It showed also that she was not disheartened, but still retained her spirits unbroken.

As he eagerly directed the attention of his companion to the discovery, the Scout's eye brightened, and a complacent smile lighted up his features, as he remarked, in a barely audible whisper, — "Ay, the gal has a quick wit and a courageous heart, though she is a darter of mine. She is worth fighting for, boy, and when the time comes, I hope your heart won't fail you."

"I hope you don't doubt me, sir!" said the youth, reddening slightly as he spoke.

"Distrust you, youngster?" replied the Scout, in a tone of honest sincerity, "never you think of it. I only thought I would give you a hint of what is before us. There may be blood spilt before we see the end of this business. One or both of us may lay our bones in the forest; there 's no saying, for these redskins have a sure eye and seldom burn powder for nothing. If either of us fall, I pray I may be the one, lad, for in the course of natur' I can't last long, and the old tree can be better spared than the young. Howsomever, as long as I can raise my rusty old friend here — ha!" said he, with a sudden start, "what is that?".

A slight rustling of the dry leaves was heard a little distance off, as if some one were making their way cautiously through the thick underbrush which sprang up in every direction.

"To cover, James!" whispered the Scout. "To

cover, and lie close!" and he crept softly behind the
huge pine against which he had been leaning. The
young man followed his example, darting behind a
dense thicket, where he could observe the Scout's motions, as well as reconnoitre the spot he had left.

He had barely secreted himself, when a tall savage
was seen to advance, with a snake-like motion, into a
little opening just beyond the small enclosure we have
mentioned. He paused for a moment after emerging
from the bushes, and then, glancing furtively around,
he bent down and applied his ear to the ground. The
slightest sound, even the mere movement of a foot,
so keen is the sense of hearing in the Indian, might
have betrayed them. Scarcely drawing a full breath,
the concealed party watched with no little anxiety the
motions of the wary savage.

From where young Mayberry stood he had the Indian completely in his range and at his mercy, and he
turned his head inquiringly towards the Scout and
made a motion to that effect. The old man shook his
head negatively, and he turned again to observe the
further movements of the red man. In the mean time
the savage, as if satisfied with his scrutiny, raised
himself from his bent posture, and crept silently away
in the direction whence they had come.

For ten minutes or more the white men remained
perfectly motionless in their coverts, at the expiration
of which the Scout left his post, and, after throwing
careful glances around him and bending his ear to the
ground, beckoned the young man to follow him.

"I could have brought him down without fail," said
the latter, in a cautious whisper, as he joined his companion.

12

"Yes, and brought the whole pack upon us at the same time, perhaps," added the old man, in the same under-tone. "There's no telling how many of the sarpents there are about here. The woods may be alive with them. But I don't understand the meaning of this fellow's lurking so slyly in this direction," he continued, with a doubtful shake of his head.

"Perhaps," suggested the younger, "he was sent back to ascertain about the firing."

"I b'lieve you're right, James; that must be it. And the cunning dog will return on our trail, and try to sarcumvent us that way. But he's run by the game to a dead sartainty this time, and now let us profit by it."

After again cautioning his companion to be silent and wary,—an admonition the latter felt to be entirely useless,—the two started briskly forward on the trail they had been so long following, and which promised to lead them ere long to the objects of their pursuit. The day was fast drawing to a close as they struck again into the woods, scarcely affording light sufficient to discern the faint tracks by which their steps were guided.

CHAPTER VI.

By the margin of a little stream, which flowed from a gradual descent and wound its noiseless way around the roots of old trees, now trickling unseen through the green herbage, whose fibres it nourished in return for the protection afforded, and now lapsing gently under the fallen and decaying trunks which extended

across but did not obstruct its course, and at last stealing its way through a broad open space, — a green
little forest nook, fit spot for fairy gambols in the pale
moonlight, which now shed its mild radiance over the
scene, — by the margin of this quiet watercourse, part
way up the slight ascent, was seated, or rather reclined,
a young maiden on a mossy knoll, just out of the shade
of a wide-spreading elm. Her dress was somewhat
rent and wayworn, and her countenance, as revealed
by the full harvest moon, betokened much exhaustion
and not a little anxiety, although there was something
in the expression of her features which spoke of a
spirit unbroken. Her face was singularly handsome,
and her form, notwithstanding the disarrangement of
her dress, betrayed much natural grace.

At the moment we have introduced her to the
reader, her glance was directed to the many little
openings in the surrounding forest, watching the
curious effects of the light and shade, the deep shadows of the trees and the tall bushes falling sharp and
distinct on the turf, forming a grotesquely checkered
scene, as well as a picture of unrivalled beauty.
Agitated and burdened as was the heart of the maiden,
it was not insensible to the softening influence of the
scene. As her gaze lingered on the different points
of attraction, for the time she forgot the terrible scenes
she had but recently passed through and the horrors
of her present situation. Her captivity and the probable fate that awaited her wholly passed from her
mind.

In this dreamy state of forgetfulness, her eye was
following down the meanderings of the rivulet, which
in the bright moonbeams, appeared like a stream of

molten silver, until its course was lost in a dark clump
of bushes which bounded the small opening, when she
gave an involuntary start, while an exclamation of
delighted surprise arose to her lips; ere it found utterance, she had the presence of mind to restrain it. The
next moment the dark form of a savage rose stealthily
in the shade behind her. The deep, guttural monotone
made use of by the red man when surprised, "hugh!"
was uttered in a subdued voice, giving evidence that
the movement of the maiden, slight as it was, had not
escaped his observation.

For three or four minutes the gaze of the savage
was rivetted on the spot to which her glance had been
so lately directed, while his hand clutched the fatal
tomahawk, ready for instant action. The maiden held
her breath, while her heart beat almost audibly, half
in hope, half in fear. Some time elapsed, yet nothing
unusual met their gaze; but presently a slight rustling
was heard among the bushes, and soon after a young
doe was seen to emerge hastily from the thicket,
gazing around in a startled manner. For a moment it
stood with its head half turned to its late covert; then,
slowly stalking towards the little stream, it lapped
awhile the bright waters, and shortly after plunged
again into the bushes; and the same deep solitude as
before reigned over the scene. As if his suspicions
were lulled to rest, the savage soon after sank quietly
back on his leafy couch, and ere long his heavy
breathing assured the maiden that his senses were
again locked in slumber.

Mabel (for the reader will recognize the Scout's
daughter in the young female we have been speaking
of) listened with an eager ear to the deep respirations

of the sleeper. In order to test the soundness of his
slumber, she moved her feet so as to produce a rustling noise among the crisp leaves around her, and then
awaited in anxious expectation the result of the trial.
But the sleep of the Indian was too heavy to be thus
easily broken. Under ordinary circumstances, probably, even the slight noise she had made would have
aroused him at once; but the night previous, which
was that succeeding the massacre, as well as that in
which the fatal deed was perpetrated, had been sleepless ones, and this, with the fatigue of a long tramp,
had induced a deeper slumber than usual.

Having satisfied herself that her captor was not
feigning, Mabel again turned her eyes toward the
thicket with a beating and anxious heart. She had
not gazed long, when a dark object was seen creeping
slowly and warily in the deep shadows of the bushes,
and presently a young man stepped cautiously into
the patch of moonlight in front. Though the thicket
was at some distance, the quick eye of the girl immediately recognized the intruder. A warm blush suf-
fused her pale cheeks, and her bosom throbbed with
intense emotion, as her glance fell on the form of one
whose presence, it may well be supposed, was never
more welcome than at this trying moment. Yet, amid
the thrill of joy which the presence of her lover
inspired, there mingled no small degree of fear. She
supposed that he had come to her rescue alone; and,
though she had no doubt he might easily overcome
the sleeping savage, what if the other, who had really
been sent back, as young Mayberry supposed, to ascertain the cause of the shot, — what if he should return?
Every moment she expected to hear his footsteps, for

12*

the hour had passed when he should have been there; and what could her lover do single-handed with two such powerful foes?

Forgetting her own situation in the danger that menaced one so dear to her, she almost regretted his appearance. Not long, however, did she entertain this feeling, for a moment after, to her great joy, she beheld her father standing by his side. The gaze of both was apparently fixed on her. She was soon satisfied that she was seen by them, for, after a brief consultation, her father either made a sign to that effect or beckoned to her. What should prevent her starting away to seek their protection? In the first impulse of the moment, she vainly made the attempt. Vainly, we say, for her crafty captors had taken the precaution to guard against a flight by confining her limbs, both arms and feet, and thus rendering her entirely helpless. Answering the sign made by her father by holding up her fettered arms, she then exerted her strength to remove the thongs from her ankles. But they resisted all her efforts; and when, from sheer exhaustion, she gave over, for the first time since her captivity the poor girl wept. Finding that her struggles were impotent, she cast a tearful glance towards her friends, and again raised her imprisoned arms, thus giving them to understand that she could do nothing for herself. Shaking their heads affirmatively, as if they comprehended her meaning, the two seemingly held another consultation, immediately after which they fell back into the shade and were lost to sight.

CHAPTER VII.

It was very evident, from the cautious movements of her friends, that they were unaware of the number of her captors. Had they known the true state of the case, they would undoubtedly have taken bolder measures for her rescue, the advantages being altogether on their side. They were pretty well convinced that there were but two at most to deal with, although they were not sure that others had not joined them. Even to get the captive safely out of the clutches of two only, they felt to be a hazardous game, well knowing that if their attempt were discovered the first blow would fall on her head. Aware of this, their proceedings were marked by the greatest possible secrecy.

Knowing that some plan had been matured for her release, Mabel awaited the issue with trembling apprehension. Holding her breath, that she might catch the first intimation of the approach of her deliverers, she waited until her patience was sorely tested. Minute after minute passed away, each one seeming an age in her state of suspense, and still all was silent as death. Once only she thought she heard a scarcely perceptible rustle among the leaves at a distance; and her eyes were immediately turned upon the sleeping savage, dreading lest the noise should break his slumbers. But he still slept on, breathing heavily, and occasionally muttering unintelligibly in his sleep. At one time she thought all was lost, for the Indian suddenly half-raised himself, uttering at the same time a slight exclamation as of surprise. The action and the utterance were probably occasioned by the flitting of some wild thought through his brain, for he soon settled away again in the same depth of unconsciousness as ever.

Mabel now listened with renewed intensity for signs indicating the approach of her friends, but not a sound could be heard. There was not so much as the falling of a leaf to break the grave-like stillness. Dreading either the awakening of the sleeper or the return of the absent, her anxiety increased every moment. The feeling of suspense, of uncertainty, grew so strong that it almost amounted to torture, and she found it difficult to sustain herself amid the conflicting emotions that agitated her breast. Again and again she bent her ear in the hope of catching an approaching sound, and for the hundredth time her searching glance was rivetted on different points whence she expected the appearance of her deliverers; but all in vain. With a sickening emotion, and a sigh of disappointment wrung from the very depths of her heart, she bent her head for a moment, half yielding to the weight that oppressed her, when a slight touch on her arm almost caused her to shriek out in alarm, so sudden and unexpected was the action.

"For your life be still!" whispered her father in her ear.

It required all the effort she could command to obey him, so full and strong was the tide of feeling that rushed through her heart. A moment hardly transpired when she felt the thongs that bound her wrists giving way and at last drop from them. Her first impulse was to throw her liberated arms around her parent's neck.

The Scout received and returned the embrace in

silence, then in a low whisper said: "Here, my child,
take the knife and loose your feet. Quick, Mabe, for
time is precious! How many of the varmints are
they, gal?" he added, as she bent over to sever the
cords.

Ere she could return an answer, a slight crashing
and a hasty step among the underbrush a little in front
of them struck her ear.

"O God, father, he's returned!" exclaimed the
maiden half-aloud, forgetful in her alarm of everything
else.

The words had barely left her lips when a tall savage bounded with a shrill whoop from the bushes a
few yards in advance of them, brandishing his tomahawk in the very act of launching it at the half-stoop-
ing girl. As quick as thought, the Scout sprang to
his feet and confronted him, interposing his own body
as a shield to his child. The action of the Scout frus-
trated the purpose of the Indian, and he poised his
weapon to strike down his opponent. His arm was
thrown back, and the glittering instrument was just
on the point of being sent on its fatal errand, when
the flash of a gun lit up the deep shadows of the forest, followed by a sharp report, and a rifle ball whistled directly over the shoulder of the Scout. A dead,
crushing sound was heard, a smothered shriek, and
the tall savage bounded high in the air and fell headlong among the underbrush.

"Bravely done, my boy!" shouted the old man
exultingly, as his glance rested for a moment on the
dead Indian; "shouldn't have been ashamed of that
shot myself. But there is other work for us yet. How

many of the red devils are there, Mabe?" said he,
turning quickly around.

The scene that met his gaze checked at once every
feeling of exultation. It was his daughter darting
down the declivity and across the opening, and the
lately sleeping Indian in full pursuit, with the long
hunting-knife of the Scout held threateningly toward
her. The first impulse of the Scout was to fly to her
rescue, but a moment's thought convinced him that
before he could reach her it would be too late to save
her. A second glance also revealed to him the young
man rushing to her assistance, though the distance
between the parties was so great, there was no hope
of his being able to reach the infuriated savage in
time to prevent the accomplishment of his fatal purpose. Something, however, must be done, and that
too shortly, for the Indian was fast closing upon the
terrified maiden, who continued her flight directly
across the area.

Springing to the little hillock on which he and his
daughter had rested at the time they met, the Scout
caught up his rifle and aimed it at the savage. He
hesitated, however, for the foe was directly in range
with his daughter, and he was fearful the same ball
might carry death to her as well as her pursuer.

By this time the Indian was within a few feet of his
victim. Already his arm was extended to seize her,
when the Scout hastily lowered his rifle, and shouted,
with a voice to which despair lent strength, " Double
on him, gal! Turn this way, for your life! "

As quick as a flash, the panting maid turned short
on her pursuer in the direction of her father. The

movement was so sudden that she gained considerably on the baffled savage.

Once more the Scout raised his rifle with a deliberate aim, and, taking advantage of the very moment when the savage was on a slight rise, which brought his person boldly out to view, while the maiden, being in a small hollow, was out of his range, the trigger was drawn. If ever the Scout prayed, it was at that fearful moment. His child's existence hung on the steadiness of his nerve, yet he faltered not. One step only had the Indian taken, when the bright flame leaped from the muzzle, a ringing report followed, and when the smoke cleared away, the long hunter's knife was seen glittering in the moonbeams, flying through the air, while the hand that so lately held it was beating the earth in the paroxysms of death. In a moment after the still flying maiden was clasped to the panting breast of young Mayberry, in whose arms she rested unscathed, though faint and exhausted, and scarcely aware of her safety.

CHAPTER VIII.

"Is she hurt?" anxiously exclaimed the Scout, as he rushed to the spot where his daughter stood supported by the young man. "Mabel, Mabel, speak to me, child!"

"No, dear father," was her faint reply, throwing herself into his arms; "I am safe, thank God! But where is he, the Indian?" and she glanced fearfully around her.

"Where he can shed no more innocent blood," replied the old man with a stern solemnity. "There lies the varmint, — there, where, if a marciful Providence spares my life, many more of the accursed race will lie before I'm done with them! But come, James, we must be getting ready for a start. Pick up the knife yonder, and see that your piece is well loaded; the whooping demons may be upon us before we know it. Sit you down, my darter, and rest yourself, for we have a long and rough road before us, and you will need all your strength."

While the young man obeyed the Scout's order, the old man, after charging his rifle, stepped to the side of the dead Indian and rolled the corpse into a deep hollow, carefully covering it with the dead leaves, to conceal it from sight should the savages be drawn to the spot by the firing; for he well knew, if they discovered the bodies of the slain, they would pursue them with an untiring vigilance and wreak on them a bloody vengeance.

But a short time elapsed ere the party were on the move. Slowly and silently they threaded the gloomy forest, the Scout leading the way, stopping at short intervals to listen if aught could be heard of the dreaded foe. But no sound broke the deep silence, save the faint rustle occasioned by their passage through the underbrush. Once only was it disturbed. Far behind them, swelling faintly on the night air, was heard what at first sounded like an Indian yell.

"O God!" whispered the maiden, in a tremulous tone, a cold shudder running through her frame; "I hear them. They will soon overtake us; they are howling over the slain."

The Scout stopped short, motioning for silence, while he stood in the attitude of one intently listening. A minute or two elapsed, when the same sound was borne more loudly to their ears.

"There, father, do you not hear them?" said the maiden, in a voice of increased alarm.

"Ay," replied the Scout, in a low tone, evidently of relief, "I hear them, sure enough. They *are* howling over the dead; but cheer up, Mabe,—they are not Indians. The wolves, gal, are feasting on the varmints. 'T is a dismal sound in a lone forest, and I've known the time when it has made me tremble as you do at this moment. But we have nothing to fear from them now; the critturs are too busy over the dead to meddle with the living."

Throughout the night the party kept on their way. Their progress was very slow, for the maiden was worn down with fatigue, although she bore herself bravely, refusing to acknowledge her weariness, but urging them on when they proposed a halt for the purpose of rest, so anxious was she to reach the settlements. Nor was the anxiety of her protectors much less than her own, for they knew not but their steps were tracked, and each moment they expected to be assailed by the treacherous and blood-thirsty foe.

Morning dawned ere they ventured at last to come to a halt, when exhausted nature gave way, and the maiden fell into a deep slumber. The sun had got far up in the heavens ere she was aroused, when, refreshed by her repose, she started with renewed vigor on her toilsome journey.

It will be needless to follow them on their wild and

13

wearisome way. After a most fatiguing march, rendered doubly so by the precautions they deemed it necessary to take, — now diverging widely from the direct course in order to mislead a pursuit; now forcing their way over broken ledges and through rocky and difficult places, where they would be least likely to leave a trail; practising a thousand arts which the sagacity of the Scout prompted to baffle their pursuers, in case they were followed, — they finally, at the close of the second day, to their great satisfaction, reached the Scout's hut on the Causeway.

We will not attempt to portray the joy of the maiden when she stood once more safely within her father's humble dwelling. The dreadful scenes in which she had been a partaker seemed more like a dream than the reality, although often, as she thought of the night of the bloody massacre, a cold shudder evinced how indelibly was that shocking scene fixed upon her memory.

We presume some of our readers would hardly be satisfied unless we adverted more particularly to one incident connected with two of the personages of our humble history. We allude, of course, to Mabel and her chivalrous lover, whose bravery was in due time rewarded by the possession of her, who, when in peril, aroused in him the bold resolve of rescuing her or of perishing in the attempt. The hearty blessing invoked on the young couple by the Scout after the ceremony, and the honest sincerity with which he addressed the bridegroom, fully evinced his satisfaction on the occasion.

"James, my boy," said he, grasping his hand, "I told you you should have her, and I am more proud to receive you as a son than if you were the king's own, with all his grandeur and gold, for I know you are worthy of the gal; and may she make you as good a wife as I am sartain you will be to her a kind husband."

CHAPTER IX.

IT was but a brief time ere the services of the Scout were again called in requisition. Indeed, during that cruel war he seldom remained idle. Wherever was the point of danger, there was the Scout sure to be found, battling the common foe. The butchery of his sister was never forgotten, and whenever a savage fell beneath his unerring rifle, his exclamation, "One more drop atoned for," evinced a determination to fulfil to the letter, if possible, the threat called forth by a sight of his kindred's blood, — "A life for a drop!"

Shortly after the rescue of his daughter, he was called upon by a messenger from a small settlement a few miles distant from Falmouth, now the flourishing town of Saccarappa. He was informed that a band of savages had the night previous attacked and burnt the house of a Mr. Warren, who was severely wounded, and that his two daughters, just verging into womanhood, were carried into captivity, for whose rescue his assistance was invoked. The Scout needed no urging, but immediately accompanied the messenger to Saccarappa, whence, after gathering all the particulars of the attack and looking around him in search of a trail, he started in pursuit of the captors. He would allow no one to accompany him, saying that he should undoubtedly fall in with some who had already started ; for, as soon as the fact became known of the captivity of the maidens, a hot pursuit was made by such as could by any possibility leave their households.

Towards the close of the following afternoon two young men were seated upon a little knoll amidst a dense forest. They were fine, hardy-looking fellows, with well knit joints and brawny muscles, evidently inured to the toils and hardships of a new country. They were armed with muskets, and each wore a hunting-knife in his belt, their dress and equipments showing that they were out on no common errand. They had started with others after the savages, but their eagerness and activity had led them far in advance of their companions.

At the time we have introduced them to the reader they had come to a halt, after a fatiguing and vain search for the trail of the enemy. They had kindled a fire for the purpose of cooking the evening meal, and had been for a time resting on the small knoll, consulting in regard to their future movements, when a slight rustling in the woods attracted their attention and caused them to spring to their feet in a hostile attitude.

They had barely time to assume a defensive position, when, from a clump of bushes near which they had kindled the fire, and which was sending up thick curls of smoke, the tall form of a man dressed in the garb of a hunter suddenly emerged. Scarcely glancing at the startled young men, he hastily strode toward the burning pile, and in a moment the smoking embers were trampled beneath his feet.

"What on 'arth possessed you? are you stark, staring mad, youngsters?" exclaimed the intruder, as he ground the last expiring ember beneath his heel.

"Why, Joe, what are you about? you have spoilt our supper," said one of the party, stepping forward.

"And saved your scalp, mayhap, young man!" returned the hunter, whom our readers will recognize as the Scout.

"I don't see," said the first speaker, not relishing the idea of losing his evening meal, "how the fire you have so unceremoniously extinguished was to endanger us."

"That's all owing to your ignorance, Jim Smith. When you've lived in the woods as long as I have, you will have l'arnt something, boy, that you don't find in the books."

"But what harm could the fire do?" asked Smith, in a more conciliatory tone.

"The fire is harmless, youngster: 'tis the smoke that might play the mischief."

"I cannot perceive how," rejoined the young man, inquiringly.

"That's 'cause you don't know. Why don't you shout aloud? why don't you discharge your rifle in the air? Tell me that."

"That would be madness indeed, surrounded as we are by the Indians."

"Do you think, boy, the red-skins hain't eyes as well as ears? Look up, youngster; don't you think that that smoke-wreath whiffling over the top of yonder pine is as good a signal as the crack of a rifle? I

13*

saw it a mile off, and there are sharper eyes prying about the woods than mine, I consate."

The truth at once flashed upon the minds of the young men. They saw their folly, and the superior wisdom of the new-comer.

"You are right, Scout," remarked the other and elder of the party; "it was blind in us; but it has served us one good turn, in directing your steps hither."

"I was on your trail, youngsters, and should have found you out sooner or later. But this is no place to waste our time in. There may be others directed here whose company might not be quite so welcome as mine. Shoulder your traps, my young friends, and be off. Here, step lightly along this trunk until you reach the ledge of rocks yonder; don't turn so much as a leaf, if you can help it; and mind and keep the sun over your right shoulder as you go along."

"Are you not going with us, Joe?" remarked Smith, as he prepared to obey the directions.

"Sartainly, sartainly; what am I here for? I shall overtake you before night closes in; but I want to leave a trail in another direction, to draw off the sarpents, if so be they should come here. Keep along the rocks and ledges as much as you can, and mind and keep your tongues still. 'T is a bad member, and breeds a deal of mischief, in the woods as in the world!"

So saying, the Scout moved off in a contrary direction, leaving a well-defined trail behind him.

It was fortunate for the young men that they had been overtaken by the Scout, for, as we have said, their search in discovering the direct route of the savages had been vain. As it happened, however, they had not deviated far from the course the enemy had taken. Before meeting with the Scout, they had been consulting about giving up the pursuit and returning home, but his presence gave them fresh ardor, and they now avowed their determination to continue on until they had rescued the captives or wreaked their vengeance on the captors.

Following the directions given, they proceeded on their way, passing silently and cautiously along, keeping the sun on their right cheek until it had disappeared from sight, and the woods began to grow dim in the coming shadows of night, when they came to a halt, anxiously awaiting the re-appearance of their sagacious leader. The wary movements of the Scout had impressed them more thoroughly with the danger that surrounded them, and rendered them doubly watchful. Keeping their weapons in readiness for immediate use, they scrutinized every thicket and rising knoll, fearful that they might conceal a foe, while every sound was listened to with breathless attention, as giving warning of the approaching savage.

There was no lack of courage betrayed by either of the young men; they were naturally brave and resolute, and would have met an open foe without shrinking. It was the sense of a hidden, unknown danger impending, which aroused their apprehension. The fast increasing darkness, the gathering gloom of the forest, heightened by the low, melancholy moan of the pines, with the occasional crashing of the fallen branches, caused probably by the passage of some denizen of the wilderness, frequently thrilled their hearts with a vague sense of fear, and made them long

for the presence of one whose sagacity and experience was to them an assurance of safety.

As the dusk of twilight deepened into the darkness
of night, and objects at a little distance one after
another disappeared from sight, they began to fear
that the Scout would be unable to find them in the
labyrinth of the forest. This conviction growing
every moment more strong, they thought it time to
make some disposition for passing the night in comfort and safety. As they were moving about for this
purpose, they were alarmed by the sudden appearance
of a man in their vicinity, whose noiseless approach,
coming ghost-like from the obscurity of the wilderness, induced them to spring simultaneously to where
they had deposited their arms, in the full expectation
of having to grapple with a deadly enemy. The long
rifle and gaunt figure, which a second glance enabled
them to recognize, as quickly undeceived them, and
hearty was the welcome with which they greeted their
ally.

"We were afraid you had missed us," said one of
the young men, "and were about preparing a place
for rest."

"Whist! whist! speak low," said the Scout, in a
subdued voice. "'Tis an hour when sound travels fast
and far, and there may be those within earshot, — ha!
look to your arms, youngsters!" he exclaimed, in a
more energetic tone, without raising his voice, at the
same time kneeling behind the trunk of a fallen tree.

The cause of the alarm was a sudden rustling and
crackling of dry leaves in the distance, as by the
approach of some one. The young men followed the
example of their leader, crouching beside him, ready

for action. The noise grew louder and louder as the disturber drew near, which apparently broke through the bushes and underbrush violently, and with no attempt at concealment.

" 'T is some pesky varmint," whispered the old man. " The red-skins are too cunning to make such a rumpus as this. I 've seen 'em at all times," he continued, suffering his rifle to rest carelessly on the tree, as if satisfied that no danger was to be apprehended; " I 've been with 'em in peace and in war, when their blood was up and when cool, and they 're always the same, creeping along with the same desateful, sarpent-like motion. They 're wary critturs, and dreadful loath to leave a trail even for friends to follow. Hist! there it comes. 'T is a she panther, about the wickedest thing to be found in the woods, of the four-footed kind."

As the Scout spoke, one of those formidable animals, a huge panther, with eyes glaring like balls of fire, passed by an opening a short distance on their right, on a half-trot, half-leap, crashing through the obstacles in its path, as if they offered no impediment to its speed.

" If 't wan't for the enemy I 'd stop the tarnal crittur's frisking," said the Scout, gazing in the direction it had taken, " for I owe 'em a grudge. They 've no more marcy than a red-skin, and I shall carry the marks of their claws to my grave, if so be I find one."

" Have you any doubts in regard to that, Scout ? " asked one of his companions.

" Sartainly I have, boy. Where the tree grows, there it falls and rots; and so it is with most people burrowed in towns; there they are rooted and die, and the churchyard grows fat. But when a marciful Providence sees fit to call me, there 's no saying where I may be found. I 've a strange liking for the woods, and I should wish to rest in their solitude, with the thick boughs waving their green arms over me, and the leaves rustling and playing near. It would seem more nat'ral like. I do not hate my kind, the Lord above knows that; but I have always fancied being alone, on the chase or trail, and when I die, if so be it is his will, I would rather my dust should not mingle with the churchyard folks'. But this is a subject to be thought of in secret, and not babbled idly about. It is time we should be thinking of sleep. My mind misgives me that we have a long trail before us, and we must be astir 'arly."

So saying, the three disposed of themselves for the night, taking care effectually to guard against a surprise, either from the prowling beast of the forest or the lurking savage.

CHAPTER X.

By the first glimmer of day the old Scout was on the move. Without disturbing his still sleeping companions, he glanced cautiously around him, shook the old priming from his rifle and reprimed it, inspecting carefully the lock and barrel, eyeing and fondling it as if it were a thing to return his affection, after which he glided stealthily into the surrounding forest.

An hour, perhaps, passed away, during which the

young men had got astir, and were wondering at the disappearance of their guide, when he returned, and, in a cheerful tone, exclaimed, —

"Wal, I 've got a track of the varmints! Come, boys, we 've no time to lose: we 'll eat as we go along. There 's a fine spring — God's blessing in the wilderness — just out yonder, which will sarve to wash down the dry bread and meat." And, leading the way, he branched suddenly off from the course they had been pursuing, until, after half an hour's rapid travelling, they struck, as the Scout said, the trail, when they again changed the direction of their route.

To the young men the course they were now pursuing was quite as blind as ever. A dense wilderness surrounded them, and, though they followed their leader with an undoubted confidence in his knowledge, they saw nothing in the appearance of things which afforded the least clue to the direction to be followed. After a while, one of them remarked, inquiringly, that he could detect no signs of a trail.

"Why, youngster," replied the Scout, " 't is as plain as dame Rawson's face, and that I consate is the plainest thing in the settlement. Here, my boys," he continued, as he stopped in his rapid walk, "may be you can l'arn something that will be sarviceable to you hereafter. Look about you now, look close and sharp, and see if you cannot find out the trail."

The young men stepped forward and examined carefully every inch of the place, scrutinizing closely the bushes and fallen leaves, but all to no purpose; and they acknowledged that they saw nothing to denote the track of the savages. The Scout gave a low chuckle, evidently pleased at their failure.

"Wal, wal, 't is unaccountable what ignorance there is in the world. But man 's never too old to l'arn, they say. Here you, Hugh Sands, step this way a little; now stoop down and observe these leaves. Don't you see how this one is pressed down flat to the 'arth, and that one is bent over and broken, and all along, just the length of a man's foot, they don't look like these out here, which lay nat'ral like, just as they fell from the tree, one on top t' other, carelessly? Now run your eye along about a step and you will diskiver the same appearance. There you see the grass is slightly bent forward, while the other stands up straight. Then, ag'in, observe these bushes, this broken twig and that turned leaf: ain't it clear enough that something has brushed by them? These signs you can barely dis'arn, but I can read them as easily as I can your dad's grocery sign in the settlement, 'specially now while the dew is on."

"And here is something plainer still," said Smith, who had gone a little ahead, and who now returned, holding in his hand a comb, dropped either accidentally or designedly by one of the captives.

Their guide needed not this assurance that he was on the right course, although the discovery seemed to animate his companions, who now pressed forward with renewed vigor.

It was at the close of the third day, and many a weary mile had the three passed over, following like hounds the tracks of the savages, that we again introduce our party to the reader. They had halted on the bank of a shallow river, the outlet of a large pond, which spread out before them, fringed on either hand as far as the eye could reach with a luxurious growth of bush and tree, the foliage of which bent over and coquetted with the crystal waters, seeming, in their placid repose, like a vast mirror framed with living green. From the signs around them they were convinced that they were in the close vicinity of the enemy.

After a short consultation, the Scout went forward to reconnoitre, leaving his companions in the dense woods which skirted the stream. Creeping along the edge of the forest, for he strongly suspected that the foe were on the opposite bank, the old man proceeded some way down the river, until the fast-fading twilight gave way to the duskiness of night. Feeling secure from observation, he then cautiously forded the stream, and, plunging into the opposite woods, directed his way to the outlet of the pond.

In the mean time the young men remained in their covert, waiting impatiently to learn the result of the Scout's movements. The thought that they were in the immediate neighborhood of a crafty and cruel foe, and that they might be shortly engaged with them in deadly conflict, was fraught with exciting interest. Their anxiety was not wholly unmixed with fear. They knew not the force of the band they were seeking, while their own weakness made their pursuit seem to them like temerity.

What if the Scout should fall? With their total ignorance of their course, and surrounded by an unsparing enemy, a sure death was in prospect. Still, they were not disheartened, and their resolve to rescue the captives at all hazards remained unshaken.

Two hours or more passed slowly by, and they sat in silence and darkness, the thick foliage shutting out

14

the light of the stars, and the dirge-like moan of the pines sounding mournfully in their ears, all tending to throw a deeper shade of gloom over their spirits. For some time they had thus sat, each busy with his own fancies, without a word being spoken between them. At last, in the far distance, the faint cry of a night-owl came from the opposite bank, causing them to start to their feet in a listening attitude. After a prolonged interval the same boding cry was repeated.

"That's the Scout's signal," said Sands, in a low, hurried whisper. "We must be on our guard. He has found them."

"Pray Heaven they may not detect him," said Smith, in a somewhat anxious tone.

"There is not much danger; the old fellow knows all their ways and is possessed of all their cunning. He will be here soon, and then comes the final tug."

According to previous directions, the young men now crept noiselessly down to the river's brink, which went brawling on its way, the white foam flashing out occasionally as it broke over the rocky shallows, then darting along a smoother current, until it was lost in the gloom of the forest, into which the dark stream glided like some huge serpent seeking a covert.

CHAPTER XI.

As the young men stood side by side, gazing thoughtfully on the rippling stream, a hand was laid on the shoulder of each, and a low voice whispered in their ears, —

"Hush! not a word. They are there. Follow me."

Turning, they followed the Scout, who crept softly up the stream until they reached the outlet of the pond, when, stealing round a jutting crag which effectually concealed them from the opposite shore, they halted, and, in a subdued tone, the Scout related his discoveries. "I have been among the sarpents, and, had it not been for the gals' safety, I would have crushed one of the reptiles, for I had him at my marcy. It was a sore temptation, I tell ye. There are but five of them; the rest have not arrived, or have gone off on some other diviltry. I saw the gals, too, and they seemed to be in pretty good case. Ah! that Kate is a bright one."

"Did you speak to her?" asked Sands, with a feeling and tone of deep interest.

"Speak to her! that would have been no easy matter, youngster, with two of the varmints within earshot. No, no, Hunting Joe is not a gossiping old woman; he is too old to run his head into such a trap."

"But you contrived to let her know that friends were at hand," rejoined Smith.

"Speak low, boy; the red-skins have quick ears, and sound travels pesky far and fast in a still night like this. 'Deaf in the world and dumb in the woods,' is a maxim I l'arnt 'arly in life. Yes, I let 'em know that the old Scout was on their trail."

"How did you manage it?" asked Smith.

"Wal, if you must know, and as we have a little time to spare, I'll tell ye." He then went on to state that, after creeping through the woods, and finding out that the Indians were there, and the position of the cap-

tives, he stole round to a clump of bushes directly
behind a small knoll on which they were seated.
"When I got there," said he, "I was within a few
feet of them; but 't was a dangerous job to attract
their attention, for I could see the dark reptiles coiled
round in the open space in front, ready for a spring.
The shaking of a limb or the snapping of a twig would
have aroused them. I had the comb you found with
me, and, by a slight throw, I tossed it into Kate's lap.
It struck the girl's hand, and I expected her surprise
would give the alarm; but, except a slight start, she
showed not the least consarn. Bending down her
head, she whispered a word or two to her sister, and
then secretly made a sign, giving me to understand
that all was right. Ah, she is a quick-witted crittur,
that gal," added the Scout, in conclusion, "and I 'll
save her, if I die for 't."

"Well, what plan have you fixed upon?" asked one
of the young men, as he concluded his narration.

The old man remained silent for a while, as if revolving the matter in his mind.

"It is a resky business, but I don't see as we can
do better," he at last said, as if speaking to himself.
"If you were as well acquainted with the woods as
I am," he continued, addressing his companions, "we
might creep among the enemy and take them by surprise, for they seem to be unsuspicious of an attack.
But there 's too much at stake, for, if they should be
alarmed, the gals would be tomahawked to a dead sartainty. It is my opinion that they will stay where they
be to-night, and start 'arly in the morning up the
lake, as I detected three canoes hid among the bushes.
Now, what I think on is this, to get possession of their

canoes, destroy one, let you have the second to bring off the young women in, and I will take the other, to act as sarcumstances may turn up."

"When shall we start?" asked Sands.

"It's about time to be moving, I s'pose," said the Scout. "The moon will be up in two or three hours, and we must get them out of their clutches before then."

So saying, he commenced stripping off his garments, adding, "To save a long tramp, I must take to the water. You will stay here till I come back. Don't move about, and, if you must talk, speak in whispers, for the slightest noise might betray us."

With this caution, having laid aside his garments, he entered the water, and in a moment was lost to sight, as he swam rapidly but noiselessly away, leaving scarcely a ripple in his wake.

The distance to the opposite shore was perhaps an eighth of a mile. With long, slow strokes the Scout urged his way through the placid waters, his head laid to the surface, at times floating motionless, while his searching glance and quick ear were on the alert; then propelling himself along with renewed caution, until he approached the opposite bank, which rose somewhat abruptly, covered with a dense growth of tall bushes. Gliding into their deep shadows, he soon found the objects of his search.

It required all the cunning and adroitness he was master of, after he had reached his prizes, to launch them in the water, fasten them together, and tow them from the dangerous neighborhood. Having got them afloat, he fastened them in a line, and hugging the deep shadows cast by the overhanging foliage, he went

14*

some distance up before he shot out into the bosom of the lake. Dipping his paddle so as not to disturb the quiet of the water, and crouching low in the canoe, he finally succeeded in transferring his prizes in safety to the spot where his young partisans were anxiously awaiting the issue of the adventure.

"Privateersmen talk of cutting out craft from under the guns of an enemy," said the Scout, in a jocose tone, as he deliberately ran his knife through the frail material of one of his prizes, which he had taken on shore, gashing large holes in various parts of its bottom: "can they boast of a better cutting out than this?" and he gave the finishing stroke to his work of destruction.

"Now, boys," he added, "see to your primings. Shake out the old ones, for the dews may have dampened the powder, and a flash in the pan may prove your death."

Having made every necessary arrangement in regard to their proceedings, the arms were deposited in the canoes, ready for use at a moment's warning, and they embarked, the Scout taking the lead.

"Follow me," said he, " and be careful of your paddles when you cross the pond. For the present we must drag ourselves along a piece under the shelter of these bushes. Don't hurry; move coolly and deliberately, and when you let go the branches, mind and not let them jerk back, but slip gently out of your hands."

With these whispered cautions the Scout forced his canoe close in with the bushes, dragging it carefully along, and followed by the young men, who were admonished from time to time, by expressive signals to be on their guard. For a long distance they proceeded in this manner, and so adroitly did the old man make his way that scarcely the motion of a twig or the rustling of a leaf betrayed his movements.

When he had at last reached what he considered a safe distance, he struck out into the lake with his paddle, and ere long, with his companions, reached the shelter of the foliage of the opposite side. Abandoning the paddles, they adopted the same method as at first, and by the aid of the pendent branches and the long grass, which in the occasional openings grew luxuriantly to the water's edge, they forced their light barks along.

At one of these openings, where the land sloped gradually to the lake, and at a short distance from the outlet, they stopped, and a brief consultation ensued.

"You will remain here," said the Scout to Smith, " while your companion will go part of the way with me to lead the gals to the place. When you get them on board, don't be flustrated. Bid them sit still, for these bark things are ticklish consarns; and when you get all ready, drag yourselves along as you came, until I come up with you. But, if I am long delayed, hide yourselves under that clump of young alders which I pointed out to you as we came along. The trailing branches will shelter you completely from sight. Have your thoughts about you, youngsters. I like your actions, — you 've behaved well thus far, sartainly. Don't spoil all now at the tug of the game; be cool, be cool!" And with this repeated warning, he stepped on shore, dragging his canoe into the grass, and then moved stealthily towards the foe, followed by Sands, who accompanied him a short distance, to the edge of a slight opening, where he beckoned him to stop, while he glided with a noiseless step into the open space, and disappeared behind a thick growth of bushes.

CHAPTER XII.

THE Indians had halted in a small opening in the forest, close by the outlet. In the full confidence that all danger from pursuit was over, they had relaxed from their usual watchfulness over their prisoners, and, instead of keeping them by their sides, as they had heretofore when they slept, they had allowed them to sit apart; taking the precaution, however, to bind their ankles with thongs. In the early part of the night the sisters, as if worn out with fatigue, had feigned deep slumber. Indeed, the distance they had travelled, and the almost constant watchfulness of the preceding nights, rendered rest absolutely necessary to their worn frames. But the intimation they had received of friends lurking near aroused them. To lull all suspicion, however, they thought it best to counterfeit sleep; and so satisfied were their captors of its reality, and that it would remain unbroken, and so confident that they were entirely beyond the reach of the whites, they yielded themselves unreservedly to that repose which, from what they had lately undergone, nature imperiously demanded.

On a little mossy knoll, wholly unsheltered from the heavy dews, the captives had thrown themselves, their deep, regular breathing betokening that their senses were locked in the deepest slumber, and that they were totally oblivious to the scene around them; and yet there was not the fall of a leaf, the snapping of a twig, the faint chirp of a half-aroused bird, the low sighing of a passing breeze rustling in the tree-tops,—not one of the many sounds that disturb the silence of night in a forest,— that was not heard by those apparently unconscious sleepers.

Since the early evening, when the Scout had ap-prized them of the presence of a friend, their bosoms had throbbed with contending emotions, hope and fear alternately predominating. As the night wore away, and no further signs of rescue appearing, their anxi-ety increased. More than once was the head of Catharine, the eldest, lifted from its mossy pillow, while she cast furtive glances around, and eagerly lis-tened to catch some sign of deliverance. Who they were that had dogged them to this place she knew not, but her heart told her that one at least of the party was her cousin, Sands, while Anna, the younger, as naturally believed that young Smith was among them.

While they were thus waiting in anxious solicitude, counting the moments by the beating of their own hearts, and almost despairing of an attempt being made that night, a faint sound in the bushes behind them reached their ears, causing them simultaneously to hold their breath as they listened eagerly for its repetition. All, however, remained as still as before, and they came to the conclusion that their ears de-ceived them.

"I certainly thought I heard something, Anna,"

whispered the elder, placing her mouth close to her sister's ear.

"So did I," added her companion, in a tremulous tone.

"Listen again, dear Anna —— "

"Hist!" came a low warning at the speaker's ear, interrupting her. "Be silent as death; do not move; you have friends at hand!"

"Be calm, Anna," whispered Catharine in a joyful tone to her startled sister; "it is Hunting Joe; I know his voice. We are safe!"

Even as she spoke the tall form of the Scout rose in front of the bush behind them, just discernible in the gloom of night. Making a sign of silence, he stooped down and cut the thongs that bound them, and then whispered, "On your lives, gals, be wary! Raise yourselves — hush! hush!" he hastily added, "don't stir, nor breathe!"

The caution thus suddenly given was occasioned by the movement of one of the savages, a rod, perhaps, in front, who turned heavily on his leafy couch, muttering rapidly the unintelligible jargon of his tribe. For a moment the three remained breathlessly listening.

"The varmint is only dreaming," at length said the Scout, in a tone of relief. "Now up and follow me."

The captives did as they were bid, moving with the greatest caution, until they reached the narrow passage in the bushes which led from the opening, when the Scout stopped, but motioned them forward.

"I must stay here," he whispered to them, as they crept by him, "to guard your retreat; you will find a friend close at hand. Bid him be careful, and remember that you are treading among sleeping adders; if you arouse them, it is death!"

The two maidens nodded assent, and, passing on, soon cleared the clump of bushes, when a well-known voice, recognized, though barely audible, greeted Kate, and a well-known hand grasped hers, and guided them along the mazy wilderness to the canoe, in which they hastily seated themselves. Hardly had the trembling girls embarked in the frail vessel, and ere the young men, who followed the counsel of the Scout by acting coolly and deliberately, had got fairly arranged for a start, they were alarmed by hearing, from the direction whence they had come, the expressive exclamation used by the red man when suddenly surprised, followed by a shrill whoop which rang wildly through the forest. Grasping the pendent branches, the young men drew the canoe swiftly along, scarcely breathing until they had left the dangerous spot far behind. Their exertions were still further stimulated by soon hearing the sharp crack of a rifle, followed by a yell so wild and unearthly that the blood of the fugitives chilled as it swelled on the ear.

"It was the Scout's rifle," said Sands, in a panting voice; "one of the savages has bit the dust!" and with an extra effort he sent the canoe with accelerated speed through the water.

Not another word was uttered until they reached the spot designated by the Scout, where they drew the canoe carefully under the clustering foliage, which bent over so as to completely conceal them from the most prying observation. Here they felt comparatively safe, and in low whispers congratulated themselves on their escape.

Their thoughts and anxieties were now centred on the Scout, for they felt that their ultimate safety depended on his skill. They had not been long in their covert when they detected the sound of a faint ripple in the water, and almost at the same moment a canoe shot swiftly by their hiding-place. It contained but one person, and as it passed, a low whisper reached their ears,—"Be still, for your lives!"—and man and bark were lost in darkness.

But a minute or two intervened, when they were again startled by the hurried dip of paddles, and presently another canoe, containing four savages, darted by farther out in the lake, and shooting off at an angle greatly favorable to the Scout if he continued to hug the bank. With feelings of most intense anxiety the fugitives awaited the issue of events.

CHAPTER XIII.

An hour perhaps passed by, although to the party in waiting it appeared an age, during which they listened eagerly, dreading every moment they should hear the savage yell of triumph. Motionless and silent they sat, filled with that sickly apprehension which springs from the consciousness of an impending though unknown danger, more trying to the nerves than a bold confronting of the evil. Everything conspired to heighten their gloom,—silence and the darkness of the tomb, doubts and fears, and racking suspense.

Sitting thus in dejected reverie, a slight jar, from

some object striking their frail bark, sent a thrill of alarm through each breast.

Ere they recovered from the sudden shock, the Scout, leaping lightly from his own canoe, stood among them.

"Seize your paddles, boys," he whispered hurriedly; "the moon is up, and this is no place for us. I've sarcumvented the varmints this time;" and he gave utterance to the peculiar chuckle with which he was wont to express gratification.

Without further remark he forced the canoe from its concealment, and, following down the banks, in a short time arrived near the outlet, where he struck out on the lake for the opposite shore. By this time the moon had got above the trees and threw a pillar of light along the lake's tranquil bosom.

"Now dip in your paddles, lads, for your lives," said the Scout, as he applied himself to the same task. "Dip easy, and don't splash the water about. If we can reach the opposite bank, we shall stand a smart chance of getting out of their clutches. Keep up your spirits, gals: a marciful Providence will deliver you out of the hands of the spoilers! I tried hard," he continued, "to get to you before the moon was up, but the reptiles dogged me so close — ha! they have discovered us!"

As he spoke, a loud whoop rang over the still waters from up the lake, and in the distance, where the rays of the moon glimmered on the surface, the canoe of the savages was seen in hot pursuit.

"Don't be flustrated, youngsters," exclaimed the old man, in a loud, encouraging tone. "Put in all you know, a long sweep and a strong one, and we will dis-

15

tance them yet!" and, exerting all his skill and
strength, the canoe literally leaped over the water.

But on and on came the pursuers, evidently gaining fast upon them, and uttering yells of triumph as
the distance between them lessened.

"Ha!" ejaculated the Scout, as his quick eye detected their approach, "we must put a stop to this.
Don't lag, boys," he added, as he drew in his paddle.
"We 'll see if there 's any vartue in this;" and, seizing
his long rifle, he turned carelessly in his seat, raised the
weapon to his shoulder, and drew the trigger. The
flame leaped forth, a wreath of smoke floated astern,
the surrounding banks gave back echoes of the loud
report, and high above them arose a frightful shriek
from the canoe in chase, which fully indicated the
fatality of the hunter's aim.

"Now we are on more equal tarms," was his cool
remark, as he exchanged his rifle, after carefully reloading it, for the paddle.

Burning to revenge their comrade's death, the Indians seemed endowed with additional strength, and
their light canoe flew over the lake with the swiftness
of a swallow. Had the distance to the shore been
greater, or had not the death of one of their party
thrown them into a momentary confusion, the fugitives would inevitably have been overtaken, and have
encountered the fatal struggle in a situation in which
the foe would have had them at great advantage.
Fortunately, the lake at this place was narrow, and,
panting with exertion, the pursued reached the land
some rods in advance of the savages.

"Smith, look to the gals!" shouted the Scout, leaping to the shore, rifle in hand, followed by Sands.

"Get 'em out of harm's way. Sands and me will take care of these water-snakes!"

Yelling with rage as they saw them land, the savages swept madly on, blind to everything, thinking of nothing but to wreak vengeance, deep and deadly vengeance, on the pale-faces. The Scout and his young companion were on the bank, which rose gradually from the water's edge, the weapon of the latter resting on the trunk of a fallen tree, behind which he kneeled.

"Mind your aim, youngster. Wait for the word. Take the for'ard one; you can bring him down easier. Don't be skeared at their bellowing, 't is the crittur's natur'."

Raising his rifle slowly, as if on an ordinary occasion, the Scout gave the signal, and the reports of the two pieces were almost simultaneous. When the smoke cleared away, the Indian in the bow of the canoe was seen standing with uplifted paddle, brandishing it with wild gestures in the air like a war-club; then, giving a piercing howl, he sprang in the direction of the shore. There was a heavy plash, a momentary struggle, a groan, and the bright water closed over the sinking savage. A second glance showed the form of another in the stern of the canoe, the head lying over the gunwale, motionless and ghastly.

"That finishes two of the varmints," exclaimed the Scout, bringing the butt of his piece to the ground in the act of reloading it; "now for the other."

But, before the words were fairly out of his mouth, a shot from behind a tree, a little distance to the left and nearer the shore, where Smith had stationed himself, had finished the work of destruction, and the little, light bark rocked violently for a while on the agitated

waters, disturbed by the struggles of its surviving'
occupant as he fell headlong into the lake.

For some time the party on shore stood gazing in
silence upon the place where this scene of death had
transpired, until the waters regained their placidity,
and the frail canoe floated in the quiet moonlight, a
lone and deserted thing, to be driven with its ghastly
freight whither the winds should list. Feeling the
insecurity of the present neighborhood, preparations
were made to leave it, and in a short time the party
were moving slowly and silently through the forest
toward their distant home.

We will not follow them on their fatiguing and
dangerous journey. Enough that the settlement was
at last safely reached, and the captives restored, like
those from the dead, to their friends, who welcomed
them and their deliverers with tears and thanks-
givings.

CHAPTER XIV.

In detailing the exploits of our hero, we do not aim
to present a connected story. We purpose only to
portray him in various situations in which his peculiar
characteristics will be best brought out, and merely to
draw attention for the time being to the characters
introduced in connection with him. Instead of a continuous story, our object is rather to offer a series of
sketches in which the Scout plays the prominent part.
With this explanation (which of right should have
been made at the outset), we proceed.

The scene to which we would now direct the attention of the reader is one that we delight to contemplate, — a dense forest in the depth of summer. Through the thick foliage of the overhanging branches the sunbeams fall with a chastened and grateful light. The birds have chanted their matin songs, and all is hushed save the dreamy murmur of the pines, so like the voice of the sea, and the slight rustling of the tree-tops, amidst which a gentle breeze plays with the rustling leaves. A little green opening spreads out before us, a dimple in the wilderness, into which the rich sunlight falls with brilliant effect, flashing upon a thread of a stream, which winds itself quietly away into the heart of the forest.

> " Noiselessly around,
> From perch to perch, the solitary bird
> Passes ; and yon clear spring, that, 'midst its herbs,
> Wells softly forth, and visits the strong roots
> Of half the mighty forest, tells no tale
> Of all the good it does.''

Seated on a small hillock covered with a velvet-like moss, beside the stream, was the well-known form of the Scout. At the time of his introduction to the reader, he was making his morning meal of dried bear's meat and coarse rye bread, washed down by the crystal water that rippled by his side; and, from the zest with which he applied himself to his task, there could be no doubt, though humble his fare, never a pampered epicure ate his with better relish.

"A fresh bite of ven'son would n't go bad this bracing morning," he muttered, in soliloquy, as he vainly essayed to tear asunder a tough, sinewy morsel he had in hand; "but there are so many of these out-

15*

lying reptyles abroad, it would be resky kindling a
fire, or I'd have a steak. Wal, a good appetite is a
blessed thing, though 't is apt to be pesky oncomfort-
able when the pouch is empty. I've seen the time,
many's the day, when an unripe root or a green yarb
tasted sweeter than the juiciest cut of the tenderest
buck. Hi! hi!" he continued, with a peculiar chuckle,
"I shan't soon forget the tussle with the b'ar. 'T was
pesky hard telling which was the hungriest, and 't was
a mere sarcumstance, the turn of a leaf, whether I
should eat him or him me! · But beast natur' ain't
equal to human natur', and I won the fight, although
't was tarnal poor picking I got from his bones. It
tasted right good, though. Ah, Brave!" he exclaimed,
as a fine mastiff burst through a thicket a little in
front of the Scout, and stood in a bristling attitude,
facing the quarter whence he came, "Ah, pup, is there
any mischief brewing? Do you smell a red-skin?"

The mastiff gave a low growl, at the same time
showing by a curl of his upper lip a most formidable
set of teeth. The Scout sprang quickly to his feet,
loosened his hunting-knife, and, grasping his rifle,
stood in a listening attitude. The dog gazed awhile
wistfully in his master's face, then gave a low whine,
as if he would warn him of approaching danger.

"I understand, I understand, pup," said the old man,
walking to the side of his shaggy companion and patting his broad breast. "The varmints are abroad.
Whist! whist!" and he bent his ear to the ground.

"This way, Brave," said the hunter, in a subdued
tone, as he rose from his stooping posture. "They've
been working mischief in the settlements the past
night. We must contrive to get on their trail, for 't is

more than likely they have got some poor captive who may need our sarvices. This way, pup." And, turning to the left, he entered with a quick though noiseless step into the depths of the forest, and man and dog were in a moment lost to sight.

But a few minutes transpired after their disappearance when stealthy steps were heard in the woods, and presently a file of Indians passed with a quick pace through the foot of the little opening. At the belts of the two foremost hung the trophies of their night's work. Dangling from each was a bloody scalp, the long, pliant locks of one proclaiming the sex of the victim, and the short, abundant ringlets of the other showing that it came from the head of quite a young child. So cautious were the movements of the band, none but a practised ear could have detected the slight noise made as they glided past.

A quarter of an hour perhaps had elapsed after the disappearance of the savages, when the Scout, followed by his dog, emerged from the forest into the opening. His quick eye soon detected the trail of the Indians. Stooping down, he surveyed it with close attention, following it along the opening with the most careful scrutiny.

"There are five of the varmints," he muttered to himself, as, satisfied with the examination, he at last stood erect. "The odds are ag'in me; but that's nothing; I've sarcumvented a larger number. Come, Brave." And, followed by the faithful mastiff, who seemed to understand every motion of his master, he crept with a cat-like pace on the trail of the savages.

Leaving the Scout on the trail of the Indians, the reader will accompany us to another scene. It is a harrowing one; a scene, alas, too frequently recorded in the early annals of New England. A settlement on Casco Bay, not far remote from the ancient town of Falmouth, is the spot to which we would direct his attention.

North Yarmouth, now rich in resources and a popular seat of learning, in 1746 consisted of but a cluster of small houses. The first settlers of this place came principally from Lynn, Mass. They had formed quite a settlement here for the times, and had lived in undisturbed security until the period of our story, when the war broke out, which wrought terror and alarm in all our eastern settlements.

Willis, in his History of Portland, alluding to this war, remarks of the Indians: "This subtle and vindictive enemy being again let loose from all restraint, started up from their swamps and morasses, harassing the whole line of our settlements, and committing depredations upon the undefended plantations. * * * They hovered about the town all the summer, seizing every opportunity to plunder property and take captives or destroy life. * * * The people here were kept in constant agitation during the season by these repeated depredations; and the terror was more lively, as it was caused by an enemy who could not be confronted, and whose secret and sudden visitations were marked by desolation and blood."

One night in midsummer the few inhabitants of North Yarmouth were aroused from their slumbers by the glare of a burning dwelling, which stood a slight distance away from the settlement, near the edge of the forest, and which was occupied by a family named Greeley; and, as they rushed trembling

to their doors, wild, frenzied shrieks rose piercingly
on the night air from the scene of conflagration.
While those agonizing cries were ringing in their
ears, a terrific war-whoop shook the air, and sent a
thrill to the heart of every listener. That fearful
whoop, the exulting shout of demons, revealed all to
the trembling settlers. Well they knew that the dreadful deed was accomplished; that vain would be their
attempts to succor. Still, there were brave hearts in
that hamlet, and with one impulse nearly every male
inhabitant rushed towards the burning building.

They were, indeed, too late! By the light of the
blazing habitation the body of Mr. Greeley was found,
his skull cleft in twain by the fatal tomahawk, and his
scalp gone, and, in close vicinity, the bodies of his
wife and young daughter, hardly yet stiffened in
death, their gory, scalpless heads revealing 'the heart-
sickening, merciless barbarity of the red man.

The darkness of the night, the uncertainty of the
number of the foe, and the deep horror which had
seized on those who gazed shuddering on the harrowing spectacle, debarred all pursuit. They knew it
would be vain; they knew that the swamps and the
tangled recesses of the forest afforded a complete
shelter to the foe, and they refrained; but, as those
hardy men stood grouped around the murdered victims, leaning on their guns, their deep breathing and
half-muttered exclamations told what thoughts of vengeance were stirring within them. A more mournful
task demanded their attention. Rude biers were constructed for the slain by the light of their late happy,
but now fast-consuming home, — their funeral pyre, —

and slowly and silently their mangled corpses were conveyed to a neighboring dwelling.

There was no more sleep in North Yarmouth that night. Tremblingly the terrified wife and child clung to the husband and father, as he detailed the awful scene he had witnessed, and repeated his vows of vengeance, while the thought that the fate which had befallen his neighbor might be wrought upon his own household, shook even his stout heart with a secret dread.

The morning sun of the 10th August, 1746, rose on a solemn and gloomy scene, so late one of undisturbed peace and comfort. Its light fell on cheeks blanched with fear, lips white and trembling, eyes red and heavy with watching and weeping, on moody brows and troubled hearts, on the charred and still smoking rafters of a recently happy home, and on the mangled corpses of a peaceful and unoffending household. A sad morning was that 10th of August in that remote settlement.

Early in the forenoon a messenger was despatched to Falmouth with the mournful tidings, and a company of men, commanded by a namesake and kindred of the writer,— somewhat of an Indian fighter in his day, — was immediately sent to the scene of action, to protect the inhabitants from further assault, and, if possible, to wreak vengeance on the blood-thirsty foe.

At that period every settlement had its "Block-House," so called,—a large building, composed of huge logs, and barricaded like a garrison. Into these in dangerous times the settlers would throng for refuge; and, frequently, within these crowded quarters they were compelled to remain for years, never venturing out unless with extreme caution, and always taking care to go completely armed. Often, during a protracted siege, were the inmates of these block-houses nearly reduced to famine, and rarely did it happen that they were not subjected to the most pinching want. Little conception have we of the trials and sufferings endured by the hardy pioneers of our towns and villages.

Having assisted the settlers in burying the dead and in removing their few effects to the block-house, and after seeing the women and children safe within its shelter, the company from Falmouth, reinforced by nearly the whole settlement, scoured the neighboring country in quest of the enemy. Their search was ineffectual. The spoiler had come, executed his bloody purpose, and vanished, like a demon of darkness. But the avenger was on his track.

CHAPTER XV.

WITH a slightly stooping gait, his long rifle at a trail, and his keen eyes fixed intently on the path he was pursuing, every displaced leaf, every depressed blade of grass, every bent twig, which none but an eye like his would have detected, served as a guide to the old hunter, who followed on the track of the savages with the unerring precision of the blood-hound on the scent. Occasionally he paused in his rapid walk, and, bending his ear to the ground, listened intently for a moment or two. During one of the pauses, he patted the shaggy sides of the mastiff, which closely followed in his footsteps, and addressed him in a low tone.

"They shall rue it, Brave! they shall rue it! 'Blood for blood,' says the good book, though the varmints are but heathens, and are ignorant of the Scripters! A woman and a child — ah, Brave! there's more marcy in a brute than in them reptyles. They came in the direction from Yarmouth, and those yaller ringlets, so much like twisted gold, were torn from the head of Ruth Greeley, poor thing! or I'm mistaken. But I'll revenge her, I'll revenge her, — if I die for't! Come, Brave," and the Scout resumed the trail with the same untiring pace.

Throughout the day he faltered not in the pursuit, making only a brief halt at noon by a spring-side, where he partook of the frugal fare he bore with him, which he shared with his faithful companion. As the day began to decline and the trail became more indistinct in the gathering darkness, the Scout stopped, and addressed his dog.

"Here, Brave," said he, pointing ahead, "it is your turn to take the lead; a dog's nose is better than a man's eye at this hour."

At the voice of his master the dog wagged his tail, as if assenting to the command, and, after snuffing along the path, as if to secure the scent, he turned his head, looking into the hunter's face, with an "I'm ready" expression about his eyes. The Scout nodded his head, the dog turned his, and, with his nose close to the ground, the sagacious animal trotted ahead, his master following unhesitatingly his lead.

An hour or more the two went silently on their path, by which time the woods had become so dark that more caution was necessary in keeping the track. Still the old man followed the dog with the utmost confidence, even when the route became wholly obscured. Once only did the dog show any signs of being at fault. Stopping suddenly in his path, and diverging first to one and then the other side of the course he had been following, he ran about for a few moments, snuffing the air and uttering a low whine. The Scout watched his movements with eager curiosity.

"Have you found it, Brave?" he at length whispered to the dog, who, having struck off at nearly a right angle, after running a short distance in that direction had returned on the trot to his master's side. The dog joyfully wagged his tail, and stood in an attitude evincing an eagerness to proceed. A word from his master, and he started forward, followed by the Scout, in a direction varying essentially from the one they had been pursuing.

"There," muttered the old man to himself, after they had got fairly started, "that 'ere pup knows more than ary two men in the settlement. 'Squire Hawkes, with all his law and larning, is a fool to him. They say these critturs have no souls, and can't reason. P'rhaps not, p'rhaps not; I can't say; but, to my thinking, when that dog dies, it won't be the eend on him! And as to his reason, I ain't so clear. I've argued many a tough case with him here in the woods, and I have l'arnt to give in to him, for, somehow or other, 't 'as always turned out that he was in the right, though *my* reason was ag'in him at first. I've my notion of these things," continued the Scout, shaking his head,—"I've my notion of these things, and 't will

16

be plaguy hard beating 'em out of me. Ha, Brave! what's in the wind?" he added, addressing the animal, who had again stopped, crouching before him.

A suppressed growl from the mastiff followed this inquiry.

"Do you smell the red-skins, pup?" said the Scout, as he knelt beside the dog in a listening attitude. He remained in this position some minutes, but apparently without detecting the cause of the dog's alarm.

"The dog's nose beats eyes and ears this time," said the old man, in a whisper, "but, I'll lay my life on 't, the varmints are not far off. Go, Brave, and find 'em out!"

The mastiff rose to his feet, and with a noiseless tread kept on his way, leaving behind his master, who, carefully putting aside the foliage of a clump of bushes near by, crept into their cover.

For nearly an hour he remained in his concealment, anxiously awaiting the return of the mastiff. He reposed unbounded confidence in this faithful creature, whose sagacity was truly wonderful. The animal was of a mixed breed, combining all the qualities which rendered him invaluable to a man like the Scout. The old man had reared and trained him from a pup, and such a perfect sympathy, as it were, existed beween the two, that neither of them seemed to find the least difficulty in making themselves mutually understood.

A light patter among the dry leaves at last announced the approach of the reconnoiterer, and presently he entered the covert, and rubbed himself fondly against his master's limbs.

"Did you diskiver 'em, dog?" said the Scout, stooping down to caress the faithful animal. As he reached out his hand for that purpose, it came in contact with the soft, silken ringlets attached to the scalp of the child, accidentally dropped by the Indian, perhaps, and which the dog had brought back as a proof of the success of his mission. Yielding it to his master, he gave a low, angry growl, and turned toward the quarter whence he had come.

"Ha! what have we here?" exclaimed the old man, as he received the fearful trophy. "The child's scalp, as I live! Poor thing, poor thing!" and a moisture gathered in his eye as he smoothed the dishevelled locks. "My little playmate Ruth, so lively and frolicsome, the pet of the settlement! And that sweet little cherub so cruelly butchered! Why didn't the 'arth open and swallow the fiends? Wal, wal, it's all right, I s'pose. His wisdom and His mercy are not to be questioned by us weak and short-sighted mortals; but——"

The Scout did not finish the sentence. The tone in which that "*but*" was uttered, however, told the stern purpose he had formed. Tightening his hunting-belt and repriming his rifle, he made a signal to Brave, who stood seemingly waiting his movements, and Scout and dog glided cautiously through the labyrinths of the wilderness, now dimly lighted by the rising moon, whose rays scarcely penetrated the deep foliage of the forest.

CHAPTER XVI.

THE scene was one of gloomy grandeur. It was deep midnight. Heavy masses of clouds floated athwart the heavens, through the rifts of which the rays of the moon occasionally fell in glimmering patches on a lake's broad bosom, which spread out like a vast mirror of steel in the uncertain light. Tall trees — the wide-spread oak, the straight and slender beech and walnut, the lithe ash, and the plume-like fir — formed a dense array in the background, while the borders of the lake were fringed with bushes and thickets of alders. At one point, the bank ran up slopingly to the forest's edge, which here receded for some distance, the huge trunks standing like massy columns in the great temple of nature.

Deep silence brooded over this little green plat,— silence and darkness, save when at times a light shiver ran among the trees, as a breath of air broke their repose, and an opening in the clouds illuminated the place with the moon's transient light. At such times might be seen, drawn up in a line on the grassy bank, their prows just at the water's edge, three canoes, ready to be launched at a moment's warning; and, clustered here and there, in groups, the dim forms of sleeping savages, to the number of ten or more.

It was the temporary encampment of a war party, each member of which was apparently buried in profound slumber. A moment, however, showed that there were sleepless eyes and listening ears in that seemingly slumbering band, for one of the number might have been seen half-raising himself, resting on an elbow, in an attitude expressing keen and vigilant watchfulness. For five minutes or more the attention of the aroused savage seemed riveted in a particular direction, as if his jealousy was awakened, his restless, burning glances striving to penetrate the dim recesses of the surrounding woods, and his ears keenly sensitive to the faintest sound that might be afloat. After a while, perfectly satisfied with his scrutiny, he let himself slowly down to his former recumbent position.

Keen as were the senses of the red man, confident as he was of his power of detecting the first approach of danger, there was one in his immediate neighborhood whose skill and cunning in wood-craft were more than a match for him. In an angle of the opening was a thick clump of bushes, and towards this, prone on the ground, the form of a man might have been seen, at the very time the awakened savage was peering around with those snake-like eyes of his, worming slowly along. Not the rustle of a leaf, not the crackle of a twig, marked the wily movement, which was so slow as to be almost imperceptible.

The covert was at last reached, and for nearly an hour the figure remained as if void of life. It was now that time of night when the senses are most deeply locked in slumber, the hour generally chosen by the savage for an attack. A dead silence reigned over the scene, broken only by the heavy breathings of the red men, all of whom, even to the sentinel, were buried in profound slumber. Slowly and cautiously the prostrate figure of the man in the bushes rose upright, revealing the well-known form of the Scout.

After peering around on the sleeping savages, the
16*

hunter gave a low, serpent-like hiss, and presently the shaggy mastiff was seen treading noiselessly over the dried leaves, just skirting the forest, to where his master was secreted, the cover he had chosen being directly opposite his entrance into the opening. Arriving at his master's side, the dog stood looking wistfully into his face.

Stooping down and patting the head of the faithful animal, the old man held the child's scalp towards him and whispered in his ear, " Go, Brave, and smell 'em out ! "

In obedience to the command, the sagacious creature started, picking his way slowly and carefully along among the sleeping foes, snuffing the air as he went, until at last he paused by the side of two of the savages who were huddled a little apart from the others, and, fortunately for the design of the Scout, in close proximity to the forest's edge.

What that design was, the reader has already surmised. It was to avenge the death of the mother and child. He had been prowling around the encampment for some hours, and had ascertained the number of the enemy. Their superior force, and the great risk of detection, would have deterred a less resolute man : but the Scout knew not fear, and, once his mind resolved, no danger, however threatening, would turn him aside.

" 'T is pesky risky business, I know," soliloquized the old man, " but little Ruth shall be avenged, — that I 'm detarmined on ! "

Leaving his rifle in the bushes, and unsheathing his long knife, he prepared himself for the fearful and desperate task he had undertaken.

" I 'd rather meet 'em in a fair fight," was the tenor of his thoughts as he left his covert and warily advanced to the spot where Brave stood motionless over the unconscious sleepers,—" I 'd rather meet 'em in a fair fight, with a tree atween us, when the quickest eye and the surest aim does the job. This stabbing 'em in their sleep is ag'in my white natur', and too much like the desateful red-skins. There 's a taint of murder about it I don't like;" and for a moment he paused and hesitated in his vengeful purpose.

Then came the thought of little Ruth, writhing under the merciless scalping-knife; then, too, came the thought of his own sister, who fell beneath the murderous tomahawk, and over whose mangled corpse he had sworn that for every drop of blood shed of hers a red man's life should be forfeited. Well had that oath been kept; and should he relent now, with some of the very tribe before him that committed that deed, perhaps the very perpetrator of it, his hands fresh-stained with innocent blood? The cruel foe were in his power, and the very ground seemed to cry, " Blood for blood!"

" They shall die!" exclaimed the Scout, in an excited voice, completely thrown off his guard as these recollections thronged upon him, and totally forgetful of his perilous situation and the extreme caution necessary.

He had nearly reached the side of the Indians when these fatal words were uttered, and barely had they escaped his lips, when he was made sensible of his imprudence, for the savage nearest to him sprang half way to his feet with an expressive " Ugh!" But ere he had got his footing the old man leaped upon him,

like a panther on its prey, and the next moment his
knife was buried deep in the heart of the savage. A
gurgling groan burst from the mortally-wounded foe,
as he fell heavily across his sleeping companion.
Quick as lightning, ere the one thus suddenly aroused
had a moment for thought or speech, the dog had him
by the throat, and only released his hold when the
formidable knife of the hunter, with one swoop, had
half severed the head from the body of the victim.

Ere the reeking blade was withdrawn from the gaping wound, a wild whoop rang through the air, and a
dozen dusky forms leaped, as if by magic, from the
sward.

Aroused suddenly from a deep sleep, the bewildered
savages made a simultaneous rush towards the canoes,
two of which were hastily launched upon the lake,
filled with the startled and but half-awakened party.
Taking advantage of the momentary confusion, with
his gaunt form bent nearly to the earth, the old man,
followed by his dog, glided into the clump of bushes
where he had left his rifle. Grasping his trusty
weapon, he plunged into the neighboring forest with
rapid strides, burying himself each moment deeper
within its intricate mazes. He knew there was no
time to be lost, and that all his cunning would be
required to extricate him from the peril which surrounded him. After the first alarm had subsided, he
was perfectly aware the foe would lose not a moment
in dogging his footsteps.

He was right, for, after the momentary confusion
was over, and perceiving no other demonstrations of
an attack, the canoes were paddled to the landing, the
savages leaped on shore, and immediately made prep-

arations for offensive operations. The discovery of
their fallen companions excited them to the highest
pitch of revenge, and called forth a fierce howl of
rage, which, reaching the ears of the Scout, added
wings to his flight. His first object was to put as
great a distance between himself and the foe as possible, hoping to escape them by superior speed, not
doubting they would follow his track, urged on by hatred and revenge.

With incredible rapidity he threaded his way
through the thick woods, every little while changing
the direction of his route in the hope of throwing his
pursuers off his trail. Occasionally he would cast an
upward glance through the opening foliage. To his
regret, he perceived the clouds which veiled the moon
were rolling toward the east, and ere long her light
would be entirely unobscured. In darkness he trusted
in a great measure for his safety, and, so long as
the moon remained eclipsed, he cherished the assurance that his trail would remain undiscovered, and
even its light, he hoped, would not be sufficient to
reveal it. Give him the hour or two until daylight,
and he had no apprehensions for his safety. Worst
come to worst, we cannot say that the Scout would
have experienced much alarm, for he had often been
thrown into equally dangerous positions, in which his
cunning and skill had alone proved his salvation. As
to fear, that was a feeling which never troubled his
breast.

The hopes that his trail would not be discovered
were soon dissipated, however, for, faintly echoing
through the forest, a furious yell swelled upon the

night air, which the old man well knew was one of triumph. The foe were on his track.

"The varmints have sharp eyes, for sartain!" he muttered to himself, as presently a second and more distinct peal of triumph broke the stillness of the forest. An angry growl from the mastiff followed.

"Do you hear 'em, Brave? the reptyles are arter us! But it will be pesky hard if we can't sarcumvent 'em with this start and in the dark. Wal, 't ain't much use to be hurried now, as I knows," he added, slacking his pace; "they will want a nose like your'n, pup, to follow us in all our twistings. There's a sense, now, that dumb crittur's got, which God has gi'n to no mortal, although I sometimes consate these 'tarnal redskins have it, they follow one up so in the night."

A whine from the dog interrupted the muttered soliloquy of his master. The Scout stopped and threw himself at length on the ground, with his ear just raised from the earth.

"You're right, pup!" said the Scout, springing to his feet and composedly patting his companion. "The varmints are swift on the foot, and are nigher than I'd an idee of. Nothing's left then but to play 'possum with 'em!"

He had just entered a more than usually heavy growth of wood, — huge trees, whose interlacing branches formed a dense roof of leaves overhead. After proceeding some distance, he retraced his steps with the greatest care, and, selecting a low-limbed oak, he placed his rifle in the branches, and, grasping a limb within his reach, swung himself into the tree. With the ease and agility of a youthful nut-gatherer he passed from tree to tree, striking off to the left. He

worked his way along in this manner for a number
of rods, until he reached a broad, shallow stream.
Letting himself down from his airy perch into the
centre of this rivulet, he gave a low signal, which in
a few minutes brought the faithful Brave to his side.
The two then commenced following up the rocky
channel of the stream towards the lake for perhaps an
eighth of a mile, when the Scout again struck into the
woods in a direction which led to the very point from
which he had first started.

"I reckon 't will puzzle the varmints some to follow
my trail now," chuckled the old man to himself;
"though, for the matter of that, many 's the time I 've
tracked their steps under water. But it wants broad
daylight to do that in, and a sharp eye to boot, which
every man hain't got. 'T is a gift of natur', as Parson
Smith on the Neck said the other day. A clever man
that Smith, and a right smart one, too, on'y he is too
oncommonly gifted in prayer, 'specially in a cold winter's day. His sarmonts is very edifying, so I 've
hearn tell; and he handles a gun well, too, that I
know, — a good shot, a good shot for a parson."

Muttering to himself in this manner, totally indifferent to the dangers which surrounded him, the old
man continued his way towards the encampment of
the savages, assured that, wherever they might look
for him, they would not suspect his presence in that
neighborhood, which they had faithfully scoured on
the first alarm; after which, his trail being discovered,
four of the runners had started off in pursuit.

CHAPTER XVII.

THE first faint streaks of light were " glimmering in
the dappled east;" the lake, unruffled by the gentlest
zephyr, spread out its broad, glassy bosom, dotted
here and there with little green islets; the bordering
trees and bushes hung motionless over the still waters
in which their foliage was perfectly reflected, tinging
the edges of the lake with a deep green, like colored
crystal, — the whole forming as quiet and beautiful a
picture as ever delighted the eye of a lover of nature.
The woods were vocal with the matin song of birds,
their rich and varied warblings blending into one glorious harmony, as if the feathered choir had, in the
language of Milton,

> "Cleared up their choicest notes in bush and spray,
> To gratulate the sweet return of morn."

Far off on the lake, just seen in the dawning light,
a solitary canoe glided slowly on its way. A short
time and it doubled a point of land and disappeared
from sight. Drawn up on the bank of the little opening already described were the two remaining canoes,
and under a neighboring tree, stark and ghastly,
stretched out the body of one of the savages who had
fallen beneath the knife of the hunter. The canoe
that had just been lost to view bore the body of the
other victim, a chief of some note, on its way to the
distant tribe to which he belonged.

From the belt of the corpse beneath the tree was
still suspended the woman's scalp, which had called
down upon the perpetrator of the foul deed the dire

vengeance of the Scout. The long dark hair lay in a heavy mass upon his breast, as if, even in death, he triumphed in this fearful trophy of his cruelty.

The plat was entirely deserted. Presently, however, the tall form of the Scout might have been seen emerging from the woods. Casting quick and searching glances in every direction, he advanced with the utmost caution towards his fallen foe, occasionally pausing, listening intently, and eyeing suspiciously every bush and tree, as if they concealed a lurking enemy. Stepping as if his lightest footfall would break the slumber of the dead, he reached at last the side of the corpse.

"The marciless wretches shan't have this to exult over," muttered the old man, as he disengaged the scalp from the belt and carefully placed it in his pouch, where the ringlets of mother and child mingled in striking though mournful contrast.

He had turned to retrace his steps, when a sudden thought seemed to occur to him.

"I'll do it to madden the varmints," he remarked, in an emphatic tone; "'t will ruck them up awfully, I calkerlate."

Unsheathing his knife and stooping over the head of the corpse, with a dexterity that evinced a practised hand, he removed the scalp from the dead Indian's head, and then, having placed it in the place so lately occupied by the scalp of the woman, he noiselessly left the spot. An angry growl from Brave quickened his steps. In a moment he was again in the woods and on his way to Yarmouth, skilfully and cunningly endeavoring to conceal his trail — no easy matter — from the prying eyes of the red-skins.

17

Ten minutes had barely elapsed, during which the Scout was making the best of his way toward the settlement, when behind him there arose a yell so wild and terrific, a howl so demoniacal and unearthly, that even the old hunter, to whose ears such sounds were familiar, could not conceal a slight shudder as it went echoing through the forest.

"Ha!" he ejaculated, as he increased his speed, "the reptyles have returned and diskivered the scalp, and it has touched the raw. The sooner I get out of this neighborhood, I consate, the better."

Throughout the day, hardly slackening his pace, he continued to thread the tangled forest, until, about nightfall, he approached the settlement of North Yarmouth. In the outskirts he fell in with a number of the scouting party from Falmouth, who detailed to him the atrocity that had been committed.

"Yes, yes," said the Scout; "I knew the reptyles had been at their bloody work in the settlements. Poor little Ruth!" And the old man's voice became choked with emotion.

"But have you not seen any signs of the Indians, Wier?" asked one of the party.

"I reckon I have, the varmints!" replied the Scout; and, opening his pouch, he handed the astonished speaker the two scalps.

"Why, what are these? Where did you get them?" were the eager exclamations of the party, as they closed round him and gazed on the gory trophies.

"They are proofs," replied the old man, with deep feeling, "that little Ruth and her mother are *avenged!*"

A few more questions and replies elicited the whole story; and, with a shout of triumph, the men escorted the Scout to the block-house, where his prowess was the theme of many an admiring tongue.

To escape the compliments showered upon him, the Scout modestly remarked, " I take no credit to myself; you may thank that 'ere dog for all this, for, if it had n't been for Brave, I should never have trapped the varmints."

It is unnecessary to add, that, ever after, the faithful Brave was a petted favorite in the settlement.

CHAPTER XVIII.

THE desolating war which so ravaged our early settlements, and in which the Scout took such an active part, was caused by the struggle between England and France for the supremacy in North America. The latter had enlisted in her cause, as we have already mentioned, the aborigines of the country, over whom, through the subtle agency of the Jesuits, she exercised a powerful influence. This harassing state of affairs continued until the conquest of Quebec, in 1759. The battle on the plains of Abraham, in September of that year, in which the rival commanders, Wolfe and Montcalm, sealed their loyalty with their lives, broke the power of the French in this country, and their copper-colored allies consulted their safety by submitting to the conquerors.

During the contest, while other settlements had been frequently wasted, Buxton, then known as Narragansett Township, No. 1, although a frontier town, had remained unmolested for a number of years. Yet the rumors of the devastating inroads on the neighboring townships kept the inhabitants in constant alarm. At the time the incidents took place which we are about to record, the hamlet consisted of only seven or eight houses. In one of these, which stood a little apart from the rest on the skirts of the forest, resided a family by the name of Woodman. The parents were somewhat advanced in age, and of their numerous children one only remained, a daughter, the pet of their old age.

Annie Woodman was a bright, lively girl of sixteen, whose neat, comely figure and winning countenance had made an impression on more than one youthful heart in the settlement. Though a pet, she was not a spoiled one, for she relieved her mother of a large share of the cares of the household. Frolicsome as a kitten in her playful moods, and at all times cheerful, she was the delight of her parents and the favorite of all. And truly was Annie worthy of this regard, for beneath her brilliant flow of spirits there existed a character full of lofty energy and replete with tenderness. Unharmed by the excessive affection lavished upon her, she promised in the development of her powers to combine all those graces of mind and heart which form the perfect woman.

It is not our purpose, however, to give the entire history of Annie at this time. We have given a slight portrayal of her person and disposition merely to awaken the interest of the reader in her behalf, while we relate a single passage in her early life.

At the close of an autumnal day, shortly after the events recorded in the previous chapters, Mr. and Mrs. Woodman were seated by their open door, watching for the return of Annie, who had gone in the early part of the afternoon on a visit to a friend, living about an eighth of a mile distant. It was now some time past the hour fixed for her return, and her parents sat wondering at her prolonged absence. As the sun disappeared and the twilight deepened, their wonder grew into anxiety, and their eyes were more frequently bent upon the grassy road which opened through a dense grove of pine in the distance, whence they looked for her coming.

Still deeper grew the twilight, and still no Annie came. Her unusually protracted absence at last excited the alarm of her parents. Could she have been beset on her way by some wild beast of the forest? This was the first thought suggested; for, though a general apprehension prevailed on account of the savages, yet this township had been so uniformly exempted from their attacks that no particular alarm was felt in regard to them. Filled with terror at the idea suggested, the old man took his gun and hastened down the road, closely scrutinizing each side of the path, dreading at each step that he might detect something to confirm his fears, — some fragment of her dress, — perhaps her mangled corpse. He passed through the pine growth without discovering any trace of his child, and, hurrying along with a mind somewhat relieved, he at last reached the house of his neighbor. The tidings he here received augmented his fears a thousand-fold, and nearly prostrated him in despair. He learned that Annie had started for home nearly two hours previous. Her friend accompanied her part of the way, and parted

17*

with her at the entrance of the pine grove, as the
woods were called.

As soon as her absence was made known an intense
excitement prevailed. An anxious but fruitless discussion took place as to the cause of her absence.
Was it not probable she had left the beaten path for
the more shady woods, and loitered by the way, and
might she not have reached home after her father
had left? There was a bare probability that this
might be the case; still, so slender was it deemed,
that, while a man was despatched on horseback to
ascertain the fact, two others started off to arouse
the settlers.

The man despatched to Mr. Woodman's soon returned, but he brought no tidings of the missing one;
and in a short time six or seven of the inhabitants
had assembled, each with his gun, ready with his
service. By this time it had grown somewhat dark,
although the twilight rendered objects still visible at
quite a distance.

The agony of the father would hardly permit him
to wait for the brief consultation that took place, in
order to facilitate a plan of search. With a wild, hurried step, he paced the opening in front of the house,
unable to suppress the moans of anguish that burst
from his lips. "My child! My dear Annie!—lost!
lost!" were his broken exclamations. "O God, spare
me this crushing trial! Leave me not childless in my
old age!" and, wringing his hands, he continued to
stride in front of the dwelling, his haggard face and
quivering lips proclaiming, more strongly than language could express, the depth of his despair.

It was at length decided that the party should pro-

vide themselves with torches and make a circuit of
the forest, each man having his particular beat, which
he was carefully to explore. Certain signals were
agreed upon in case of any discovery, and a rallying
point assigned where all should meet when the search
was over. Mr. Woodman, whose advanced age rendered him susceptible to fatigue, and who had become
completely exhausted by excitement, was induced to
return home, where indeed his presence was greatly
needed, to comfort and console his aged and well-
nigh distracted partner.

Just as the party were starting on their expedition,
a loud holloa from some one at a distance caused
them to look back. A tall figure, just discernible
afar off, was seen hastening towards them with rapid
strides. Presuming it to be one of the settlers
coming to assist them, they were about to resume
their way, leaving word for him to follow, when one
of the party, a young man by the name of Elden,
whose feelings seemed deeply enlisted in the affair,
exclaimed, with a joyful voice,—

"Wait, wait! it is the Scout!"

At the name of the Scout the whole party immediately came to a halt, and eagerly awaited the approach of one whose experience and sagacity were
so well known. He was soon in their midst, accompanied by his dog, a large, shaggy animal, of a mixed
breed; and his presence was hailed with the most
lively satisfaction.

On the arrival of the Scout, the bereaved father,
who had proceeded a few rods in advance, turned and
hastened towards him. Grasping his hands with affecting earnestness, and gazing into his face with an ex-

pression in which hope and despair were strangely
commingled, he exclaimed, "O, sir, save her! Save
my child, Scout, if she is not torn by the wild beasts,
and the blessing of an old man rest upon you!"

"The wild critturs have not harmed her, old man,"
said the Scout, sensibly affected by the appeal of the
father; "the gal still lives, and I will save her, if it is
in the power of mortal man so to do."

"Bless you! May the Almighty bless you!" was
the hurried reply of Mr. Woodman, a heavy weight
lifted from his heart, — such faith had he in the words
of the old hunter.

The assurance given by the Scout that Annie lived,
although he had given no reason for the declaration,
infused new courage and ardor into the breasts of all.
Mr. Woodman left for home with a lighter heart,
although the uncertainty that still rested on the fate
of his darling child filled him with despondency.

"It was a lucky sarcumstance I happened along
this way just now," said the Scout, as the company
proceeded up the road. "I've been out hunting in
these parts lately, and stepped in to Elder Tufts' on
my way to Falmouth, an hour since, to get a bite of
something and to mention a word or two that consarns your safety around here, when I l'arnt about
this affair of the gal; and, as I know her well, and her
sire, I thought I might be of some assistance, so I
hurried on to overtake you."

"But how do you know that Annie is alive, and
where is she?" asked young Elden, in a voice whose
agitation betrayed his deep interest in the matter.

"Wal, youngster, I have two good reasons for con-
sating she is not dead. The elder's wife down yonder

told me no signs of the gal can be found in the road. Now, the pesky beasts are not so hungry at this season as to eat up a lass like Annie Woodman, duds and all, without leaving some fragments behind. So it is pretty clear she is not devoured ; and, if not devoured, where is she? That's the question, I s'pose, youngster, you wish to have answered. Wal, to tell the truth, then, boy, I don't know! I argue no wild beast carried her off, for that is well-nigh unpossible, without leaving marks, and —— "

" What, then, has become of her, Scout ? " asked two or three of the company, simultaneously, and with some degree of impatience.

" Become of her," rejoined the hunter, patting his dog on the head ; " that 's to be found out, I consate ; hey, Brave? The savages are desprit cunning —— "

" The savages, Scout ! " exclaimed his companions ; " we have not heard of their being in this neighborhood."

" Likely as not," replied the imperturbable hunter ; " they are not in the habit of blowing a trumpet to tell you they are coming. But I 've had my eyes on 'em a week or more back, and part of my business in stopping at the Elder's was to put you on your guard up here ag'in the reptyles. They have been doing bloody work in some of the settlements, and it is a marcy you have 'scaped so long. But it is time to be looking about us. Give me a torch, one of you," he continued ; " but don't a soul of you leave the road. If there 's a trail, too many steps would spile it for the sharpest eyes."

Taking a torch, the Scout walked by the side of the road, holding the blazing knot close to the grass and shrubbery that skirted it. Every now and then he would pause and send his keen, searching glances along the sward and among the bushes, noticing every pressure upon the grass and every displaced leaf or twig. He had proceeded some distance in this manner, when, stopping suddenly off against a clump of high bushes, he surveyed them closely for a moment, then, pushing his way through them, he was seen on the other side, his form bent closely to the earth. In a few minutes he returned to the roadside, with a peculiar smile lurking on his countenance.

"Here, youngster, give me another pine knot," he said, addressing young Elden. "This hunting for a trail by torchlight is pesky trying to the eyes," he remarked, in a quiet tone, after he had gone on a few steps; "but I've got scent of the varmints. They came out yonder and seized the gal," he continued, while the party gathered around him in anxious excitement, "and we shall find a broader trail presently, unless she observed them and started up the road a piece before they overtook her. Aha!" he exclaimed, after he had proceeded a rod or two, "this is as plain as a guide-board. Here, youngster," he added, addressing young Elden, thrusting his hand as he spoke among the bushes, "here is something,— a keepsake of your mistress." And he handed the blushing youth a bit of ribbon, which had got detached from Annie's dress during the struggle she evidently made with her captors.

The men all gathered around the Scout, who pointed out the trail he had discovered, and a number of them proposed starting immediately in pursuit of the captive.

"What, follow that trail by torchlight? that's a bright idee," said the Scout, in a slightly derisive tone. "Had n't you better take a drum to beat on the way? An Injun ain't like an owl, to be blinded by light, nor a partridge, to be stopped by noise. No, friends, the best thing we can do is to go home and to bed. I will meet you 'arly at Father Woodman's in the morning, and see what is best to be done."

The majority of the company concurred in the decision of the old hunter, but two of them insisted on following up the pursuit that night, in spite of his remonstrances; and, supplying themselves with fresh torches, they plunged into the woods.

"Wal, let them go," said the Scout, turning with the rest to retrace their steps; "a wilful man will have his own way. They 'll l'arn their mistake before long, and trust to old Joe for the future. In ten minutes they 'll lose the trail, and all the harm that will come of it will be a tiresome tramp, and p'rhaps the frightening of the birds from their nests."

The old fellow's words proved true. In less than the time specified they had lost the trail, and, after wandering about an hour or more in the mazes of the forest, found themselves in the road again, at no great distance from the place whence they started.

"Consarn it all!" said one of the individuals, as he ascertained his whereabouts, "I believe the old man's advice was correct, after all."

"Guess that p'int ain't worth an argument," briefly rejoined his companion; and, with these extorted compliments to the superior knowledge of the Scout, the party bent their steps homeward.

CHAPTER XIX

EARLY the next morning, at the first glimmer of dawn, a number of the settlers met at the house of the parents of the missing one. The countenances of the aged pair too plainly told the distress of their minds. No sleep had visited their eyes during the night, whose long, weary watches had been passed in prayers, supplications, and tears. The party had been assembled some time, and yet the Scout did not make his appearance. His prolonged absence had just begun to excite remark, when he entered the house, with Brave at his heels.

"We began to fear you had left us and returned to Falmouth," said the mother, in a voice weak and tremulous with emotion.

"What, and Annie in the savages' hands? No, no, ma'am; Joe Wier don't leave this business until he has restored the lost one safe and sound into your arms."

"But will they not murder her, Scout? My poor Annie, would to God I could die for thee!" exclaimed Mrs. Woodman, in tones of bitter anguish.

"Hush, wife, hush!" said the husband, in a tone of tender rebuke; "she is in God's hands. His will be done, Eliza; he will order all things aright."

"Don't distress yourself, ma'am," chimed in the Scout, with his rough consolation; "they will not harm her. Why should they destroy the gal? They are a fiend-like set, I know, when their blood is up, and think no more of dashing a tomahawk into a man's skull than I would of crushing a worm, — and less, too, for that matter, for I never do that intentionally. No, Mrs. Woodman, their object is to take her to Canada and sell her to some of them infernal toad-eaters, who put them up to this diviltry. But it's time to think of startin'," added the Scout, tightening his belt and whistling his dog to his side.

The men now gathered around him, proffering their services; but he shook his head.

"No, no, friends; too many cooks spile the broth. I've been out on the trail this morning and found there were but three of the critturs; and Brave and I are a match for ary three red-skins that ever lived; hey, puss? You had better stay at home, for there may be more out-lying varmints about the settlement to work mischief. Keep a good watch, for they are desateful sarpents, and almost before you know it will have your scalps dangling at their belts."

After three or four had vainly urged the Scout to accept their services, particularly young Elden, who would hardly consent to remain at home, Deacon Hazleton, who had spent the night with the bereaved parents, administering such consolation as was in his power, of whom the ancient chronicle says that he prided himself on having more spiritual discernment than his minister, arose and said:

"Be it as the Scout says; he surely knows what is best, and may God grant that success attend him. But, before he leaves, brethren, let us unite in asking the blessing of Heaven on his perilous undertaking. Peradventure the Lord will listen to our prayers, unworthy as they are, and make our friend the humble instrument of restoring to us the damsel, even as

18

Abram of old brought back his brother Lot from his captivity in the land of Hobah."

With this intimation, those present assumed devout attitudes, the Scout reverently lifting his wolf-skin cap, and leaning on his long rifle, at the butt of which, with his head uplifted, his ears thrown back as if listening, and his eyes fixed on the face of his master, crouched his faithful companion, Brave.

The good deacon wrestled long and fervently in prayer. He first invoked blessings on the aged parents, beseeching that comfort might be vouchsafed to them in this their hour of affliction; that they might be strengthened to bear up under the cross laid upon them, and that, whatever might be the issue of this trying dispensation, they might be enabled to say, "Thy will be done!" He then alluded to the captive, and prayed that the maiden might be sustained in her captivity; that her life might be precious in the sight of the Lord, and she be returned at length in safety, a monument of God's abounding mercy. Particularly did he invoke the blessings of Heaven on the Scout, supplicating that his steps might be directed aright, and his arms strengthened; that the Lord would be his shield and buckler, and compass his pathway by day and by night, and make him the instrument in his hands of working out the deliverance of the captive, and thus bring joy again to the hearts of his aged serv'nts. Nor were the captors forgotten. He prayed that their hearts might be softened; that the heathen might be returned to repentance; that the bow and the spear might be broken, and they who wielded them be brought to delight no more in shedding blood.

"It was a powerful, s'arching prayer," the Scout

was wont to say, "quite equal to any he had heard
from Elder Tufts, and almost a match for one of Parson Smith's, down to the old meetin'-'ouse in Falmouth,
who had a nat'ral gift that way, praying often two
hours on a stretch, without once breaking down. But
it was a complete waste of words," the Scout would
add, "to pray for the convarsion of the red-skins. I
would as soon think of convarting a she-catamount any
day."

Before the long petition was over, the Scout began
to show signs of impatience; and, as soon as the sono·
rous "Amen" fell from the lips of the rapt deacon, he
took the hand of the weeping mother. "Be of good
cheer, ma'am," he said, in a voice full of tenderness;
"there's a good God above us all, and he will not
suffer the child of so many prayers to perish. If so
be," he added, in a sterner tone, "she does come to
harm, trust to the old Scout, the varmints shall rue it."

Thus saying, the old man shouldered his rifle, and,
whistling to his dog, left the house, and walked, with
long swinging strides, along the road, until he reached
the trail, when he plunged into the forest and was lost
to sight.

We will not follow him in all his movements. Suffice it that, day after day, he continued the pursuit,
dogging the footsteps of the Indians with unerring
precision, until late in the afternoon of the fifth day,
when, by certain signs, he was made aware that he was
in the immediate neighborhood of those he sought.
From this moment his movements were guarded by
the strictest caution. Every sense seemed to be on
the alert, as he crept stealthily forward, now gliding
from tree to tree, and sending his quick, observant

glances into the surrounding forest, anon bending his
ear to the earth, listening to catch the faintest sound,
his face the while expressive of the keenest excitement, like that of the sportsman in the moment of
securing his prey.

CHAPTER XX.

"Whist! whist! Down, Brave, down! Have you
lost your senses? don't you hear them? can't you
smell the varmints?"

In obedience to these whispered commands, the dog
crouched lowly at his master's feet, wagging his tail,
and giving him an intelligent look, which said, as much
as look could say, "I understand you now: forgive
my inconsiderateness."

The Scout was creeping up a wooded ascent, and
had nearly attained the summit, when he addressed his
companion, who was a little in advance of him. The
southern and eastern aspect of the hill presented a
gradual though broken slope, well studded with trees,
but whose occasional openings permitted glances of
the surrounding country. On the northern and western side, a precipice fell a sheer descent of forty feet,
with scarce a shrub to relieve the nakedness of the
smooth rock. Trees and bushes grew to the cliff,
some of the former leaning far over, as if falling, menacing whoever chanced beneath with instant death.
But their tough, talon-like roots clung to the rocks
with a tenacity which defied the blasts of the tempests
to unloose them. At the base of the cliff, half-buried

among the shrubbery and half-hidden by the trees whose branches swept its naked side, huge blocks of stone, that had from time to time fallen from the hill-side, might be seen strewed around. At the extreme northern part of the hill, these blocks were heaped upon each other in a manner to afford a difficult and somewhat painful passage to the plain below.

Motioning his dog to remain behind, with a wary movement, so guarded that not the crackling of a twig betrayed his step, the Scout proceeded to the edge of the precipice. When there he crept along the trunk of a tree that inclined fearfully over the abyss, his body partly concealed by the foliage of the trees, but mostly by the bushes near by that threw their protecting branches around him. From this position he had an uninterrupted view of the scene below.

A momentary smile lighted up the old man's countenance, as his keen eye took in at a glance the objects presented. On a spot of greensward, directly beneath him, seated and lounging in easy attitudes, were three natives of the forest, apparently enjoying the luxury of rest, after a fatiguing tramp. The fragments of food scattered on a block of granite, whose smooth surface answered the good purpose of a table, indicated that they had just finished their evening meal. In a cavern-like recess, formed by the mass of fallen rocks, on a couch of dried leaves and grass, reposed a white girl, the long-sought Annie. . Her countenance bore the marks of intense grief, and every appearance denoted extreme fatigue. She had fallen asleep, but the short, quick sobs which frequently broke from her lips too plainly evinced that hers was a restless slumber. As they reached the ear of the Scout, his eye

18*

glistened, and an expression of tenderness, immediately succeeded by one of fierce resolve, flitted over his countenance.

While the Scout was revolving in his mind a plan to rescue the captive, his attention was directed to a sudden movement among the savages. Starting from their listless attitudes, they sprang to their feet, and, seizing their bows, which reclined against a neighboring block, two of them, after gazing at a broad opening in front of them for a moment, struck off to the left with a quick and wary step.

For a time the Scout was at a loss to account for this strange movement. The cause, however, was shortly revealed to him. From the base of the cliff the land spread out in a broad plain, covered here and there with thick bushes and clumps of low-growth trees. Casting his eye over the different openings, in one of them, a long distance off, he saw a herd of deer, some of them nibbling the grass, while others were sporting around. The remaining Indian was gazing at the same objects, the sight of which was too tempting to permit him to forego the sport so dear to the huntsman. Throwing a hasty glance towards his sleeping captive, he carefully selected an arrow from his quiver, and, taking one of the two bows that remained, he started in pursuit of the coveted prey.

The feelings of the Scout had become so deeply enlisted in the issue of the sport, that he forgot for a moment the object he had in view. His gaze was wistfully directed towards the distant opening, watching the deer, and it was not until he saw the herd first .ick up their ears in alarm, and then bound swiftly away over a small knoll, that his thoughts reverted to the business he had in hand.

Lifting himself carefully from the tree, and putting aside the branches that intercepted a full view, he threw rapid and searching glances in every direction. Satisfied with his scrutiny, he left his perch, and with a quick step hastened to the northern extremity of the hill, where the fallen rocks permitted a perilous descent.

Shielding himself as much as possible behind the huge blocks, with the agility of an Alpine goat he sprang from point to point, and in a short time accomplished the difficult passage. Loosening his formidable hunting-knife in its sheath, in case he should have occasion to use it, for he had left his rifle on the hill, he crept among the rocks with the utmost caution to the resting-place of the captive. To awaken without startling her, and thus leading to an exclamation of alarm which might prove fatal to his errand, he felt to be a difficult task. He knew there was not an instant to be lost, for the savages might return at any moment, although he trusted that, led away by the ardor of the chase, they might be absent some time.

Leaning forward, he touched the shoulder of the sleeping girl. She started at once, and, in the first confusion and alarm, not recognizing the intruder on her slumbers, would have raised a cry of fear; but the broad palm of the Scout was placed unceremoniously on her mouth, thus sealing her lips, while he stooped forward and whispered hurriedly in her ear, "Speak not, for your life! Be not frightened,—look at me! It is the old Scout, come to save you."

The bewildered girl turned her terror-stricken face

towards him, and seeing in truth it was one whom she had frequently seen at her father's house, she clung to his arm with a desperate grasp, murmuring, as he lifted his hand, "Save me, Scout! O, save me!"

"That will I, poor gal, or die in the attempt!" said the Scout, deeply affected by her beseeching tones and looks. "But, quick; follow me, for time was never more precious. Say not a word, and tread lightly, for the varmints have sharp ears as well as eyes."

Leading the trembling maiden along the rocks, and cautioning her not to tread on the grass, or, if possible, brush the bushes with her dress, lending his assistance, when it was necessary, along the broken way, the laborious ascent was at last safely accomplished. On his first ascent of the southern slope, the Scout had discovered by accident an opening in the hill-side, near the base, a sort of natural cave, the entrance to which was completely concealed by a cluster of bushes. Hastening to this spot, he carefully put the bushes aside, and bade Annie enter. The room was rather limited, but the interior was dry, the floor and sides of the cave being of a rocky formation.

"They are rather snug quarters, Miss, but all the safer for that," said the Scout, in a low tone. "You must remain here a spell, while I mislead the reptyles. Do not move so much as a foot if you can help it, for the sarpents will be creeping about in sarch of you. But don't be skeered, gal; keep up a good heart; it will be a miracle if they diskiver you; nor don't be oneasy at my absence, for I may have to take a long tramp to sarcumvent the varmints. I will trick them yet. Courage, gal, and trust in the Scout; he will

take you safe home again out of their clutches!"
With these encouraging admonitions, he replaced the
branches with the utmost care, and stole softly from
the place.

CHAPTER XXI.

TREMBLING with apprehension, yet buoyant with
hope, Annie awaited the issue of events. The deepening twilight rendered her place of concealment
nearly dark. This she did not regret, for she felt that
the obscurity of the place gave a better assurance of
her safety. Literally obeying the warning of the
Scout, she did not dare to move a foot, and she sat
holding her breath, listening to catch the least floating
sound.

Her rescuer had not long left her when she thought
she heard a footstep creeping in the vicinity of her
hiding-place. A moment afterwards a slight rustling
among the bushes in front caused her blood to run
cold with terror, for she immediately ascribed the
noise to some prowling savage in search of her. The
very pulsations of her heart momentarily ceased, as
the movement of the branches showed that some one
was forcing an entrance into her retreat, and she
crouched in the back of the cave, as if she would
bury herself in the very heart of the naked rock.

But her terror was of short duration, for, just as
she was resigning herself to despair, by the aid of
the dim light she discovered the noble Brave, who
was well known to her. Wagging his tail with a dignified air, after he had worked his way in, he laid

his shaggy head in Annie's lap, as if to give her assurance; he then placed himself at her feet, with his face towards the opening, in a watchful attitude, giving her to understand that he had constituted himself her guardian. And much rejoiced was the lonely girl at his presence, for his company was a great relief to her, and she breathed more freely as she patted his head, feeling that she had in him a defender.

The Scout, in the mean time, had gone back to the Indian encampment, and seizing the bow and some arrows he found there, — for he had, for certain reasons, left his rifle on the hill, — he started off, leaving a broad trail behind him. He had not long left the place ere the savages returned, bringing with them a noble buck, the fruit of their expedition. Some minutes elapsed before they noticed the absence of their captive, when the whole party rushed to the spot where they had left her asleep. A single glance revealed to them the trail purposely left by the Scout, and two of them started in pursuit. They had proceeded but a rod or two when an expressive "Ugh!" from the third savage, caused them to look back. He had been on his knees, closely scrutinizing the trail, and, with animated gestures, he now beckoned his companions towards him, pointing to the discovery he had made. With countenances in which astonishment and fear were equally blended, they bent their gaze on the trail, particularly on the spots pointed out by the one on his knees. An unpractised eye would have detected nothing to attract his notice, not even the trail itself; but the more acute perceptions of the Indian revealed to him that the foot-prints

before him were larger and wider apart than their
captive could have made.

A hurried consultation immediately ensued, after
which they scattered around the spot, surveying intently every inch of the limited space. Their inspec-
tion was of no avail, and they once more huddled
together in low and earnest debate. They were evidently at fault. The only trail they could discover
was the one before them. That was made by a man,
—this they were perfectly sure of. Which way, then,
had their captive fled? They conversed for a while
with rapid tones, perplexed with the mystery of the
affair, until at last one, who appeared to be chief of
the party, seemed suddenly to fathom it. Pointing,
with expressive gestures, to the rocks which were
piled along the northern ascent of the hill, he issued
a few commands, when his companions started again
on the trail, while he leaped along the mass of rocks,
like a panther in pursuit of its prey.

The Scout had, in the meanwhile, been making the
best of his way in a direction leading from the hill.
Chance led him to a spot where was a narrow slip of
bog, which terminated in a ridge, or ledge, that ran
off to the north for a long distance. Having reached
this ledge, he made a few steps upon it, so as to leave
his foot-marks; then, carefully stepping backward,
placing his feet lightly in the tracks he had left, he
retraced his way across the bog, until he reached
more solid ground. Stepping back to a spot completely overshadowed with trees, whose branches
were interlaced, with the utmost caution he swung
himself into the nearest tree, and creeping along lat-
erally from limb to limb, with the agility of a squirrel,

until he had attained some rods from the trail, he dropped to the ground, and concealed himself behind the trunk of an ancient oak.

He had not been long there before he discovered the two savages gliding among the trees, dogging his steps like slot-hounds. He saw them cross the bog, hesitate a moment on the ledge, and then dart along the ridge, as if secure of their track.

"There go two of the varmints," said he, with a low chuckle, "like blood-hounds on the scent, little thinking I've played them a 'possum trick! I have the other reptyle now at my marcy. 'Twas well I found the bow, for the report of a gun would bring the whole pack on me." So saying, he started in the direction of the hill, and ere long was stealing warily up its southern slope.

He was not there a moment too soon, for the other savage, on attaining the summit, had been prowling around in search of Annie. The deepened gloom of the evening, rendered still more dense by the heavy growth of trees that crowned the hill, prevented a discovery of the trail which led to the cave. But in searching around, the Indian accidentally approached its neighborhood, and would probably have passed it unnoticed, had not Brave, whose ear had caught his step, and who stood in a bristling attitude at the foot of Annie, given a low growl. The quick ear of the savage immediately detected it, and grasping his tomahawk, with a snake-like motion he was approaching the mouth of the cave at the same moment, and with the same wary movement, that the Scout was approaching it in another direction.

From tree to tree, from bush to bush, the wily sav-

age crept towards the cave, until he had reached its
entrance. Annie heard not his approach, nor could
the sharpest ear have detected it; but the noble
Brave, now silent as death, stood behind the leafy
enclosure, gathered for a spring, his bristling hair,
flaming eyes, and formidable row of teeth, together
with his attitude, warning her of the impending
danger.

The Scout, too, had approached near the scene of
action, with the fatal arrow drawn to its head, ready for
instant flight. As the unsuspecting Indian reached
forth his hand to remove the bushes that concealed
the entrance to the cave, the twang of the bow broke
the silence, and the well-directed shaft pierced the
side of the savage, at the same moment the dog, with
one bound, burst from his covert, and buried his fangs
in the throat of his victim. There was a momentary
struggle, and the athletic son of the forest lay a rigid
corpse.

"Well done, Brave! Nobly done, pup!" exclaimed
the Scout encouragingly to the dog. "But leave the
varmint. Here, sir!" he added more emphatically, as
the dog seemed reluctant to quit his hold, "leave him,
Brave; he'll work no more mischief, I consate."

CHAPTER XXII.

DURING the enactment of this scene of blood on
the outside, Annie remained pale and terror-stricken
inside the cave, every moment expecting to feel the
rude grasp of the savage. Her fears were soon

19

changed to the most intense joy, as the low call of the
Scout met her ears.

"Gal, gal! come forth; 't is time we should get
clear of this place."

Gladly did Annie obey the invitation, and with trembling steps make her way from her hiding-place. On
reaching the entrance, she started back, while a low
exclamation of horror escaped her lips, as the bleeding
form of the savage lay at her very feet.

"Don't be skeered, Miss; the reptyle can't hurt you
now," said the Scout, in a subdued but still exultant
tone; then adding, as he noticed Annie's pale face,
"but you look sick, gal; won't you be able to go along
a piece, for this is not a safe neighborhood just now?
— not but that Brave and I could manage the two if
we were alone."

Annie hastened to assure him that it was but a momentary faintness that paled her cheek, and that she
felt perfectly able to travel, signifying her readiness
to start immediately.   Indeed, the assurance of escape,
with the excitement of the occasion, endowed her
with new strength, and banished all sense of fatigue.

Night had now fallen, and, shaping his course by the
north star, the Scout led the way, followed by Annie,
Brave bringing up the rear. For an hour or more
they proceeded on their way in silence, with occasional halts to afford Annie a little rest. At last they
made a final stop, and in a short time the Scout had
arranged a couch of dried leaves and fern, canopied
with branches of trees, for his wearied companion.
Annie was very glad to avail herself of this opportunity for repose, for the fatigue she had undergone

since her captivity had taxed her strength to the utmost.

"There, my child," said the Scout, as he completed her rustic sleeping-place, "you can rest here as securely as if you were in your own father's house. Don't let a single fear keep you awake, for Brave and I will protect you from harm."

Thanking her preserver for his services and kind care, and commending herself to One mightier than man for protection, she threw herself on her leafy bed, and in a few minutes was buried in a deep sleep. The noble Brave stretched himself at the feet of the sleeping girl, while his master sat on a knoll, a little apart, his back resting against a tree.

If, during the night, the Scout dozed at intervals, the frequent inclination of his head in a listening posture showed that he was on the alert to detect the first signs of approaching danger. At the earliest glimmer of dawn he aroused himself, and, ordering Brave, in a low voice, to remain at his post, he started off on the route he had passed the evening previous. He had two objects in view in revisiting the scenes of his last night's exploit. He wished to ascertain if the savages were still lurking in the neighborhood, or, as he trusted, had become alarmed and retreated, as was their wont on receiving a rebuff; besides, he said, he wanted to secure a part of the buck killed by the Indians, "for it was a pesky shame to leave such a feast to the tarnal wolves."

On arriving at the foot of the precipice, he found a trail leading around the hill to the spot where the savage received his death. The body had been removed, but he discovered it a little distance from the cave, covered with branches, and hedged around with blocks of stone, evidently disposed to protect it from beasts of prey. From this hasty and rudely-built sepulchre he found a trail branching off in the direction of Canada, which convinced the Scout that he had no more to fear from the party. After scouring the woods awhile to assure himself, he went back to where the dead buck lay untouched, and, helping himself to some choice bits, hastened to retrace his steps to the camping-ground.

The sun was well up ere Annie awoke from her slumbers, by which time the Scout had prepared a rich repast of venison steaks, cooked as only an old hunter like him can cook them, which proved a most acceptable dish to the half-famished girl. Brave also came in for his share of the spoils.

After a hearty meal, the party again took up their line of march. Refreshed by her night's rest, and impatient to reach her home, Annie won largely on the good graces of her companion by her spirited endurance of fatigue. Indeed, freed from alarm, the novelty of her situation gave a buoyancy to her spirits; and, in listening to the adventures of the Scout, in witnessing his skill as a sportsman, in wandering amid the grand old woods, enjoying the beautiful scenery constantly breaking upon the vision, as well as the excitement of a forest life, all combined to relieve and almost make her forget the weariness of the rugged journey.

It was the evening of the eleventh day since Annie was taken captive, and her aged parents sat in the doorway, conversing of the absent one. No tidings

had been received from the Scout, and, from his prolonged stay, it was feared that he, too, had fallen into
the hands of the red men, or a victim to their barbarity. Day after day he had been anxiously looked for,
and, as disappointment succeeded disappointment, the
hopes of the parents were fast giving way to despair.
If their child was not dead, a long, hopeless captivity,
perhaps a fate worse than death, was reserved for her.
Indulging in such forebodings, the aged man sat bowed
in grief. So absorbed were they in their gloomy med-
itations, they did not observe the approach of two
persons, who emerged from the forest that skirted the
side of the house, one of whom sought, with light step,
the back entrance to the dwelling. A slight noise
made by the approach of the latter attracted their
attention; and, as they started in surprise to their
feet, the Scout stood before them — but alone.

"O, God! he has returned, and alone! Annie —
our child — where is she?" was the hurried exclamation of the mother, as, starting forward, she seized the
arm of the Scout.

"For the love of Heaven, tell us — tell us, is she
living?" gasped the father, in trembling accents, as
the Scout hesitated to reply, his silence confirming
their worst fears.

"Dead! dead!" said the mother, dropping the
Scout's arm, and burying her face in her apron, while
her aged frame rocked in agony.

At that moment, a light hand was laid on her shoulder, and a well-known voice, half-choked with emotion,
said, "Mother! father! I am here; here, safe and
unharmed, — thanks to that brave man!"

A wild cry of joy burst from the lips of the aged

19*

couple, followed by convulsive embraces, passionate exclamations, and tears of joy. Taking advantage of the excitement of the moment, the Scout stole away unperceived; and, when the bewildered parents turned to thank the preserver and restorer of their child, he was not to be seen. With rapid strides he was hastening up the road on his way to Falmouth, to escape the gratitude of those he had benefited.

"The sight of the meeting of the poor gal and her parents doubly repaid me for the little trouble I had taken," was the simple response of the Scout whenever this subject was alluded to.

The return of Annie spread joy throughout the settlement. Public thanks were returned on the next Sabbath; and, at the evening meeting, Deacon Hazleton made her return a subject of especial remark, taking for his text the words, "For this my son was dead, and is alive again; he was lost, and is found;" which he made the ground-work of a very profitable and acceptable exhortation, although, in so doing, many thought he infringed upon the prerogative of the minister, — in fact, anticipated a discourse which he was preparing for the next Sabbath.

It need not be added, that the Scout never visited the settlement without receiving a hearty welcome from all the inhabitants, more particularly from Annie and her parents, while the noble Brave was petted to the top of his bent.

Here we leave the Scout. During all our Indian troubles he was always foremost to redress the wrongs of the whites. When peace ensued, he continued to follow his wood-craft, not scrupling, we fear, when a red man came within range of his rifle, to execute upon him his long-cherished vengeance.

THE LIGHT-KEEPER.

CHAPTER I.

I love to stand on some high, beetling rock,
Or dusky brow of savage promontory,
Watching the waves, with all their white crests dancing,
Come, like thick plum'd squadrons, to the shore,
Gallantly bounding.

SIR A. HUNT.

HE who has never stood upon our rough, rocky coast of the North, and gazed upon the wild Atlantic when the breath of the tempest has aroused it to fury, has yet to behold one of the most awful and sublime pictures in the great gallery of Nature. The mountain and the waterfall, the forest and the wide-flowing river, the green valley and the calm lake, awaken emotions of beauty and grandeur; but, if we would learn aright the might and majesty of Him who "taketh up the isles as a very little thing," and saith to the proudly vaulting wave, "thus far and no farther," we must stand upon the border of the ocean when the spirit of the storm is abroad, when deep calleth unto deep, and the mad billows rush in from the illimitable expanse, and break in thunder-tones on the rocky battlements which oppose their

(223)

fierce career. We have often stood thus, over-whelmed with awe, when the very earth beneath our feet trembled, and the atmosphere was filled with clouds of foam from the watery avalanches which dashed in fury around us. And O! how utterly weak and impotent at such times has seemed the boasted power and skill of man, when his noblest work, the brave bark, has been tossed like a plaything amid the "hell of waters."

The scene to which we would invite the attention of the reader is a spot on our northern coast, a bar-ren and desolate one to him who has an eye only for the beautiful in nature; but to him who loves the bold and rugged features which she presents, a scene of exciting interest. For miles along the coast, stern and jagged cliffs stand like giant knights, — earth's guardians, battling forever against the encroachments of the sea. Here and there huge fragments of rock, piled promiscuously along the shore, show where one and another have yielded to repeated attacks of the foe, still offering their scattered masses as a rampart and shield against the onset of the wave.

Bordering the coast, all is sterile; no green thing relieves the monotony of the scene. Occasional inlets, however, offer to view a clean sandy beach, or white pebbly shore, up whose easy slopes the billows glide with a graceful sweep and murmur, and linger among the tinkling shells and glistening stones as if loth to retire from the gentle caress, — Earth and Ocean embracing in amity. Passing a short distance in-land, and the delighted eye would, perhaps, run up a beautiful opening, luxuriant with vegetation and lined with stately trees, crowned with the deepest verdure;

Eden-like spots, appearing a thousand times more charming from the barrenness of the surrounding scenery.

Into one of these picturesque openings would we invite the reader, where, sheltered from the sea air by a rising knoll, from which a cluster of maples and walnuts have sprung with interlaced branches, stands a log hut, rude, it is true, in its construction, but still looking as if made on purpose for the spot on which it is reared, nestling there as quietly and unobtrusively as if part and parcel of the scene. The murmur of the waves as they kiss the shore, or the perpetual roar of the sea breaking in foam against the more distant headlands, come with a gentle and soothing tone to the ear. A few steps from the door give you a fine glimpse of the sparkling waters on the beach, while a neighboring bluff affords an unbroken view of the ocean in all its vastness and glory.

This is the light-keeper's dwelling; and if ever humble content, if ever unalloyed happiness, dwelt under one roof, it surely finds a home there. The family consisted at the time of our story of the gray-haired keeper and his wife, together with three children, who were nearly grown to man and womanhood. A small enclosure some distance up the glen contains three or four mounds of various lengths, showing that one and another of the little household had loosed the silver tie. On a distant headland, which juts boldly into the sea, rises the white tower which nightly sends forth its beacon-light to guide the ocean wanderer on his course. For nearly half a century has the aged keeper daily trimmed and nightly lighted the lamps that send their star-like rays far over the waste of waters; and never, when the wild tempest is raging, does he leave that stone tower without offering up an earnest prayer for the mariner abroad in such a night, and time and again will he hurry through the dark storm to his post, to see if the lights are in good order, and that no duty has been neglected; for well knows that old man the value of these ocean guides.

The extreme beauty of this isolated spot, and the stern grandeur of the surrounding scenery, render it one of the most pleasant retreats during the summer months that can be found. An additional attraction is offered in the glorious sport here to be obtained; for, from the shelving cliff or low reef, the angler finds abundant employment for his rod, and the aged partner of the keeper stands ever ready to serve up in a most acceptable manner the spoils you are sure to win.

CHAPTER II.

A wreck complete she rolled
At mercy of the waves : whose mercies are
Like human beings' during civil war.

BYRON.

"WE cannot be too particular," said the old keeper, as we stood one afternoon with him in the lantern of the lighthouse, while he busied himself in his daily task. He was then burnishing, for the tenth or twelfth time, the reflectors, which were already of dazzling brightness.

"Humble as is my duty, there is a responsibility attending it only appreciated by those who can realize the importance of a good light. There have been keepers through whose neglect many a noble ship has been wrecked, and many a valuable life lost. Well do I know, too, by my own experience, young man, the value of these beacons to the bewildered and storm-driven mariner.

"Years agone," continued the keeper, as he carefully wiped a faint speck from one of the glass chimneys, "before the coast was dotted with lighthouses, a merchant ship by stress of weather was driven out of her course. For a week the captain had not been able to get an observation, nearly the whole of which we had been lying to under a mere rag of sail. Our captain, who was an experienced navigator, judged that he had plenty of sea-room, although sensible that the ship had made a great lee-drift. From what happened, it was evident that we were in a strong current, which set us all afloat in our reckonings.

"One night, soon after eight bells, the captain was aroused with the startling intelligence of land under our lee. The gale was then at its height, and a tremendous sea running; and sure enough, as we rose on a wave, the dim outline of coast could be seen through the dusk and mist of night. Where were we? Alas, no friendly light streamed its welcome beams over the troubled waters, but all was darkness, uncertainty, and dread. With characteristic coolness, the captain took those measures which the fearful emergency demanded. But skill could little avail us. All the sail the ship could possibly bear was put upon her, in the hope of being able to claw off the land; but scarcely had she begun to feel its influence when the harrowing cry, 'Breakers under our lee-bow!' sent a chill through every vein. The ship was immediately hove on the other tack, and, as she came slowly up in the wind, and was falling off, a loud report was heard aloft. The foretopsail was blown clear from the bolt-ropes. At the same moment, and while the ship shivered in the wind, from a rift in the clouds a few sickly moon-beams revealed a long line of breakers both ahead and astern. But one course was left. The anchors were let go and the masts cut by the board.

"With fearful anxiety did we watch the strain on the cables, and we all breathed more freely as we found, after a time, that the anchors held. Thus we remained for a number of hours, until the first faint light of morning revealed more fully the horrors of our situation. But a few cables' length astern of us the billows, seething and foaming, were driven mast-head high, as they burst in thunder-tones on a long line of craggy cliffs as far as the eye could reach. Save this little cove, into which the huge waves rolled with an earthquake roar, the eye rested upon nothing but frowning rock, cliff piled beside cliff, throwing back the ghastly foam, till sight became lost in the distance.

"With a shudder," continued the old man, solemnly, "which the bravest could not dispel, we turned from this despairing view toward the only hope which remained to us. The anchors held their ground bravely, but the parting of a single link in either of the cables we well knew would seal our destruction. With what deep intensity, as the ship rose on the broad billows, would we watch the long scope straightened out like a whip-cord, the chains stretching far along the surface, under the immense strain, while the ship,

like a frightened courser, would leap and plunge as if
striving to break away from the power that held her.
Had our cables been made of hemp instead of iron,
we might have rode out the gale in safety; but with
the morning flood immense rollers hove in, burying
the ship from stem to stern. At last one of unusual
size came rushing on like an avalanche, and the captain had just time to shout 'Hold on all!' when it
burst upon us. A sudden tremor shook the vessel as
she rose heavily from beneath her watery shroud,
then a piercing cry burst from every lip. The chains
had parted! Heavenly Father, may I never witness
another such a scene!

"Hope did not wholly leave us," added the keeper;
"the dying still cling to it. If we drifted on to the
rocks our fate we knew was inevitable, but if we
could run the ship into the cove and beach her, our
chances, desperate as they were in that heavy sea,
would be more favorable. When the tackle parted
the ship fell off into the trough of the sea, and was
driven with fearful rapidity towards the shore. For
a time we were cheered with the hope that we should
drift into the cove, as it laid dead to the leeward
of us.

"On and on we went, now struggling on the top
of a billow, and now wallowing in the deep trough,
each man holding his breath, awaiting in agonizing suspense the final catastrophe.

"We were nearly at the mouth of the inlet, and
hope had almost ripened into assurance that we
should escape the breakers churning around us, when
a giant surge came heaving in, a perfect wall of
water, crested with a lurid foam. I was on the quar-

20

ter-deck, clinging to a remnant of the mizzen-stay, as this monster billow swept toward us. A moment before it reached us a sudden and fearful crash shook the ill-fated vessel to the centre. She struck on a sunken reef that makes out from the cliff yonder. Simultaneously with the shock the wave met us, and, scarcely knowing what I did, I sprang upon its very top, as it rolled thundering by the wreck. That leap saved me.

"Whirled about on the very edge of its curve, I was borne into the cove, the waters hissing and roaring about me, and yet, above all the noise of the elements, there came distinctly to my ear the last agonizing shrieks of my poor companions. Once only I remember of hearing them, and they were so piercing that even I shuddered, though death at the very moment was staring me in the face. All after that was chaos. There was a sound in my ears like ten thousand thunders; I felt myself darting forward with the rapidity of lightning; then came a strangling sensation, and I knew no more until I found myself high up the beach, clinging with death-like tenacity to the coils of sea-weed washed in by the sea."

CHAPTER III.

A beam of comfort, like the moon through clouds,
Gilds the black horror, and directs my way.
DRYDEN.

"IT was all through God's mercy," continued the aged narrator, "that I escaped. Truly may I say

with the Psalmist, 'He sent from above, he took me,
he drew me out of many waters.'"

"And were you the only one that reached the shore
alive?" we asked, as he paused in his narrative.

"You see the cliff yonder, at the base of which a
low reef runs out, just visible on the top of the tide.
Half-way up or more, you perceive that it shelves in,
forming a narrow platform. Well, on that small shelf
one of the crew was thrown by that wave, but shockingly maimed, poor fellow. He was nearly dead and
quite helpless when I discovered him, and it was only
after repeated attempts, and the most persevering
efforts, that I at last succeeded in rescuing him from
his perilous situation. All the rest of the ship's crew,
numbering fourteen souls, perished.

"You may imagine my situation, far away from my
fellow-men (for at that time the region about here
was entirely uninhabited, and my nearest neighbors,
as I discovered by chance some years afterward, being a few small fishing hamlets, scattered along the
coast, seventy or eighty miles distant); thus isolated,
as it were, with my unfortunate companion; no shelter, no food, no hope of relief from my kind. A dismal
fate seemed to await me. But man's extremity is
God's opportunity. Never, my young friend, in whatever situation you may be placed, in the darkest hour
of adversity, under the deepest misfortune, never distrust his providential care. He that feedeth the
young ravens, and marketh the sparrow, that it fall not
unheeded to the ground, watcheth with especial care
over those who put their trust in Him ; thrice blessed
be his holy name !

"My first care, after rendering my suffering com-

panion as comfortable as circumstances would permit,
was to cast about for food. Fortunately, a fine spring
of water was discovered early, near which, on a bed
of leaves, I placed the sufferer. I then went to examine the wreck. With the turn of the tide the gale had
abated, and an off-shore wind was fast knocking down
the sea. To my great surprise (for I did not expect
that a fragment of the ship would be left), I found that,
though the forward part of the wreck was entirely
gone, from her main hatch aft she was wedged into a
chasm in the cliff, and there remained. This discovery
infused new hope into me, and I hastened back to my
companion with the cheering news. The beach, too,
was scattered with fragments of the wreck, and, among
other useful articles, a barrel of bread, slightly damaged, was seized upon as a treasure. The dread of
starvation had now vanished, for, with bread and shell-
fish at our command, we had not much to fear on that
score.

"When the sea had become calm, which was not till
the second day, I formed a raft from the drift-wood,
and, after considerable difficulty, succeeded in boarding
the wreck, which at low tide was high out of the
water. My object was to secure what the sea had
spared, and my search was well rewarded. The tool-
chest, some spare sails and rigging, the captain's and
mate's chests and bedding, were prizes I had not calculated on. These were transported to the shore
during the day, and that night we slept under a comfortable tent. For a week or more, while the weather
was fair, I made repeated visits to the wreck, and in
the run of the vessel found abundance of provisions,
beef, pork, and vegetables. Among the latter was a

small quantity of beans and corn, which I preserved with care, for seed, in case I should be compelled to remain long in this place.

"My last trip liked to have proved fatal to me, for the weather had changed and threatened a storm, and, there being a pretty heavy swell heaving in, my raft was thrown among the rocks and shattered. I succeeded, however, in reaching the shore, considerably bruised. That night a furious gale set in, and in the morning not a vestige of the wreck was seen. I felt sad at its disappearance, I assure you, although I had saved pretty much all that was valuable from it. When that fragment of the ill-fated ship was gone, I know not why it was, but I felt more than ever isolated. It seemed as if the last link that bound me to my distant land was severed.

"My whole attention was now devoted to preparing a suitable habitation, and in arranging matters for the future. My wounded companion was getting along better than we had reason to expect, although the nature of his wounds was such as to render him a cripple for life, if not entirely helpless. It was the spring of the year, and, selecting a patch of ground easy of cultivation, I broke it up as I best could, and sowed it with beans and corn. Everything worked favorably; and, while I was busied in rearing a more comfortable habitation, and in cultivating the soil, the time passed pleasantly away. I began to grow attached to the spot; and, as there existed no kindred ties to draw my affections away (for, though young, I was a lone man in the world), I grew to look upon the place as my future home.

"Early misfortunes, perhaps a constitutional fondness for retirement, rendered the world less alluring to me than it generally is to those of my age, consequently my isolated situation was not so irksome as it otherwise might have been. It was different with my companion; his heart was knit to many friends, and to a pleasant home, and he pined in his solitude with a heart-sick yearning which rendered life anything but a blessing to him. Poor Tom! he found rest at last."

CHAPTER IV.

All comfort go with thee !
For none abides with me : my joy is — death.
SHAKSPEARE.

The desert, forest, cavern, breaker's foam,
Were unto him companionship ; they spake
A mutual language, clearer than the tome
Of his land's tongue.
BYRON.

"But I am tedious in my details," remarked the old man, as he cast a last look on the blazing lamps, which he had lighted during the conversation, and prepared to leave the lantern. "I had no idea, when I commenced these reminiscences, of spinning out so long a story. It is hard to stop an old man's tongue when it once gets going."

We begged him to continue, assuring him of the interest we felt in his narrative, — an interest we trust the reader shares with us.

"Well, then, we'll continue the story as we walk along toward the house," added the keeper. And we left the lighthouse together.

"This part of the coast," continued he, as we slowly proceeded homeward, "was at that time rarely visited, it being out of the track of ordinary trading-vessels. Since then a large sea-port has risen up, as if by magic, in its neighborhood; but then it was entirely uninhabited, save, as I said before, by a few scattered fishermen. For my wounded companion's sake, who was pining for those who mourned his absence, I kept a diligent lookout for any chance passing vessel, and on the bluff yonder I hoisted a signal, to attract attention should one approach when I was not on the watch. But days grew into weeks, weeks into months, and still no sail appeared, until poor Tom resigned himself in despair to his fate.

"In the mean time, busied with the cultivation of my little patch, which thrived wonderfully, and in erecting a log hut, the time passed rapidly away with me. My companion rendered but little assistance, and it grieved me to notice that he daily grew more feeble. I soon became sensible that he would ere long leave me; and, as the conviction was forced upon my mind, the full sense of the loneliness of my situation stared me in the face. For his sake, I could not regret his departure, for life had nothing to tempt his stay. Here physical suffering and mental anguish embittered his existence; but in the grave he looked for rest. He had placed an anchor ahead, with plenty of scope to ride out the storms of life and the dark billows of death. He had a well-grounded faith that he should be safely moored at last in that haven where tempest and shipwreck are unknown. For my own sake, however, I grieved the fast approaching event. His very helplessness had endeared him to me; and, in nursing

him and trying to alleviate his sufferings, in cheering
his despondency and sharing his hour of triumphant
joy, my mind found employment and relief.

"The hour came at last; and, with a prayer and a
blessing on his lips in my behalf, poor Tom left me.
I felt a lone man then, and for hours I sat by the bed
of death, with my hand clasped in his stiffened grasp,
as he held it in the last struggle. God knows I have
passed many a sad hour, but none so sad as those.
Life seemed a dreary blank, a terrible void spread out
before me, and I would gladly have lain down beside
my friend in the embrace of death.

"It was a hard task for me to perform the duties to
the dead; and, in digging his grave under his favorite
tree, and in shaping his rude coffin, I would often
pause in my work, filled with bitter repinings, and
sometimes fearfully tempted to make one grave
receive us both.

"The melancholy task was at last accomplished, the
green turf heaped upon the mound, and then the evil
spirit departed from me. With a chastened heart, I
bowed in humble resignation to His will with whom
are the issues of life and death. The concerns of life
again gradually engrossed my attention. I felt the
necessity of constant action, of keeping my mind employed on something besides vague thought, anything
to keep down that listless yearning for companionship
which is natural to all living beings. I sought the
acquaintance of Nature, and she did not repel me. I
made the rocks and the trees my companions, the birds
grew friendly to me, and their sweet minstrelsy touched
a chord in my breast in unison with their own pure
melody, and the wild flowers came to me with mes-

sages of love, and the golden corn in my garden whispered to me of the goodness of Him whose care is over all, and whose blessings never fail. A new sense was given to me, new fountains in my heart were opened, and instead of being a solitary man, I found myself surrounded everywhere with a 'co-existence and community.'

"Sometimes, for a change of scene, I would wander away up the glen, or along the coast, and not return until nightfall, when I was sure to be welcomed by a robin, which I one day rescued from a bird of prey and cherished until its wounds were healed. Ever after that, the little thing courted my acquaintance, eating crumbs fearlessly from my hands; and, whenever I returned from my walks, it would fly toward me, alighting on my shoulders, fluttering its little wings, and chirping caressingly as I spoke to it and stroked its plumage. Sometimes it brought its mate with it, who was a little more shy; and I was greatly affected, one day, when, after missing my little warbler for some time, it flew from a neighboring tree, and, perching on my hand, commenced a peculiar cry, a warbling call, which was immediately answered from the tree, and presently two little robins, but a short time fledged, lit on the turf a short distance from me. The affectionate creature flew down to them, and absolutely urged and coaxed them toward me, appearing to me as if she had brought her offspring to thank the protector of their parent. Truly, 'God tempers the wind to the shorn lamb.' In my despondency, after the death of poor Tom, I had murmured at the loneliness of my lot, and He here had sent the birds of the air to cheer my solitude. Not more welcome

were the ravens to Elijah in the wilderness than were
these little nestlings to me. I received them as messengers from heaven, and knelt in gratitude for the
gift.

"On one of my excursions, I discovered a little
sandy cove, and, on visiting it, to my great joy found,
high up the beach, and half-buried in the sand, a large
yawl boat, which, save a small hole stove in the bow,
was not materially injured. By great labor, in a
few days I repaired her, got her afloat, and with a
small sail succeeded in safely mooring her in ' Glen
Cove,' for that was the name by which I had chris-
tened the place of my residence. I immediately
fitted her with a suit of sails, made from the spare
canvas saved from the wreck, and frequently took trips
up and down the coast. The only result of these
voyages was a deeper conviction that the region was
wholly uninhabited. I found a number of other coves
of inviting aspect, but not one spot on which nature
had lavished so many beauties and advantages as the
one where a merciful Providence had cast me, and I
always returned to my pleasant home more satisfied
with my lot.

"I must confess to a bitter feeling of sadness when
the changing aspect of nature announced the approach
of the colder seasons. The fall of the leaf and the
departure of the birds stripped my desert home of its
principal attractions, and filled my mind with emotions
of melancholy and induced feelings of loneliness which
it is difficult adequately to portray. But in securing
my crop, which was very abundant, in arranging my
household, supplying little necessaries to increase my
comfort, and in adopting plans for the future, the

dreaded season wore away more agreeably than I had dared to anticipate. The absence of my feathered companion was a hard trial to bear, but I cheered myself with the hope that with the spring she would return.

"I have already, I fear, fatigued you with my trifling details; but I must confess to you it is a source of pleasure to indulge in these reminiscences. I look back upon those days, solitary as they were, as among the happiest of my existence. My life was indeed monotonous, but if the smooth current bore not on its bosom the sparkle of worldly pleasures, neither was it disturbed with the angry turmoil of worldly contention. Peace, like a white-winged angel, brooded over the scene. My wants were few and simple, and abundantly supplied; and, though I yearned for one to whom I might whisper, 'Solitude is sweet,' yet I had every reason to thank God that my lines had fallen in such pleasant places.

"A severe winter was followed by an early spring, the snow rapidly disappeared, and you may imagine the gush of joy I experienced when, one morning, I was greeted by the warbling of a bird. Hurrying to the door with that nervous haste with which we go to welcome an unexpected friend, conceive if you can the thrill of happiness I felt, as from its perch on a neighboring tree my little absent warbler flew to my bosom, fluttering and chirping as if overjoyed at the meeting. Can you wonder that the deepest fountains of my heart were stirred, and that tears, warm tears, gushed freely from my eyes, and that I sobbed in very ecstasy of feeling? It was even so. My heart swelled almost to bursting as I caressed the affectionate little creature; and, if ever pure and perfect happiness dwelt on earth, it was my guest on that blessed morning. The world wore a new aspect to me, the sun looked brighter, the sky purer, and a universal smile of cheerfulness appeared to rest on nature, responding to the sense of joy that pervaded my being. Solitary as was the life I there led, I doubt if the wealth of the world would have tempted me on that day from that spot. I was indeed a happy man. You may not be able to enter into my feelings. You must be placed as I was placed, surrounded by the same circumstances, shut out from the world, with no living thing near you, and then suddenly have a guest, like an angel from heaven, come to you, with demonstrations of love and confidence, and that guest a tiny bird, the most innocent thing under heaven, and who finds in man his most cruel foe,—you must experience all this to fully realize the strong tide of emotions that flooded my heart.

"If time and your patience would permit, I could detail a thousand little incidents connected with that period of isolation: of my employments and enjoyments,—for, as you have seen, I was not without the latter,—of my improvements in husbandry, and the many comforts which gradually clustered around and in my home. But I will spare you these, and pass over two years of my life, to incidents which gave a new coloring to my existence."

CHAPTER V.

O'er the lone waters, without sail or oar,
She drifted on at mercy of the waves.

OLD PLAY.

A rotten carcass of a boat, not rigged,
Nor tackle, sail, nor mast.

SHAKSPEARE.

"You would scarcely have known 'Glen Cove, after two years had elapsed, so altered was it. I had enlarged and finished my house, pretty much as you see it now, my kitchen garden was extended and highly cultivated, and I had a beautiful flower-garden, into which I had transplanted all the variety of wild-flowers I could find. This was a delightful task, and threw a charm over many an hour devoted to it, which otherwise would have passed in weariness. During these two years, three times only I caught sight of passing sails; but they were at such a distance they only flitted along the horizon like passing clouds, and were soon lost to view.

"One morning in early summer, I took my accustomed walk to the bluff yonder, whence, as you are aware, an extended and unbroken view of the coast and sea may be had. I did not visit this spot with the expectation of seeing a vessel, scarcely with the hope, for I had grown so attached to my new home and quiet life that I hardly had the desire to change it. It had been my daily practice, however, to saunter to this lookout, and I had gone thither on the morning in question and taken my favorite seat. It was a beautiful morning; there was no breeze, and the ocean was as calm as a summer lake, except the long, smooth swell, which came in and broke with a soothing murmur at the base of the cliff.

"I sat longer than usual this morning, gazing out upon the placid deep, indulging in those reveries which such a scene would naturally inspire. As I arose to leave, I thought I detected a small object in the offing, a little to the eastward, — a dark speck merely, hardly visible. Riveting my eyes upon it as it rose upon the swell, it struck me as resembling a boat. It was evidently drifting with the current, for I could not detect the movement of an oar, or anything indicating life on board.

"A boat adrift on the wide and solitary ocean is always an object of interest, and the imagination immediately invests it with a thousand romantic associations. Situated as I was, the sight of such an object naturally excited an intense interest. Scarcely waiting to take a second glance, I hastened to the cove, and, having placed some water and provisions on board my yawl, I shoved from the shore. The distance of the supposed boat from land was great, much greater than I had anticipated; but, with an eagerness I can hardly account for, I plied the oars, and slowly urged my way toward the object of my search.

"As I approached nearer to it, I saw plainly that it was a boat, and I watched eagerly, as it rose on the top of the swell, to see if any one was on board. But it appeared to be completely deserted. It was a large yawl. The painter hung dragging over the bows, and a piece of what appeared to be a sail in the stern sheets lay over the gunwale and flapped carelessly with the motion of the sea. There was something in the appearance of this apparently deserted boat, as I ap-

proached it, drifting thus solitary on the great deep,
that awakened reflections of a sad and melancholy
nature. What dark history was connected with this
little craft? How came it thus abroad upon the
waters? Was it swept from the storm-drenched deck,
or was it launched from the foundered ship, — the forlorn hope of the wretched crew? If so, where were
those who embarked in it? Had they been rescued
from their perilous situation, or had they perished mis-
erably, their last husky cry being a prayer for ' water?'
Who can tell? Such was the tenor of my thoughts,
as I slowly advanced towards the stranger.

"After nearly three hours' toilsome labor, my boat
grazed alongside the object of my search. Merciful
Heaven, what a spectacle was presented to my sight!
My very blood ran chill, and for a moment I stood horror-struck as I gazed upon the scene before me. The
first object that attracted my attention was the form
of a man, bent nearly double, face downwards, over
the bow-thwart. His head did not quite touch the
bottom of the boat, and his long, matted hair hung
wildly over his fleshless face. The position of the
body, the fearful expression of the face, the blackened
and shrivelled tongue protruding between his thin and
parched lips, presented a horrid and sickening sight.
In the bottom of the boat was another, lying on his
back, his feet over the thwart, as if he had fallen back-
wards from his seat, his ghastly and despairing look
too plainly evincing the agony endured before death
came to his relief. O God! it was a terrible sight, —
a terrible sight. As I stood gazing, in a sort of stu-
pefaction, upon the harrowing scene, a low moan

caught my ear, and drew my attention to another quarter.

"A piece of a sail was spread over the stern sheets, which, with trembling hands, I hurriedly lifted. Underneath the covering I discovered two persons: one the mere skeleton of a man, so emaciated that it seemed impossible the breath of life could linger in him, and by his side a female form, her attenuated hand clasped in that of the man, and her face buried in his bosom. The glaring eyes of the former rolled wildly in their sockets, as, with a feeble, husky voice, he exclaimed, 'Water! for the love of God, a drop of water!' As he spoke, the female turned her head toward me, with a low, heart-breaking moan, and fixed on me such an imploring look that the tears blinded my sight.

"Trembling with eagerness, I hastened to obey his prayers. But I felt the necessity of extreme caution in administering relief. As I presented the wooden bowl, the man motioned me toward the female, but, in a low tone, she said, 'My father first.' And her eyes glistened at the prospect of relief. I did not dare to let them drink, but first bathed their parched and blackened lips with the cooling liquid, suffering but a small quantity to be swallowed. At first, the man clutched feebly at the bowl, as if he would drink off its contents at once; but I checked him, and warned him of the consequences of a too free use of water in his present exhausted state. Frequently moistening their lips, and cautiously administering to their wants, I was rewarded by perceiving in both faint signs of improvement.

"My thoughts were now directed towards home.

Fortunately, a light breeze had sprung up; and, spreading my sail, with the yawl in tow, I arrived late in the afternoon in the cove. My first care was to get the sufferers to the house. They were mere skin and bone, and entirely helpless, but a child could have lifted them. After preparing for them such sustenance, suitable to their condition, as my limited means admitted, I left them, in the edge of the evening, comparatively comfortable, murmuring blessings on my head.

"A melancholy task called me forth, — the last sad duties to the dead were to be performed. In a retired spot I made a wide grave, and in it deposited the bodies of the two unfortunate seamen. With saddened and subdued feelings, I heaped the green turf over them, and left them to their last sleep, thankful that the mournful privilege of giving back ' dust unto dust' was granted me. On returning to the house, I was glad to find the sufferers had fallen into a sound slumber. The excitement produced by what I had witnessed, and the anxiety I felt for my patients, banished all inclination for sleep, and I watched through the night by their bedsides. Grateful was the prayer I breathed over them, that I had been the instrument in rescuing them from their dreadful situation, and ardently did I beseech the Father of mercy to crown with success the means used for their restoration to health. The sleep of the father seemed to be deep and undisturbed, but frequently through the night would the young lady utter broken exclamations, in all which a lively and affecting concern for her father was manifest. Once she exclaimed, in piteous accents, ' Water, water! O God, have mercy upon my poor

21*

father!' And in all the workings of her mind there appeared to be a total forgetfulness of self; her whole thought and care seemed to centre in her parent, and all her prayers were invoked in his behalf. It was a beautiful and touching display of filial love, and my heart thus early took a deep interest in one who unconsciously betrayed so endearing a trait of character. The tones of the human voice, though tremulous and sorrowful, were to my unaccustomed ears sweet and musical, and awoke in me all the instincts of humanity, and restored anew that interest for my kind which continued solitude had nearly banished from my heart.

"A night's rest greatly refreshed and improved my new tenants, and, after three or four days' careful nursing, the daughter was so far recovered as to assist in tending on her father, whose improvement was slow and doubtful. His health, I was informed, had been for a number of years feeble, and the dreadful trial he had passed through had shattered it still more, rendering the chances of his recovery extremely uncertain. From the lips of his daughter I learned the sad story of their suffering on the sea, and their previous history was revealed to me afterwards.

"Mr. Morton, the father, was a retired merchant of one of our Northern States. The death of his wife, to whom he was most ardently attached, and the subsequent loss of the greater portion of his property through his own unfortunate speculations and the villany of others, had preyed upon his spirits, and seriously affected his health. His physician had advised a short residence in Santa Croix, an island considered peculiarly adapted in its climate for persons in ill health. In accordance with this advice, he had visited the island, taking with him his only child, a daughter, just entering on the bloom of womanhood. After a protracted residence of two years or more, finding that his disease continued to grow upon him, he concluded to return to his native land, that, in case of his anticipated death, he might rest beside the partner he so constantly mourned.

"Accordingly, he took passage in a freighting brig, on board of which he also shipped the small remnant of property misfortune had spared to him. The brig, which was an old one, was heavily laden with sugars, and encountered very boisterous weather on her passage, which caused her to leak badly. They had been out about twenty days, when one night a fresh leak was discovered, and it was found that the hands at the pumps, wearied by incessant toil day and night, could not keep her free. The water gained fast upon them, and in despair the crew left the pumps, and proposed abandoning the brig. But little time was left for consultation, for it was found that the water was working in so rapidly, the brig was liable every moment to go to the bottom. The long-boat and yawl were prepared for the last emergency. There were other passengers on board, and a division hastily took place. The father and daughter, with five of the crew, were assigned to the yawl; the remainder took to the long-boat, on board of which the bulk of the provisions and water was stowed, a small quantity only being retained in the yawl, as it was deemed expedient to keep her as light as possible.

"The fated vessel began shortly to settle by the head, and the boats were launched in the gray of morning. They left not a moment too soon, for they had rowed but a short distance off, when, with a lurch and a plunge, the brig was buried beneath the billows. The boats were then shaped toward the nearest land, and slowly and toilsomely did the weary crew ply the oars. Day followed day; no land, no vessel appeared. Provisions grew short, and, to add to the horror of at least one party, one dark and blustering night the boats got parted from each other, and when the morning came, those in the yawl looked round in vain for their companions. Now, for the first time, did the full sense of their miserable situation stare them in the face. With hardly bread and water sufficient for one day's sustenance, with no knowledge of their position, a fearful fate was before them.

"It is unnecessary that I should follow them through the appalling scenes that ensued up to the time I discovered them. In their delirium, brought on by want of food and water, three of the crew plunged into the sea at different times, two died on board, and the father and daughter were left the only survivors. The father ascribed his preservation to the fact of his being in feeble health, so that he felt not that craving for food which tortured his robust and hearty companions. As for the daughter, she was sustained by that mysterious power of endurance which God has seen fit to bestow on woman, and which enables her to bear up triumphantly amid scenes and in situations where man, with all his boasted superiority of nerve and strength, is crushed. So they two lingered, witnessing one strong man after another fall before them, until they alone of all that company remained. When the last man fell from his seat in the agonies of death, the daughter placed herself beside her father, and, drawing a part of the sail, which her father from the first had used as bed and covering, over their faces, she had laid herself down to die. Hope had fled, despair itself had fled, and both were fast sinking in that deep lethargy which precedes death, — the only boon they now looked for, — when my providential presence awoke anew the love of life.

"Such, in brief, was the sad history of the two persons thrown on my care. Need I say that its relation excited a deeper interest, if possible, in my breast toward them? My own history was given in return, from the day of my first being thrown upon this spot down to the hour I met them; and, in mingling our sympathies, in uniting our grateful aspirations to Him who had so wonderfully preserved us, our hearts became knitted together."

CHAPTER VI.

With thee all toils are sweet ; each clime hath charms ;
Earth, sea alike, our world within our arms.

BYRON.

O, if good Heaven would be so much my friend
To let my fate upon my choice depend,
All my remains of life with you I 'd spend,
And think my stars had given a happy end.

OLDHAM.

"WHILE Mr. Morton continued with but very little perceptible change in his favor, Emma (for that was the name of the daughter) rapidly regained the bloom

of health and beauty. With the most tender devotedness would she attend upon her parent, hovering
ever by his bedside, anxious to anticipate his slightest
want.

"At times, however, at his urgent request she
would walk abroad for exercise; and together would
we ramble up the glen, searching out its hidden beauties, the little green nooks and fairy-like spots with
which it abounds, returning loaded with wild flowers,
with which our dwelling was decorated like a floral
palace. At other times we would stroll by the sea-
shore, gathering the delicate and curious shells washed
up by the sea, or roam amid the caverns and cliffs, listening to the unceasing roar of the waters. And she
possessed a spirit to enjoy these various aspects of
nature, and with an unaffected delight and unstudied
eloquence she gave expression to the emotions which
the changing scene awakened; whether she was bending over the tiny wild flower, half-hidden in its cushion
of moss, or stood upon the brink of the dizzy cliff,
gazing with a kindling eye upon the waters whirling
and seething with foam far below her. And as I accompanied her amidst places so familiar to my footsteps, and conversed with her in relation to the
grandeur and beauty that met us on every hand, I
wondered that never before had I felt such an interest, never before had discovered so many secret
attractions in objects so constantly presented to my
observation.

"In process of time Mr. Morton so far regained his
strength as to be able to leave the house and take
short excursions with us; and it was with no small
degree of pleasure, mingled with pride, that I ob

served the undisguised delight he took in the picturesque beauties of the glen, and the strong interest he
manifested in all that concerned the arrangements of
the place, and listened to the encomiums he passed
upon the taste displayed in its improvements. He
was a man of strong, enthusiastic temperament; a close
and critical observer; his mind had evidently been
highly polished; and, above all, he possessed that pure
and lofty spirit of Christianity which sheds such a
beautiful halo around the character. He had been
chastened, severely chastened, by affliction; he had
bowed beneath the rod, but not submissively. But
now a new and better light dawned upon him; the veil
which had so long shrouded his vision was withdrawn;
he groped no more in shadows: and, with the poet, he
was ready to exclaim, 'Sweet are the uses of adversity,' and to acknowledge that ' through danger safety
comes, through trouble rest.'

" With such companionship, need I say that a new
coloring was given to my life, that the cup of my happiness was full to overflowing. Even so. I trembled
at times lest it should be suddenly dashed from my
lips. I dreaded now every day that some vessel
should draw nigh and rob me of those in whose society centred all my happiness; and it was with a
shrinking feeling allied to fear that I daily approached
the cliff whence the broad ocean spread out before me,
apprehensive that some vessel might by chance be in
sight, with whom communication might be had. I
know not why these feelings oppressed me, for my
companions had never even hinted a desire of leaving, but on the contrary had frequently and always
favorably alluded to the happy seclusion in which we

lived. Still, I was uneasy, and dared not question them particularly on the subject.

"One day I had visited the look-out in company with Emma, and, as we stood gazing out upon the ocean, our conversation turned upon our isolated situation, and I alluded to the possibility of some passing sail approaching the coast, affording to herself and father an opportunity of returning to the home from which they had been so long separated.

"O, what a weight was lifted from my heart, as in an earnest tone my companion quickly replied, 'Home? We have no home, we want no home, but this!'

"'And could you be content,' I asked, in a manner which at once arrested her attention, 'to remain in this solitude, away from the world, from your friends, and forever debarred the allurements of society?'

"A blush overspread her face as she replied, 'The world, why should I regret it? I had but few friends of my age, and they have probably long ago forgotten me. Where my father is, there is my home. He is happy here, and why should not I be also?'

"'But would he not leave if an opportunity offered?' I inquired, with an anxious earnestness I could not conceal.

"'Not if he could persuade you to permit him to remain,' was her reply. 'This he told me yesterday, as we were conversing upon this subject; and, my dear friend, if you have been fearful, as I judge from your late saddened tone, that we should be so ungrateful as to desire to part from one to whom wo are indebted not only, under God, for life, but for all the kindnesses which render life a blessing, dismiss such thoughts from your breast, and set your heart at rest.'

"And my heart was at rest. Nay, nay, not at rest, for it was agitated by a thousand blissful emotions. The kind — more than this, the affectionate — tones in which Emma conversed with me as we slowly walked homeward, the air of confidence she assumed, the warm terms in which she spoke of the attractions of Glen Cove, and the glowing picture which she drew of the happiness here to be found, away from the glare of the world, the bitterness and strife which there exist, with no distracting cares, no mocking pleasures to win us away from those lofty and ennobling thoughts which a constant contemplation of the grand and beautiful in nature tend to excite, — all this thrilled me with feelings as new as they were strange, and awakened in my bosom sweet hopes which ere this I had not dared to entertain."

CHAPTER VII.

He says he loves my daughter.
I think so too; for never gaz'd the moon
Upon the water as he 'll stand, and read,
As 't were, my daughter's eyes: and, to be plain,
I think there is not half a kiss to choose
Who loves another best.
SHAKSPEARE'S WINTER'S TALE.

"You have doubtless, ere this," continued the keeper with a warm smile, "detected the nature of the emotions thus kindled in my breast. Yes, I loved Emma with no common love. My whole being was

22

wrapped up in her. Her presence was as necessary to me as the light of heaven, nor was it denied me. Even my little bird seemed instinctively to partake of my feelings, for in a short time it became as familiar to her, perching on her hand with the same freedom with which it sought mine.

"Under her fostering care the very flowers seemed to bloom with increased loveliness. Together had we searched the glen, transplanting such rare plants and flowers as attracted our notice, until my little domain appeared like a fairy scene. With the suggestions and assistance of Mr. Morton, aided by the good taste of Emma, a thousand little improvements were made in and about our dwelling, all tending to enhance the comfort and beauty of the place. Destitute of many of the conveniences of domestic life, we resorted to numerous contrivances to supply the deficiency; and never was a gold plate on a monarch's table more valued than were the humble dishes of stone, wood, and shell, which graced our board. Nor was that board illy supplied. Our garden afforded us all necessary vegetables, the sea yielded us fish, and the glen abounded in wild fruits, so that we enjoyed not only the necessaries but many of the luxuries of life.

"A few days after my conversation with Emma on the cliff, Mr. Morton took occasion to allude to the same subject. Possibly, he said, an opportunity might offer to leave the place, but he had now nothing to draw him back to society. His property was gone, his relish for worldly intercourse had left him, and all he desired in life, peace and contentment, here surrounded him. He would not say he regretted being a burden on me, for he felt assured that I did not con-

sider the presence of himself and daughter in that
light. In alluding to his daughter in connection with
the precarious state of his health, an opportunity was
offered, which I had long desired, of making him
acquainted with the state of my feelings in regard to
her. Frankly and fully I unfolded to him the secrets
of my heart, unreservedly informing him of the feelings with which she had inspired me, and of the hopes
I had cherished.

"He heard me throughout without interrupting me,
and when I had concluded he said, with a smile, 'All
this is no new thing to me, Robert; months ago it was
revealed to me.'

"'Revealed to you!—months ago!' was my astonished reply.

"'Yes, my dear young friend,' he answered. 'Even
before, I suspect, you yourself was fully aware of it,
I knew it. The heart too often betrays itself to others
ere it is aware of its own secrets. Actions have a
very forward tongue, and babble many things of which
the individual himself has hardly as yet dreamed. Yes,
I knew it all, for a father's sight is keen; and,' added
he, taking my hand affectionately, 'I rejoiced in it all.
Need I say, Emma's heart is yours; take her, and, with
mine, may the blessing of Heaven rest upon you
both!'

"It is common with all story-tellers," continued the
aged keeper, as we reached the precincts of his humble dwelling, and seated ourselves by the doorway,
"to wind up with a wedding or a funeral, and I suppose you will not be contented if I deviate from the
prescribed method. I need not say that the 'blushing
consent' of Emma was without difficulty obtained.

Our preparations for the wedding were very few, and
were soon completed. But then came the question,
who will perform the marriage ceremony? We had
gone on making our arrangements, until, all of a sudden, this serious obstacle presented itself on the very
threshold of Hymen's temple. Never shall I forget
the moment when Emma, who was intently engaged
on some little preliminary affair, looked up from her
work, with a perplexed air, and said, 'But how shall
we get married?'

"There was something in the tone in which this was
uttered, something so ludicrous, I suspect, in the expression of each of our countenances, as this wholly
unthought-of dilemma suddenly occurred to our minds,
that both of us burst involuntarily into a hearty
laugh, in which Mr. Morton, who at that moment came
in, as heartily joined.

"After we had sobered down a little, we began more
seriously to consider the unforeseen obstacle. What
should we do? was the question repeatedly asked;
and it was the very question we could not for the life
of us answer. We talked it over a long time, and
Emma and I began to grow a little sad on the subject —— "

"Nonsense, Robert; you was the only sad one," said
the keeper's wife, as she took her seat beside her
husband, and looked up into his face with an affectionate smile; "what cause had I for sadness, pray?"

"Well, well, wife," said the old man, kindly, "if you
were not sad, I was, and should have been still more
so, had not your father helped us out of the dilemma.
'Where there is a will there's a way,' said he; 'and it
will go hard if we do not accomplish your wishes,

even without the aid of a minister. Let me think,'
continued he: 'my justice commission holds good
until next year, if I am not mistaken; and I can bind
you as legally together as all the ministers in Christen-
dom. So stand up, my children.' And, joining our
hands in his, he performed the necessary rites, invoking at the same time a blessing on our heads,—and
we were husband and wife! It was a hurried wedding, but it was a happy one, and the blessing of
Heaven has rested upon it from that hour to this.
And now," continued the keeper, as he arose from his
seat and turned to enter the house, "after this long
story, let us see what the good woman has prepared
for supper. We have kept you waiting, wife, but we
have not been unmindful of you, for I have been giving our young friend a history of our lives,—a history which, though shadowed in its commencement,
hath ever since beamed with the radiance of Heaven's
choicest blessings."

22*

THE SETTLERS.

A TALE OF THE FOREST.

CHAPTER I.

THE month of October, to us of the North, where the scene of our story is laid, is one of the most delightful in the year. Then Nature is robed in her most magnificent garments. He who has never seen a New England forest after the first frosts of autumn have touched it, has yet to behold one of the most gorgeous spectacles the eye ever rested upon. Suddenly, as if by magic, the green woods undergo a wonderful change. The different trees, with the exception of the hardy evergreens, with the manifold varieties of the same species, each assume a distinct livery, embracing every hue, from the rich scarlet and crimson of the oak and maple to the pale gold of the beech. Words are inadequate to describe the pomp of the unrivalled display, nor is it in the power of the pencil to portray it. No palette could produce such a combination of colors, such delicate blending of tints, such brilliant contrasts, and all commingling so harmoniously and producing such a perfect whole that the eye is never wearied with gazing upon it.

We know of but one other scene here at the North that can approach it in rivalry: it is that presented after one of those warm rains we frequently have in the depth of winter, followed by a clear, cold night. The next morning you look out, and a miracle of beauty meets your eye. You see the trees everywhere bending gracefully to the earth with their fruitage of sparkling gems, like a bride weighed down by her burden of jewelry; flashing with dazzling splendor as the sunbeams fall upon them, while every object, from the tall spire to the minutest shrub and tiny blade of grass, is encased in crystal armor. In a night, by the touch of magic, as it were, the bleak and barren aspect of nature has been metamorphosed, and a scene of inconceivable splendor is unfolded to your view.

There is yet one more spectacle, not so gorgeous, perhaps, but " beautiful exceedingly," that glorifies our winters. It is beheld when a warm, misty day is succeeded by a moderate cold. The congealed vapor settles on every limb and twig, so that every object, all its outlines distinctly marked, seems delicately embossed with silver, rivalling the most cunning workmanship. The woods at these times present a singularly attractive appearance. Veiled in their snowy, gossamer-like robes, they seem like huge foam-drifts, or clouds of feathery spray, thrown up and transfixed in the air.

A short time since we witnessed an exhibition of rare splendor, surpassing anything that we had previously beheld. It combined both of the features just described. A rain had fallen, and all the trees were cased in ice, when there came on a fine snow, which, lodging on the glittering and still dripping trees, soon became amalgamated with the icy covering. When the weather cleared off, and the rays of the sun fell upon the trees, the spectacle presented was one of which words utterly fail to convey an idea. Every limb, to the minutest, flashed with dazzling brilliancy, while each was surmounted with its fringe of snow, clinging there like swan's down, and softening the glare of the scene. A more splendid sight than that presented by State street, with its double row of elms, on the morning in question, never yet was witnessed on earth.

"Infinite splendor! wide investing all."

But to our story.

We would invite the reader to step back with us about a century, say to the year 1755, and permit us to introduce him into the wilds of the then province of Maine. It is in this same beautiful month of October, of which we have spoken. The delicious "Indian summer" had arrived, and the woods were flushed with the hectic of the dying year. Through this portion of the country there flowed a narrow, placid stream, running in a very serpentine direction. At one point on this stream, called Royal's river, a clearing had been made and a settlement commenced. This primitive village consisted of ten or a dozen log huts, scattered here and there, from an eighth to a quarter of a mile apart, and a small meeting-house, built of the same material. On a rising ground, some distance from the river, stood a block-house, as it was called. This house, or fort, was built of heavy, rough-hewn timber, and surrounded by a high palisade. These houses, our readers are already aware, were used as places of refuge by the early settlers, when fearing an attack by the savages, in which the inhabitants of the threatened settlements were frequently confined for years, or only ventured out, well armed and in squads, to attend to their husbandry, or to bring down a passing deer or some other wild game.

The disadvantages under which the early settlers labored were enough, one would suppose, to have discouraged the hardiest and bravest of men. They had not only to contend against the stubbornness of a virgin soil, not remarkable for its richness, but they had also to contend against merciless foes, ever lurking in ambush to wreak their vengeance on the whites. In the first settlement of New Gloucester, Me., prior to the subjugation of Canada by the English, the inhabitants of this then isolated spot were in continual peril; so much so, that, according to an ancient chronicler, "they had not been able to clear or raise anything, only as the men went altogether armed to their work, within reach of the shot of the large swivel guns of the fort, keeping good sentinels of men and large dogs, and leaving the women to keep the fort." *

It was previous to their being in the block-house, however, that our story commences. Although there came evil tidings, from time to time, from the neighboring settlements, of the incursions of the savages, the settlers of New Gloucester still remained in their habitations, busily engaged in securing their crops, and making preparations for the approaching cold season. But as, day after day, fresh accounts were

* "An Account of New Gloucester," by Isaac Parsons.

received of the depredations committed by the Indians, many an anxious thought was directed to the fort, and eager consultations held about resorting to it. Already large quantities of provisions had been transported thither, and most of the families had made arrangements to take up their abode there at a moment's warning.

Some two miles from the settlement, but as the bee flies a somewhat shorter distance, — situated about midway between Royal's river and the Little Androscoggin, — stood the solitary dwelling of a man by the name of Millet. His family consisted of a wife, a son, some twenty-two years of age, a daughter about three years younger, and a niece, an orphan, the child of a deceased sister, of about the same age. At times, and at this particular time, he had a "hired man" to assist him in harvesting.

It must be borne in mind, however, that, although receiving the wages of a laborer, the servitude of Henry Worthly was no detraction to him. It was common in those days for the young men to let themselves out during harvest-time, when their services were not required at home. Worthly was of nearly the same age of George Millet, between whom a strong friendship existed. They were co-laborers in the field, and sharers of each other's bed. Worthly was also a general favorite in the family, and a particular one, if certain signs were to be relied on, with Ellen Millet. Not that she too openly displayed her partiality, — she had too much true womanly delicacy to do that, — but, as the poet says,

"There is a language by the virgin made,
Not read but felt, not uttered but betrayed;

> A mute communion, yet so wondrous sweet,
> Eyes but impart what tongue can ne'er repeat."

Although reared in the wilderness, there was nothing coarse or hoydenish about Ellen Millet. She was a fine specimen of a country lass, full of life and spirit, ready to assist in all household duties, and in the haying season more dexterous with the rake than most youngsters. She was of a medium stature, with a finely moulded person, and a countenance blooming with health and vivacity. As the expression of her face betokened, she possessed a quick, active mind, excitable, but not frivolous. Her temperament was lively and hopeful, but her judgment was firm and discriminating. Her education was limited, but not neglected. She was one of those characters who grasp knowledge intuitively, as it were. A select collection of books, though small, possessed by her father, aided materially in the development of her intellectual powers.

Young Worthly's character was somewhat akin to Ellen's, and perhaps it was their mutual thirst for knowledge, and their mutual studies to obtain it, that biassed their hearts towards each other. He was a well-knit, manly-looking fellow, possessed of that natural grace which lends ease to every motion, whether in swinging an axe or a scythe, or in passing a cup of tea. It did not require a very close observation to detect a strong growing attachment between this couple, so eminently fitted by character and position for each other.

It was not long, however, before a circumstance transpired which revealed to the full the deep interest which Worthly felt for his fair companion. And that

same thrilling incident, which we shall presently relate, threw a light on the secret workings of other
hearts.

Being cousins, there had always been, of course, an
open show of affection between George Millet and
Annie Wilson, but no one dreamed at the time that
any stronger than a cousinly regard existed.

Annie Wilson was like and yet unlike Ellen. In
many characteristics there was a marked resemblance.
She evinced the same aptness for study, and exhibited the same household virtues; but her spirits were
not so exuberant as Ellen's. At times a shade of
melancholy would veil her usually lively features.
The loss of her parents had thrown a shadow over
her early life, and although she had found an affectionate father and mother in her uncle and aunt, a
warm-hearted sister in Ellen, and something more
than a devoted brother in George, a feeling of loneliness would at times steal over her, not amounting to
unhappiness, but sufficient to slightly check a flow
of spirits naturally lively and excitable. In person
she was more delicately moulded than Ellen. Although enjoying excellent health, it was not so robust
as her cousin's. She possessed no common share of
beauty, and it would be difficult to determine which
bore the palm, she or Ellen. There was a witchery
in the laughing eyes and playful expression of Ellen's
features, which fully balanced the more quiet charms
of Annie. They were both lovely girls, and lovable
as lovely.

As for George, he was a happy-hearted fellow, with
a full share of his sister's lively disposition. He
was more impulsive than Worthly, and lacked, per-

haps, a little of his firmness and decision of character. He loved a merry joke, and it would have done one good to hear his hearty, jovial laugh. The staidness of his father, who was a deacon in the church (and a deacon in those days was a very dignified body, to be sure!) was frequently severely tested by the good-natured pranks he was fond of playing. His fond mother doted on him as the apple of her eye, and was always ready with an excuse for him when his frolicsome propensities carried him beyond the bounds of propriety, and rendered him amenable to the good deacon's rebukes.

Such were the characters, hastily portrayed, and such the relation in which they stood to each other, of the inmates of the small log hut we have mentioned.

CHAPTER II.

THE day was drawing to a close; the horn had been sounded, with a lively tra-la-la, by the rosy lips of Ellen, calling the laborers from the distant field to the evening meal. Right readily had the summons been obeyed; the cattle had been put up; and now around the table the family had gathered, and the good deacon was about to ask a blessing on the plain but substantial fare before him, when footsteps were heard approaching the house.

There was a pause, and the eyes of all were turned curiously towards the door. It opened, and a tall figure dressed in hunting gear, with a formidable rifle in his hands, entered the room, followed by a powerful

23

dog. A smile of recognition and silent welcome greeted the new-comer, who paused as he noticed the prayerful attitude of the family, and, raising his cap, he bowed his head reverently as a signal for the deacon to proceed.

As he will perform an important part in the following sketch, it may be well to describe him as he stood there leaning on his long rifle. He was above the middling height, with broad chest and shoulders, and though spare in flesh, his well-developed muscles denoted great strength and powers of endurance. He was apparently about sixty years of age. His face was bronzed by the sun and the weather, and somewhat scarred with age, but his eye had lost none of the fire of youth. His features betrayed a remarkable vivacity when he entered the room and returned the mute salutation of the family. But, composed as they were now, in every lineament could be read a firm, unwavering resoluteness. Though there was sternness, there was nothing like harshness or coldness in his countenance. It was one of those faces that indicate a bold, self-reliant man, full of shrewdness, and accustomed to depend on his own resources in whatever circumstances he might be placed.

His dress was of a half-savage, half-civilized fashion. His cap was made of the skin of some wild animal, and was evidently the work of his own hands. He wore a short hunting-frock, girt around the waist by a broad belt of undressed hide, suspended from which was a sheath of the same material, containing a formidable hunting-knife, and a capacious pouch. His lower limbs were cased in leggins of deer-skin, and his feet in moccasins, like those usually worn by the Indians.

His appearance, as he stood there, his dog crouched at the butt of his rifle, was singular in the extreme. There was not the movement of a limb or a muscle until the deacon had finished his somewhat prolix blessing. That over, with a quick, active motion he deposited his weapon in the corner of the room, his face lighted up as if by magic, and in a moment he was shaking hands at one and the same moment with Mr. and Mrs. Millet, while exclamations of "Welcome, Scout!" "Glad to see you, Scout!" "Take a seat at the table, Joe!" burst from the different members of the family.

The personage thus introduced to the reader was celebrated far and near, not only as a huntsman, but as a leader of excursions sent out to punish the oft-repeated depredations of the savages. The greater part of his life had been spent in the woods, and he had acquired all the cunning and subtlety so characteristic of the aborigines. His eye was as quick to detect and to follow a trail as the sharpest among the red men. His services were always ready when required to head a war party, to warn distant settlements, or to watch the enemy, and a great portion of his time was employed in following them up single-handed. He evidently harbored a strong animosity against the whole race, and a ferocious fire would burn in his eye when speaking of them. He was not naturally cruel in his disposition, although he has been portrayed as such; but some early wrong he had received from the hands of the Indians had implanted in his heart an implacable enmity toward the whole race.

"Well, Scout, what news is there stirring?" asked the deacon, after having bountifully helped his unexpected guest; "are the settlements all quiet?"

"Just now, round here, deacon," replied the Scout. "But the varmints have been at their bloody work down to Falmouth. One Sweat was shot there while riding on horseback, the other day, and I l'arn that Greeley, of Yarmouth, has been murdered by the reptyles."

"Do you know the name of the tribe that committed the deed?" asked young Worthly.

"The Androscoggin, youngster, the most treacherous and blood-thirsty of them all. The out-lying sarpents are spread all over the eastern sections. They carried off a young gal down to Freeport not long since, besides killing one Means, and his babe at its mother's breast, wounding the woman with the same ball that killed her child."

"Are there any signs of them at the west of us?" asked the deacon, without inquiring farther into the particulars of the murders, for they were too common in those days to excite more than a passing remark.

"Wal, now, that's part of my business here. There's a stir among the Ossipees, and I consate they are bent on some mischief. I've been in their region, and things don't look right, any how. There was a mustering of the critturs on the Saco, and they were all daubed up with their infernal war-paint."

"Did you dare to venture among them?" inquired Annie.

"Wal, I've been out hunting thereaways, and I reckoned 't would be as well to keep my eyes open, and look round to see what the varmints were about."

"Were you not afraid of being caught?" asked Ellen.

"Ha, ha! when you catch a weasel asleep, gal, you may trap old Joe when he is on the trail! I've not lived in the woods so long to be sarcumvented by a pesky copper-skin, — hey, Brave?" and he patted the head of the dog, which stood by his chair receiving a share of his supper, giving utterance to a low chuckle at the same time.

"But, see here, deacon," he added, rising from the table, "I've a word to say to you outside. Stay where you are, Brave, and finish your supper." So saying, he unceremoniously placed his plate on the floor before the dog, then turned and left the room with Mr. Millet.

After they had got outside, and a short distance from the house, the Scout commenced, in a low tone: "'T was no use in skeering the women folks in there, so I thought it best to call you out."

"How does any danger threaten us, Scout?" asked Mr. Millet, with no small degree of anxiety.

"Wal, deacon, 't ain't no use in covering on it up, but, the fact is, the Ossipees are on the path, and likely's not the skulking rascals will be along this way. Nay, I'm sure of it. I saw enough to convince me that it was their intention to send war parties off in different directions, and in course some will come this way. I l'arnt as much as this, and then started off to put the settlements on their guard. I warned them at Hollis and Buxton and Gorham, as I came along; and

23*

the sooner you get into the block-house the better, I consate."

"We will do it this very night. I will go and make preparations to leave immediately, while you, Scout, can go forward and notify the neighbors of their danger;" and with evident alarm Mr. Millet was turning to go back to the house, when the hunter took him by the arm.

"'T ain't at all necessary, deacon, to be in a hurry. Any time to-morrow will do. You are not in the slightest danger to-night. I had a good day's start of them, and I can out-travel ary red-skin in these parts, I reckon. I will go and notify the other settlers, and you go home and sleep to-night, and move in the course of the day to-morrow." With this injunction, the Scout turned and accompanied the deacon to the house.

He was pressed hard by the inmates to remain for the night, as the evening by this time had quite shut in; but, taking his rifle from the corner and calling to his dog, he declined, saying that he had some business down the road, which it would not do to leave until morning. Bidding the family good-night, with long, swinging strides he left the house, and was soon buried in the gloom of the forest, on his way to the settlement at New Gloucester, to which a rough road led him.

After his departure, Mr. Millet revolved the matter in his mind, whether he should reveal to his family the unwelcome tidings he had received, that night, or wait until the morning. And yet he wished to consult with them, for he was strongly inclined to remove to the block-house that night.

The family noticed his unusual gravity and abstraction of manner as he slowly paced the room; and, after a while, his wife addressed him in a tone of some apprehension.

"Husband, what is the matter? There is something preying on your mind. I am fearful the Scout was the bearer of bad news."

"It is too true, Abby," said Mr. Millet, taking his wife's hand; "I have received unwelcome tidings by him." And he related to the eager listeners the information given him by the Scout. "And now what had we better do?" he added. "Shall we remain here to-night, or —— "

"To the block-house, by all means to the block-house, my dear husband," broke in the wife, who was constitutionally timid.

"Yes, dear uncle," added Annie, with lips a little pale, "let us go. Remember the poor family at Gorham, whose delay of one night proved their destruction."

"What say you, George and Ellen?" asked the deacon, wishing to hear each one's opinion.

"I hardly know which is most advisable," replied the son. "Perhaps —— "

"What do *you* think of it, Henry?" asked Ellen, turning to Worthly as George hesitated, evincing by her tone and manner that she should be governed by his decision.

"As for myself," replied Worthly, "I have such full confidence in the Scout that I should follow his advice and remain. If the danger were imminent, he is not the man to lull us into false security. Besides, it is now quite dark, and it would take us some time to get

ourselves ready for a start. The road, too, is very
bad; and, if there is danger abroad, we should be
more exposed to it on the way than here. My opinion
is that we had better remain. George and I will keep
watch through the night, and I will answer for it that
no harm shall befall us."

After some little discussion, it was finally decided
not to leave the house. The doors were strongly barricaded, fire-arms were placed ready for instant use,
and, after a fervent prayer from the deacon, all retired
save the two watchers. The night passed without
disturbance; but the sleep of the inmates was broken
and restless.

CHAPTER III.

WITH the first dawn of the day, the household were
astir and in active preparation for removal; and, soon
after the sun was up, the little party were crossing the
rude, rustic bridge over Royal's river, bearing with
them their household treasures. The inhabitants of
the settlement were actively engaged in transporting
their goods and furniture to the block-house. Although the fort was of a sufficient size to admit them
all, it must be confessed the accommodations were
rather close.

Throughout the day there was a passing to and fro
of teams and persons conveying provisions, and all
were busily employed in this work and in disposing
of the articles they were obliged to leave behind
for want of room. Notwithstanding the apprehen-

sions felt by all, the excitement of removing and adjusting the household utensils created not a little animation, amidst which the light, merry laugh of Ellen, and the jovial humor of George, tended not a little to enliven the spirits of those who might otherwise have given way to despondency.

"By jabers!" said a son of the Green Isle, who was employed by one of the settlers, after one of Ellen's lively sallies, "she's a broth of a girl, and thinks no more of the bloody h'athens' tomahawks than I do of facing a Connaught boy with his shillalah. She's true grit, anyhow." Pat was right. Ellen was not one to borrow trouble or to give way to unnecessary fears.

"It is time enough to turn pale and have your teeth chatter, you silly puss, when the war-whoop is ringing in your ears, and the scalping-knife is flashing before your eyes," she said, laughingly, to her cousin, whose nervous agitation was too apparent to be disguised. It was not out of bravado that Ellen made light of the matter. She did it for the purpose of cheering her mother and Annie, both of whom needed something to enliven their spirits.

By noon the work of removal was completed. The cattle were driven inside the palisade, and a watch detailed.

The block-house was some fifty feet square, consisting of two stories, the second of which jutted a short distance over the lower, and was pierced with a number of narrow windows. A tower rose from the centre, in which was a mounted swivel on a pivot. The stockade that surrounded the house was so high that the Indians could not climb over it, and the timber of which it was composed placed so close together that they could not get through it. Care was taken that it should not be of a size sufficient to afford a shelter to the foe. It was impossible for a man to place himself in any position without exposing some part of his body. The cattle were protected by a pen of logs well fitted together.

After the bustle consequent upon the change of quarters had subsided, and the inmates found time to reflect upon their situation, a spirit of gloom settled upon the company. The uncertainty as to the duration of their imprisonment was the principal cause of their depression. It might be months, nay, years, before it would be safe for them to leave the garrison. In repeated instances, they well knew, the inhabitants of other settlements had been kept close captives for two and three years, not daring to venture out to till the ground, and suffering the most pinching wants, to such a degree, as the old chronicles inform us, that for months they did not taste bread or meat. Such, in all probability, would be their fate; and they brooded despondingly on sufferings to be endured, on fields running to waste, on habitations destroyed, and on cattle shot down or driven off. The latter was of frequent occurrence, as it was impossible to lay in provender sufficient to keep them any great length of time inside the stockade. When, therefore, the fodder failed, there was no other resource left but to drive them out to seek their own food.

The result of an attack on the block-house they did not much fear. It was so strongly fortified, that, with due watchfulness, they felt it to be impregnable. Sometimes these fortresses had been carried, when fire was resorted to as one of the dreadful agents of destruction; but they apprehended no danger from that source. As a general thing, the Indians would lurk in ambush about a garrison, with a dogged perseverance, for the purpose of starving out the inmates, or of shooting or making prisoners of those who should rashly venture out. It was impossible to designate whence the attack would be made. Every clump of bushes might conceal a foe, every tree prove a covert. In the very grass at your feet, snake-like they might hide, springing up and attacking you unawares. You only knew that you were surrounded by a merciless, unseen foe, — and how much more terrible from being invisible ! — and that you were liable at any moment to be attacked, not in open, honorable warfare, but secretly, treacherously, as the midnight assassin strikes down his victim.

The afternoon wore away without any signs of the enemy. Indeed, they had no fears of their appearance during daylight, although it was not uncommon for a man or woman to be shot down at the very threshold, or a child to be snatched away from the door-steps. Generally, however, the savages selected an hour or two before daybreak for the time of attack, as they deemed that then the slumber of their intended victims would be the soundest.

Young Worthly and Millet assumed the duty of watchmen the first night. Their station was in the tower, which commanded a view of the whole settlement, as well as a long reach of the river, which at this point of view assumed the width and character of a much more important stream than its general features proved it to be. Before ascending to the lookout, all the inmates were assembled in the largest room, where the evening devotions were performed, conducted, in the absence of the minister, by Deacon Millet. The services were closed by all uniting in a hymn of praise, after which, at an early hour, they all sought repose, and silence reigned throughout the fort.

It was a lovely night. The moon was quite at her full, and field and forest and river were bathed in a flood of light. Every object was distinctly visible in the clearing, and the distant river spread out like a vein of burnished silver, save near its banks, where the shrubbery obscured the rays of the moon, producing an inky blackness. Every tree and bush threw a deep shadow on the ground, and often would the young men imagine that they could detect in those black patches a crouching foe. A deep calm prevailed, but occasionally a slight breath of air would float by, just stirring the tree-tops. A profound silence reigned, which was almost oppressive, save once in a while there was borne to the ear that mysterious flutter or shiver which is often heard in the woods in a still night, like the passing of a spirit, and, at distant intervals, the melancholy hooting of the night-owl coming faintly from the depths of the forest.

It was getting near midnight, when the attention of the watchers was aroused by what sounded like the baying of a dog afar off.

"Do you hear that, Worthly?" asked George, in a whisper, holding his breath, and listening for a repetition of the sound.

"Yes," replied Henry, after a pause; "it sounded like the baying of a dog. But it cannot be that."

"Why not?"

"Because the Indians would not bring their dogs with them on a night attack, or, if they did, they have trained the animals so well they would never betray their presence in such a noisy manner."

"What could it be, then?"

"Probably the cry of a wolf, or some other night animal. But, by Heavens! there is something moving under the bushes yonder!" and Henry pointed to a small clump that stood in an open space, a few yards distant from the skirts of the forest.

"The wind stirs the foliage," whispered George, "causing the shadow to move. I have been deceived a number of times by the same cause."

"No, I'll stake my life that was not it. Look, look,—there it is again! See to the priming of your gun."

The eyes of the young men were now fixed intently on the clump of bushes, but for a while nothing could be detected to confirm their suspicion. In a short time, however, a figure was seen creeping slowly across the patch of moonlight towards the forest, and ere long was lost to sight in the deep shadows.

"They have come! they are prowling around us!" said George, in an excited voice. "Had I not better arouse the garrison?"

"Not yet; let us wait a while," rejoined Henry, calmly. "The fellow is evidently reconnoitering; he was edging this way. Step back in the corner there,

24

out of the moonlight, or you may get a touch of the rascal's cold lead."

A half hour or more passed by and nothing was seen of the skulker. The most searching glances were sent in every direction, while the young men bent their ears to catch the slightest sound, but all in vain. They scarcely drew a long breath, so completely was their attention absorbed.

"He must have gone in another direction," said George, in a scarcely audible tone.

The words had barely left his lips, when a slight noise was heard outside the palisade, in the rear of the block-house, where the shadows rested, and presently a low hail was heard: "Holloa, there!"

No reply was made, and again the voice was heard: "In the tower, there! are you asleep?"

The voice was immediately recognized, and a joyful exclamation burst simultaneously from the young men: "The Scout! the Scout!"

"Whist! whist! youngsters; there may be more ears in the neighborhood than mine. It's terrible risky to move the tongue in the night, 'specially when near the water. But one of you come down to the palisade a moment. Don't disturb the elders, for my errand does not consarn them at present."

Henry immediately descended to the enclosure and joined the Scout.

"You need n't unfasten the gate; I can say what I have got to say just as well here."

"But you will come in and spend the night here, Scout?"

"No, youngster," said the hunter, "I must go along a piece further, where I shall camp out. My old bones could not rest well on a softer couch than pine boughs."

"How did you approach the block-house?" asked Henry, with some interest. "We kept vigilant watch in all quarters, but did not see you."

"Wal, my lad, that is one of the tricks I have l'arnt of the cunning sarpents. They are snaky critturs, them red-skins. They're a pesky sight worse than rattlesnakes, for *they* do give warning before they strike, but an Injun never does."

"All seems quiet to-night," said the young man. "What brought you here? is there anything astir?"

"There's no telling, the varmints are so desateful. But I reckon they will not disturb you to-night. I've been scrummaging round here these two hours or more, and have seen no signs of them. I was glad to find the houses empty, and that you were all safe in here. My object in calling was to caution you to be on your guard."

"We shall endeavor to be so," said Worthly.

"Yes, youngster, you may be for a while, but people grow venturesome after a time. Finding that you have taken the alarm, the savages may hang round here for weeks, watching an opportunity to pounce upon you. I know the reptyles well,— I know all their diviltries,—and I charge you, and mind tell all the people, to be watchful, always watchful, by day and by night. When you think yourself most secure, destruction may be staring you right in the face. Don't venture outside on any account. I shall be along this way one of these days, and will tell you how matters stand. Good-night, youngster, and keep in mind what I have said."

Thus saying, the old man dropped slowly to the ground, and for a little while was seen worming himself along in the direction of the forest. In a few minutes, however, not a sign could be discovered to indicate a living thing in the neighborhood. Young Worthly again ascended to his post, not a little relieved from the anxiety that so lately disturbed him.

CHAPTER IV.

Would the reader like to take a midnight flitting through the forest? We feel greatly inclined to follow in the footsteps of the Scout, it is such a glorious night, and the moonbeams, falling on and through the parti-colored leaves, present such fine effects. The foliage is somewhat thinned out, so that the forest paths are illuminated with that " dim religious light" which so tends to impress the heart with chaste and hallowed feelings.

Nowhere is the mind more affected with a solemnity almost amounting to awe than in the depth of a forest, particularly in that season when the leaves begin to fall. At each step you take there rises a muffled sound from the dry foliage displaced by your feet, and all around you, as the light breeze soughs through the tree-tops, withered leaves come flitting through the air,—gentle monitors, reminding you of decay, and whispering in your ear with startling emphasis the prophetic declaration, " We all do fade as the leaf." Men talk of being subdued and awed when treading the aisles of lofty cathedrals; but what are

these puny works of man in comparison with the vast
forest sanctuaries, "God's first temples?" Beautifully has our own Bryant said:

> " The groves were God's first temples. Ere man learned
> To hew the shaft, and lay the architrave,
> And spread the roof above them ; ere he framed
> The lofty vault, to gather and roll back
> The sound of anthems ; in the darkling wood,
> Amidst the cool and silence, he knelt down
> And offered to the Mightiest solemn thanks
> And supplication. For his simple heart
> Might not resist the sacred influences
> Which, from the stilly twilight of the place,
> And from the gray old trunks that high in heaven
> Mingled their mossy boughs, and from the sound
> Of the invisible breath that swayed at once
> All their green tops, stole over him, and bowed
> His spirit with the thought of boundlessness and power
> And inaccessible majesty. Ah, why
> Should we, in the world's riper years, neglect
> God's ancient sanctuaries, and adore
> Only among the crowd, and under roofs
> That our frail hands have raised? "

It is not the educated and the refined alone who
are subjected to the influences spoken of by the
poet; the unlettered and unpolished share in them.
The rude hunters of the period of which we write —
dwelling mostly apart from men, and in constant warfare with the wild beasts of the forest, or the as wild
savage — were touched by them. There was some
thing in those dim twilight solitudes that solemnized
their hearts and moulded their spirits to worship.
Rude as they were, and habituated to the rough, solitary life of the wilderness, they could not " resist the
sacred influences " of the place.

24*

In the westerly part of New Gloucester, there is a pretty sheet of water bearing the singular cognomen of "Sabbath-day Pond." Tradition says that this pond derived its name from a number of hunters who used to hunt for beaver on the streams in its neighborhood, and who agreed to meet at this pond to keep the Sabbath. This was the destination of the Scout; and the main purpose of his journeying so late on the night in question was to meet his brother hunters the next morning at the chosen spot. We mention these facts, not as having any particular connection with our story, but merely to give the reader a clearer insight into the character of one who will be a prominent actor in it, and to show that, although belonging to a semi-civilized class, leading a wild, unrestrained life, he, too, was touched with those reverential feelings which Nature in some of her aspects strongly inspires.

We said we felt greatly inclined to follow in the footsteps of the Scout; but, leaving him to pursue his solitary journey, we must return to the block-house, where the main interest of our story at present lies.

As the Scout surmised, the night passed without disturbance. The following day being the Sabbath, a marked stillness prevailed throughout the fort. Every movement seemed regulated by the sanctity of the day. There was a staidness of deportment and conversation among the inmates, from the oldest to the youngest, that evinced the deep respect they cherished for the holy time. The religious sentiment predominated among the early settlers, and marked them as a "peculiar people." The historian tells us that "the proprietors of the towns, when they had but their fort and garrison, took care to have the public worship of God maintained in it on the Sabbath."

Divine service was performed both in the forenoon and afternoon, conducted in a very acceptable manner by Deacon Millet. After the services were over, Worthly and young Millet ascended the tower, where they were soon joined by Ellen and Annie. It was in the depth of the Indian summer, and was one of those warm, delicious days peculiar to the season. There was a slight haze in the atmosphere, not enough to obscure the view, but just sufficient to soften down and mellow the scene. It was like a delicate veil on a beautiful woman, not concealing but enhancing her charms.

The view spread out before the party was surpassingly grand and beautiful. On three sides of them the forest stretched away for miles, gorgeously colored, as if a thousand rainbows were entangled in its meshes, while bounding their vision far in the distance the misty hills shot up their purple heights into the golden air. It was such a scene as Bryant painted :

> " The mountains that enfold
> In their wide sweep the colored landscape round
> Seem groups of giant kings, in purple and gold,
> That guard the enchanted ground.''

In front of them, with here and there a tree interspersed, was a clearing to the margin of the river, which in graceful bends flowed now calmly in gleaming splendor, and now in sparkling ripples as it broke over some mimic fall; while all along its banks the still water reflected the variegated hues of the trees

and shrubbery that bent over it. It seemed like some
enchanted stream, whose bed was paved with gold
and encrusted with myriad gems, the brilliant colors
of which lent to the tide their varied dyes. Not a
breath of air was stirring, nor a sound heard to disturb the holy tranquillity of the scene.

"Beautiful, gloriously beautiful!" exclaimed Ellen,
in a subdued tone, after gazing a while spell-bound
with the sight.

"You look sad, Annie," said George, stepping to
the side of his cousin; "how can you be sad with
such a scene before you?"

"Not sad, George, but there is a strange feeling
that thrills me when I gaze upon such a splendid
scene as we now behold. I feel oppressed with vague
yearnings for I know not what;" and a faint smile illu-
mined her countenance.

"They are common to us all, Annie, I believe,"
remarked Worthly. "Who has not been oppressed
with the gorgeousness of an autumnal sunset, and, as
the light slowly departed, felt almost a willingness
that his life should flow out with the fading light?"

"The emotions we experience at that hour, Henry,
are vastly unlike those excited by the present scene,"
said Ellen; "at least, it is so in my case. As the light
dies away over the distant hills, and the shades of
evening thicken gradually over the scene, I am filled
with an overpowering dreariness. The deepening
shadows seem to penetrate and veil my heart, shrouding it in gloom. I feel as if standing before some
vast sepulchre, — as if a visible eternity were spread
out before me. No wonder you smile, Henry, to hear
me talk thus."

"And how does *this* scene affect you, Nell?" asked her companion.

"It raises my thoughts to a brighter, purer, more glorious world, of which it seems the type; only in that higher sphere there will be no change."

"I believe it is the very idea of the transitoriness of the pomp that surrounds us," remarked Annie, "that imbues me with melancholy. We sigh to think that such a show of magnificence will in a few days pass away like a dream."

"But only to be succeeded by other, though varied displays. There is cheer in that thought, Annie," added George.

"Let us have a hymn," said Ellen, suddenly. "Think of one, Henry, appropriate to the time and the scene around us."

The proposition was at once acceded to, and soon the four voices in rich accord were blended in one of those old German chorals, which seem to embody the very soul of harmony. This was the opening stanza of the hymn:

> " O Lord, our heavenly King,
>   Thy name is all divine;
>   Thy glories round the earth are spread,
>   And o'er the heavens they shine!"

Their voices were musical and well balanced, and the scene, the hour, and the words, that were so appropriate to the occasion, seemed to inspire the singers. As the song arose on the stilly air, first one and then another of the inmates of the block-house came out into the enclosure, until at last all were gathered in front of the building, listening with rapt attention to the sublime strains.

"It is well, my dear children," said the deacon, in a tone of gratification, as the last note died away; "it is a most fitting song, and we trust an acceptable one to our 'heavenly King.' Let us now all unite in my favorite hymn." And, taking the lead from those in the tower, the whole assembly joined in singing that grand composition, Luther's celebrated "Judgment Hymn." As the tones swelled upon the air, the sun dipped behind the distant hills, and so closed the first Sabbath in the block-house.

CHAPTER V.

MORE than a week passed away without bringing any signs of the Indians. Frequently those to whom confinement was irksome would venture outside the palisade, taking care to go well armed. Growing more and more bold as the enemy did not appear, they would linger around their fields and dwellings; some of them would resort to the river for the purpose of fishing, and others, more hazardous still, would roam into the forest in search of game.

It may be supposed that, to the younger portion of the Millet family, the restraint to which they were subjected was borne very patiently. They found relief in each other's society, and the constant contact into which they were thrown tended to mature those mutual sentiments of regard at which we have hinted.

A fortnight had nearly elapsed since they had taken

refuge in the fort, when, one morning, Ellen proposed
to her brother that they should visit their home, from
which they had fled, for some article which she had
not brought away. George readily agreed to the proposal; but Worthly, who at the moment entered the
room, strongly advised their not risking the venture.

"There is not the least danger, Henry," said young
Millet. "A number of the people have been out all
day, and some of them have scoured the woods. I
have my doubts, after all, if the Scout was not mistaken, and raised a needless alarm."

"No, no, George, he is not the man to do that," replied Worthly, with much earnestness. "Depend upon
it, there is danger abroad. Remember his parting injunction. He knows, better than we do, the character
of the Indians, and the arts they employ to lull their
intended victims to a sense of security."

"There can be no danger, Henry," said Ellen, turning towards Worthly, "else why have you ventured
out for the last two days? Even now you have just
come from the woods. What you have said was only
intended to frighten us."

"I went out on an errand for my father, and I had
the means to defend me. I took a little circuit in the
woods to assure myself that the savages were not
lurking in the neighborhood."

"And you detected no signs of them?"

"Not the least."

"Then I may surely go in safety," rejoined Ellen,
laughingly. "Ah, Henry, you are fond of teasing
one." And she gave him an arch smile.

"No, dear Ellen," replied Henry to her, aside, in a
tone which brought the warm blood to her cheeks,

"not teasing; but, when not only your life but my happiness is at stake, can you blame me for undue apprehensions? But go, if you will; I shall wait anxiously for your return. Would that I could accompany you."

"Do not be troubled about us," said George, gayly. "We shall be back in good season, to laugh at your fears." And, shouldering his gun, he and Ellen left the block-house and proceeded on their way.

Worthly was half tempted to follow them; but his father required his presence at the time, and he reluctantly remained behind. Although satisfied by personal scrutiny that no imminent danger threatened them, yet he felt ill at ease, and, after an hour had elapsed, he frequently resorted to a port-hole in his room, which commanded a view of the clearing, to watch for their return. Nor was he the only anxious watcher. Annie had not heard of the excursion until the parties had been gone some time, and her apprehensions were tenfold greater than Henry's. Immediately on being informed of the fact, she ascended to the tower, and kept her eyes fixed on the small opening in the woods, by the rustic bridge, whence they would issue on their return.

"How could he be so rash?" she murmured to herself, with pallid lips; "and after all the warnings that were given him!" And, leaning her cheek on her hand, with her eyes fixed in one direction, she gave way to every fear which an active imagination could conjure up. She imagined George a prisoner in the hands of the savages, bound and scourged. She pictured him, now lying bleeding and lifeless, a ghastly corpse; and now chained to the stake, amid the burning pile, and surrounded by his infuriated captors. So wholly absorbed were her feelings in-him she had not a thought for the fate of Ellen. George alone was the object on which her thoughts were concentrated, and for whom her sympathies were enlisted.

She sat there for some time, buried in a painful revery, when she was startled by two distant reports, fired in rapid succession. This she knew had been agreed upon when danger was near. As she rose wildly to her feet, her fears were confirmed by seeing a young man on horseback crossing the bridge at a furious rate, and making signs, evidently of warning, to others in the vicinity. Scarcely waiting to take a second glance, with trembling limbs and tottering steps Annie rushed from the tower, and in a few moments, with a face of ashy whiteness, stood in the presence of Worthly.

"He is attacked! he is attacked! O God, save him!" she cried, in agonizing tones, wringing her hands distractedly.

Henry did not stop to hear more, but, rushing into an adjoining room where were two or three other young men, he shouted, "My rifle, my rifle! Follow me, all of you! Ellen Millet is taken by the Indians." And, darting from the room, he was soon outside of the defences, and far down the clearing, ere those whom he had addressed had sufficiently recovered from their surprise to obey him.

With a speed almost rivalling that of the deer, Worthly pressed towards the bridge, while, far in the rear, three or four others followed in hot pursuit, vainly endeavoring to overtake him. With panther-like springs he crossed the bridge and dashed along

25

the road leading to Mr. Millet's house. His brain was
in a whirl, and it was some time before he checked his
speed and strove to collect his thoughts to form some
plan of action. Precipitation he knew might ruin all;
and he felt the necessity of acting with coolness and
deliberation. Proceeding on the road with a less rapid
pace, he struggled to subdue the tumult within, for his
mind was excited almost to frenzy at the idea of Ellen's
seizure.

As Annie's sole thoughts were centred on George
when she implored Henry to save him, so were the
thoughts of Worthly wholly concentrated on Ellen.
It was her peril alone that filled his mind. He had
not stopped to question Annie's statement, but had
rushed forth on the first impulse, supposing Ellen was
in danger; and now, as he drew near to the house,
observing the perfect quiet that reigned around him,
seeing nothing to indicate the presence of the foe, it
first occurred to him that Annie might have been mistaken. He had not heard the report of the guns, nor
had he observed the horseman; and the query now
arose in his mind, how should Annie have been informed of the attack?

He had now arrived within sight of the house, the
door of which stood open, as if the party in whose
safety he was so much interested were inside. His
fears in a great degree subsided, as he saw no signs
of a struggle in the neighborhood; and, as he drew
near, he listened, expecting to hear Ellen's well-known
voice, while he watched the open door, anticipating
her appearance. He had not proceeded many steps,
however, before his worst fears were realized. A few
rods from the door, on the edge of the forest, he dis-

covered the corpse of an Indian, his brain crushed in
by a bullet. Fluttering in one of his hands, held by
the strong death-clutch, was a portion of Ellen's dress.
The truth at once flashed on Henry's mind. The savage had seized Ellen, and had met his death from
George's rifle. But where were they?

He wildly shouted their names. Again and again
he called upon them; but no answer was returned. A
stillness as of death succeeded his cries, and brooded
over the spot. His brain reeled as the terrible truth
was forced upon him that they had been murdered.
He shuddered as he looked around him, fearing that
his glance might fall on Ellen's mangled remains.
Racked with almost insupportable agony, he stood by
the body of the dead savage, gazing distractedly
around him, when the young men who followed him
came panting to his side.

"O God! what shall be done, Stevens?" he said, in
a hollow tone, addressing the foremost. "Look — tell
them to look for her body." And he leaned for a
moment against a tree, completely prostrated in body
and mind.

He had not the slightest doubt of Ellen's fate, for,
maddened by the fall of one of their band, the savages would not hesitate to despatch her at once. He
was naturally of strong nerves; but the certainty he
felt of soon being called to gaze upon the idol of his
heart, horribly despoiled by the cruel scalping-knife,
the fair temple of her brain shattered by the murderous tomahawk, for the time entirely overcame him.
The weakness soon passed away; but the pallor on his
cheeks too plainly told of the inward struggle.

A few minutes had elapsed, when one of the party,

who had gone a short distance further on toward the
Little Androscoggin, called the attention of the rest
to a discovery he had made. All of them rushed
eagerly to the spot. Among the underbrush, by the
side of a broad trail, evidently thrown there to attract
attention, was a ribbon, which Ellen was known to
have worn around her neck that day.

"She is not only alive," said Stevens, pointing to
the discovery, "but she has her wits about her, and
has contrived to give us a hint of the direction her
captors have taken."

"Let us follow on," said Henry, a burden rolling
from his mind as he seized the treasured token; and
the party immediately pressed forward in pursuit.

They were not long in reaching the banks of the
Little Androscoggin, and a simultaneous exclamation
told of a new discovery. Far up the stream, close in
shore, as if to avoid observation, a canoe was seen,
urged rapidly forward by two savages. In the bows
sat a female, readily recognized as Ellen. Casting one
glance at the fugitives, Worthly started from the spot
and plunged into the forest at the left.

There was a long bend in the river at this point,
which swept round so as to leave but a narrow passage of land between the two points of the stream.
Henry's movement was at once divined.

"He 's going to head them off," said young Stevens.
"I will follow him, and the rest of you had better be
looking round to see if you can discover anything
of George."

Leaving them to this employment, — which we may
as well say was fruitless, — we, too, will follow in
Henry's steps.

Scarcely noticing the obstacles which beset his path, the young man pressed forward with incredible speed. Leaping over fallen trees, over broken rocks, forcing his way through thicket and bush, on he went. But not a moment too soon. As he broke through the last clump of bushes and stood on the margin of the stream, the canoe was nearly abreast of him. The moment he appeared, one of the Indians dropped his paddle and sprang forward. As quick as thought Worthly levelled his rifle, but, before he could sight it, the Indian had seized Ellen, and, raising her up in front of him, he shouted in the ear of the terrified girl, "Speak! Tell him, shoot 'em Indian, me kill 'em squaw!" and he brandished the tomahawk menacingly over her head.

"Do not fire, Henry; he threatens to kill me if you do!"

An instant more, and the caution would have come too late, for already was Henry's finger pressing hard upon the trigger. But the consequences of such an act suddenly flashed upon his mind, and he refrained. Well he knew that it was no idle threat of the savage; that, at the flash of his rifle, the tomahawk would be buried in the brain of Ellen; and with almost a shudder he lowered his weapon. The Indian, however, as if distrusting his intentions, still stood with the tomahawk raised ready to give the fatal blow. In the meanwhile his companion still urged the frail bark on its course.

"Ellen, dear Ellen!" exclaimed Henry, in an agitated voice, "must I leave you in their hands? God knows I would willingly sacrifice my life to save yours."

25*

"I do not doubt it, Henry, and I am grateful for it. But courage! I do not think my life is in danger. Comfort mother as well as you can, and let us hope for the best."

The courage displayed by the heroic girl was not without its effect on Worthly. The canoe was fast receding from him, and, wishing to learn the fate of George, he asked, "What of your brother, Ellen?"

"He was wounded, and has gone ahead of us in another canoe. Good-by, Henry. Perhaps you can find some way to release me. Keep up your spirits; I shall try and not despond."

"Good-by, and God bless you, dear Ellen! I will rescue you or die in the attempt."

Just beyond this bend, the river takes an abrupt turn around quite a high bluff. Worthly stood watching the canoe as it approached this point with feelings more readily imagined than described. The Indian had lowered his weapon, but he still retained his position back of Ellen. Just as the canoe passed around the bluff and was lost to sight, Ellen raised her hand and gave a parting signal; the next moment the little bark was hidden from view. As she disappeared, Henry turned with a bitter sigh to retrace his steps.

CHAPTER VI.

The agony of the good deacon and his wife, and of Annie Wilson, we should vainly attempt to describe. As one after another of the party who had gone out in pursuit returned to the block-house, they were met by Mrs. Millet and Annie, who, striving to catch some gleam of hope, wildly importuned each in regard to the missing ones. When at last Worthly returned, bringing certain tidings of their captivity, their cup of anguish was filled to the brim. In the frenzy of her grief, the mother rapidly paced the room, wringing her hands and calling distractedly the names of her children, while Annie sat by a table, pale and tearless, a moan of distress from time to time breaking from her lips. Occasionally she would press her hand to her forehead, and look around bewilderingly, in a piteous manner, as if inquiring the nature of the great woe that had come upon her. Mr. Millet strove hard to restrain his emotions, that he might minister comfort to his partner; but the struggle was a hard one, and the strong man shook like a reed.

Henry, after announcing his information, had left the room. In a short time he re-entered, accompanied by two other young men, by the names of Stevens and Eveleth, all completely armed and equipped for a journey.

"God be praised!" said Mrs. Millet, springing to Henry's side. "You will save them, you will restore them to us!" and she clung convulsively to his arm.

"We shall make the attempt, Mrs. Millet," replied Henry, "but God only knows what will be the issue. What men can do, we have resolved to accomplish, even to the sacrifice of life, if necessary."

"Bless you! bless you, young man! A mother's prayers will follow you."

"Deacon Millet," said Henry, after a moment's hesitation, "the fate of your daughter is at this moment uncertain, and I am about to peril my life in her behalf. The probabilities of my safe return are slight. This, then, is no time for concealments. The life of Ellen, sir, is as dear to me, more dear, if possible, than it is to you. I do not ask you at this inauspicious moment to sanction these sentiments so long entertained; I only allude to them to afford you assurance that nothing will be left undone to insure her safety."

"Restore her to us, young man," said the deacon, pressing him cordially by the hand, "and Ellen is yours."

With a kindling eye Henry turned and approached the aged man, and, kneeling before him, said, "Father, your blessing."

The old man placed his hands reverently on the youth's head, and, in a voice trembling with emotion, said, "May God Almighty bless you, my son, and prosper you in your perilous undertaking."

As young Millet arose from his knees, a bustle was heard in the adjoining room, words of surprise and welcome were uttered, the door opened, and the tall form of the Scout entered. His presence was hailed with exclamations of joy.

"Wal," he said, in his own rough way, when an opportunity was afforded him to speak, "there 's been purty doings here, I l'arn. Did n't I warn you about the pesky varmints? Did n't I?—But that 's neither here nor there, now," he continued, after a slight pause. "Let us hear the sarcumstances."

He was soon put in possession of all the facts, and then Henry informed him of the expedition just setting out.

"Let us consider first, let us consider a while," said the old hunter, sedately. "The woods are swarming with the reptyles, and it won't be no child's play. We must go to work with our eyes open."

" Then you will assist in rescuing them?" said Mrs. Millet, hurriedly.

" Sartain, ma'am! I've a grudge agin the whole race, and mean to pay it, too. Give yourself no consarn about the young folks; we'll return 'em to you all safe, I reckon. Come, boys, let us see what preparations you have made;" and, bidding the rest good-by, the party left the room.

On consultation, the Scout was opposed to having any but Worthly with him; but, when he heard that George was wounded, he changed his mind.

" If the party are Ossipees, as I consate, — and we can tell by the dead Injun, — I know where their camping-ground is. Let us go down the road, and we can talk the matter over as we go along."

So saying, the company left the block-house and proceeded to the scene of attack. It was getting late in the afternoon when they arrived at the Millet house. The Scout immediately sought the corpse of the savage.

" I consated so," said the old man, as he stooped and removed a portion of its dress, thus exposing the naked breast. " 'T is an Ossipee; here is his *totem;*" and he pointed to the figure of a tortoise imprinted on the skin. It was the custom of the Indians to wear the badge of their tribes on their persons, — a " totem," as it was called, being the figure of a bird, fish or reptile.

" Now, youngsters, I will give you my idees when we reach the river. I've a canoe hidden away there somewhere among the bushes. Follow me, and be as

still as possible;" and the Scout took the lead through
the forest, with whose intricacies he appeared to be
perfectly familiar. Having arrived at the banks of
the stream, the Scout entered a thicket of evergreens,
and soon returned, bearing a birchen canoe.

"This, now, is my plan. You two," addressing
Henry's companions, "will take to the river as soon
as it gets darker, and go as far up as the upper falls,
and when you get there, draw your canoe close to the
left bank under the foliage, where it will be out of
sight. Mind, boys, what I say to you: keep a still
tongue in your heads. You've hearn tell of a whisper among the mountains bringing down an avalanche
on travellers' heads: I tell yer, a whisper on the river
in such a still night as this may bring down upon you
something worse than a heap of snow. Be careful,
too, of your paddles; keep in the shadows as much as
possible; and, above all, keep your eyes and ears open.
I will meet you at the falls. Can you remember
this?" and the Scout gave a cry so resembling that
of a night-owl that the most practised ear would have
been deceived. "That will be a signal that I am in
the neighborhood. Can either of you reply to it?"

Young Eveleth made the effort, and succeeded so
well as to win the commendation of the Scout.

"Very well done! You must answer my call. You
and I, youngster," he continued, addressing Henry,
"will take to the woods; and, as the sun is about
down, the sooner we are off the better."

Cautioning the two young men not to start until
the shadows fell on the stream, and whistling his dog
to his side, the old man and Worthly entered the

woods. Leaving the young men to pursue their course, we will follow the Scout and his companion.

After proceeding for some distance in silence, the old man said, in a low voice: "It was a good shot that the young man made, clean through the crittur's skull, and yet it may prove a bad one for him. We must get him out of their hands to-night, at all events."

"Shall we not rescue both?" asked Henry, with much interest.

"That we'll detarmine on as things appear, but we must get the boy clear first."

"But why George, and not Ellen?"

"Don't yer see," said the old man, emphatically, "there's blood been spilt, and life for life is their doctrine; as though one of those hathens," he continued, in a sort of parenthesis, "was worth as much as a nat'ral-born Christian."

"I had no fears for his life," said Worthly.

"You told me the youngster was wounded, did you not? Wal, now, is it reasonable to suppose that the varmints would trouble themselves to carry him off, unless it was to wreak their vengeance on him?"

"But why did they not kill him on the spot?"

"That wouldn't satisfy the bloody sarpents. You've hearn tell of the stake, of pitch splinters, and such like devilish tortures, I suppose? That's why they didn't kill him on the spot, youngster."

"And will they not subject Ellen to the same fearful treatment?" asked Henry, shuddering as the terrible thought shot across his mind.

"There's not much danger of that. The infarnal scamps, though they delight in blood, love money better. The worst they will do will be to carry her to Canada and sell her to the French. They'll never kill women as long as they can find a good market for them.

"Cheer up, my boy," added the hunter, noticing, after a pause, the dejection of his companion; "there's no saying but we may get them both off. My idee is, to make sure of the youngster, get him safely out of their clutches into the canoe, and start him down the river. If we do this without disturbing the venomous snakes, we will attend to the gal's case. But hist! Brave smells mischief. What is it, pup?" whispered the Scout.

The dog, which was a little in advance of them, suddenly stopped and gave a low growl.

"Is it a red-skin, pup?" said the Scout, approaching the animal.

The dog lifted his nose in the air and snuffed eagerly for a moment; then, as if satisfied, looked his master in the face and wagged his tail, as much as saying, "All right!" and kept on his way again.

"Thar now, that 'ere dog," said the Scout, following him unhesitatingly, "knows more than any human being in the settlements. He's been my constant companion this many a year, and I have l'arnt his ways, and he has mine, so that we perfectly understand each other. I will tell you some day of a trick he played upon the red-skins when they thought they had me in their clutches; it was a 'cute one. But it is getting dusky, and I must not forget the caution I gave the youngsters about a still tongue."

After this the Scout proceeded in silence, all the way throwing quick and searching glances in every direction. For miles he travelled in this manner, until darkness had completely fallen. By this time they had again struck the banks of the stream, and, leaving the woods, they moved close in their edge up the river.

They were evidently approaching the neighborhood of the Indian camping-ground, for every movement of the old man betrayed the utmost watchfulness. Time and again he turned and whispered in his companion's ear, "Not a word, for your life! Step lightly, or the whole pack may be upon us!" and similar cautions. Occasionally he would stop short and bend his ear to the ground, listening eagerly to catch the slightest sound. After proceeding in this manner for some distance, the party halted beside a clump of high bushes. Softly displacing them so as to afford an entrance into the thicket, the old man bade Henry enter.

"Some of the out-lying varmints may be skulking in the neighborhood, but you will be safe here," said the hunter, in suppressed tones. "I am going into the reptyles' nest to see how things look. Be on your guard, and do not stir a limb if you can help it. If I had this dog's nose now, it would be worth a dozen pair of eyes. Come, Brave, lead the way."

As if fully comprehending the nature of his errand, the noble dog took the lead, stepping with a cat-like tread, and followed in like manner by his master. A moment, and their forms were not to be seen, and Worthly could not detect so much as the crackling of a twig to denote the presence of a living being. He was alone and in darkness.

CHAPTER VII.

THE place selected by the Indians for their camping-ground was in a bend of the river, forming a pretty cove. The forest here receded a short distance from the stream, leaving a clear, crescent-shaped spot, which ran down slopingly to the water's edge. On this opening some dozen lodges were scattered, in the usually disordered manner of an Indian encampment. The tents of the wandering tribes that annually visit our neighborhood at the present day are made of canvas or stout cotton cloth, and present quite a comfortable appearance; but those of which we are writing were rudely constructed of such material as the forest afforded. Some of them were made of pine boughs laid over rough poles or young saplings, but the outer covering of the majority was of birch bark, broad strips of which are obtained from the birch tree.

In one of these, on the night in question, sat, or rather half-reclined, Ellen, on the skin of some wild animal, which, with some regard to her sex, her captors had provided her. Her arms were confined behind her back by withes, and her ankles bound by strips of skin. Pinioned as she was, she could not long retain a recumbent position with any degree of comfort. A little hillock that rose in one corner of the tent afforded her a leaning place. Situated thus, the reader can better imagine than we can portray her feelings.

She was a brave-hearted girl, and not one to give way to trifling weakness; still, she could not repress the half-sigh, half-moan, that from time to time arose from her lips. What added to the poignancy of her distress, was the certainty of the terrible fate that awaited her brother. Of her own life she had not the least fear, so long as she retained her strength, for she knew that the worst fate that awaited her would be a long, tedious journey through the wilderness, and it might be a few years of servitude among the French Canadians, an escape from which was frequently obtained by ransom or artifice.

We said that she had no fears for her life, if her strength should hold out; for she well knew that it was a common practice with the savages, when a captive gave out on a journey by reason of weakness, or detained them much by not being able to keep up with them, to despatch him at once and take his scalp. In those days the French paid the Indians a bounty for an English scalp, as some States pay a bounty for the ears of a wolf or a wild-cat. This horrible traffic was not confined wholly to the French. Our mother State at that time paid a stipulated price for Indian scalps; and it is well attested that many Indians belonging to friendly tribes were shot down by lawless rangers of the woods, merely for the bounty paid for scalps. Who could tell by the scalp whether it was taken from the head of a friend or a foe?

The great distress experienced by Ellen, we have said, was on her brother's account. She knew that he had killed one of the tribe; she had heard of their inexorable law; and she had been a painful witness of the manner of his reception at the encampment. She had seen the savages dancing around him, brandishing their tomahawks in fearful proximity to his person, their eyes glaring with almost demoniacal fury, while their wild howls of vengeance shook the air. More dreadful than all, she had seen, in the early evening, from the door of her lodge, a stake planted in the centre of the encampment, and heaps of dry brush brought from the forest and placed near it. This was hardly needed to confirm her worst fears; still, a sight of the terrible preparations struck a sickening chill to her heart. How could this horrible fate be averted? She revolved in her mind all possible contingencies, but not a ray of hope pierced the very blackness of darkness which surrounded her. A cold despair settled upon her heart. All her sympathies enlisted in behalf of her brother, she forgot her own sufferings.

How would her heart have leaped for joy had she known that even then there were friends near at hand, brave and determined men, ready to risk life in rescuing them from bondage. Her thoughts, it is true, often reverted to Worthly, and his promise to do all in his power to rescue her, and she did not doubt that he would make the attempt. But would he appear in time to save George from his impending fate? She endeavored to obtain a gleam of hope from that thought; but, when she reconsidered the matter, the improbability, nay, what she deemed the utter impossibility, of his tracing their route in season, and bringing a force sufficient to overmaster the savages, convinced her at once that to entertain such a hope would be sheer madness.

"No, no," she murmured to herself; "he will come too late — too late! and George must die! and O God, such a death!" And a moan of anguish broke from her lips.

In another lodge, nearer to the river, bound hand

and foot, so as to be almost incapable of motion, stretched on the cold sward, was George Millet. In his encounter with the savages he had received a severe wound, which would have been excessively painful had not his mental agony rendered him insensible to physical suffering. He knew he had but a few hours to live, — the coming morn would witness his death. Young, buoyant with life and hope, death in any shape would have been terrible to him; but from that which awaited him he shrunk appalled.

With a refinement of cruelty, his captors had pointed out to him the stake to which he would be bound, and had exhibited the splinters with which they intended to pierce his body and add to his torture. He did not harbor the slightest hope of an escape from the fearful doom; and for hours he remained in a state of agony, with the fated stake, the burning pile, and the flaming splinters, continually in his mind. At times prayers burst from his lips, wild and incoherent, the ravings of despair, that death would come and save him from the fiery trial. And then would come thoughts of his home; and for a while he would be with his parents, or sitting with Annie in the tower, relating to her, as a horrible dream, his present sufferings. O, it was terrible, terrible beyond description, when the delightful vision passed away, and his mind recurred to his real situation. Great drops of agony would force themselves from his brow; and, bound as he was, he would writhe as one in mortal struggle. After these momentary paroxysms, calmer feelings would steal over him, and he would strive to nerve himself to endure with unflinching courage the doom before him.

We have exhibited the captive in some of his dark-

26*

est moments, when his spirits were bowed in the depth of despair. It must not be inferred from this that ho was devoid of manliness,—a spiritless coward. His situation was peculiar: wounded, bound, exhausted, in darkness and solitude, with the certainty of an ex-cruciating death within a few hours pressing upon his mind, no wonder he quailed. What man, under the circumstances, would not have quailed? And yet, when the hour of trial should arrive, George would probably face his enemies without shrinking, and laugh at their savage cruelties. We all instinctively shrink at the thought of being subjected to the surgi-cal knife, but when brought to the test we submit to the most painful operation unflinchingly.

It was in one of these calmer moods of mind, some-where about midnight, his car detected a slight move-ment outside the lodge. He listened eagerly, but for a while all was silent, and he concluded that his car must have deceived him. No, there was another movement. This time it was no deception. What could it be? An animal prowling in the neighborhood, or an enemy come to deal in secret the death-blow? He remembered now that a brother of the fallen In-dian was with difficulty restrained from wreaking his vengeance on him when he first landed; he remem-bered the fierce, revengeful look the savage gave him, with a secret threatening gesture, as he was led reluc-tantly away from the lodge into which George was thrust. Was he coming at this hour to avenge his brother's death?

George had besought death, but the idea of its near approach, there in the darkness and solitude, startled him. Whoever was seeking him, he was in their power, for he was incapable of resistance, and would prove an easy victim. With all his senses on the alert, he again listened. The same movement continued, as if some one were trying to obtain entrance through the boughs of which the lodge was composed. He heard the bushes carefully put aside, and then a sound as of some one forcing a passage. George remained perfectly still, holding his breath with suspense, every moment expecting to receive the crushing blow of the tomahawk or the sharp thrust of a knife. His position was near the entrance of the tent, while the intruder came from the rear. The young man could hear, almost feel, the slow approach of his mysterious visitor, and a cold, clammy sweat burst from every pore. Seconds seemed hours, minutes ages, in that fearful crisis. The hand of the unknown touched his arm; and O! what a revulsion of feeling did he experience, how did his heart throb, and his whole frame thrill, as his ear caught a just audible whisper:

"Boy, boy! where on 'arth are you?"

"Here. God be praised, God be praised!" exclaimed George, every nerve quivering with intense joy.

"On your life be silent. Would you bring the whole pack on us?" was whispered, in the same cautious manner. Even as the well-known tones reached his ears, George felt the fastenings that bound his feet give way. "Hold out your arms," continued the unseen speaker, and immediately the withes, that had cut deeply into his flesh, were severed, and he was free.

"Heaven bless you, Scout!" said George, fervently, imitating the cautious tones of the old man.

"No thanks now, youngster. Follow me, and move

warily: the scorpions are easily aroused." And, prone on the ground, the old man twisted himself, with a snake-like motion, out of the lodge and in the direction of the river.

With stiffened limbs, every movement of which caused intense pain, George followed close on the heels of his leader, until they reached a clump of bushes on the edge of the forest, in front of which, as if standing sentinel, was the old man's dog.

"I must leave you here," said the Scout.

"To rescue Ellen, I trust, Scout," said George.

"We must get you off first, boy. If it was n't for that pesky wound of yours we 'd do it at once. But don't worry about the gal; t' other youngster and I will see about her. Brave will lead you to the spot where I will meet you. Go, pup." Thus saying, the Scout rose to his feet and glided silently into the forest.

As the hunter disappeared, the noble dog commenced moving slowly along, turning, from time to time, his head, as if to ascertain that he was duly followed. Finding that his wound would not permit of his walking, George crept along as he best could, dragging his maimed limb painfully after him. His progress was necessarily slow, and his admiration was not a little excited at the sagacity displayed by his canine companion, who seemed to be aware of the difficulty his follower labored under, and timed his pace to suit George's.

The stars shone brightly, but not a ray of light penetrated the covert in which Henry was secreted. Worthly waited, with no little anxiety, the return of his companion. He felt no fear, but there was a wild beating in his heart which he could not control. He thought of Ellen in her loneliness and gloom. He pictured her sitting bowed with grief in her rude wigwam, and he yearned to make his presence known to her. He thought what a solace it would be to her could she but know that friends were at hand, working for her deliverance. Buried in these reveries, an hour or more passed away.

The distant cry of a night-owl broke his train of thought. The ill-omened sound, so in keeping with the surrounding gloom, did not tend to dissipate the depression which had settled upon his spirits. It was not until he heard the cry repeated in another direction that he remembered that it was the signal agreed upon between the Scout and those in the canoe. When this occurred to him, the sound struck him as anything but one of ill omen. Henry now impatiently awaited the issue of events. Intently he listened to catch the returning footsteps of the Scout. Minute after minute passed slowly, but still no sound met his ear. Half an hour perhaps rolled by, when a movement among the bushes sent a sudden thrill to his heart.

"Wal, youngster," said the Scout, thrusting his head into the opening, "most tuckered out? I've seen the gal's brother. He was most cruelly bound, and has got an ugly wound in his thigh. But I cut his thongs, and directed him how to proceed. The sly dog made them think he was worse hurt than he is; and so, fastening him with their cursed withes, they thought they had him safe enough, and did not guard him so carefully as they otherwise would."

"And you will get him clear, then?" asked Henry.

"Speak softly, boy. You 've no idee how sound travels in the night. If nothing turns up, we shall get him out of their clutches, and the gal too, I consate. But come with me, and mind, you are treading among sleeping adders, which the slightest noise may arouse."

Stepping out from his hiding-place, Worthly followed in the lead of the hunter. Occasionally the old fellow would give utterance to a low chuckle. At last he said, in his usual cautious tone, "I declare, that pup of mine knows more than ary human crittur."

"Where is he, Scout?" asked Henry.

"Guiding the youngster down to the canoe."

"Guiding him?" asked Henry, in some astonishment.

"Yes; and enough sight surer guide than I should be. I 'd trust that dog's nose anywhere."

"How did you find where George was?"

"'T was all that pup's doings. Says I, 'Brave,' says I, 'lead me to the white boy.' At that he went snuffing along, until the crittur stopped before one of the tents and began wagging his tail. You need n't tell me that such dogs ain't reasonable beings: I know better." After this, the party proceeded in silence on their way.

They were not long in reaching the river's bank, at a spot just above the encampment. Soon after their arrival, Brave made his appearance, followed by George, who was heartily welcomed by the Scout and Henry. Truly thankful was George when he reached the stream, and many were the congratulations exchanged between the young men at the success which had thus far attended them, while equally lively were they in their gratitude to the Scout.

" Save your thanks, save your thanks, youngsters," said the old man. " Wait till we get out of the varmints' clutches. Remain here a while, and do not speak above your breath, while I go and find the canoe." And the Scout went up the stream.

Just below one of the falls in the river, hidden beneath the overhanging branches, swung a canoe, in which were seated young Eveleth and Stevens.

" They 're a long time coming," remarked the latter.

" We must not speak too loud, Stevens, although the roar of the rapids serves to drown our voice Hark! what is that?"

There was a disturbance of the limbs overhead, followed by the low tones of the Scout. " Drop your canoe down to where the banks are sloping, lads. Move cautiously, and keep snug in shore."

The directions were obeyed; and in a few minutes, with the assistance of Henry and the hunter, George was placed in the canoe and arranged as comfortably as the circumstances would permit.

" Now, youngsters," said the Scout, giving them a parting word of caution, " all depends on yourselves. Move warily. I see the mist is rising; keep in that as much as you can. The moon will be up soon, and some of the varmints may be abroad. Keep your eyes and ears open, and your mouths shut, and by daybreak I trust you will be safe in the block-house."

" And tell your mother, George," said Henry, as the canoe floated from the bank, " that Ellen will not be long in following you, I trust." And, bidding the voyagers a whispered good-night, the Scout and his companion, followed by Brave, turned and plunged into the forest.

CHAPTER VIII.

THE light bark shot rapidly and noiselessly down the stream. The mist soon began to grow more dense, into the thickest of which the canoe was guided. For some time they continued their voyage without meeting with anything to excite their alarm, and their hearts were cheered in anticipation of the successful issue of their expedition. The most profound silence was observed by the party, and their paddles were handled so carefully that only the light dripping of water from the blades could be heard as they raised them from the stream.

It was not long before the moon arose, and, although her light aided to guide them on their way, they would very gladly have dispensed with it, for they felt that they were more secure in the darkness. If the mist had continued unbroken the entire length of the river, they would not have regretted the presence of the "queen of night," for the vapor hung low, shrouding them completely from view; but there were certain portions of the stream, broad patches here and there, on which the moonbeams fell unobstructed. In crossing these they were completely exposed; still, by hugging the shore, they could sometimes take advantage of the deep shadows of the trees and shrubbery that lined the banks, and so escape from observation.

They were crossing one of these openings, which occurred at a bend of the river, where a point of land run out, leaving the water so shallow that they were forced to edge off into the channel, when the dip of paddles was heard on the opposite side, and in a few moments a canoe, containing three savages, bound up stream, shot out of the mist into the open space.

"Down, both of you!" whispered George; "they may pass without discovering us."

The young men crouched immediately into the bottom of the canoe, which floated silently and apparently deserted on the water.

For a time they hoped to escape without being perceived, but presently a low, guttural "Ugh!" came across the stream, and the direction of the strange canoe was seen to change, her prow heading toward them. For a minute or two the savages rested on their paddles, as if scrutinizing the newly discovered object, during which the young men could hear them holding a murmured consultation, and see their significant gestures. They were evidently at fault, and suspicious that the seemingly lone bark might not prove a harmless prize. George watched their movements with the most intense anxiety. For a while the two canoes remained equi-distant, but presently it struck him that the space between them was diminishing.

"By Heavens, they are stealing slowly upon us!" said George. "Up, boys, and strike out for your lives!"

The young men sprang to their feet and plied their paddles with desperate energy. A loud whoop from the savages rang over the water, followed by the report of a gun, and a ball whistled directly over the head of Eveleth.

"A miss is as good as a mile," said George, cheeringly. "Plunge into the mist as soon as possible; we have got a good start of them. This infernal wound of mine," he continued, in an excited tone, "gives

27

them the advantage over us, but we may succeed in
eluding them.   Bend to it, with a will."

In a few minutes the canoe containing our young
party shot into the mist and was lost to sight.   With
the rapidity of a swallow skimming the surface of the
stream, the pursuing bark dashed on, the wily savages
slightly changing its direction so as to intercept the
fugitives at a certain angle.   The young men, however, were as crafty as their pursuers, for as soon as
they had got well into the mist, they, too, changed the
direction of their flight, and made a straight wake for
the opposite bank.   Fortunately for the success of
this manœuvre, the moon just then was obscured by a
passing cloud, and the vapor, being unusually dense,
served effectually to screen them from observation.

"There they go!" said George, in a whisper, as the
quick strokes of paddles were heard crossing their
track astern.   "Dip softly but strongly, and we may
give them the slip, after all.   Would that I could aid
you.   I can pull a trigger, though, if I cannot handle
a paddle;" and he raised a weapon to a position for
instant use.

To enable the reader to understand the position of
the young men, we must explain a little.   Just below
the point we have mentioned as making out into the
river, a quarter of a mile or so, there is a fall, or a
series of falls.   Perhaps the term "rapids" would be
the most correct, as the fall of the stream is gradual,
the angle of descent being about twenty degrees.
Near the centre of the rapids there is a passage, both
difficult and dangerous, even to those acquainted with
its navigation.   From the first dip the current runs
some rods in glassy smoothness, until its bed becomes

broken, when it rushes in boiling whirlpools, seething and foaming over sharp rocks, darting rapidly through narrow passages, whirling and tossing about in the wildest tumult, and threatening instant destruction to whatever should attempt the passage, especially so frail a thing as a birchen canoe. Still, a dexterous hand could carry one through in safety, and, fortunately for our party, George was well acquainted with the intricacies of the passage.

There is near the eastern bank of the river a comparatively smooth and easy channel, which offers no serious impediment. In ascending the river, the rapids are avoided by a narrow portage.

With this brief description, the reader will perceive the position of our party. In doubling on their pursuers, they had crossed to the western bank of the stream, where no channel existed, and from the nature of the ground where no transit could be found to the still water below the rapids.

For a while the young men remained stationary, listening eagerly to catch any sound indicating the presence of the foe, but all remained quiet.

" We had better have kept on," said Stevens, in a low tone, " and run down the eastern passage."

" No," replied Eveleth, " we should have been overhauled before we reached it, or, if we had got into the channel, they would have followed us."

" Well, I do not see that we are any better off, cooped up in this bight."

" There is the central passage," rejoined Eveleth; " worst come to worst, George can take us through that."

" It will be risky business, as the old Scout says,

especially in the night," said George. " But we may
be forced to make the attempt, and, in anticipation of
such an event, you had better prop me up so that I
can guide the canoe."

This was done; and, after waiting some time without hearing or seeing anything of the enemy, they
commenced slowly crossing the river, keeping just in
the edge of the rapids. They had got about in the
middle of the stream, when a slight passing breeze
dispersed the mist, and left them fully exposed to
view in a broad patch of moonlight. To their consternation, there appeared, some few rods up the river,
the other canoe, evidently in search of them. Again
a defiant war-whoop broke upon the stillness of night,
as the party of savages dashed in pursuit.

"There is no help for it now, Eveleth,—push for the
rapids!" shouted George, seizing a paddle to guide
the boat.

They were soon in the quick current, where the
guiding paddle was only required. The savages
were evidently acquainted with the passage, for
they did not hesitate to follow in the track of the
fugitives.

"Are they following us?" asked George, whose
whole attention was devoted to the management of
the canoe, which began to be tossed upon the troubled
waters.

"Yes, yes, close in our wake!" was the simultaneous reply of his companions.

"This will never do," exclaimed George. " See to
your rifles, boys; we must give that helmsman a dose.
Wait a moment until they get into the most dangerous
navigation, and aim only at the one who steers. If

you can bring him down at the proper moment, we shall be saved."

The young men grasped their pieces ready for instant action. The surges were breaking furiously around and under the frail vessel, while the white foam creamed over her sides in thick masses, threatening to swamp her. At one moment she rushed forward with the speed of a race-horse, the next she was tossed amid the struggling billows like an egg-shell. At times it seemed as if she would be dashed on some point of craggy rock and swept to destruction, but almost as soon as the danger was seen it was passed. It required a steady hand and a cool, calculating head to guide a bark through that "hell of waters;" and fortunate for the fugitives was it that young Millet was equal to the task. He knew that it was a matter of life and death, and that all depended on his skill. He forgot his wound; his quick eye took in all things at once, and his ready hand held the quivering vessel in subjection to his will.

"Now, my good fellows," said George, in a calm, determined tone, "we shall presently be a little more quiet for a moment, and they are about entering upon the most dangerous part of the rapids."

The young men sprang to their feet.

"Steady, steady, or you will capsize us. Brace yourselves firmly, and don't waste your shot. Let them have it!"

The young men had taken deliberate aim, and, at the word, a flash and a report followed. Instantly and shrilly above the roar of the rapids a death-cry rang out upon the air. The shot of one of the young

27*

men took effect in the breast of the helmsman, who, throwing his arms wildly in the air, gave one fearfully agonizing cry, and toppled over into the raging waters.

Left to her own guidance, the frail canoe was borne through a narrow channel, and, before the other Indian, who sprang to execute the task, could obtain the mastery of her, was dashed against a point of jagged rocks, against and over which the mad waters beat in clouds of foam. It was but an instant, and the birchen vessel was crushed like a shell, — torn in shreds, — and the two savages were hurled by the force of the current against the sharp ledges, and whirled helpless in the foaming eddies, their mangled bodies catching now on some slippery projecting rock, and now jammed tightly in some narrow crevice, while the laughing billows leaped around them, as if exulting over their prey.

With a triumphant shout the young men shot safely on their way, and were soon gliding once more over the smooth surface of the stream. Nothing further transpired to interrupt their passage, and soon after daybreak the canoe touched the landing-place. The walk thence to the block-house was one of great difficulty and pain to George, but, supported by his companions, they reached the gates soon after sunrise. We need not dwell on the enthusiastic reception they received, nor on the joy their presence inspired.

Annie did not meet George at his entrance. It was not until he was alone in his mother's room that the interview took place. Hastily entering and rushing towards him, she flung herself on his bosom, weeping convulsively.

"Dear George!"

"Dear Annie!"

There was a world of meaning in the tone and manner of utterance of that brief salutation, which expressed more than we could crowd into a volume.

Leaving George in the care of his cousin, who, it may be presumed, proved a tender and devoted nurse, let us turn our attention to Ellen, and those who were seeking her rescue.

CHAPTER IX.

"I NEVER knew the varmints to be so unguarded," said the Scout, in a subdued tone, as he and Henry left the bank of the river. "They thought the youngster was hurt worse than he proves to be, and they reckoned they had him safe enough, I warrant you. How it will ruck them when they find that their intended victim has escaped their infarnal tortures!" and the old fellow chuckled as if he enjoyed the disappointment that awaited the Indians.

"But what do you propose to do for Ellen?" asked Henry.

"Wal, I've been turning the matter over in my mind. I see the moon is 'bout rising, and it will be risky business. I'm not sure but that it will be best to take another night for it."

"For Heaven's sake, do not think of that!" hastily replied Worthly, who shuddered at the idea that they might wreak their vengeance on her when they had ascertained the escape of George.

"Whist, whist, youngster! not too loud! Your feelings are nat'ral, young man," rejoined the Scout, who conjectured the fears of his companion, "but I know the nater of the red-skins better than you do. They will not touch a hair of her head. Howsomever, I will see what can be done. You wait here, and I will go and look round a little. Come, Brave, let us look for the gal!" and, after a few directions to Henry, he glided off in the direction of the encampment.

He had not been absent but a short time when he returned, and, in somewhat hurried tones, said: "The dogs are astir, and the pack will open on us directly. Come this way, a little more into the woods; we'll watch the varmints;" and he led off at a rapid pace into the forest.

They had proceeded but a few steps when an infuriated yell burst upon the night air, as if a herd of demons had broken loose. A low laugh burst from the Scout, as yell after yell rang through the forest. "That's just like them critturs," said he; "when they're riled, the only way they can spit out their spite is to set up an infarnal howling, just like a pack of painters or wolves."

Just then momentary gleams flashed through the woods, as of torches borne hurriedly to and fro.

"Ha, ha! they'll find him, I consate! It was a lucky sarcumstance we got him off as we did. If the boys hain't been interrupted, he's safe out of their clutches by this time."

"But will not this discovery operate against us?" asked Henry, who saw in it a destruction of all hope of rescuing Ellen, for the present at least.

"I'm not sartain about that," replied the old man.

" By what I observed, all the party were not in camp,
— off working mischief somewhere else, I s'pose, the
infarnal hounds! You'll observe, by the clustering
of torches, they have diskivered something, probably
the trail to the river."

" Well," said Henry, as the old man paused and
gazed in the direction of the lights.

" Wal, it is reasonable to calculate, don't you see,
that some on 'em will start in pursuit, and much good
may it do 'em! That, in course, will leave so many
the less to contend with."

" But will not those who remain keep a stricter
watch?" asked Henry.

" Undoubtedly, youngster, but we must throw wool
over their eyes. We must contrive some plan to
draw off their attention, and then seize upon the
moment to get the gal off. Let me consider a moment;" and the old man mused a while, buried in
thought.

" Yes, that may do," he muttered to himself; " 't will
be purty risky business, though;" then, addressing his
companion, he continued: " My mind is this. There's
a cluster of lodges near the river which are empty,
save one, which contains their stores and skins. Now
if we could set fire to one of these, the whole would
soon be in a blaze. Nat'rally they would all rush to
save their property; then would be your chance to
rescue the gal. But, boy, it's a bold trick, and there's
some risk in it. If we did not succeed, the gal's
life might be jeopardized. The malignant devils might
brain her in their rage. Dare you attempt it, youngster?"

Henry was silent for some moments. The probably fatal consequences attending a failure pressed heavily upon his mind, and he knew not how to decide.

"Dare you attempt it?" again asked the Scout.

Fearful of assuming a responsibility pregnant with the life or death of one so dear to him, the young man replied: "I cannot decide; I know not what to say, Scout. I leave the whole matter to you. You know what is best, what risks we shall run, and what are our chances of success."

"Wal, then," rejoined the Scout, "if you leave it to me, I decide to follow the plan I mentioned. I acknowledge there is danger, but there can't be many of the varmints left, and, worst come to worst, we can fight it out with the reptyles. Should it come to that, they will not show a fair stand-up fight, but skulk. Then, you see, Brave and I can keep them at bay, while you and the gal can escape."

"But there is your own risk, Scout," said Henry.

"That, young man, I don't count much on. I've lived through worse skrimmages than this is likely to be. I consate that the ball that is to reach my life is not moulded yet. But, if I do fall, what matters a year or two off a lonely old man's life, who has got not a kin in the world to mourn his death? But I can't go before the good God calls me. There are so many grains of sand put in each man's glass, young-ster, and that sand must run out in its nat'ral course; you can't hurry the grains, you can't check them. Man has his allotted time, and all the bloody red-skins on airth can't cheat him out of a single second. If I am to fall, I am to fall. That's the doctrine we preach, down to the Sabba'-day Pond meetings. So don't be consarned about me, youngster."

While the old man was thus unfolding his creed, they had been making a circuit of the woods, so as to obtain a position in the rear of the encampment. Their progress had been slow, and by the time they arrived there the hubbub in camp had subsided, and quiet once more reigned in the place.

" Now," said the Scout, " I will go and see if the snakes have crawled into their holes. It's my idee that the young woman's lodge is the farthest one back, near the edge of the forest. If so be it is, it will be all the better. Brave will point it out to me. Come, pup." And the old man and his dog moved off in the direction of the encampment.

The young man, thus left alone in the forest, felt ill at ease. It was natural, now that the crisis of his adventure was approaching, that he should be somewhat excited. The emotions that agitated him were various and opposite in their characters. Hope struggled with fear. The thought of speedily releasing Ellen from her bondage thrilled him with joy. Then came apprehensions of the difficulties that surrounded him, of the probably fatal consequences that would follow a failure of their plans, shadowing his joy and filling his heart with despondency. Dark forebodings stole over his mind, and his excited imagination pictured the captive a victim to his rashness; and he half-regretted that he had not postponed the attempt until a more favorable opportunity. But would a more favorable one be presented? Would not the attempted rescue be at all times fraught with danger? Revolving the subject in his mind, Henry concluded that it was no

time to falter now, and he nerved himself for the task
before him. In the course of half an hour he was rejoined by the Scout.

"The reptyles have crept into their dens," said he;
"but 't ain't likely they have gone to sleep. I 've
ascertained the lodge where your sweetheart is, but I
did n't venture to go near it. Come this way (tread
softly, for they have sharp ears!) and I will point it
out to you. The moon is getting up, which will be
of some sarvice, although for such a job as this darkness would be best."

The moon, however, had not risen above the tree-
tops, and it afforded just light enough to allow them
to distinguish the situation of the lodges when they
had arrived at the edge of the forest. The Scout then
pointed out the wigwam which Ellen occupied, and
gave directions to Henry how to proceed.

"You will keep your station here, and Brave will
remain with you — (do you hear, pup?) — while I go
and fire the lodges. When the flames burst out and
the varmints rush towards them, then is your chance.
Keep in the rear of the lodge, in the shade, and cut
your way through and release the gal. Mind and have
your thoughts about you, youngster. Don't be rash,
don't be excited: one can't be too cool on such occasions as this. A false move might ruin us all."

"But where will you join me?" asked Henry, in
the same cautious tone employed by the Scout.

"That depends on sarcumstances. I may have to
show myself to draw off pursuit. At any rate, you
will plunge into the woods, keeping the moon over
your right shoulder, — over your right shoulder, remember that, boy. If I lose your trail, Brave will

bring us together, without doubt. Be wary and collected, and, when the rush happens, make quick work of it." Saying thus, the old man crept silently off to the left in the skirts of the woods.

Henry stood by a little thicket somewhat in advance of the heavy timber, and but a few rods before him, dimly discerned, rose the lodge in which Ellen was confined. He had left his rifle leaning against a tree, but he held in his hand a large hunting-knife, ready for instant use. The moment was one of thrilling interest, and, as he stood there, his gaze fixed on the cluster of wigwams, scarcely perceptible, by the river's side, waiting for the signal, every nerve seemed strung to its utmost tension. There was no quivering of the muscles, no trembling of the limbs. He was calm, almost preternaturally calm.

Beside him stood the faithful Brave. At times the sagacious animal would seem to be gazing steadfastly on the lodge ; then, raising his head toward Henry, he would wag his tail, as if to assure him that he was aware of all that was going on. At one time he gave a just audible growl, and, with bristling hair, he crouched in a springing attitude. At that moment Henry perceived the dusky form of a savage lurking in the neighborhood of Ellen's lodge. He saw him but for an instant, ere he disappeared behind one of the tents. The dog crept slowly forward a few steps, and, after snuffing the air a while, returned to the young man's side, as if satisfied that no danger was to be apprehended. It was very evident that the savage had been prying around to see that all was quiet, and, finding nothing to excite suspicion, had retired.

28

Some considerable time elapsed, and Henry waited anxiously, wondering at the delay of the Scout. Like all impatient waiters, when some important crisis is impending, the moments dragged slowly by. At last he thought he detected a small point of light, a mere spark. He strained his eyes in the direction of the lodges. It disappeared, then it shone out more distinctly, and presently he observed tiny tongues of flame flickering out of the side of one of the central lodges. In a few moments a slight explosion was heard, and the birchen side of the lodge was rent apart, while from the curling bark a vast volume of flame spread out in every direction; at the same instant a rush of feet was heard, and a terrible yell rose on the air.

With a beating heart, Worthly dashed forward at the sound. It was but the work of a moment to cut a passage through the frail material of which the lodge was composed. As he forced his way through the opening, a shriek of terror burst from the captive.

"Ellen, dear Ellen, be not alarmed. I have come to save you. Quick—follow me."

"Henry, Henry, can it be you?" exclaimed the trembling girl. "I cannot move; I am bound."

Springing to her side, Worthly cut the thongs that confined her feet and arms, and, raising her to her feet, he bore her through the entrance he had made. The whole air was now illuminated with the blazing lodges, and the infuriated cries of the savages rang through the encampment. Scarcely glancing at the conflagration, Henry darted towards the forest. At this moment an athletic young savage sprang from behind a neighboring wigwam, brandishing the deadly

tomahawk, directly in the path of the fugitives.
Henry did not perceive that he was pursued, and in
another moment the fatal weapon would have been
buried in his head. But there was a deliverer at
hand.

The first notice the young man had of the threatened danger was a deep growl from Brave, and, hastily turning his head, he saw the powerful animal leap
panther-like from the ground and seize the Indian by
the throat; a second glance revealed to him the dog
and savage struggling furiously on the earth. His
first impulse was to go to the assistance of his faithful
ally, but a thought of the momentous interest he had
at stake restrained him, and without checking his
speed he kept on, and in a few moments reached the
forest and was in possession of his rifle. Without
pausing a moment, he hurried his companion into the
depths of the woods, stopping not until the light from
the burning camp was lost to sight. He then selected
a dense thicket, in the centre of which he found a
slight opening, into which he made his way with his
companion, and made a brief halt, to enable the
affrighted girl in some degree to recover herself. "I
can keep on still farther," said the panting girl. "Let
us not wait here; they will pursue us."

"We will stop but a moment for you to recover
breath, Ellen. They will not follow us at present, I
think. Thank God, we have succeeded thus far so
well."

"Yes, yes, we indeed owe Him our thanks. But
O, Henry, what will become of poor George? They
will surely murder him."

"He is safe out of their hands by this time, I trust,

my dear girl;" and in a hasty manner he informed her of his rescue, and of the means they had taken to effect her escape.

While they were thus conversing, they were startled by a rustling among the bushes in which they had sought refuge, as if some one were forcing an entrance. Springing from the little mound on which he had been sitting, the young man stood with levelled rifle, prepared to receive the intruder. A low, joyful bark caused him to lower it on the instant.

"It is the noble Brave," said he; and the faithful animal broke into the enclosure, and, bounding to Ellen's side, placed his head on her lap, seemingly testifying by mute signs his joy at her escape. Henry and his companion caressed the noble animal, to whose services they probably owed their lives, rejoicing heartily at his escape from the struggle with the savage.

In that struggle, however, the dog had not run much risk. When he sprang upon the savage, he seized him in his huge jaws directly by the throat, and brought him at once to the ground. The Indian was entirely powerless in his grasp, and in a short time was completely throttled. Not until his victim had ceased to struggle did the dog quit his hold, when, being apparently satisfied that he was dead, he shook himself, and running awhile to and fro until he caught the scent of the fugitives, he bounded rapidly into the forest on their track.

CHAPTER X.

"Had we not better continue on, Henry?" said Ellen; "I feel quite rested. Every moment we remain in the neighborhood is full of danger."

"I think we had," replied her companion, "and Brave seems to be of the same opinion. See, he stands ready to lead the way."

Cautiously the party made their way out of the thicket. Ascertaining the position of the moon, glimpses of which could now be caught through the trees, Henry followed the direction of the Scout by getting it over his right shoulder, and then with his companion moved rapidly forward.

They had not proceeded far when the report of a gun came faintly echoing through the forest from their rear, followed shortly after by a second.

"The Scout is engaged with them," said Henry. "Pray Heaven no harm may befall him, for without his aid I fear it will be difficult to find our way."

When the reports were heard, Brave gave evident signs of uneasiness, turning his head in the direction whence they came, and whining repeatedly.

"The dog knows that his master is in danger," said Ellen, "and evidently wishes to seek him."

"Yes, and I think he had better go," rejoined her companion; "he will be of more use to him than to us. Go, Brave, and seek your master."

The dog jumped joyfully in the air, and then with the speed of a deer dashed toward the Indian camp, while Henry and his companion continued their toilsome journey.

28*

As the young couple, doubtless, will have no objection to being left by themselves, we will leave them to proceed on their way, and go back and see how it fares with the Scout.

When he left Henry to fire the lodges, he crept along the edge of the forest until he was near the river. To accomplish his object required the utmost wariness, for every step was encompassed with danger. Leaving his gun in the woods, the old man crept stealthily toward the cluster of lodges, which were so close together that the bark of which they were composed came in contact at the base.

Selecting the central lodge, he was not long in effecting an entrance. He had brought with him a quantity of dried brush and leaves, which he placed against the sides of the tent, and then striking a fire with a flint and steel, which he always carried with him (for loco-foco matches were unknown luxuries in those days), after some time he succeeded in kindling a blaze, which soon seized upon the inflammable material of which the wigwam was composed. Leaving a package of powder in the centre of the lodge, he hastily took his departure, closing every aperture whence the light could be seen. He then started for the woods, but before he reached them the explosion took place, and the yell of the savages burst upon his ears. Startling from his stooping posture, he rushed to the place where he had left his rifle. Once more under cover, with the knowledge he possessed of forest life, he had no apprehensions of pursuit.

Hovering in the skirts of the forest he saw the savages, four in number, after they had made an attempt to secure their skins and stores, suddenly rush to the rear of the encampment, where they gathered in a state of great excitement. One of them hastily entered the lodge in which Ellen had been confined, and as hastily emerged, gesticulating and speaking in a most excited manner. Presently a wild outcry burst from one of the number, who had gone toward the forest, which drew the rest to his side. To the Scout's surprise, he saw them stoop down and lift up what appeared to be a dead body. Could it be that the captive or the young man had fallen? — this was the first thought that darted into his mind. The mystery was shortly solved, for the savages soon bore the corpse into the centre of the camp, and placed it on a mat in front of one of the lodges. As they laid the body down, the Scout saw by the glare of the burning wigwams the torn and ghastly throat.

"That is some of Brave's doings," the old man chuckled to himself. "The varmint was on their track, no doubt, and the dog seized upon him. That pup is worth his weight in gold."

The attention of the Scout was soon attracted to the movements of the savages. He saw them looking around diligently as if in search of the trail of the fugitives, and presently he knew by their actions that they had discovered it. Two of the party were evidently about to follow it up. This the old man determined to prevent, even at the risk of his own life.

Stepping out into the clearing, he levelled his piece at the foremost Indian. Was he ever known to miss a shot? The woods echoed with the report, and the Indian fell headlong to the earth. During the confusion that ensued, the old man deliberately reloaded his

rifle, and then started off in a direction contrary to
that taken by the fugitives.

With a yell of rage the savages rushed in pursuit,
one of whom discharged his gun at him, but without
effect, although the ball split a sapling close by his
side.

"A good shot," muttered the Scout to himself, "a
capital shot, if aimed at the sapling. But you can't
expect much from such a breed."

The old man led the chase some distance in the
woods, until, coming to a large fallen tree, he dropped
suddenly to the ground, and crept under its trunk,
where the branches grew the thickest. His pursuers
soon arrived at the spot, and two of them kept on,
while one of them sat down on the butt of the fallen
tree, evidently to rest himself. The Scout could hear
him breathing heavily, as if exhausted with the pursuit.

It was a critical moment with the old hunter. The
least movement on his part would betray his hiding-
place. In case he should be discovered, he deemed it
best to be prepared for the struggle; he therefore
cautiously felt for his hunting-knife. In drawing it
from its sheath, he accidentally struck his arm against
a small dry limb, which broke with a slight noise.
This at once attracted the attention of the savage,
who sprang to his feet and threw suspicious glances
around him.

The Scout had no fears of coping with the savage
single-handed, and would have made the venture, did
he not know that the whoop of the Indian would recall his companions, thus making the odds too much
for him. He therefore kept quiet, and fortunately for

him,—as the Indian was creeping warily towards him, and was on the point of reaching out his hand to remove some of the branches that sheltered him,— a partridge, or some other bird, broke from among the limbs, seemingly frightened from its nest, and took refuge in some underbrush in the vicinity. The sight of the bird at once allayed the suspicion of the savage, and after a short halt, to the Scout's great relief, he started in the direction taken by the others.

Waiting until the sound of his retiring footsteps was lost, the Scout crept softly from his covert, and with a light step retraced his way to the encampment. Just before he reached the open space, he heard a quick movement behind him, and he immediately sprang behind a tree for a cover. He might have succeeded in concealing himself from an enemy, but he could not from the faithful Brave, who rushed toward and leaped upon him with the most lively manifestations of joy.

"Ha, pup! you come in good time!" said his master, patting him heartily. "I 've started the reptyles on a wrong scent, Brave, and you must put me on the right one. Come, old fellow!" and the Scout followed around the edge of the forest, until he arrived in the vicinity of the lodge recently occupied by Ellen.

The embers of the burnt lodges still emitted a lurid light, and a heavy smoke still hung over the ground and curled among the trees. Occasionally the cinders would flame up, throwing a momentary light upon the surrounding objects; then die away, leaving the place enveloped in a ten-fold gloom. A grim smile played over the old man's face as he gazed upon the scene of desolation.

"The varmints have had their bonfire," he muttered to himself, "but 't ain't such a one as they calkerlated on, I reckon! If 't wan't for the youngster and gal, now, I'd wait here jest to enjoy the rage of the sarpents who have gone down the river, when they come back and find what's been done."

The Scout was gratified, for, as he turned to leave the spot, he heard the quick dip of paddles, and presently two canoes shot into the cove, from which some seven or eight savages leaped to the land. They were met on landing by two or three squaws. There was a noisy jabbering and violent gesticulations on both sides, followed by a howl of rage that made the forest ring again. In their frenzy some of them leaped around the ruined lodges like maniacs, twisting their faces into the most diabolical contortions, gnashing their teeth like famished wolves, and brandishing their tomahawks fiercely in the air, as if in the presence of their hated foe.

"Come, pup, let's be off!" said the hunter. "That, now, is something worth hearing and seeing. To call them critturs human beings! Why, a pack of starved catermounts wouldn't cut up such awful freaks!" With these remarks, the old fellow followed the dog, which had caught the scent of the fugitives, into the woods.

Henry and Ellen had continued their way through the mazes of the forest. At the first he was particular in following the direction given him in regard to keeping the moon over his right shoulder. Had he not paid attention to this he would probably have made but little progress. There is no place where one can be so easily lost as in a forest; and in the night-time, without something especial to guide you, one cannot take ten paces without being completely bewildered in regard to the proper direction to be followed.

As our young couple journeyed on, their conversation was naturally directed to the exciting incidents connected with the circumstances in which they were placed. But gradually the topic was changed: Ellen whispered of gratitude, which her companion responded to as any young man would in such a situation, until at length, insensibly, as it were, Henry found himself breathing in the ear of the blushing maiden that tale which, the poet tells us,

"Must be told by the moonlight alone!"

It was a very pleasant mode of whiling away the tedium of a night tramp, and from our heart we cannot blame the young man, who, no doubt, was prompted to it by a desire to make his companion forget the dangers that surrounded them. And most admirably did he succeed. We doubt whether, if a savage had started up by their elbows, they would have given him more than a careless glance, perhaps a reproving one, for his intrusion.

They were wandering along in that happy reverie in which it is said young lovers are apt to indulge when taking a walk by moonlight, when Henry was startled out of his elysian dream by feeling a heavy hand laid on his left shoulder.

"Ha, youngster!" and the voice of the Scout was

toned with good-humored irony, "is this your *right* shoulder? The moon up yonder seems to be peeping over it, at any rate! Wal, wal, it is n't strange, when one's head and heart get turned, that the body should turn with them. It's risky business, Miss, for young folks to be roving abroad in the forest at night; they 're mighty apt to mistake their way. I was young once myself;" and the old man chuckled over his remarks.

"But the night is fast waning," he continued; "we have a long tramp yet before us, and had better hurry on. It's lucky the Injuns have n't their dogs with them to follow up our trail. I make no doubt, as soon as there is sufficient light, they will be upon it."

"We heard the report of guns, and were fearful that something might have happened to you," said Ellen.

"Yes, I had a bit of a skrimmage — not much to speak of. You will be glad to hear that the party which went down the river have returned without bringing the boy; so I consate he 's safe. They were awfully riled when they found the lodges were destroyed. I hope, Miss, you 'll be able to go along a piece farther, for the varmints have got their blood up, and will surely be on our heels."

Ellen assured him that she felt perfectly able to keep on, and urged their doing so. Striking into an Indian file, the Scout taking the lead and Henry bringing up the rear, while Brave acted as a sort of escort, they proceeded rapidly on their way. The utmost caution was exercised by the Scout to prevent, as much as possible, leaving any marks to indicate the route they had taken. Every artifice was resorted to in order to perplex those who might follow them.

CHAPTER XI.

AFTER the return of George, the whole interest of the inmates of the block-house was concentrated on Ellen and those who were seeking her rescue. The fears of her parents were in some degree allayed, and they hardly entertained a doubt but that her deliverance would be effected. All eyes were now bent on the bridge, in expectation of the appearance of the party. Henry's message to Mrs. Millet, that Ellen would not be long behind George, had greatly excited the hopes of all, and she was confidently looked for before breakfast, which had been put off to a late hour on her account.

But hour after hour passed by, and still there were no signs of her coming. Slowly the time crept on until noon, and with every passing hour the anxiety of the inmates increased. Doubts began to fill their minds of the most painful nature. Had the attempted rescue failed? And if so, would not the savages, to prevent any further trouble, as well as to avenge their disappointment by reason of George's flight, murder Ellen at once? These were the questions they asked of each other, with a fearful apprehension of the worst.

A watch had been stationed in the tower to give notice of the approach of the absent party; and, as the recently excited hopes were giving way to despair, it was announced that a report of a gun was heard afar

29

off in the woods. All assembled to listen, and again a report was heard, followed by still others. A hasty consultation was instantly held. The party were evidently near at hand, but had been followed and were now attacked by the Indians.

Six young men immediately volunteered their services to hasten to their assistance, and, led off by Eveleth, they started at a rapid pace in the direction whence the reports came. As they crossed the bridge and struck off through the woods, repeated shots told them that the party were hotly engaged, and guided their steps to the combat. They pressed on at great speed, nerved with excitement, which was not a little heightened by hearing a wild outcry that sounded to their ears like the triumphant yell of the savages.

"Press on, press on!" shouted Eveleth, as he dashed ahead with renewed speed. "We may be too late to save them. That shout spoke of some advantage on the part of the Indians."

It was not long before they reached the scene of action, and their arrival was not a moment too soon, for they found the Scout and Henry engaged with some eight or ten Indians in a desperate tree fight. The fugitives had been forced to take a devious course in order to blind pursuit. Fortunately they had arrived nearly within gunshot sound of the fort before the Indians came up with them. Finding that they could not escape them, they had slowly retreated, keeping the enemy at bay, until they reached a heavy growth of timber, where they came to a halt. Through this dense wood, fortunately for them, there ran a windrow of trees, caused by one of those tornadoes which often pass through a forest, like some huge monster, treading down the tallest trees in its path.

This windrow served admirably as a barricade ; and, stationing themselves behind this defence, they kept the foe in check, trusting that the report of their guns would be heard at the block-house, and bring a party to their relief. Ellen, in the meanwhile, was concealed in a deep grassy hollow, where, by crouching down, she would be protected from any chance shot. Henry urged her to proceed on alone, but she persisted in remaining.

" I cannot leave you here in danger," she replied to his remonstrances. " If you lose your life, I do not wish mine to be saved."

As the supply of ammunition was getting low, the party had to be sparing of its use, and only fired when they were sure their shots would be effective.

The savages, who were on a slightly rising ground, took advantage of the trees, skulking from one to another, gradually drawing nearer to the fallen timber, on which it was their evident intention to make a rush, when they should succeed in drawing the fire of the little party.

" We must resarve our shots," said the Scout, coolly taking a piece of dried meat from his pouch and eating it. " The varmints are mighty tricky. Here, now, is a trick of theirs when they want to waste the powder of their foe." So saying, the old man raised his cap a few inches above the logs by means of a stick. No sooner was it up, than there was a discharge from the Indians, and a ball went humming through it. " There, you see, youngster, is so much powder burnt for nothing," said the hunter, as he picked up his cap as composedly as if he were safe in the fort; " therefore don't fire at the imps unless you are sure of them."

While he was speaking, the Indians raised a shout of triumph at the result of the shot, and two or three of them started forward from their covers. Worthly caught the movement, and a shot from his rifle brought the foremost savage to the ground.

" Well done, my boy!" exclaimed the Scout. " They will l'arn a lesson from that, I consate, that a white skin has cunning as well as a red one."

The late shout of triumph was exchanged for a yell of rage, as the enemy saw one of their number bite the dust, and became aware of the trick that had been played upon them. It is a custom with the red men, when one of their number falls, to proclaim their loss by wild shouts of rage. With the white man it is different. He will stand in stern silence and witness battalion after battalion mowed down, as at Waterloo, the only sounds that are heard being the groans and cries of the wounded and dying.

After the yell that attended the fall of the Indian, an ominous silence prevailed among the band. Not a sound was heard nor a sign perceived to denote their presence.

" I don't like this," said the old man, after waiting some time. " Keep a sharp lookout, youngster; I mistrust the varmints are planning some mischief."

At this moment a cry from Ellen startled them. " Henry, Henry! Scout! O Heaven, they are creeping over the trees — there at the right!"

It was too true. Three or four of the savages had stolen away unperceived to the right, and were scaling the fallen trees, thus out-flanking the little party.

Their case now appeared desperate, and Henry looked to the Scout, with an anxious, inquiring look.

There was a ferocious fire gleaming in the old man's eyes, and the expression of his features evinced a bold determination. "There 's no help for it, boy!" he muttered, between his clenched teeth: "we must take each of us to a tree, and sell our lives as dearly as possible. I would n't mind it much if the gal was out of harm's way. Lay low, Miss, so that the shot shan't hit you. They shall have my life before a hair of her head is touched."

"And mine, too, if a thousand were linked with it," said Henry, firmly, who in this great extremity still remained unshaken in his courage.

At the bidding of the Scout, Ellen crouched tremblingly to the earth, while the old man and his companion each took to a tree for a cover. They could see the Indians gliding from one trunk to another towards them, but they did not dare to venture a shot until they were secure of their men, and the woods here were so dense that the savages could approach them more safely.

After a time the Scout discharged his piece at one of the five, whose body was not wholly covered. A cry of pain told that the shot had taken effect, although not a fatal one. At almost the same moment, happening to cast his eye to the left, Henry detected a savage creeping up to attack them in the rear. He immediately fired at him, and the Indian fell mortally wounded. No sooner was the report heard than a rush was made by the savages in front, with brandished tomahawks. There was no time to reload.

"Club your rifle, boy," shouted the old man; "let

29*

us sell our lives dearly." And the two stood with clubbed pieces, determined to defend themselves to the last, while, close in the rear of the hunter, stood Bravo, with hair erect, and showing a formidable row of teeth, ready to join the melee.

So absorbed had been both parties in the others' movements, that they had not perceived the company of young men, who were cautiously making their way through the woods. The first notice that they had of their presence was a ringing .volley, which was nearly simultaneous with the charge made by the savages, followed by a loud shout, as the young men rushed into view of the astonished and delighted Scout and his companion.

The volley was well directed, for three out of four of the savages plunged forward and fell to the earth in the struggle of death, the tomahawk of one of them flying through the air and burying itself in the very tree behind which Henry had taken refuge.

"To cover, youngsters, to cover!" shouted the Scout, reloading his rifle, while an exulting smile played over his countenance. And, springing to the barricade, his example was immediately followed by the rest.

But the danger was passed. The few remaining savages, seeing the fall of their companions, retreated precipitately, leaving four of their band on the ground. When this fact was ascertained, loud and hearty were the congratulations that passed between the parties, the rescuers and the rescued, in which Ellen, though pallid and shaking with recent affright, joined as heartily as the rest. The old hunter, meanwhile, busied himself in securing the spoils, that is, the arms and

ammunition, not forgetting the scalps, of the fallen.
This accomplished, with joyful steps the company
started for the block-house.

As they drew near the bridge, three shots fired in
rapid succession gave notice to those in the fort of
the success of the expedition, to which the swivel in
the tower immediately sent back a booming response.

With what emotions of joy did Ellen recross that
rustic bridge and emerge into the clearing! Half
way down the slope Annie came flying rather than
running, and with wild exclamations of joy threw
herself into the arms of her cousin. Just outside
of the palisade stood Mr. and Mrs. Millet, ready to
receive their daughter, while gathered within clustered the inmates, eager to welcome the rescued
one, but standing apart, out of respect to the feelings of the parents, whose agitation was too great for
concealment.

As the party drew near, Henry, with a face glowing with happiness, stepped out from the little group,
leading Ellen by the hand. In silence he conducted
her to her father, who stood with outstretched arms
to receive her. Folding her to his breast in a warm
embrace, he raised his hands devoutly, and said, in
tones almost too full for utterance: "Verily, God
hath heard me; he hath attended to the voice of my
prayer. Blessed be God, which hath not turned
away my prayer, nor his mercy from me!"

Choking back her tears, — tears springing from a
heart surcharged with happiness, — Ellen left her
father's arms to be received into her mother's passionate embrace. Not a few eyes, unused to tears,
grew moist over that tender meeting, — a scene we

should vainly endeavor to portray, although it is one
we delight to linger over.

The reception given to the Scout and Henry you
may be sure was not wanting in warmth and hearti-
ness.   Such grasping and shaking of hands, and such
noisy congratulations, are not witnessed every day.

The following morning, as the Scout was about
taking his leave (for he was not a man to remain long
inactive), Ellen went up to him, and, placing her hand
in his, renewedly thanked him for his services, and
added, "How shall I repay the great debt I owe
you, Scout?"

"That depends on sarcumstances, gal," said the old
hunter, fondling the plump little hand in his broad
palm as he would a young bird.   "Have you squared
accounts with the youngster yonder?"

"He says he is satisfied," said Ellen, with a glowing face, casting a bright glance towards Henry.

"Yes, I dare say the rogue has forestalled me,"
rejoined the Scout.   "Wal, then, I s'pose I must be
content with an invitation to the wedding, which, in
course, will come off one of these days.   He is worthy
of you, Miss, and may God bless you both!   Come,
pup;" and, followed by the dog, he left the block-
house, and soon struck into the woods.

The main interest of our story is over.   Disheartened by their losses, the Indians did not make their
appearance again that winter.   In the spring the men,
under protection of the guns of the fort, ventured
out to see to their farms.   But it was not until the
year 1760 that they finally left the block-house, and
returned to their long-deserted homes.   During this
time two of the men had been seized by the savages,

and carried prisoners to Canada, and one was killed and scalped in the lower part of the town, after which the settlement received no further trouble from the Indians.

We suppose we should not be pardoned if we omitted to describe one pleasing incident which took place the fall after the rescue of the captives.

One fine autumnal evening there was an unusual stir in the block-house. All the elderly persons were dressed in their go-to-meeting clothes, and all the young folks decked out in their holiday attire. A great event was to come off — a double wedding to take place. We are half tempted to describe the young couples, as they stood up there, flushed with the glory of youth and of anticipated bliss. But all brides are "beautiful," and as for bridegrooms, who cares a fig for them?

Conspicuous among those who witnessed the ceremony was the tall form of the Scout, with his noble dog by his side. When the rites were performed, the old man took the hands of Henry and Ellen with a hearty grasp:

"God bless you, young folks!" said he, with no little emotion. "You little dreamed of this, I consate, one year ago this night, when you were tramping in the woods, with the infarnal red-skins arter you!"

Henry and Ellen glanced archly at each other, as their thoughts reverted to the moonlight walk.

"Ha, youngsters," said the Scout, who surmised their thoughts, "you're thinking of the moon's getting over the wrong shoulder! There was something warmer than moonshine on 't other shoulder, I consate! Did n't I tell you that it was risky business for young folks to be abroad in the woods by moonlight? and you see here what has come of it."

We leave our principal personages with the cup of happiness at their lips, trusting that we may hereafter meet them again under not less agreeable auspices.

THE LIBERTY POLE.

A TALE OF MACHIAS.

O for the swords of former time !
O for the men who bore them !
When, armed for right, they stood sublime,
And tyrants crouched before them.   MOORE.

CHAPTER I.

ON an evening in the latter part of April, 1775, a number of persons were collected in a small tavern in the town of Machias. A day or two previous the inhabitants had received the proclamation of the Provincial Congress of Massachusetts, authorizing and requiring preparations and efforts to be made incident to a state of hostility. The people of Machias had, from the first, been strenuously opposed to the usurpations of the British Government; and the sole topic of conversation, whenever a few met together, was this exciting subject. On the evening in question, a much larger number than usual had assembled to talk over the stirring news recently received from Boston.

Conspicuous among the rest were two young men, brothers, by the name of O'Brion, sons of Morris

(347)

O'Brion, who came to this country from Cork, in Ireland. Seated around the ample fireplace, enjoying their pipes and cans, the all-engrossing topic of the hour was canvassed by one and all.

At last the elder of the brothers, Jeremiah O'Brion, spoke out: " Well, neighbors, what do you think of this rumor that is flying about?"

" What rumor do you allude to?" asked a man by the name of Foster, who sat near by, and who held the dignified office of colonel in the militia.

" Why, that the first blow has been struck, Colonel, and American blood spilt at Lexington and Concord."

" Where did you get that news?" was the immediate inquiry of nearly all present.

" I know not how the news reached us, but such is the report."

" And what followed?" rejoined Colonel Foster, in a tone of great earnestness. "Did our people submit to the outrage? Were they so dastardly as not to retaliate?"

" You must mistake the spirit of the people of Lexington and Concord, Colonel, if you think they patiently submitted to such an act of violence. Not they; many a red-coat bit the dust in consequence. Men, bowed down by age, forgot the weight of years; and boys, scarcely able to hold a musket, rushed forth to avenge the blood of their countrymen; and all along, so says the report, the road was strewed with the dead bodies of the retreating enemy."

" God grant it may be true ! " was echoed from several parts of the room.

" I move," said O'Brion, when the agitation whi h

this news had excited had subsided, "that to-morrow we raise a Liberty Pole in front of the town-house."

"Agreed! agreed!" was the animated response from every quarter.

"And that a Committee of Safety be appointed," he added, "who shall have a supervision of all the affairs relating to the proclamation lately received from the Provincial Congress."

"You will pardon me, gentlemen, for interfering, as I am not an inhabitant of the place," remarked a gentleman present, by the name of Jones, who belonged to Boston, but who had a store in Machias, and exercised in consequence considerable influence; "while I cordially approve the spirit manifested on the present occasion, yet permit me to suggest if it would not be more advisable to call a town-meeting, to act on the propositions that have been made this evening. To give weight to acts of this character, they should be legally sanctioned; and from what I know of the good people of Machias, I doubt not they will unanimously coincide with your views."

This seasonable proposition won the assent of all; for it is a noted fact, that the men of the Revolution were a "law-and-order" loving people, and all the acts which preceded that great movement were in conformity to a previously authorized "vote."

Accordingly, the next day a public meeting of the inhabitants was called, at which it was voted to comply fully with the requisitions of the proclamation of the Provincial Congress. A Committee of Safety was forthwith appointed; and as a symbol of their resolutions, it was carried by acclamation that a Liberty Pole should be immediately erected.

30

On the adjournment of the meeting, the O'Brions and a number of the more active spirits set about the work. Selecting the tallest tree they could find, they stripped it of its branches, leaving a tuft of verdure at the top. In the mean time, a deep hole had been dug, in which to plant it; and long before sunset, amid the shouts of the assembled inhabitants and the discharge of muskets, the lofty pole was set and secured. This work accomplished, the people gathered around it and solemnly pledged themselves to resist the oppression of the mother country, and, if occasion called, to sacrifice their property, and shed their hearts' blood, in defence of the colony. After this exciting scene, they gradually dispersed, firmly but anxiously awaiting the course of events.

CHAPTER II.

A few days after the occurrence of the events related in the last chapter, two merchant vessels, in British employ, arrived from Boston, for the purpose of obtaining pickets and plank, to be used by the English in the defence of that city. By this arrival, confirmation was received of the battle at Lexington, and the people of Machias were made acquainted with the actual state of affairs in that quarter, regarding which there had existed a great degree of uncertainty and anxiety.

The merchant vessels were convoyed by a British armed schooner, named the "Margaritta," mounting four four-pounders and sixteen swivels. She was commanded by a spirited young Irishman, by the name of Moore, who, notwithstanding his coming in the character of an enemy, by his gallantry and gentlemanly conduct won largely the esteem of the inhabitants.

Immediately on his arrival, observing the Liberty Pole, Captain Moore landed, and demanded of a group who had collected around the landing-place, who had erected it.

"That pole, sir," answered John O'Brion, "was erected by the unanimous approval of the people of Machias."

"Well, sir," rejoined the officer, "with or without their approval, it is my duty to declare it must come down."

"*Must come down!*" repeated O'Brion, with some warmth. "Those words are very easily spoken, my friend. You will find, I apprehend, that it is easier to make than it will be to enforce a demand of this kind."

"What! am I to understand that resistance will be made? Will the people of Machias dare to disregard an order, not originating with me, gentlemen, but with the government whose officer I am?"

"The people of Machias," replied O'Brion, "will *dare* do anything in maintenance of their principles and rights."

"It is useless to bandy words," rejoined the officer, a little nettled at the determined spirit manifested around him; "my orders are peremptory, and must be obeyed. That Liberty Pole must be taken down in one hour, or it will be my painful duty to fire on the town."

As the young officer turned to re-enter his boat, he was accosted by Mr. Jones, the merchant we have alluded to, who prevailed upon him to suspend his determination until the people could assemble in town-meeting, when perhaps the town would agree to remove the objectionable object.

During this conversation, the group around dispersed, with the understanding that the Committee of Safety would meet that afternoon and consult about this new and exciting state of things.

At an early hour in the afternoon the Committee met. Being composed of such men as the O'Brions, Foster, and like spirits, it may readily be imagined what their opinions were in regard to taking down the pole. Instead of discussing that question, they busied themselves in forming plans to repel an attack, should one be made. They advised that a town-meeting should be called, to take the sense of the inhabitants on the subject of removing the pole, feeling perfectly sure that they would vote to keep it up. In the mean time, they made arrangements to send off next morning to Pleasant River Village, distant about twenty miles, and to a few other villages, requesting the people to come to Machias to help them defend the symbol of liberty.

The next day, which was Saturday, the town-meeting was held, and the subject laid before it. It needed not much discussion. There was the demand and the threat. "Let those," said the chairman, "who are disposed to obey the one through fear of the other say Ay."

A silence as of death prevailed throughout the hall,

until the chairman interrupted it by submitting another question.

"Those who are opposed to taking down the Liberty Pole will please say No."

With the suddenness and almost with the force of a thunder-clap, one loud "No!" seemed to spring simultaneously from every lip.

"The noes have it," quietly remarked the chairman, whose voice had unconsciously mingled with his fellow citizens' when the vote was determined.

Captain Moore was somewhat exasperated on learning the vote of the town, and would have put his threat into immediate execution, but for the interference a second time of Mr. Jones. That gentleman represented to him that the meeting was not fully attended, and that the vote was not a fair expression of the sentiments of the town. By urgent persuasion, he succeeded in obtaining a respite until another meeting was called, which was to be held on the following Monday.

"It will grieve me, Mr. Jones," said the officer, on taking leave, "to resort to extreme measures; but you may assure the people that, unless they vote to remove the pole, in one hour after their meeting breaks up I will open on the town."

With this understanding, and with expressions of mutual respect, they parted: the one to pace the quarter-deck of his little craft, the other to report the result of his errand.

30*

CHAPTER III.

THAT same evening a party of five met at the house of a Captain Lambert, consisting of the two O'Brions, Colonel Foster, Mr. Wheaton, and the gentleman at whose house they met.

"Well, gentlemen," said the elder O'Brion, "Mr. Jones informs me that unless the tree is taken down on Monday, the town is to be fired upon."

"So we were threatened yesterday," rejoined Captain Lambert, significantly; "and yet the tree stands."

"Yes," added Colonel Foster, "and will stand in spite of the King's authority."

"Have you heard from the messengers sent to Pleasant River and the other settlements?" inquired Wheaton of O'Brion.

"One of them returned this afternoon."

"And what word does he bring?"

"Every man who can possibly leave will be here to-morrow or early Monday morning."

"I hope they will come well provided with ammunition," remarked Colonel Foster.

"I am afraid not," said O'Brion; "the messenger says there was a great scarcity of powder at Pleasant River. However, they are coming, and those who cannot obtain muskets will come armed with pitchforks and scythes. They are all fired with the true spirit, and swear the pole shall not be taken down." .

"You said you had a proposition to make," remarked Captain Lambert, addressing John O'Brion, who as yet had kept silent.

"Mr. Jones informs me," said the person addressed,

"that it is the intention of Captain Moore to attend religious worship on shore to-morrow. About that time our friends from abroad will have arrived, and my proposition is that a number of us carry concealed arms to meeting, and, when services are over, seize upon the captain, and after that capture his vessel."

"It will be a bold measure, an open act of rebellion," remarked Mr. Wheaton.

"I am aware of that," continued O'Brion; "but we have the example of the Old Colony people to back us. The King and Parliament may call it 'rebellion,' if they please, but we who are engaged in it know but one name for it, and that is — *Revolution.*"

"Well, gentlemen, what do you say to my project?" said the same speaker, breaking the silence which followed his bold declaration.

"I say ay to it, with all my heart," exclaimed Col. Foster, in which assent all the rest joined.

"But who will be the one to seize the captain?" asked Lambert.

"I claim that privilege," said John O'Brion. "I will have an eye on him, and place myself in his near neighborhood. You, gentlemen, will stand ready to aid me."

"We must make the people acquainted with our design," said Lambert, "so that we may act in concert."

"And I propose," said Mr. Wheaton, "as we compose a majority of the Committee of Safety, that between this and morning we ascertain what quantity of powder and balls we may rely on."

"You need not trouble yourself about the balls," said Jeremiah O'Brion. "All the women in the village have been busy the whole afternoon melting up lead to cast them. My mother, I know, in her zeal, melted up an old pewter teapot for that purpose, in spite of our remonstrances, for it was a sort of heirloom. The women, if possible, are more crazy about keeping the pole erect than are the men."

A long conversation followed these remarks, having reference to their future proceedings, after which the company separated for the night.

The next morning, before the usual hour for religious worship, here and there men could be seen straying along singly and in pairs toward the church, each bearing a musket, so carried as least to expose it to view, for the church stood a short distance from the river, and directly opposite the church the Margaritta lay at anchor. As the men reached the church, they immediately concealed their weapons in various parts of the house, ready for use, and then disposed of themselves in such a manner as not to excite suspicion.

At the appointed hour, Captain Moore came ashore and entered the church. John O'Brion was on the lookout for him, and entered the house soon after, taking a seat directly behind him. There were no pews in the church, the house being unfinished, but temporary seats had been fitted up, without backs, for present accommodation. The weather being somewhat sultry, the windows of the church were thrown open, and from where the English captain sat, he commanded an extensive view of the river.

The services commenced. The prayers and the singing were gone through with, and the sermon was commenced, which, like a majority of the sermons of those stirring times, resembled more a political harangue than a discourse on ethics, — a mistake sometimes made by ministers in modern times, although in those days it was expected, and chimed in with the views of the people.

In the course of the sermon, happening to glance his eyes through the window, Captain Moore was surprised to see, at the distance of half or three-quarters of a mile up the river, men crossing the river on logs, with guns in their hands. These were the men the people of Machias had sent for, coming to take part in the affray. Realizing at once the peril of his situation, but without betraying alarm, or appearing to notice the strange sight, the young captain again turned his eyes upon the speaker, apparently deeply engrossed in the sermon.

Little did he heed, however, the impassioned words of the speaker. His mind was fully intent on escaping the snare which he felt was set for him; for, now that his suspicions were aroused, he could see furtive glances bent upon him in all directions. Near where he sat was an open window, the height from which to the ground was trifling. Taking advantage of a more than commonly stormy sentence in the discourse, which served to rivet the attention of the congregation, he started from his seat, and, leaping across the intervening benches, dashed through the window, and made his way directly to his boat.

In a moment the whole church was in an uproar; but, in the crowding and confusion that ensued, instant pursuit was prevented; and by the time the men had secured their guns and were ready to follow him, he had succeeded in getting on board his boat and pushing her off into the stream. A few minutes' rowing carried him on board his vessel, when he immediately commenced firing on the town, the men on shore briskly returning the compliment. After a few discharges, the vessel made sail down the river, followed by the people, however, who kept up an incessant fire of musketry, until she soon was beyond their reach. Very little damage was done on either side in this affray, but the excitement of the people was aroused to the highest pitch. The church was wholly deserted in the afternoon, and during the remainder of the day men might be seen collected in groups, earnestly discussing the affair, and proposing plans for future action.

CHAPTER IV.

DURING the day and evening, straggling parties from out of town continued to arrive in the village, some with muskets, some armed with pitchforks, and some with scythes fastened on poles, — formidable weapons, and used with much effect, as we are informed by a Polish officer, during the Polish Revolution. On Monday morning Machias was a scene of great excitement. Men paraded the village with their various weapons, while the women searched every nook and corner for powder and lead. As a proof of the spirit which animated the latter, an incident is related, which, as the writer declares, is well "worthy of being recorded."

It seems that the men who came from Pleasant River

settlement were greatly in want of powder, having but two or three charges each. The wife of one of the party, having found a horn of powder after they were gone, followed them twenty miles through the woods (there being at that time no roads) to bring it to her husband, and arrived with it the next day after the party had reached Machias.* Early in the forenoon it was decided to take possession of a lumber sloop in the river, and go in pursuit of the schooner. About sixty volunteers mustered on board, among whom were six brothers by the name of O'Brion, — Jeremiah, Gideon, John, William, Dennis, and Joseph. The father of this heroic family also insisted upon accompanying them, but he reluctantly yielded to the wishes of his sons, and remained on shore. The sloop, which was afterwards called the Liberty, started in pursuit, and overtook the schooner, which was becalmed, about two leagues distant from the head of Machias Bay.

When they came in sight of the Margaritta, the pursuing party were without any organized head. But before coming up with the enemy, who was now about three miles distant, Jeremiah O'Brion was unanimously chosen captain. On taking command, his first exercise of authority was to give permission to all who were afraid to follow him at all lengths to go on shore. Three men, who had blustered the most when on the land, availed themselves of this offer, and, amid the

* We may as well here state that this fact, and indeed all the leading incidents connected with our story, are borrowed from a paper communicated to the Maine Historical Society, being a narrative of the events of that period, taken down from the lips of John O'Brion, an actor in the scenes, who, at the time of making the communication, twenty-five years ago, resided in Brunswick, at the advanced age of eighty-one.

ill-concealed contempt of the rest of the crew, took to
a boat alongside, and left the vessel.

"Now, my brave fellows," said Captain O'Brion,
"having got rid of those white-livered cowards, our
first business will be to get alongside of the schooner
yonder, and the first man who boards her shall be
entitled to the palm of honor."

By the aid of boats towing ahead and the use of
sweeps, the sloop was soon brought alongside of the
schooner, but, having no grappling irons, they almost
immediately separated, yet not before John O'Brion,
who stood in the bows of the sloop ready for a spring,
had leaped upon the schooner's deck. On looking
around, he found the sloop had drifted off some
twenty or thirty yards, leaving him standing alone on
the quarter-deck of the enemy. Before he had much
time to reflect on his situation, "seven of the English
discharged their guns at him, almost at the same moment," but not a ball touched him. They then charged
upon him with their bayonets, when, to save his life,
he jumped overboard, and swam towards the sloop,
and soon stood, to the wonder of himself as well as
his companions, unharmed on her deck.

"Brother John, you have won the palm!" said
Jeremiah, shaking him affectionately by the hand.
"But man the sweeps, my hearties, and lay us alongside once more, and stand ready to fasten on to him
when you reach him."

Twenty men, armed with pitchforks, were now
selected to board the schooner, and when the vessels
were again brought in contact, amidst a fierce discharge from the enemy, they rushed over the schooner's side, followed by the rest of the crew. A sharp

contest ensued. The English bravely stood their ground, but they could not withstand the impetuous onset of the Americans, and, after a spirited struggle, they were forced to submit, having lost about ten killed and the same number wounded. Among the latter was Captain Moore, who in the early part of the action was shot through with a brace of balls, from the effects of which he died the next day, "much lamented." * The loss of the Americans was four killed, and eight or nine wounded.

When the sloop appeared in the river, with the Margaritta as a prize, those on shore were perfectly wild with excitement. Men, women and children gathered on the banks, shouting and exhibiting every demonstration of joy. The Liberty Pole was decorated with evergreens, and throughout the day, and long into the night, might be heard the sounds of revelry and rejoicing.

As a mark of distinction for the bravery he had displayed, the Committee of Safety appointed John O'Brion as bearer of despatches to the Provincial Congress of Massachusetts, at Watertown, to report what had been done, and to receive directions for the future. The news was received with the most lively interest, and the Congress expressed their approbation of the conduct of the people of Machias in the highest terms, and passed a vote of thanks to the individuals concerned in the battle. †

* Captain Moore is said to have been the first English naval officer who fell in the American Revolution.

† Cooper, in his Naval History, speaking of this action, says : "This affair was the Lexington of the seas ; for, like that celebrated conflict, it was a rising of the people against a regular force ; was characterized by

CHAPTER V.

IF the news of the capture of the Margaritta was received with a lively interest at the head-quarters of the Provincial Congress, not less lively, although of a different nature, was the excitement caused on its reception at Nova Scotia. Two schooners were immediately fitted out at Halifax for the purpose of retaking her. These vessels were called the Diligence and Tapnaquish, the former mounting eight or ten guns, with a crew of fifty men, the latter sixteen swivels, with a crew of twenty men.

About a month had elapsed after taking their prize, when the people of Machias were notified of these vessels coming up the bay. Instead of being alarmed at the news, preparations were immediately made to give them battle. The armament was taken out of the Margaritta and placed on board the Liberty, which, with a full crew, under the command of Jeremiah O'Brion, proceeded down the bay to meet the enemy. As they entered the bay they met a coaster coming in, which they took possession of, placing thirty-five men on board, under the command of Colonel Foster.

It was agreed that O'Brion should attack the Diligence and Foster the Tapnaquish. In accordance with this arrangement, they bore down upon the enemy, and each at about the same time boarded. Five minutes were not required to settle the matter.

a long chase, a bloody struggle, and a triumph. It was also the *first* blow struck on the water, after the war of the American Revolution had actually commenced."

Both of the English vessels surrendered at the first attempt at boarding them, without making the least resistance. On his return with his prizes, Captain O'Brion fell in with a boat containing his father and a surgeon, whom the old man had brought off. Happily there was no occasion for his services.

The news of this second capture created intense feelings at Halifax, and, to wipe off the stigma of former defeats, and to punish the authors of them, in the course of three weeks another expedition was fitted out from that place, consisting of a frigate, a twenty-gun ship, a brig of sixteen guns, and several schooners, containing about a thousand men.

The news of this formidable flotilla being on the way caused not a little apprehension in Machias, and some of the more timid advised that the place should be abandoned. This proposition, however, was immediately scouted, and the O'Brions, with about one hundred and fifty volunteers, determined to resist the approach of the enemy, overwhelming as they were in numbers.

About three miles below the town, on the eastern side of the river, at a place called Scott's Point, a breastwork was hastily thrown up. They had no cannon to defend it; all they had to rely on were common muskets.

Hearing that the fleet was coming up the bay, the brave little band, under the command of Jeremiah O'Brion and Colonel Foster, took up the line of march for Scott's Point, resolved, if they could not check the advance of the enemy, they would pour out the last drop of their blood in the attempt.

All the inhabitants had gathered in the vicinity of

the Liberty Pole to see them start. Mothers and wives were there, with heavy foreboding hearts, but there was no shrinking on their part, — no urging a son or a husband to remain. On the contrary, struggling with the emotions that filled their breasts, they exhorted them not to falter in their duty, and without a sign of weakness bade them farewell. Such were the women of the Revolution.

Soon after taking possession of the redoubt, a party of observation was sent out, which shortly returned, bringing intelligence that the squadron had anchored in the bay, with the exception of the brig and a number of boats, filled with men, which were advancing towards the town. It was not long before they came in sight, and, when opposite the breastwork, a large body of men, about five hundred, landed.

As this formidable number drew up on the banks, their bright arms glistening in the sun, O'Brion and Foster made their preparations. At this juncture Captain O'Brion addressed his men: "You see, my lads, what you have got to contend with. The odds are greatly against us; therefore, if there is one man here who is sick of his bargain and wishes to leave, in Heaven's name let him be off!"

Not a man moved from the ranks.

"You will find no skulkers this time," said a voice from the centre.

The light laugh which passed through the ranks at this remark was the best proof the captain could have of the coolness of his men. It gave him confidence in their stability.

"They are stirring," exclaimed Colonel Foster, pointing towards the moving mass, coming up in a compact body. "Be careful, men, and don't waste your powder," he added. "Be cool and steady, select your man, and do not fire until the word is given."

The Americans were drawn up in double rank, O'Brion having charge of the front and Foster of the rear division. The front rank were to deliver their fire, and then fall back, giving place to the rear rank, while the former reloaded, the second rank going through the same manœuvre.

The enemy pressed on at double quick time, and seeing the small number opposed to them, they burst into a cheer of anticipated triumph, while they commenced an irregular firing.

"Steady, my lads, steady!" said O'Brion, as the balls began to whistle around them. "Let them come a little nearer, — we cannot afford to throw away powder."

The men stood firm as though hewn from the solid rock, patiently waiting the word. At last, when the English had arrived within one hundred feet of them, the command was given. A sheet of flame ran along the breastwork, and, as the leaden shower fell among the assailants, a terrible gap was made in their number.

Immediately as the report of the first volley rang in the air, the stern voice of Colonel Foster was heard above the din: "Rear rank, advance! Present! Fire!" and another death-dealing discharge poured from the breastwork.

In spite of the efforts of their officers, the English broke and retreated towards the bank of the river. Here after a while they succeeded in forming them, and again they advanced towards the handful of men.

31*

But this time no triumphal cheer accompanied their onset.

On this occasion the assailants rushed on at a charge, with the evident intention of carrying the breastwork at the point of the bayonet. Not a shot was fired until they arrived within point-blank distance, when again the fiery storm was hurled upon them, and again they broke, while another well-directed volley threw them into perfect disorder. A general rush for the boats immediately ensued; and, while crowding into them, the Americans left their cover and poured discharge after discharge into their disordered ranks.

During the action, the British brig had caught aground within musket-shot of the shore, and, when the retreating foe had gained her decks, they were exposed to and experienced severe loss from the Americans, who continued to throw their fire into her until she floated and was removed down the river.

In this battle three Americans only were killed and a small number wounded, while the killed and wounded of the British amounted, as near as could be ascertained; to one hundred. After this repulse the English did not make a second attempt, but, hastening to get their wounded on board, they weighed anchor and stood out of the bay on their return to Halifax.

We will not attempt to describe the joy of the inhabitants of Machias at the unexpected result of this battle. They had made up their minds for the worst, and they looked upon the little band that had gone forth to cope with the adversary as a sort of *forlorn hope*. When the tidings of the overwhelming defeat of the enemy reached them, they could scarcely credit the report; but when the little band marched back to the village, with apparently undiminished numbers, their joy knew no bounds.

After this decided repulse, the people of Machias rested in perfect security, feeling confident that another attempt at invasion would not be made. But they were mistaken. About six weeks after this, a third expedition left Halifax, and landed a thousand men at Passamaquoddy, with the intention of marching through the woods and attacking Machias by land.

On learning the fact, the people again mustered, and preparations were again made to waylay and resist the enemy. From the prowess they had already exhibited, there is no doubt that they would for the fourth time have come off victors. The British, however, on the second day of their march, meeting with so many obstacles, became disheartened and retreated.

After this, the town remained unmolested. The Liberty Pole, which first drew on them the ire of the British, remained a long time standing, a cherished memento of their unyielding firmness and heroic bravery.

We cannot close our story without alluding to the O'Brion family, whose noble patriotism should have immortalized their names.

After the transactions we have recorded, the Liberty and Diligence were commissioned by the State of Massachusetts and sent out on a cruise. Jeremiah O'Brion commanded the former, his brother William being lieutenant. Captain Lambert commanded the latter, with John O'Brion for first lieutenant. For two years they did good service on the northern coast, affording protection to our navigation, after which they were laid up. After this, John O'Brion, with a number of others, built at Newburyport an armed ship, letter of marque, called the Hannibal, mounting twenty guns. On the completion of one voyage, she was fitted out as a cruiser, manned with one hundred and thirty men. Unfortunately, off New York she fell in with two frigates, and after a chase of forty-eight hours was taken. O'Brion was detained in the famous guard-ship Jersey about six months, suffering many privations, when he was taken to Mill Prison, England, whence he escaped after a number of months' confinement.

His brother, in the mean time, was not idle. He had command of one or two armed vessels, and in a number of successful combats did the State good service, and proved himself worthy the name which he bore.

THE STORM AT SEA.

CHAPTER I.

THE day was almost preternaturally calm. The heavens were clear, not a film of a cloud could the eye detect, and there was not motion enough in the atmosphere to flutter the lightest leaf, or to impel the volatile thistle-down, so sensitive to the faintest breath; yet a heavy ground-swell vexed the sea, and the vaulting billows came rolling in from the great deep, breaking with an unceasing roar on the coast, and deluging its rocky ramparts in heavy masses of foam, giving the whole line of shore the appearance of being ridged with drifting snow.

The stillness that brooded in the atmosphere contrasted strangely with the turbulence of the ocean. There was no apparent cause for this watery tumult. There had been no recent storm to provoke it; on the contrary, for an unusual length of time, the weather had been remarkably pleasant. A novice on the sea-shore would naturally ask, Why, then, this strife of the waters, this oceanic riot? To one born on the brink of the rough Atlantic, it is no strange sight, although always an exciting one. Common as is the scene to

us, familiar as are the tones of the lofty anthem of
the great deep, we can never behold the one or listen
to the other without experiencing a thrill akin to awe,
nay, of absolute awe, mingled with profound reverence,
when we reflect on the terrible power of the raging
sea, and the might and majesty of Him whose slightest
word "maketh the storm a calm, so that the waves
thereof are still."

The present agitation of the ocean was the effect
of some distant storm at sea. The heavy ground-
swell was what is called in nautical parlance an "old
sea," the undulations not being so rapid and violent,
nor the ocean wearing such an angry aspect, as during
a storm. The huge billows came heaving in from the
outer deep, formidable in size, it is true, but with a sort
of tired motion, as if in the storm-struggle they had
spent their fiercest energy. They did not,

> "With all their white crests dancing,
> Come like thick-plumed squadrons to the shore
> Gallantly bounding,"

but more like battalions from the field after a desperate and exhausting fight, — until just as they reached
the shore, when, gathering themselves as it were for
a final charge, they leaped forward, with a hoarse
shout, and dissolved in foam.

On a high, rugged cliff, that jutted boldly out from
the main land, against which the billows surged with
fearful violence, clothing, with each assault, its steep
front nearly to the summit with a mantle of spray,
stood two females, gazing intently into the offing.
The eldest might have been fifty years of age, although
exposure to wind and sun, superadded perhaps to toil

and care, gave her the appearance of a more advanced
age. The younger had just entered the bloom of
womanhood. She was not what is called beautiful,
but she possessed one of those *good* countenances,
which is far more attractive than mere beauty. But
a cloud of sorrow now rested on that sweet face,
which seemed only made for smiles and sunny looks.

With their aprons twisted not ungracefully over the
backs of their necks and heads as a covering, the two
stood for some moments in silence, their eyes wandering restlessly over the broad expanse of waters, as if
in search of an expected object.

The youngest first broke the silence. "There is no
sail in sight." And a desponding sigh followed the
sadly-uttered words.

"What is that?" exclaimed the elder. "Look yonder, Maggie (your eyes are better than mine), there,
just over Bulwark Rock, — is not that a sail?"

For a minute the glance of the young woman was
riveted in the direction pointed out, when she answered, in the same tone in which she had first spoken:
"No, mother, it is but the combing of a wave over the
sunken ledge. God help me! I am afraid that we shall
never see him again."

"God help *him*, and restore him safely to our
arms," responded the mother, in a more hopeful tone.
"Cheer up, my daughter, and put your trust in One
who is mighty to save, and who will not willingly afflict
and grieve us."

"It is sinful, I know, mother; but, when I think of
the many widowed hearts, the childless mothers, and
fatherless children, which the late dreadful storm has
made, I am almost led to doubt His goodness and

mercy, and to ask, why did He permit this great affliction?"

"Hush, hush, my dear daughter, and do not give
way to such thoughts. Would you arraign your
Maker? Shall a humble worm of the dust question
the wisdom of his decrees? O, my child, trust in the
Lord. Yea, Maggie," she repeated, in a solemnly emphatic tone, "though he slay thee, still trust in the
Lord, and all will be well with thee." And, with this
pious admonition, she turned, and with her companion
sought their humble dwelling.

Good cause had that young heart to be weighed
down. The heavy burden of fears that rested upon it
was well grounded, and the booming of the waves
might well sound to her ears as a funeral knell. She
had waited and watched, day after day, for the return
of her husband and the father of her babe, until her
heart grew sick with hope deferred. Tidings had recently reached her of a terrific gale at the eastward,
and of the wreck of a large fishing fleet. Rumor, it
is true, had magnified the extent of ruin wrought, but
it was ascertained that nearly a hundred sail had been
lost, and that in many instances not one of the crew
was saved. Every day came fresh reports of the coast
being strewed with wrecks. and of the washing ashore
of dead bodies.*

Among that fleet was the vessel in which was her
husband. Nothing had been heard from him since the
gale. In the list of vessels lost and of those that rode
out the storm in safety, the name of the "Curlew"
was not mentioned. She was reported among the

---

* This was written in 1851, and the gale referred to occurred in the
Bay of Chaleur

missing. "Missing!" what a terrible import had that simple word to many an anxious heart; how pregnant with sickening hopes, with prostrating fears. The dread certainty that the worst had befallen her husband could not have filled the heart of the young wife with intenser misery. The torture of suspense, the conflict of hopes and fears, agonized her more than would have the knowledge of her loss. In the latter case she would have bowed in resignation to the tempest of sorrow; as it was, she stood up distractedly amid the storm, struggling piteously against its violence.

CHAPTER II.

THAT evening, as the mother bent in silent agony over her sleeping babe, there came to her a vision of the absent one. Her mind went back to the day of his departure. This is what she recalled:

It was a beautiful autumnal morning. The heavens were unstained by a cloud; the sea sparkled in the bright sunlight; the breeze was fair, and every auspice favorable. The "Curlew," a fine new fishing-smack, floated gracefully in the waters of the cove, everything about her looking neat and trig as the youthful skipper and owner, who bustled about, buoyant with life and activity, making preparations for the voyage.

A fine specimen of manly beauty was the young fisherman, Henry Stanwood. He was of middling height, well proportioned, and his countenance bore an expression of quick intelligence and an amiable

32

disposition. How the young wife's heart beat as she
watched the cheerful smile so rarely absent from his
face, and read in his beaming glance a depth of affection answering to her own, while his cheery, sonorous
voice, softened to love's cadence when addressing her,
thrilled her with a strange delight.

In the hurry of preparation, young Stanwood found
frequent opportunities to bestow all these on his wife,
who watched his work with a sadness which she vainly
endeavored to conceal. Why was it? She had frequently seen him depart before without experiencing
such depth of feeling. Was this unwonted reluctance
to part with him a foreboding of evil? No, this was
not its nature. The babe which she bore in her arms
had riveted her heart more closely to her husband,
had opened new and deeper fountains of affection.
This it was that saddened her. It was in part sympa-
thetic sadness. New ties, new chords of love, had
been thrown around the heart of her husband to bind
it more closely to his home. The little outstretched
arms of their first-born she knew were tugging be-
seechingly at his heart-strings; and she shared with
him the double pain of separation. Her regrets were
as much for him as for herself. Does not the young
mother sympathize with and appreciate these feelings?

The hours flew by; the work of preparation was
finished; the stores were on board; everything was
stowed away, and the white sails, and the weather-
vane, the work of her own hands, were flapping and
fluttering in the breeze, beckoning the skipper on
board.

They all stood on the beach — Mrs. Stanwood, the
widowed mother, the young wife, and husband, the

latter folding to his heart the little nestling, as if he would hide it there forever. It was one of those moments when language fails to express the emotions of the overcharged heart, whose only interpreters are the heaving breast and the speaking countenance.

"Take good care of yourself while I am gone, dear Margaret," at last said the young skipper, breaking the silence; and, placing the babe in the bosom of its mother, he folded the twain in a fond embrace. "Goodbye, mother. I shall be back in a few weeks, and then no more of these sad partings for this season, for this will be my last cruise. Come, cheer up, Maggie," he continued, with assumed gayety. "It is better to part with a smile than a tear. Good-bye, and God bless you!" And, snatching a kiss from mother and child in the same moment, he hurried on board of the boat and soon gained the deck of the vessel, which, in a short time, with a favoring breeze, and under full press of sail, stood out to sea. A silent wave of the hand was the parting token of the young captain to those on shore, as an intervening cliff shut the vessel from sight.

Long did the unhappy wife linger on that sad, and, as she now felt, final parting. Slowly in thought she went over the incidents of the day. She busied herself over the chest of her husband, arranging his clothing, and seeing that nothing was lacking; she stored therein a few articles without his knowledge which she thought would be luxuries at sea. She tasked herself in every way to insure his comfort. Then came the hour of departure. She stood again on the beach; she heard his parting words; she felt the pressure of his embrace, the impress of his warm kiss; she saw him on board of the vessel, she caught the last wave of his hand, and the vision vanished. Then followed the dreary first evening, then the succession of weeks, then the tidings of storm and disaster. She lived it all over again up to the present hour, when hope had well-nigh perished, and despair was brooding over her soul. Starting from this retrospect as from a dream, she pressed her hand to her heart as if she would force down some feeling too agonizing for endurance.

The sun had gone down, and she sat in the gloom of twilight, listening to the roar of the breakers, which sounded more loudly as the night deepened. It seemed to mock her grief. Those merciless waves which had engulfed the whole wealth of her affections, which had made wreck of her entire freight of happiness, now came, with their hoarse shout of triumph, exulting in the ruin that they had wrought. Often ere this had she listened, with heart all astir, to the grand music of these same tramping billows, which now crushed her with an overwhelming sense of desolation. Ah, many a sad evening like this had the mourning one passed!

CHAPTER III.

THE aged mother seemed to forget her own sorrow in the endeavor to cheer and sustain the heart of her son's wife. In conversing with her she always spoke hopefully of his return. His vessel might have been driven on some island remote from the main land, and from which no tidings as yet had been received; or she might have been dismasted at sea, and thus prevented from reaching the shore. But as day after day passed by, bringing no news of the missing one, she, too, began to betray the despondency which from the first had burdened her soul, but which she had studiously concealed from her daughter. In her privacy her heart was bowed down with grief, for Henry was her sole remaining child, her youngest born, and the only tie that bound her to earth. Yet, though her sorrow was great, her anguish was not so keen as Margaret's.

The elder Mrs. Stanwood had been disciplined by trials. She had passed through the furnace of affliction, which, if it had not blunted her sensibilities, had taught her resignation. It had given her a more realizing sense of the uncertainty of life and the transitoriness of human happiness. In a word, it had loosened her hold on earth, and fastened her hopes and aspirations on a higher and better state of existence. Therefore the cup now presented to her lips had lost some of its poignancy, because she had often been compelled to drink from it; but to the young wife it was drugged to its very depths with the gall of bitterness.

This was Margaret's first affliction; for, though an orphan, her parents had died when she was too young to feel their loss. It may be from this very cause, the early loss of her parents, that she experienced the present intensity of grief. She had grown up from childhood a stranger to those gentle affections which the young heart craves. Her aunt, who adopted her, was an austere woman, with a really kind heart, if one

32*

could but find one's way to it, but whose forbidding manner checked those effusions of childish love in which the youthful heart delights to indulge. Thus she grew up to womanhood amid chilling influences, although her heart beat with kindly impulses; and thus it came to pass, when one was presented to her whom she might love, — one who courted her love, — that she lavished all her hoarded affections upon him. Never did wife bestow upon husband a richer dowry of love than did Margaret Newton on Henry Stanwood, and never was that sacred deposit entrusted to worthier keeping. Their very existences seemed bound in each other, and hence the acuteness of that sorrow which now wasted the heart of the young wife.

I would not undertake to say how far the effects of this grief might extend. To one of Margaret's peculiar organization, with susceptibilities so alive to the tender passion, the sudden shattering of an idolized object of worship too often scathes, as with a lightning stroke, the devotee. Love thus suddenly checked worketh like madness on the brain, and its subject thenceforward is reduced to that most pitiful of all states, a "wreck at random driven."

Margaret was fast verging towards this deplorable condition. On that dismal evening, when she sat alone with her child in the gathering gloom, the sullen waves mocking her, in the paroxysms of her grief her reason tottered. She was like one walking bewildered on awful heights, along the dizzy brinks of precipices, reckless of the fearful abysses that yawned beneath her, nay, feeling an almost irresistible desire to plunge into their terrible depths. What prevented her? What but that one tiny hand withheld her? The outstretched arm of her nursling interposed to save her, and its feeble cry caused an entire revulsion of feeling, restoring, in a measure, the equilibrium of her reeling brain. Like the ancient Voice, whose "Peace, be still!" rebuked the troubled sea, so did that infantile plaint quell the raging billows of her soul. She felt that, though clouds of wrath had gathered about her, and the very blackness of darkness brooded over her future, yet earth still had ties to bind her to it, — that life was not wholly valueless. That feeble wail seemed to reproach her selfish sorrow, seemed to plead for that existence of which she had grown so weary.

"No, my poor fatherless one!" she exclaimed, pressing the little one with passionate fervor to her breast, "I will not leave you as I was left! For your sake I will struggle to sustain this weight of woe! God help me, — it is a sore one to bear!"

"And God *will* help you, my dear child!" said the aged mother, who had entered unperceived. "He is a very present help in time of need. Once and again have I said, and again do I say," she continued, in a voice tremulous with emotion, "'The Lord gave, and the Lord hath taken away; blessed be the name of the Lord!'" and, folding the disconsolate one in an affectionate embrace, the tears of the mother mingled with those of the daughter.

Magic potency of tears! whose sparkling flow sheds a reflex light upon the darkened soul, and rids the heart of that "perilous stuff," which saps the mind's strength, and poisons the springs of life! The mother had often shed them in secret, but to Margaret they

had been denied. Her great grief had lain like a
stone on the fountain of tears, and her overburdened
heart was well-nigh shattered by the pressure; but
now that the stone was rolled away, giving vent to
her pent feelings, she experienced a very perceptible
sense of relief; the fever of her brain was assuaged,
the blinding mists that enveloped her mind were dissolved, and reason again resumed its sway. She had
reached that fearful point when her whole mental
organization hung in the balance. A straw would
have overturned it. That tiny hand of her babe,
nestling in the folds of her dress, touched the secret
spring of feeling. Nature asserted her rights. The
noble temple which had been racked as with the throes
of an earthquake again became stationary, as the lava-
flood gushed forth in a burning, impetuous torrent.

CHAPTER IV.

THENCEFORWARD the life of Margaret was marked
by a calm resignation. She had her seasons of despondency, when she would gladly have laid down her
burden and sought rest in the grave; but she struggled to overcome these prostrating feelings, and nobly
sustained herself under her trials. The whole aspect
of the world, however, had become changed to her.
She took no pleasure in her former favorite haunts.
The shady grove, whither she was wont to resort,
seemed clothed now in deep, funereal gloom. Particularly at this season was it sad to her, when the
fallen and faded leaf reminded her so constantly of

her own withered hopes. The heart untouched by sorrow cannot view these emblems of a dying year without melancholy emotions; how much greater influence, then, must this scene exert on one rendered painfully sensitive by a recent affliction. From her sea-shore rambles, too, she always returned with a deeper cloud upon her brow. The gleesome music of the waves now came to her ears with a mournful cadence, and the glittering spray, which to the undimmed eye presents forms of exquisite grace and beauty, to her tearful vision bore the likeness of cold and ghastly shrouds. Although calmly resigned to her fate, she could not shake off this morbid state of mind.

Notwithstanding the sound and sight of the sea awoke in Margaret the most gloomy associations, she felt an irresistible impulse to be by the seaside; and often, on the calm moonlight evenings which then prevailed, she would ramble away for hours, lingering on the hard, sandy cove, listlessly watching the heavy rollers as they came breaking in foam at her feet; or traversing the rocky coast, now standing on the brink of some dark, gaping chasm, and now gazing on the splintered rocks and black ledges, at one moment deluged with spray, at the next left bare by the receding wave. More often she would seat herself on some prominent cliff, and gaze earnestly into the offing. Sometimes a solitary sail would slowly cross the rays of the moon, which, reflected in the placid waters, stretched like a path of light along the ocean; or for a moment would suddenly appear in the little sparkling patches that glimmered here and there, then phantom-like vanish from sight. Ah! what deep, intense yearnings, what vague, momentary-thrilling hopes would those transient glimpses awaken in her breast, followed by pangs of keenest anguish, as the shadowy sail receded from her strained sight, to be seen no more.

Depressing as was the effect of these lonely rambles on her spirits, and well aware as Margaret was that her indulgence in them only served to feed her grief, yet there was something in the brooding stillness of the night, something in the solitude of those cavernous rocks, something in the profound tranquillity of the infinitude of ocean, that won her steps abroad.

On one of these excursions, tempted by the splendor of the night, she had remained out longer than usual. The moon was at her full, and flooded the whole visible expanse of ocean with her beams. There was a slight in-shore breeze, a faint fanning of the air, not enough to create a ripple. Far off at sea the eye could dimly descry a small vessel heading toward the shore, but so light was the wind it appeared to be stationary.

For a long time, motionless as a statue, Margaret had stood, her gaze fixed upon the vessel. So absorbed was she in thought, she did not notice the approach of her mother, who, uneasy at her prolonged absence, had come out in search of her; nor was she aware of her presence until her voice aroused her.

" Come, my child," said the aged matron, "the dew is falling, and the sea air comes chillingly in; let us go home."

" Look yonder, mother," said Margaret, pointing to the distant sail; "there are happy hearts on board that vessel, anticipating the joys that await them, and there are happy hearts on shore, eager to welcome them to their embraces."

"Yes, yes, my daughter," said the mother, in an agitated voice, divining the thoughts of her young companion; "let us pray that their joys may soon be realized."

"God grant it. But, alas, mother, no such joy awaits us, no such prayer will avail us. I have been thinking, mother, how often I have here awaited the return of Henry, and how I have impatiently watched his approaching sail, as I have been watching yonder vessel, and how my heart has leaped as I heard his cheerful voice swelling over the sea, as just now a joyful shout came on the air."

"O, my daughter," said the mother, tears nearly choking her utterance, "you know not the wounds you have opened. Often and often have I, too, waited for Henry's father in this manner; often from this spot given him the joyful welcome home. But there came a time, Margaret, when I waited in vain. In storm and in calm, at early morn and late at night, I watched for him, but he came not; and only when the sea shall give up its dead shall we meet again!" and, bowing her head on the shoulder of her daughter, the aged mother gave free vent to her feelings.

"Mother, dear mother, do not weep!" exclaimed Margaret, in a broken voice, folding her arm around the aged form of the matron, striving to act the comforter, although her own tears flowed freely. "I have been too.selfish; I have thought only of my own sorrow, and have leaned on you in my affliction, when I should have sustained you. Do not weep, mother."

"Lean on me still, my child," said Mrs. Stanwood, lifting her head and somewhat recovering herself. "I

am but a poor bruised reed, but God in his infinite
mercy has upheld and will continue to sustain me.
Look to him, Margaret," she continued, in a voice
already rendered firm, "and all will be well. The
night of our sorrow will soon be over. Let us
rejoice with the Psalmist, where he says, ' *Weeping
may endure for a night, but joy cometh in the morning.*' "

With these and other comforting words, the stricken
ones retraced their steps homeward.

CHAPTER V.

" *Joy cometh in the morning* " — prophetic words!
The chapter from the inspired volume had been
read; the lowly prayer, the incense of humble hearts,
had ascended to the throne of God; the light had
vanished from the casement of the fisher's dwelling;
and the sister angel of Death, Sleep, had sealed the
eyes of the mourning ones.

Slowly over the gently-heaving sea came that solitary vessel whose appearance had awakened such
painful emotions. Slowly but steadfastly she headed
for the little inlet, and, just as the early dawn flickered
in the east, she reached the haven, and noiselessly
dropped her anchor. In a short time her sails were
lowered and furled, and presently a boat left her side,
propelled by a single oarsman.

That safely-moored vessel was the " Curlew," and
that oarsman was the long-mourned Henry Stanwood.
In the terrible gale which had proved so disastrous

to others he had been dismasted, and for many days
had been tossed about at the mercy of the waves.
Without the means of rigging a jury-mast, after the gale
had subsided, he had drifted hither and thither, until
at last he succeeded in reaching a small island remote
from the main land. Here, after much delay, and with
considerable difficulty, he succeeded in procuring new
masts, and, having spare tackle on board, he soon had
them rigged. This done, he started homeward, stopping just long enough in a by-port to obtain cable
and anchors to replace those he had lost. A succession of calms retarded his voyage. His anxiety to
reach home may be imagined, when he learned from a
vessel which he fell in with that the " Curlew " had
long been given up as lost. He pictured to himself
the agony which Margaret must endure. Knowing
the depth of her affection, he too well knew what her
sufferings must be. He greatly feared the effect of
her sudden grief, and tortured himself with a thousand
apprehensions. If impatient sighs could have filled
his sails and propelled his vessel, he would have made
a short passage.

But at last he drew near the wished-for spot, and,
catching a distant sight of the headland at the entrance of the cove, he could not repress a shout of
joy. That was the longest night of his life in which
he slowly crept toward the shore. When at last he
reached his anchorage, and had flung himself into the
yawl, impatient to reach the shore, he bethought him
that sudden joy was often as fatal as sudden grief, and
he felt the necessity of proceeding cautiously.

Walking hastily up to the house, he tapped gently
on the low window of the room in which he knew his

33

mother slept. The summons was not answered, and, fearing he knew not what, he rapped again with more force. With a beating heart he heard the movement of one within, and he stepped aside in the shade of the building. Presently the window opened, and his mother's form bent over the sill. He could scarcely refrain from springing to her embrace; but, commanding himself, he spoke, in a low, altered voice: " I have ventured to arouse you thus early, Widow Stanwood, believing the bearer of good news —— "

" Of good news ! " exclaimed the widow, interrupting him. " Then it is of Henry. O tell me, is he alive? "

" Both alive and well."

" Where, sir, is he ? " she continued, in an agitated voice.

" Here, dear mother, here in your arms ! " said Henry, no longer able to contain himself, springing as he spoke into her embrace.

Pressing him convulsively to her breast, the aged woman raised her eyes to heaven, and, in a tone of solemn fervor, exclaimed: " Almighty God, I thank thee ! *For this my son was dead, and is alive again ; he was lost, and is found.*"

That meeting in the dim night-air, — the mother suddenly aroused from her sleep to fold in her arms the long-mourned son, that passionate embrace, that fervent outpouring of thanks, — O, it was a scene over which angels might shed tears of joy.

Henry was the first to break the silence. He could utter but one word, which was pronounced in an inquiring tone, as if dreading the answer. " Margaret? "

" She is well, my dear son. But I fear this happiness will be too much for her, for it has almost been more than your aged mother can bear." And she again strained her son to her bosom, while the warm tears fell on him like summer rain-drops. "But come within the house, Henry. Come in the back entrance and step lightly. I must prepare her for what is to come." And, closing the window, with trembling haste she lighted a lamp, arranged her dress, and admitted her son.

The sight of her beloved son once more safe within his own home filled her heart with an oppressive sense of joy. But, putting a restraint on her emotions, and wiping away the tears that dimmed her sight, she took the lamp and crept to her daughter's room. She lifted the latch, and stood for a few moments gazing on the scene before her.

The young wife was in a deep slumber. Her face was partly turned one side, toward the babe who rested on her arm. A large tear glistened on the cheek of the sleeping one, but a radiant smile played around her lips.

As the aged mother hesitated a moment, a voice whispered in her ear, "One moment, mother, let me look upon them but one moment." And the husband and father bent over the wife and child, yearning to clasp them in his arms. With no small effort he checked the impulse; but, softly touching the cheek of his wife with his lips, he stepped back into the entry.

Slight as was that touch, it awoke her, and starting up she exclaimed, in a tone of surprise, "Why, mother, what are you here for?"

"I came to see how you rested, my child," commenced Mrs. Stanwood, in an assumedly grave tone, although she found it difficult to repress the emotions that agitated her.

"O mother," said Margaret, interrupting her, "I have had such a pleasant dream! I thought Henry had come back, and we were all happy once again, — O, so happy! But it was only a dream," she continued, sadly, after a brief pause, — "a dream, to be followed by tears on awaking."

"Do you remember, my daughter, what I repeated to you last evening: *Weeping may endure for a night, but joy cometh in the morning*"? Then, stepping to the window and lifting the curtain, "See here, Margaret," she said, in an earnest tone, pointing to the east, now glowing with the beams of day. "The morning has come."

"I see it has, mother," rejoined the young wife, turning her eyes in that direction; "alas! what is it but the dawning of another day of sorrow? The morning bringeth no joy to —— "

She stopped suddenly and gazed fixedly for a while, as if some unexpected object had met her sight; then, springing up and pointing toward the cove, she exclaimed, in hurried, bewildered accents, "Look, mother, look! there, in the cove! There are the masts of a vessel; and, O God, there is the vane I worked for him! Tell me, mother, tell me, I beseech you, am I deceived?" And she clung wildly to the aged widow, as if life or death was in her reply. "Is it not Henry's vessel? Is Henry safe? Is he here?"

"Be calm, my daughter," replied the mother, almost as much agitated as the one she admonished. "Re-

strain your feelings. That is Henry's vessel. He is
alive, and well, and here, — blessed be God!"

"Margaret!" said a well-known voice behind her.

With a wild, almost frenzied cry of joy, the young
wife turned and threw herself into the arms that were
extended to receive her.

*   *   *   *   *   *   *

It is one of the most difficult things for a writer to
wind up the threads of his story in a compact manner.
But as ours is a simple tale, we have no such difficulty
to contend with. We cannot do better than to leave
the young wife, as we have left her, happy in the arms
of her husband.

33*

THE CANADIAN CAPTIVE.

A LEGEND OF FREEPORT

CHAPTER I.

In a beautiful location on Casco Bay, at a place called Flying Point, in what is now known as the town of Freeport, there stood in 1756 a neat and commodious log house, reared in the fashion which generally prevailed among our early settlers, who consulted as much their safety from lurking foes as they did their comfort. The scenery of the neighborhood, both seaward and landward, was unusually attractive, rendering this spot one of the most charming on the coast. A number of acres had been reclaimed from the wilderness and made productive; and for a series of years this had been the happy residence of the owner, Thomas Means, who had a young and interesting family growing up around him.

Thus far, amid the wild, savage wars that devastated the early settlements, he had remained unmolested; yet, as the depredations of the merciless Indians became more and more frequent, and every day brought rumors of their nearer approach to this hitherto peaceful spot, his mind became troubled, and he began anxiously to make preparations to remove his family to a place of security.

At the distance of a mile or so from his dwelling was one of those garrisons, or block-houses, which were erected for places of refuge in those troublous times, into which whole settlements would cluster for safety, and oftentimes for years endure all those privations which attend confined quarters and limited provisions. But little conception have we in these later days of the trials and sufferings of those who first reared their homes in the wilderness of Maine. If we, their posterity, can say, " the lines are fallen unto us in pleasant places," not so could they, the early pioneers, who sacrificed comfort, ease, and too often life, in laying the foundation of our prosperity.

At the close of a day in the latter part of June, 1757, just at dusk, the family of Means had gathered around the supper-table. His household consisted of himself, his wife Alice, and three children, — two girls, Alice and Jane, the one six and the other four years of age, and one son, Robert, some sixteen months old. Besides these were the sister of Mrs. Means, Mary Finney,* a beautiful, spirited maiden, in the bloom of early womanhood, and a Mr. Martin, who was an employee of Mr. Means.

" Well, Alice," said Mr. Means, addressing his wife, " have you got everything prepared for removal tomorrow ? Martin and I have put everything to rights, I believe, out o' doors."

" I think all is ready, Thomas, so that we can start early in the morning."

---

* Her real name was Molly. We have taken the liberty to substitute the more euphonious one of Mary.

"That is right, my dear. The sooner we are all safe in the block-house the better. Every moment we remain out I feel is like courting our destruction. I regret," he added, with unwonted seriousness, "that we did not take neighbor Skolfield's advice, and remove the first part of the week."

"Why, husband, have you seen any signs of the Indians, that you are so anxious?" asked Mrs. Means, with much interest.

"Not in our immediate neighborhood. Alice, but the settlements are swarming with them, and they may be upon us at any moment. If you and Mary and the children were in safety I should feel more easy in my mind;" and a gloomy shadow settled on the brow of the speaker.

"I wish to Heaven I were a man!" suddenly exclaimed Mary Finney.

"And if you were, my pretty Molly, what then?" asked the husband, with a faint attempt at a smile.

"What then!" said the spirited girl. "I would scour the woods and shoot down every cowardly, skulking red-skin I could find. I would join old Miers, of Yarmouth, and hunt them down by night and by day, — the barbarous wretches."

"This would do if no one was dependent upon you, Mary; but a man cannot chase Indians and support a family at the same time."

"To think we have got to leave this beautiful spot," said Mrs. Means, after a moment's pause, "just as everything is coming forward so finely."

"Yes, and be cooped up in that close, gloomy block-house, afraid to move an inch outside," said Mary, in a tone of vexation. "It is too bad, Thomas. I would not stir an inch. Remain here. I will practise with a gun, and, if the Indians attack us, fight them off;" and the determined tone and flashing eyes of the beautiful girl evinced that she was in earnest.

"Ah, my brave sister, this talking about fighting the Indians, and a real battle with them, are different things. With their hideous forms and brandished tomahawks before you, and their infernal war-whoop ringing in your ears, bold as you now are, I imagine there would be a quaking of your heart and a blanching of your cheeks."

"There might be both, brother; I do not say there would not be; but put me to the test, and see if I flinch. What do you say, Alice?"

Mrs. Means made no reply, but shook her head doubtfully, while she smiled at the enthusiasm displayed by her sister.

Mr. Means answered: "I do not doubt your courage, Mary, but I think it will be best not to put it to the trial. The Indians seldom engage in a fair, stand-up fight, but work mischief by stratagem and treachery. So you will have everything ready for an early removal in the morning. I shall be uneasy until you are all in a place of safety. I would that we were in the garrison this night."

"Hist! Thomas, what is that?" suddenly exclaimed Mrs. Means; and as the whole party held their breath in a listening attitude, a slight rustling of leaves and a crackling of bushes could be heard, as of some one moving stealthily near the house.

The window of the supper-room was open, and, being nearest to it, Mary sprang up and rushed toward it. Leaning over the sill and gazing around, she for a time saw no moving thing; but presently her eye detected, in the deep shadow of the trees which skirted a little valley that ran in the rear of the house, a dusky form, which was retreating slowly into the woods. She watched it narrowly and suspiciously, until it was lost to sight. What could it be? Was it the dreaded red man? It was so dark she could not recognize the form, and she felt her heart beat quicker as the thought flashed upon her that the foe might be lurking around the house. But presently a wolf, or some other animal, burst from near the same place, and, bounding across the clearing, plunged into the valley.

"It was but a wolf or a deer," said Mary, returning toward the table, from which the others had risen. "I really believe our conversation about the Indians has made us all nervous. But we do not care for the red-skins, do we, Bobby?" and, taking the youngest child in her arms, the light-hearted girl tossed him in the air, chirruping to him the while, as if a thought of danger had never troubled her.

The buoyant mirth of his frolicsome sister failed, however, to remove the weight that pressed on the heart of Mr. Means. He could not himself account for the unusual despondency of his spirits. In vain he strove to shake off the gloom which had gathered around him. It clung to him in spite of his efforts. He strove, also, to conceal the feelings which oppressed him, but his too evident uneasiness threw a shadow upon the little circle.

At an early hour the family retired. The bedroom of Mr. and Mrs. Means was on the lower floor, as was also that of Mary Finney, with whom slept the two little girls. Mr. Martin, the hired man, slept in the chamber.

CHAPTER II.

Do coming events cast their shadows before? Does an unknown pending doom mysteriously affect the heart, blanching it with vague fears, and filling our whole being with a gloomy unquietness, with strange, undefined terrors? Is there such a thing as *presentiment?* Or are all those depressing forebodings which oftentimes precede a calamity but instances of disordered mental action, which by singular coincidences happen on the eve of some misfortune? Philosophy holds to the latter, although facts and experience stubbornly support the former, proposition.

The gloom which enwrapped the spirit of Thomas Means on that June evening was but the foreshadowing of his awful fate. Evil influences, in which his destiny was involved, were at work around him, unseen and unknown by those connected with him, but *felt* by himself. The nature of the danger that threatened him, of the doom that hung over him, he could not fathom; but that some fearful calamity awaited him, or those that were dear to him, he had not a doubt. And yet he was far from being a superstitious man. He strove to shake off the conviction, he arrayed reason and common sense against it, but all to no purpose. When he had retired for the night, it was long before his disturbed feelings found repose in sleep.

The reader will remember the noise that attracted the attention of those at the supper-table, and which was supposed to be occasioned by the harmless tread of some animal of the forest. It was a more dangerous animal than wolf or panther. The noise was made by the retiring footsteps of one of a band of savages that had been prowling in the vicinity of the house during the afternoon, who had crept near to the open window during supper-time, and heard the conversation in regard to the intended removal to the block-house the next morning. On learning this fact, the Indians made preparations to attack the house that night.

The early part of the night passed away quietly; midnight went by without disturbance; but about three o'clock in the morning the foe by some means forced an entrance into the house. They immediately proceeded to the bedroom of Mr. Means, seized him, and dragged him from his bed out of the house. Startled from a deep sleep by the noise, Mrs. Means caught up her son, when a bright flash illuminated for a moment the apartment, followed by a sharp report in front of the house. Rushing to the door to learn the fate of her husband, another gun was discharged, the ball from which passed directly through the body of the child she held, killing it instantly, and lodged in her breast.*

In the mean time, others of the band had entered the house and seized upon Mary Finney and little Alice, — the younger sister, Jane, having succeeded in escaping from their hands by creeping into the ash-hole.

* Literally true.

Perceiving that her husband was dead, Mrs. Means, who, instead of sinking under the accumulating horrors which surrounded her, seemed to be endowed with supernatural strength and nerve, closed the front door, and effectually barred it; then, placing her dead child on the bed, she loudly called over a number of names, for the purpose of leading the Indians to suppose there were other men in the house. She also aroused Martin, ordering him to fire from the back window on the savages, which he did, severely wounding one of them in the back.

The report of Martin's gun and the fall of one of their number alarmed the Indians, and the one who held Alice by the hand for a moment let go his hold. Taking advantage of her freedom, quick as thought the brave girl darted from his side, and, rushing up the narrow valley we have mentioned, succeeded in effectually hiding herself in the rushes. Too much alarmed to spend long time in search of her, the Indians immediately dragged the body of Mr. Means some forty rods from the house, where they tore off his scalp, and then hastily left the place, bearing with them the wounded Indian and Mary, to whom they gave, with unexpected kindness, a blanket, her only previous covering being her night-clothes, part of which had been despoiled in the rough handling to which she had been subjected.*

---

* We have detailed the circumstances of this attack precisely as they were related to us by a descendant of the murdered man. Parson Smith, in his Journal, in a brief notice of this affair, places the time one month earlier. Under date of May 18th, after mentioning the capture of a man in Brunswick by the Indians, he says, "They killed one Mains and ****, at Flying Point, and carried away a young woman, but

With the retreat of the Indians and the cessation of danger, the strength of Alice Means forsook her. She had seen her husband murdered· in cold blood; she had borne her dead child in her bosom unfalteringly. In the short but terrible conflict she had not a thought for herself, for the unspeakable woe that had befallen her. Nay, in the early morning light she had gone out, and, with the assistance of Martin, had borne the gory corpse of her husband and placed it on the bed by the side of the weltering body of her youngest born. All this she had done with a heroic firmness truly marvellous in one to whom such sights of horror were unknown. But when all was accomplished; when she stood by that gory bed, and heard the blood of the two so dear to her heart plash, plash, slowly upon the floor, her courage gave way, and her gentle woman nature all returned.

Language is inadequate to portray the anguish that rent her heart. So late a happy wife and mother, she now stood there bereft of all by one cruel stroke, — widowed, and, for aught she knew, childless. What wonder, as she gazed on the bleeding, mutilated forms before her, that she should covet their deep, unbroken repose? At times she would stand pale and silent as a statue, not a word or a tear betraying the agony of her feelings; and then, giving way to the paroxysms of grief, she would frantically call upon her husband and child not to leave her alone in her sorrow, and

they also left an Indian there, a man firing down through the chamber floor, and killing him on the spot." Our account says nothing of killing one of the attacking party, but merely states that one was wounded, as we have related.

on her God not to prolong a life that was a burden to her.

In the midst of one of these paroxysms a tiny hand nestled amid the folds of her dress, and at last clasped her own. It was that of her little daughter Jane, who had ventured from her hiding-place, and now stood gazing awe-struck on the fearful scene before her. Bewildered, and nearly heart-broken, the poor woman seemed to be unaware of the presence of her child. Presently there was a pattering of bare feet over the floor, and in another moment, with haggard face, and rent and soiled night-clothes, Alice stood by her side.

"Mother! mother!" said the trembling little one, forcing herself on her notice, "we are here, little Jane and Alice. Will you not kiss us, dear mother?"

The sound of the child's voice reached the mother's ear, and touched the mother's heart. Starting as if from a trance, she strained the little ones to her throbbing bosom, while, in a broken voice, she exclaimed: "Not all gone, — not wholly forsaken! God, I thank thee!" and the bereaved one bowed her head, while plentiful tears relieved the pressure of heart and brain.

But why dwell on the sad scene?

The bodies of the murdered ones were committed to the earth, and the widow and her children removed to the block-house, where she received all that sympathy which her situation could not fail to call forth. Here it was, some seven months after the scenes we have related, Mrs. Means gave birth to a son,* to

* From this child descended those bearing the name of Means in Freeport and in Portland, to one of whom we are indebted for the facts of our story.

whom was given the name of his ill-fated father. But it is time we should see what has become of our captive.

CHAPTER III.

AFTER leaving the scene of their butchery, the Indians with their captive made their way to Samoset Point, on the Kennebec. To relieve their wounded companion, who was severely though not mortally injured, they were obliged to travel slowly, which was a great relief to the young captive, whose bare feet and unprotected limbs suffered greatly on the journey.

On their arrival at the Point they were joined by another band of savages, who had been on a marauding expedition to New Meadows, the scalps dangling at their belts too plainly intimating that their bloody work had been crowned with success. Here, after a fiendish exultation over their trophies, in which they manifested their joy in the most demoniacal manner, whooping, shouting, and dancing around their gory spoils, and brandishing their tomahawks around the head of their captive, menacing her with a death which she would willingly have accepted at their hands, they finally held a consultation as to their future course. The result of their wild and riotous debate was, to take the nearest route to Canada. Preparations were immediately made for the journey. The wounded Indian was given in charge of Mary, with directions to attend upon his wants, and with the agreeable assurance that if he died her life would

be forfeited. Before starting, the captive was enabled
to secure a pair of moccasins and leggins, which she
found a great protection to her limbs.

On their journey, the party frequently halted for
the purpose of hunting, at which times Mary would be
left alone with her savage patient, whose wound, rendered painful by exertion, often worked him into almost ungovernable fits of rage, during which he time
and again menaced her life. On one of these occasions
he seized Mary by the hair, and, brandishing a tomahawk, would no doubt have buried it in her skull
had not some of the party opportunely arrived and
wrenched the weapon from his hands. So resolved
did he appear to take her life, that Mary was kept in
a continual state of anxiety and excitement. Determined, however, to shield herself to the best of her
abilities, she had secreted a hunting-knife, which she
resolved to use in her own defence should the occasion
demand it. More than once, when left with the disabled savage, was she tempted to make her escape; but
when she reflected on her situation, in the depths of a
wilderness, without a guide, and with no means to
procure food, her path beset with prowling foes, the
hopelessness of succeeding deterred her from the rash
undertaking.

Fortunately, our captive was blessed with a hopeful
disposition, and possessed no mean share of energy; so,
bracing up her courage with the determination to make
the best of her situation, she plodded on her toilsome
way. It would be difficult to form anything like a
true conception of the trials and sufferings to which
she was daily and hourly subjected. Severe as they
were, she bore up under them bravely, displaying such

34*

an indomitable spirit that she won sensibly on the regards of her captors, all save the wounded savage, to
whom she was anything but a tender nurse. Indeed,
we are not sure that she did not take a mischievous
delight in prolonging his sufferings.

We will not follow her through the route. Suffice
it that, after a fatiguing journey of six weeks, the
party arrived in the vicinity of Quebec, and right glad
was Mary, although wholly uncertain as to what her
future fate might be.

At the time of which we are writing, the Indians
always found ready purchasers for their captives in
the French, who bought them for servants. This will
account for their preserving the lives of so many, in
their ruthless attacks on the whites. Still, it was a
frequent occurrence, when their captives gave them
much trouble by their attempting to escape, or, worn
down by fatigue and suffering, they were unable to
keep up with them, for the savages to despatch them
at once, knowing well that their scalps would be a
source of profit to them. It is well authenticated that
the French encouraged the savages in their cruelty by
paying a bounty for the scalps taken, as our Legisla-
ture does for the heads of wild-cats. It seems incredible that a professedly Christian nation should have
become a party to such an inhuman, such a horrible
traffic; but the fact cannot be gainsayed. The life-
blood of thousands has attested to the degrading
truth.*

---

* It may be well to curb our indignation against the French, until we
learn if our own skirts are not stained with gore. In Belknap's History
of New Hampshire, speaking of one of Lovewell's or Lovel's fights, the
author says of those engaged in it, " The brave company, with the ten

A purchaser was soon found for our captive, and
Mary gladly left her savage companions to enter the
service of Monsieur Lemoine. Her life she felt would
now be secure, while the chances of regaining her
liberty were much in her favor.

This Lemoine, on the whole, did not prove a bad
character, although at the outset he displayed that of
the unfeeling task-master. At the first, he set her to
work in his fields, a species of labor common enough
to French women, but at which the high-spirited girl
at once rebelled. She soon evinced her determination
not to be subjected to the rough usages of a field-
servant, by uprooting his crops and destroying whatever came within her reach. Remonstrances had no
effect on her; the more her master reproached her
heedlessness and sputtered over her carelessness, the
more perverse and reckless she grew; and, finding
that he had no control over her, and that she was
worse than useless at out-of-door work, he wisely concluded to try her in doors.

He took her into his kitchen; and her excellent
domestic qualities became so soon apparent, that, in a
very short time, Madame Lemoine installed her as
mistress of the cooking department, the duties of
which she performed to the entire satisfaction of the
household, proving herself an invaluable servant, to
whom, in a brief period, the whole family became
much attached.

Matters moved along very smoothly for a while; and,
had it not been that her thoughts constantly reverted

scalps stretched on hoops and elevated on poles, entered Dover in triumph,
and proceeded thence to Boston, where they received the bounty of one
hundred pounds each, out of the public treasury."

to her former home, and to the dreadful uncertainty of the fate of her sister's family, she might have lived comparatively happy. When that uncertainty was removed, and she had learned the result of that fearful night-attack, she yearned to be with the widowed one, whose bruised heart she felt she might strengthen if she could not heal.

We have intimated that Mary possessed a good share of beauty. She was, indeed, we are told, remarkable for her personal charms. To a graceful, well-developed form were added features of uncommon loveliness. But it was not merely a set of features nor a faultless complexion that won admiration. There was a glow of intelligence in those features, an expression of sportive archness playing around the mouth and the eye, such a depth of character shadowed forth in every lineament, —

"The mind, the music, breathing from her face," —

that few could resist the bewitching spell of her beauty.

These charms soon made an impression on the susceptible heart of a young Frenchman, who was in the habit of visiting the house. So enamored did Monsieur Bovais become of the beautiful English servant, that he was not long in betraying his passion to Mary. We believe there was a spice of coquetry — not a rare thing, we apprehend, in her sex — in our heroine's disposition. At all events, she did not dislike a little admiration; or, if she did not encourage, she certainly did not discourage, the addresses of her admirer, who was not a bad-looking fellow, take him all in all.

We know not how long a period elapsed after this

conquest ere the old Frenchman, her master, began to suspect how matters were going on, or what objection he had to the flirtation, — for such only, we are convinced, did Mary consider it. But it appears his eyes were at last opened, and a great pother he made about the affair. He at once peremptorily forbade Mary having anything to do with Bovais, prohibiting all intercourse by word or look. Finding, however, that she proved refractory, and showed a disposition to slight his commands, he instituted a strict watch over her conduct during the day, and when evening came he carefully locked her within her chamber.

What would have been the result of these harsh measures it would be difficult to say, knowing that "Love laughs at locksmiths," and opposition to the tender passion but serves to feed the flame, had not a new character appeared on the stage, whose introduction to the reader we beg to reserve for another chapter.

CHAPTER IV.

IT chanced about this time that an English transport ship, commanded by Captain William McLellan,* of Falmouth, arrived at Quebec. Captain McLellan had heard of the capture of Miss Finney before he left home, and was determined, if possible, to rescue her. Soon after his arrival, therefore, he commenced making inquiries respecting her, but in a manner so

* Father of the late Captain William McLellan.

guarded as not to excite suspicion of his real design.
To cloak his intentions, in his conversation he maintained a show of indifference rather than interest in
her fate, yet not the slightest hint that might serve to
give him a clue to her did he suffer to escape his notice. For a long time his endeavors to ascertain her
place of abode were unsuccessful, and he began to
doubt of his success. But being young, energetic,
and of a sanguine temperament, he was not one to be
easily discouraged.

The first intimation he received respecting her was
one evening in a coffee-house, where he accidentally
overheard two or three Frenchmen bantering one of
their companions for worshipping at the shrine of a
certain English serving-maid, whose beauty was confessed by all. In the course of the conversation, the
names of "Mary" and "Lemoine" were often mentioned.

"Ha!" said the captain to himself, "steady as she
goes; this must be the right course. I'll sail on this
tack a while."

So, seating himself a little apart from the group, he
ordered some refreshments, and busied himself apparently in discussing their merits, while not a word that
the party uttered escaped his attention.

When they had left, our young captain, in a careless
manner, inquired of the hotel-keeper if he knew of a
person by the name of Lemoine in Quebec.

"Monsieur Lemoine? O yes! I know him well."

"What is his occupation, Monsieur Dumont?"

"An Indian trader, a dealer in pelts and fur."

"Is he a man of wealth?"

"Oui, very rich. He owns lots of land in the vicin-

ity of Quebec. A very prosperous man. Would
Monsieur like an introduction to him?" asked the
lively Frenchman.

"O no," said the captain, indifferently. "I had
heard of him as an enterprising merchant, which was
the occasion of my inquiry."

Finding the landlord disposed to be loquacious, the
captain thought he might venture a step or two
further.

"Is Monsieur Lemoine married?" he asked.

"Yes, he has quite a family."

"Does he keep an establishment?"

"Certainly, quite a large establishment," said the
garrulous host; "but Monsieur Lemoine is one very
odd man."

"Where did you say he lived?"

"O, close by, on the corner of —— street, not a
stone's throw distant."

"So far so good," thought our shrewd captain.
"We have got possession of the outworks; now for
the citadel!"

"So Monsieur Lemoine is an eccentric character, is
he?" continued the captain.

"One very queer man indeed," rejoined Boniface.

"I judged as much from what the young men said
who left us a short time since."

"Ha! ha!" chuckled the good-humored host;
"Mons. Duran, Mons. Fonbanc, Mons. Bovais!"

"Exactly; they joked one of the party about a
pretty serving-girl, a flame of his, I should judge."

"Oui, oui! Mons. Bovais. He is very much —
what you call it? — smitten with Mademoiselle."

"Is she very pretty?"

" Beautiful ! " was the laconic response.

" What did you say was her name? " asked the
crafty captain.

" Mary — Mary Feeney : one beautiful girl ! "

Here, his services being required elsewhere, the
landlord moved off, rubbing his hands, as he repeated
to himself, " Oui, one beautiful, one very beautiful
girl ! "

Our worthy captain, having gained all the information he desired, soon after took his departure, well satisfied.

The whereabouts of the object of his search ascertained, the next purpose was to obtain an interview
with her. This he found would be rather a difficult
matter, for her master, he learned, kept a jealous watch
over her. Frequently during the day he would saunter in the neighborhood in which Lemoine lived, hoping he might get sight of Mary, but for a long time he
was doomed to be disappointed.

At last, one morning, when his patience was well-
nigh exhausted, as he slowly walked by the door, it
opened, and a young woman appeared with a broom
in her hand. There was no time to lose, and stepping
hastily into the recess in which the door was placed,
the captain asked : " Does Monsieur Lemoine live
here ? "

" He does, sir," said Mary, surprised at hearing herself addressed in her native tongue.

" Is there a girl by the name of Mary Finney living
with him ? " continued the captain.

" That is my name, sir ! " replied Mary, while a flush
of mingled joy and astonishment mantled her cheeks.

" Take this, then," returned the stranger, handing

her a note. " I will be passing here at the same hour to-morrow morning, when you can give me your answer."

Mary had barely time to conceal the note, and the stranger to leave the alcove, when the shrivelled face of Monsieur Lemoine protruded through the half open door, and his querulous voice was heard, ordering her to hasten her task of sweeping the steps, and return to the house. Not less impatient than her master to get through with her work, she made the broom and the dust fly, and hastened into the house, her heart in a flutter of curiosity to learn the contents of the note so strangely and unexpectedly thrust into her hands. Never in her experience did the hours seem so long, until she found leisure and opportunity to retire to her chamber, where she could read the mysterious note undisturbed. The coveted opportunity came at last, and with a beating heart Mary sought her room.

Having secured the door, to prevent intrusion, she eagerly broke the seal of the note. The brilliant glow of satisfaction that lighted up her countenance, and the sudden glistening of her eyes as she ran over its contents, plainly evinced the interest they had excited, and that they were in the highest degree agreeable to her. The note read as follows:

"Miss MARY FINNEY,—Though personally a stranger to you, the writer is a friend and a countryman of yours. He is in command of the English ship Jane, and is bound for Falmouth, Maine, his native place, for which port he expects to sail in the course of a week. Previous to leaving home he had heard of your captivity, and his object in writing is, to devise some plan for your release and restoration to your friends. He is aware of the strict seclusion in which you are kept, and of the difficulties which surround you ; but if you could by possibility contrive a per-

35

sonal interview so as to arrange matters, it would greatly facilitate the purpose he has in view.

"Precisely at seven o'clock to-morrow morning, the writer will pass the house for the purpose of receiving your answer. Should anything occur to prevent your being at the door, he will again pass the house at five in the afternoon.   With respect,

"WILLIAM McLELLAN."

A tide of tumultuous joy rushed through the heart of Mary as she finished the perusal of the note. The prospect of deliverance from her irksome captivity, and restoration to friends and home, excited such intense emotions that for a time the obstacles to be overcome before her deliverance could be accomplished were wholly unthought of.

Leaning her head on her hand, in a delightful reverie her thoughts wandered to her far-away home. She was again amid familiar and cherished scenes, surrounded by loved friends, urgent to welcome her back, and eager to hear her story of sufferings, peril, and escape. Then came thoughts of the one to whom she was indebted for all this happiness. Although she had, in fact, caught but a partial glimpse of his person, still that passing glance prepossessed her in his favor, and fancy endowed him with all those manly qualities and graces so attractive to the female eye and heart. Gratitude had already endeared him to her, and what gratitude had commenced, a deeper and tenderer sentiment was perfecting. In truth, our captive was building a very charming castle in her busy brain, when the wheezing cough and shuffling feet of Monsieur Lemoine, as he passed her door, and, as was his custom, turned the lock upon her, demolished at once the airy fabric, and hastily recalled her roving thoughts to the unpleasant reality of her situation.

An entirely new direction was now given to her reflections. What should she write in reply to her proposed deliverer? How could she manage to grant the desired interview? The surveillance of her master had of late grown so strict she felt it would be extremely difficult, if not impossible, to elude it. She could not meet the stranger in the evening without the house, for Lemoine never permitted her to step out of doors after nightfall. She might invent a thousand excuses for going abroad, but she well knew they would not be listened to for a minute. If he came to the house in the daytime and inquired for her, it would be at the risk of at once arousing the suspicions of old Lemoine, without at all accomplishing the object she had in view; for she was convinced she would not be permitted to see him alone, as, from certain circumstances that had transpired, she had not the least doubt that some of the domestics were placed as spies on her conduct.

Mary now regretted the rather defiant spirit she had of late been in the habit of exhibiting toward her master, and that she had not won his confidence by a more compliant disposition, a more ready acquiescence in his wishes. But there was no help for it now. "It is too late to repent of that," thought Mary, as she sat perplexed in mind in regard to the proposed meeting. A thousand plans arose in her mind, which were no sooner suggested than discarded as impracticable. After pondering over the subject she resolved that she would clandestinely leave the house at the appointed hour in the morning, running the risk of her short absence being detected. Then came the reflection, if her absence should be noticed,—and the chances

were as a hundred to one that it would, — would not
the consequences be fatal to her final escape by cre-
ating new and insurmountable obstacles to it?

Half bewildered by the many projects that floated
through her brain, she passed her hand rapidly over
her forehead, as if to efface the frown of vexation that
was gathering there, when a new idea flashed upon
her mind.

" Why could I not have thought of that before?"
she said, with a low, merry laugh, which evinced that
the difficulty had vanished.

On one side of Monsieur Lemoine's house was an
avenue open to the street and running back the whole
length of the building and out-houses. Mary's chamber was in the second story, and a window opened on
this place. The sleeping apartments of the family
were on the opposite side of the house, looking upon
the street. Those of the servants were in the third
story. The thought suggested to Mary was, to invite
the stranger to an interview beneath her window,
after the family had retired for the night. Acting
upon this, she immediately wrote him a note, in which
she sketched a plan of the house, pointing out the
window of her chamber. She also informed him of
their usual hour of retiring, and mentioned the time
when she would be at the window to receive him.

But little disposition for sleep had our captive that
night. Her busy thoughts kept her wakeful and restless; or, if she fell into a brief slumber, her imagination rioted in the wildest and strangest dreams, all
relating to her proposed flight. Every possible inci
dent that could attend her escape, and a thousand im
possible ones, mingled fantastically in her thoughts,

keeping her mind constantly on the stretch. Heartily rejoiced was she when the lagging day at last appeared, and she could leave a couch which had proved anything but refreshing to her.

With feelings so intensely excited, Mary found her usual routine of duties to be exceedingly irksome. She exerted herself to restrain her emotions and to assume her wonted air of indifference. As the appointed hour drew near when she was to return her answer, she became nervously sensitive, imagining that her movements were scrutinized more closely than usual. Anxiously she counted the minutes and consulted the clock, and, as the time approached, she took the broom, as had been her custom, and commenced sweeping the entry. When the clock struck seven she opened the door and descended the front steps. Casting her eye down the street, she recognized the person who had accosted her the morning previous, coming towards her. At the same moment, to her dismay, she heard the steps of Monsieur Lemoine in the entry, making towards the half-closed door. His appearance at the door and that of the stranger in front of it she saw would be simultaneous, and that it would be impossible to deliver the note into the stranger's hands, with her master's prying eyes fixed upon her, without detection. What should she do? Let a woman alone in an emergency. With the ready wit of her sex, she dropped the note on one of the lower steps at the very instant the old man opened the door, at the same moment busily resuming her employment, as if unconscious of observation.

As she foresaw, the stranger was directly in front

35*

of the door as Lemoine stood on the sill. With a dexterous sweep of the broom she managed to twirl the note over the lower step and up the pavement directly in front of the stranger, whose significant glance as he passed assured her that he understood the manœuvre. The door, as we have said, being in a recess, the old man could not see what followed; but Mary, stepping out in front to sweep the walk, had the satisfaction of seeing the stranger secure the object of so much anxiety.

"Come in, girl! come in!" said old Lemoine, as for a moment Mary paused in her work, her eyes unconsciously following the stranger. "What are you looking at? Eh, eh, hussy, was not that the same young man who passed yestermorn while you were sweeping?"

"I did not notice that it was," replied Mary, blushing at her duplicity, and striving to avoid the jealous gaze of her master by stepping into the somewhat darkened entry.

"Did not notice him? I thought he looked as if he knew you," rejoined the old man as he closed the door and shuffled after her.

"He is a perfect stranger to me, I assure you, sir," said Mary, with such a tone of candor that her master appeared satisfied that she spoke the truth.

With feelings of relief Mary now went about her daily avocations, yet disturbed by many an anxious thought in regard to the interview of the coming night.

CHAPTER V.

THE evening of what had been to Mary a long and weary day at last arrived. Her household duties had all been performed; not entirely to her satisfaction, it is true, for she had been in a perturbed state all the day, and her heart was not in her work. She felt somewhat fatigued, for she had accomplished much more than the usual task allotted to her. Impatient for the coming night, she had hurried her work as if by that means she could hurry the hours; passing from this thing to that with such celerity that Madame Lemoine noticed it, and laughingly remarked that she seemed to be seized with a new fit of industry. Most heartily did Mary rejoice when the last duty of the day was performed, and she was permitted to retire for the night.

Seated in her chamber, she waited in suspense for an hour or two, anxiously listening as one after another of the household retired. At an earlier hour than usual she was delighted to hear the footsteps of her master in the passage-way that ran by her chamber, and never was sound more welcome than the click of the lock which notified her that she was a prisoner for the night. She could not restrain a gay, laughing exclamation: "Ha! ha! Monsieur Lemoine, you will find your bird flown, one of these mornings, in spite of your lock!"

Having extinguished her light, she sat in silence and darkness another hour or so, intently listening if all was still in the house. She then took her place at the window. Although the night was cloudless, owing to a peculiar state of the atmosphere the stars shed but a feeble light. Conflicting emotions, hopes and fears commingling, agitated her breast as she leaned upon the sill and gazed on the darkened scene. Not a sound disturbed the stillness of the hour, until the tones of a neighboring bell, throbbing solemnly on the midnight air, startled Mary from a reverie into which she had fallen, and sent the blood coursing through her veins. It was the hour appointed for the meeting. With senses all alert, Mary leaned eagerly over the sill, and presently her ear detected the sound of distant footsteps. They came nearer and nearer, but at last they suddenly ceased, and the same deep silence reigned.

"It was some one else," murmured Mary, with a sigh of disappointment. But the words had barely escaped her lips, when her eye detected a dusky figure stealthily moving down the avenue. It halted beneath her window; and, with a thrill, Mary heard her name softly whispered. She replied. Then, in the same cautious tone, a consultation followed, the result of which was, that the ship would be ready for sea in three days, and that on the second succeeding night Captain McLellan would be on the spot provided with means for her descent. This and other matters agreed upon, the captain took his leave undiscovered, and Mary sought her pillow, her thoughts filled with the one all-absorbing subject, though in a more composed frame of mind than she had been throughout the day. Now that the affair was settled, and but one more obstacle to be overcome ere she effected her escape, she could look the difficulty more calmly in the face.

The idea of leaving clandestinely caused a momen-

tary feeling of regret, for a mutual attachment existed
between her and the members of the family, all of
whom treated her with kindness. Even old Lemoine,
whose jealous suspicions subjected her to frequent
annoyances and restrained her freedom of action, was
by no means a harsh and unkind master. It was but
the petty tyranny exercised by a foolish old man, who
feared that her pretty face might win admirers, and
in the end subject him to the loss of a valuable servant. It may be that Monsieur Lemoine was not himself wholly insensible to the tempting, blooming charms
of his servant-maid. There is no saying. Some of
these white-headed old fellows retain the fervor of
youth to a remarkable degree. Their hearts are like
the famous Geyser springs, boiling with internal heat
amid polar snows and ice.

The regret, as we have said, was but momentary;
for on the one side was, it might be, a life-long servitude, an ignominious bondage, — for the sphere into
which she had been forced was not congenial to her
feelings or her station in society; on the other side,
freedom, restoration to friends and home, and all the
endearing associations that cluster around and within
the domestic circle. There was still another influence
in operation, hidden within the depths of her heart,
and as yet scarcely recognized. Mingling with and
coloring by its passionate hues all the joys which
awaited her deliverance from captivity, came this
secret feeling, an unbidden, almost as we have said
unrecognized, yet not an unwelcome, guest. Twice
only had she caught passing glances of the stranger
who had so disinterestedly volunteered in her behalf;
yet it was but natural she should cherish his image

with no small degree of interest. Her sympathies
were of course deeply enlisted in his favor; and, when
a woman's sympathies become thus rooted, they are
very apt rapidly to run to seed.

The intervening days were passed by Mary in no
enviable state of mind. The hours flew by swiftly,
however, for every moment she could steal away from
her household cares was devoted to preparation for
her flight. Her small stock of clothing was gathered
and got in readiness for her departure. A few hours,
indeed, would have been sufficient to have effected all
her little arrangements, for she could boast but a
scanty wardrobe, the whole of which might be contained in a small bundle. Yet the arranging and re-
adjusting of the few articles served to employ her
mind, and to relieve the tedium of suspense to which
she would otherwise have been subjected.

At last all was completed, and the eventful night had
arrived. The last duty of the day was discharged with
a feeling of joyful relief as she thought that *that* was
the last time she would be subjected to the perform-
ance of an involuntary servitude. As the hour drew
near, her spirits recovered their wonted buoyancy;
and when, after retiring to her chamber, she heard the
key turn as usual in the lock, she broke out into a
smothered laugh, and gayly muttered, "Ah, Monsieur
Bovais! when the cage is found empty, you will have
the credit of this night's adventure; on your poor
head will be poured the wrath of Monsieur Lemoine."
Then, as if a thought had at that moment suggested
itself, she took a piece of paper, and, writing upon it,
" *Ce que femme veut, Dieu le veut. Bon jour, Monsieur Lemoine!* " affixed it to her unpressed pillow.

Having indulged in this malicious prank, she arranged herself for flight, extinguished the light, and took her place at the window to await the arrival of her deliverer.

It was a favorable night for their purpose. There was no moon, but the stars gave light sufficient to aid without betraying their movements. It would be difficult to analyze Mary's feelings as she stood there counting the moments that brought nearer and nearer the designated hour. Rapidly her thoughts ran over all that had transpired since the night of her seizure. The terrible death-scene of her brother-in-law, her painful journey through the wilderness, the perils and sufferings which attended every step, her arrival at Quebec, and her long servitude under Monsieur Lemoine, all passed through her mind. Then came thoughts of the home and the dear ones from whom she had been so long separated, and of the surprise her unexpected return would create, and of the joy which would await her. Absorbed in these reflections, time passed unheeded, until the midnight-bell proclaimed the hour in which her captivity was to end.

Barely had the sound died away, when, prompt to the moment, the young captain stood beneath her casement, and, after an exchange of salutations, whispered, " Is the coast clear ? "

" All clear," was Mary's brief response.

" Have you everything in readiness ? "

" Yes."

" Good! take this, then," said the captain, " and be sure and secure it well." And, by the aid of a long pole, a rope was placed within Mary's reach. A slip-noose had been prepared in the end, which Mary threw over the bed-post, previously placed in a suitable position near the window.

"Wait a moment, Miss Finney, and let me see if all is right," said the captain. And, seizing the rope, with scarcely an effort, he mounted to the chamber window. "It will answer to a charm," said he; "although I fear, Miss Finney, you will find it rather an awkward mode of descent. However, I have spliced in billets of wood; at intervals, which will serve as footholds, and aid your descent."

Instructing her how to proceed, and cautioning her not to be in too much haste, the captain returned to the ground.

"Now, Miss Finney, throw us your bundle," said the captain. "Be sure and grasp the rope firmly," he continued, "and plant your feet securely on the bits of wood;" adding, jocosely, for the purpose of encouraging her, "like most important undertakings, you will find the first step to be the most difficult."

Our fair readers will appreciate the embarrassing situation of poor Mary, and readily award to her their meed of sympathy. She made many fruitless attempts before she succeeded in obtaining egress from the window; but, when she fairly got the "hang of the rope," she almost equalled the activity of the captain in reaching terra-firma.*

"Bravo!" said he, as he stood by to assist her as she let go of the rope. "That feat would do credit to Jack himself! Now take my arm, Miss Finney; we have some distance to walk. We must leave the rope," said he, with a light laugh; "it may come in play as a

* The flight of Miss Finney from the house was through a window, as we have described it, aided by a rope furnished by the captain.

halter, should old Lemoine feel in the hanging mood when he discovers your absence."

With what feelings Mary took the proffered arm, and proceeded through the darkened streets of Quebec towards the river-side, we must leave the reader to imagine.

CHAPTER VI.

AFTER a rapid walk our adventurers arrived at a quay, where a boat with four oarsmen was in waiting, the ship being in the stream, having dropped down the river a little distance below the city in readiness to trip her anchor early in the morning. Having seen his companion safely on board, Captain McLellan handed her a cloak.

" Take this, Miss Finney," said he, " and wrap yourself close, for you will find the night air on the river damp and chilly." Then, taking the tiller, he addressed his men: " Now, my good fellows, give way with a will. Dip your oars lightly, lads, and let not a word be spoken."

Scarcely a sound was heard, save the ripple at the bow, as the boat shot rapidly from the shore and proceeded down the river, the row-locks having been muffled to prevent noise. Not a word was uttered by either party as the boat glided on her way. The feelings of Mary were too intense to permit her to enter into conversation. The sense of freedom, of having escaped from a hated bondage, of being in entire safety, surrounded by friends, ready with stout arms

and brave hearts to protect her from harm; the knowledge that she was even then on her way towards her
long sighed-for home ; these, with the circumstances
which surrounded her, the obscurity of the night, the
swift though lulling motion of the boat, all served to
flood her heart with emotions too deep and vivid for
mere words. Tears swelled to her lids, but there was
no bitterness in those tears. The source whence they
sprung was one of unalloyed happiness, from those
deep fountains of joy which rarely in a life experience,
often never, are opened.

Appreciating her silence, her companion did not
obtrude his conversation, and it was not until the
order was given to unship the oars, and the boat
grazed the side of the ship, that Mary was aroused
from her reverie. When she stood on the deck, the
captain cordially congratulated her on her escape, and
welcomed her on board. Then, leading her to the
cabin, she was invited to partake of some refreshments which were in readiness, after which he introduced her to an airy, commodious state-room, which
he had furnished with every convenience that could
conduce to her comfort.

As he was on the point of bidding her good-night,
Mary extended her hand, and, with a voice tremulous
with emotion, said: "If I have been backward in
thanking you for your disinterested services in my
behalf, Captain McLellan, be assured, sir, it is not
from lack of grateful feelings ; but solely because I
could not find words to express my gratitude ―― "

"Poh! poh! my dear Miss Finney," exclaimed the
captain, interrupting her; " say not a word about grat
itude. There is not a man who would not have

jumped at the chance of doing what I have done. Rest assured that the satisfaction of restoring you to your friends will more than repay me for the little trouble I have incurred. Good-night, or rather good-morning!" and, squeezing the plump little hand he held, the gallant captain turned away with a glow on his cheek, and a warmer glow in his heart.

At an early hour in the morning Mary was awakened by the tramping of feet over her head, and the hearty "yo-heave-ho" of the men at the windlass. For a while she was bewildered, and could not account for the strangeness of her situation. A moment's reflection was sufficient for her to realize the change in her condition. The thrilling emotions that agitated her heart would not suffer her to remain quiescent; and, leaving her comfortable berth, she hastily arrayed herself preparatory to going on deck.

The sun had just risen as she ascended the companion-way. A slight breeze rippled the river, and under a cloud of canvas the ship was gliding swiftly down the St. Lawrence. Behind her lay Quebec, the scene of her weary captivity, while before her the broad river stretched far away, glistening in the early beams of the sun. The scene was both strange and beautiful to Mary. The white-winged ship moving in graceful majesty, the passing shore clothed in the fresh livery of early summer, the glittering expanse of water in front, and the long wake, catching and reflecting the sun's rays, as if the ship's keel had turned up a furrow of snowy pearls and blazing gems,— on these as they opened to her sight she gazed silent and spell-bound, and was only roused from her abstraction by the cheery voice of the captain.

"Good-morning, Miss Finney. We have a fair breeze aloft, and a promise of favorable weather. The Jane bowls off as if conscious of having a fugitive on board. I did not expect to see you stirring at so early an hour. I trust you rested well?"

Mary responded to the salutation, and tendered her acknowledgments anew for the services he had rendered. The captain bowed, and then, as if to divert her mind from the subject, led her aft and directed her attention to the various striking views as they successively presented themselves.

But it is not our purpose to detail all that transpired during the voyage. Suffice it that, after a very favorable passage, the good ship Jane arrived safely at Falmouth, now Portland. We will not take it upon ourselves to say that the captain or his passenger was much rejoiced when the ship cast anchor in Falmouth harbor. The truth is, those charms of person and mind which our heroine so eminently possessed, and which were sufficiently potent to have won the admiration of a landsman less impressible than our worthy captain, proved at sea — where such things are rare luxuries indeed — all-sufficient to secure his warmest devotion.

Although lately in the condition of a captive serving-girl, Mary had been reared and educated in quite a different sphere. Knowing this, the captain had from the first treated her with the respect of an equal. The interest which her friendless and forlorn situation had excited in the outset soon ripened into a tenderer and deeper feeling, which Mary, whose heart was already gratefully enlisted in his favor, was not slow to reciprocate; so that the thrill of pleasure which the pre sure of hands sent to each heart as the captain assisted his charge over the ship's side into the boat, clearly enough betokened that they vibrated in unison.

We might possibly add to the interest of our story by describing the arrival of Mary at her home, and of the joyful welcome she received from her family and friends; by portraying her feelings as she again took her accustomed place in the endeared domestic circle, and related to eager and untiring auditors the story of her seizure, long captivity, and final release. But all this, for want of space, we must leave to the imagination of the reader.

There is another point in her eventful life on which we would willingly dwell, did we not apprehend that we have already been too prolix in our details; and that is, the occasional visits of her rescuer at Freeport, which in a short time grew more and more frequent, until, one fine day, he left the place, taking with him our heroine, a happy, blushing bride.

That Mary proved an excellent housewife, who can doubt, having "served an apprenticeship," as she often laughingly remarked, " in a Frenchman's kitchen." That she loved and was beloved by her lord, we have abundant living evidences in their numerous descendants, who serve to swell the list of our most worthy and respected citizens.

A word in regard to the other characters introduced into our story. Little Alice grew up to be a fine, noble-hearted girl, and in process of time became the wife of Mr. Clement Skolfield, of Harpswell. Jane was married to Mr. Joseph Anderson, of Freeport. We have already mentioned that the son born subsequent to his father's death was the progenitor of those bear-

36*

ing his name in Freeport and Portland. The widow, we are informed, afterwards wedded Colonel George Rogers, of Georgetown, who removed to Freeport after his marriage. Though the wife of another, the scenes of that fearful night were never effaced from her memory. She bore to her grave the scar in her breast occasioned by the bullet which caused the death of the child in her arms. The wound in her heart that grave alone healed.

THE END.